se retu

DAUGHTER OF DARKNESS

Four years after being drugged and tricked into marrying the fourteen-year-old Willow Givanchy, a suspected witch and unwanted daughter of his deadliest enemy, Gerard Lytton returns home to find his wife and family much changed. Having lost none of her fiery independence, Willow has become a well-loved member of Lytton's family. But although nobly born, she cannot belie her mother's dark reputation, and her father's dishonour. Having transformed herself from a child bride to a beautiful woman, Willow eventually falls in love with her husband but is her love deep enough, to overcome the obstacles of her parentage and reputation that threatens to tear them asunder.

DAUGHTER OF DARKNESS

DAUGHTER OF DARKNESS

by

Janet Woods

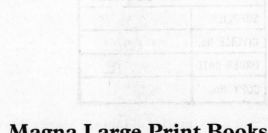

Magna Large Print Books
Long Preston, North Yorkshire,
BD23 4ND, England.

British Library Cataloguing in Publication Data.

Woods, Janet
    Daughter of darkness.

    A catalogue record of this book is
    available from the British Library

    ISBN   978-0-7505-3623-3

First published in Great Britain in 2002 by Robert Hale Limited

Copyright © 2002 by Janet Woods

Cover illustration © Marta Bevacqua by arrangement with
Arcangel Images

The moral right of the author has been asserted

Published in Large Print 2012 by arrangement with
Janet Woods, care of Kate Nash Literary Agency

Magna Large Print is an imprint of Library Magna Books Ltd.

Printed and bound in Great Britain by
T.J. (International) Ltd., Cornwall, PL28 8RW

For my daughter, Carol, with love.
Keep smiling.

PROLOGUE

London – New Year's Eve – 1750

An icy stream of wind blew through a broken window behind the altar. The candles spluttered. The stench of burning tallow caught in Gerard Lytton's throat as the bishop's sonorous voice droned on.

The viscount was not paying attention to the words. His head was pounding and his eyes refused to stay open without effort. All his concentration was focused on keeping his nausea under control until the service reached a conclusion.

'I pronounce you husband and wife in the sight of God.'

Gerard's powerful frame swayed as he shifted from one foot to the other. He gazed down at the figure of the veiled woman beside him. Her small hand trembled inside his. When he smiled at her she jerked it angrily away.

His lips curled wryly at the gesture: Daphne de Vere had every right to be angry. Although their marriage had been ordained since childhood, this clandestine affair was not what she'd envisaged. Unfortunately, his dalliance with Daphne on the eve of his departure for America had left them with no choice.

He'd been caught in Daphne's chamber. The invitation had been hers, a chance to say farewell in private. Her kisses had been surprisingly seductive for a maid – the wine he'd consumed, heady.

His mind was a blank to what had actually taken place between them, but his state of undress had told its own story when her stepfather had aroused him with a well-placed foot.

Daphne had been huddled in a chair; her eyes red from weeping, her bodice torn. She'd avoided his eyes as he'd been hustled away by her stepfather and his two male companions.

He rubbed a sore spot on his jaw. They'd been none too gentle with him, but under the circumstances he considered he'd got off lightly.

'The ceremony is over, sir, I bid you good night.'

Spots appeared before Gerard's eyes as his head jerked towards the voice. Clutching the back of the pew he waited until the accompanying dizziness abated before allowing his eyes to focus on Daphne's stepfather.

Contempt painted the pale, glittering eyes of the marquess. His smile was a sneer, as were those of his two companions – men who'd sell their souls to the devil if there was a guinea to be earned.

'Lynchcross.' Gerard's acknowledgement of the marquess bordered on insolence. There was a long-standing feud between their two families – one that would end only when the marquess was dead.

'You seem loath to kiss your bride,' the marquess mocked. His fingers closed around Daphne's wrist. 'If you don't want her, I'll take her to France with me.'

'No!' A terrified sob came from beneath the veil.

Gerard's lips tightened in distaste as he knocked the man's hand aside. The marquess's château in France had as unsavoury a reputation as its owner.

'As you will.' The marquess yawned as he turned away. 'My daughter is your responsibility now. May you find pleasure in each other. Her servants and chattels will be dispatched to your residence forthwith.'

'Daphne is not *your daughter*,' Gerard reminded him, as the three men retreated towards the door. 'Had your blood flowed in her veins I'd not have considered marriage – whatever the circumstances.'

Raucous laughter greeted his words as the door slammed shut.

Throwing his cloak about his shoulders Gerard turned to his bride. 'Come, Daphne, stop your weeping. I'll take you to my grandmother's house.'

Her veiled head turned slowly towards him. 'I'm not Daphne de Vere.'

Impatience darkened his pewter-grey eyes. He was in no mood for jesting. The hour was late, his luggage and servant already aboard the East Indiaman that would convey them across the Atlantic. He should have met Charles, his friend and travelling companion, an hour ago. 'And I'm not Gerard Lytton, Viscount Sommersley, heir to the earldom of Lytton.'

'You've been duped, My Lord.'

Puzzled, he gazed down at her.

'I'm Willow, daughter to the Marquess Lynchcross.'

'What foolishness is this?' His eyes narrowed. 'Rumour has it the daughter of the marquess died in childhood.'

'Then rumour is wrong. I am she.'

The simple statement shafted dread into Gerard's heart. 'Remove your veil, madam.'

Fear was evident in her every move. Her hand fluttered upward like a bird against her chest. She gave a cry when he reached out and plucked the veil from her face.

'*God's truth!*' The soaring, vaulted roof sent the blasphemy echoing back at him.

The maid was young, about fourteen. Violet eyes fringed with dark lashes dominated a pale, tear-stained face. A torrent of dark hair poured down her back in shining ripples.

'What devil's mischief is this?' he muttered. 'Who are you?'

'That, My Lord, you've already been informed of.'

The pert answer displeased him. His eyes blazed a warning at her.

She shrank from him, then sinking on to a stool, closed her eyes. Tears trickled from beneath her lids as she whispered, 'The wine you drank was drugged. Daphne de Vere is to wed Eduard, the illegitimate nephew of my father.'

A void opened in the pit of Gerard's stomach and a pulse beat painfully in his temple as he stared at her. 'This is a jest, a New Year's prank, yes? You and this' he gestured towards the cleric

– 'this mock bishop, are part of the theatre company. You've been hired by the marquess to fool me, is that not so?'

The maid said nothing. Such abject misery was written on her face he knew she'd spoken the truth.

The cleric averted his eyes, and moving into the church began to snuff the candles.

The girl flinched as he dragged her by the shoulders to her feet. 'Why?'

'I had no choice, My Lord.' She started to sob. 'You were the lesser of the two evils. I pray you, stop shaking me.'

'The devil I was!' He avoided the temptation to crush her frail bones beneath his hands by releasing her. His palms came away sticky. *Blood?* For a few moments he stared at it uncomprehendingly.

The situation became clear when the girl whimpered.

Tight-lipped, he eased the cloak from her shoulders. Her gown hung in bloodied strips from her back which was crisscrossed with whip lashes. She would be in agony.

'The marquess did this?' Anger burned in him. Before anything else she needed comfort and medical attention. 'Why?'

Her eyes came up to his, luminous with tears. 'I reminded him of my mother.'

'Your mother?' He still didn't understand. 'What has your mother got to do with this?'

'She was Marietta Givanchy.'

Gerard spun round as a strangled gasp came from behind him.

The cleric was grey-faced as he snatched up a

cross. 'God save me from hellfire,' he cried. 'Banish this demon from Your house, Lord.'

'What are you gibbering about?' Uneasiness pricked Gerard's spine as snippets of drawing-room gossip came to his mind. They didn't seem so amusing now. 'Speak, man.'

The bishop's eyes rolled upwards and he sank to his knees. 'Marietta Givanchy was in league with the Devil and cursed the marquess on her deathbed. That's why he has no male heirs. His infant daughter was banished to Ireland lest she inherit the evil eye.' He started to moan. 'Go, My Lord. The church is no place for heretics.'

'I'm no heretic,' the girl said indignantly.

'Be quiet,' Gerard snapped, as he hauled the man to his feet. His wits all but restored, his grey eyes impaled those of the cleric. 'The marriage was illegal. It must be annulled immediately.'

The bishop shook his head. 'There was no illegality. The documents were duly signed and witnessed, vows were exchanged at God's altar.'

'Damn it, man! I was under duress. Besides, she's hardly more than a child.'

The bishop's glance shifted away. 'There was no duress and the maid is of marriageable age. I perceived only that you'd partaken of too much wine.' He shrugged from Gerard's grasp and backed towards the door, the cross held aloft. 'The marquess is responsible for my living. If need be I shall testify to the legality of the marriage in Parliament. Take your bride and depart, sir.'

'The only place I shall take her is back to her father's house,' he snarled. As the door closed behind the priest he set off up the aisle. 'Come,

14

child. I'll escort you safely home and we will sort this matter out.'

'I'd rather die.'

The desperation in her voice made him spin round. His heart leapt in alarm when the light from a solitary candle glinted on the silver blade of a dagger.

'Stop, don't be foolish!'

Several rapid strides took him back to her, but too late. The knife stabbed against her chest in a slashing downward motion. It struck against a brooch on her bodice, shattering the stone into glinting shards. She screamed as he twisted the knife from her hand, striking out at him with her fists.

'Please let me die, for my life will be spent in suffering should you return me to my father.'

Gerard's heart went out to her. Drawing her close he held her until her hysteria became shuddering sobs. She was too slender, her bones gaunt against her skin. In all conscience he couldn't abandon her to her father's care. She'd not survive another beating.

As for her bloodline? His forehead creased in a frown as he tipped up Willow's chin and gazed at her again. She was of good birth. Her mother was reputed to have been born from a liaison between a French duke and one of his mistresses. He was relieved she bore no resemblance to her father.

This skinny little maid was not one he'd have taken by choice, but now he must make the best of the match and provide Lytton estate with heirs from her. He was no debaucher of children though. He could afford to wait until she grew up.

'Hush,' he soothed. 'Once my grandmother has been made aware of the situation she will care for you whilst I'm abroad.'

'You promise you will not return me to my father?' Her violet eyes were wounded beyond trust.

'My word of honour.' Testing the blade of the dagger with his thumb he flicked her a grin. 'You'd best get it honed. This would not slice through butter.'

She gave a weary shrug and, stifling a yawn, rested her head against his arm.

The gesture was touching, the rush of tenderness he experienced unexpected. She made no protest when he hefted her slight figure up in his arms, just nestled her head on his shoulder.

Anger built up in him as he strode from the church and picked his way through the clutching hands of the beggars huddled on the steps. Tomorrow, he'd be the laughing stock of London. The Lytton and Lynchcross families united by marriage? It was unthinkable!

'Yet it's happened,' he muttered, hearing the girl whimper as he stumbled in a pothole. 'This unloved, and unwanted child is now my responsibility.'

His fierce, hawklike gaze and powerful body did not encourage liberties from the human flotsam who littered London's dark streets. The moon was full, the night cold enough to glaze the mud with ice.

Gerard's feet hardly made a sound as he moved with a fast catlike gait, his eyes searching the shadows for danger.

Within minutes he'd reached his destination. Depositing his sleeping burden on a couch he quickly explained the situation to his astonished grandmother.

He gave Willow a troubled glance. 'She is too young to be a wife.'

His grandmother smiled. 'She will grow. Her mother was a childhood friend of your dear mama. The notoriety Marietta gained was without substance. I shall enjoy having her daughter as a companion. May God go with you, Gerard.'

His grandmother's parting words brought him comfort.

As he was leaving the house, Willow's servants arrived: a young maid, and an Irish groom leading a mare.

He took a moment to admire the horse. A coat of black satin shone as the groom held a lantern aloft. Vapour snorted from her nostrils as she pranced nervously upon the cobbles, and sparks flashed from beneath her hooves. Her grace and beauty awed him.

The mare was too spirited for a girl of Willow's small stature. In fact, Willow looked hardly old enough to have graduated from a pony.

Without more ado, he instructed the groom to remove the horse to the Lytton estate in Dorset, where she could be used for breeding purposes.

'May God speed you safely home, sir,' the Irishman called out when they parted in the stable-yard.

Silently, and with more sincerity, Gerard echoed the sentiment as he took long, loping strides towards the docks.

He reached his destination just after the ship had been released from its berth. Charles was gazing over the side and cheered him on as he raced down the wharf and leapt across the ever widening gap. He managed to hold on to a rope net hastily thrown over the side by his servant, and was hauled aboard.

As the ship made its way down the River Thames the two men watched fireworks burst overhead. Faintly came the sound of church bells. The citizens of London were welcoming in the New Year.

He exchanged a smile with Charles. Off to seek adventure, neither of them realized it would be four long years before they set foot on English soil again.

CHAPTER ONE

Summer 1754

'Not that cloak. Fetch the blue velvet with the white fur trim. It's more becoming with this gown.'

And a match for your eyes, you vain child. Lady Edwina gazed at Willow with more than satisfaction as the maid scurried to do her bidding. Just eighteen, Willow was a beauty. Her body trembled on the brink of ripeness, her eyes sparkled with life.

Raised on an isolated estate in Ireland by a male tutor, she'd been without grace when she'd arrived. Maturity and discipline had toned her rebellious nature, but not completely obliterated it.

When Gerard returned from America, her pert charm would intrigue him, as it did all men. Lady Edwina concentrated on her charge as the cloak was draped round her shoulders. 'You will wear your fichu over your gown,' she said sternly. 'The grounds of St James's Palace will be full of officers for the King's parade. I won't have them peering into your bodice.'

Willow's expression took on a teasing quality. 'They are only men, Grandmother. What harm can it do when I am well chaperoned and out in the open?'

'*What harm!*' Lady Edwina almost shrieked. 'The harm done to your reputation could be incalculable. Gerard would expect you to behave with modesty.'

'As if he cares,' Willow muttered, stung into mutiny. 'He's not sent me one letter, nor has he enquired after my welfare in all this time. Truly, I'd not be at all surprised if he'd forgotten my existence.'

'No doubt he has. What's equally certain is that the sight of you will soon remind him.'

Willow's pout became a sunny smile. 'Is this shepherdess style becoming, Grandmother?' The straw hat trimmed with cornflowers and embroidered silk ribbons sat jauntily above a white lace cap that matched the flounces on her sleeves.

'You know it does, you vain creature.' She smiled as she caught the girl's eyes, thinking, I pray Gerard hastens home before some rake turns her head. I will take her to the country out of harm's way. Ambrose and Caroline will welcome Gerard's bride.

The ride down the Mall to St James's Palace drew many admiring eyes towards her. Willow's eyes sparkled as an officer presented her with a red rose.

'Lieutenant Hugh Macbride at your service, ladies. My commanding officer sends his compliments and begs your company in the refreshment tent.'

'And who exactly is your commanding officer, sir?' Lady Edwina fixed her most chilling gaze on the hapless young man.

Willow smothered a giggle when he blushed.

'General Robert Marriot, ma'am.' Hugh Macbride snapped to attention. 'He sends his compliments and...'

'Yes – yes, we've been through all that already. Why did you not say your commanding officer was Robert Marriot in the first place?'

His blue eyes wandered back to Willow. Placing his hand over his heart, he smiled. 'I was struck senseless by your daughter's beauty.'

'You'll be struck senseless by my cane in a moment,' Lady Edwina murmured under her breath. 'Why does my cousin send a junior officer to escort us? Is he too grand now to greet us himself?'

'He's taking refreshment with the King.' Hugh Macbride offered Lady Edwina his arm. 'He begs leave to apologize in person.'

'The King, you say?' Interest lit Lady Edwina's eyes as she turned to Willow. 'Make sure you mind your manners if you are lucky enough to be presented. It would be unwise to be frivolous in His Majesty's presence.'

'I do not need reminding, Grandmother.' She lowered her lashes to hide the flare of rebellion in her eyes.

The blue and white striped marquee reserved for guests of the regiment was hot and crowded. She stood meekly whilst pleasantries were exchanged with Lady Edwina's tall, gruff cousin, though it was hard to ignore the handsome, young officer, who seized every opportunity to engage her eyes.

Eventually, the general barked an order at him and he scurried off to fetch refreshments.

The smell of humanity was suffocating against her nostrils. The marquee was ablaze with a crush of silk and velvet. Men talked loudly, women smiled and nodded and eyed each other's diamonds and frills.

She had seen two children huddled together outside a silversmiths that morning. Gaunt-cheeked and hollow-eyed, they'd held out grimy hands to beg for coins. The shopkeeper had set about them with a stick.

Suddenly Willow hated London – its squalor, its fogs and the poor spilling like rats from the filthy alleys. Her mind drifted back to Coringal Estate, and a childhood free of restraint.

She sighed, longing to feel her horse gathering its muscles together between her thighs as she put it to a jump. She craved the soft Irish mist against her face, damp grass beneath her feet and the experience of coming home at dusk to see

Coringal – once the home of her exiled paternal grandmother – waiting with shabby gentility to welcome her.

Summer at Coringal had been a delightful profusion of flowers amongst the green wooded hills, and soft perfumed air. Winter had brought cold to battle with, and days of hunger. But although her body had often gone without warmth and comfort, her mind had been kept nourished – and she'd never had to beg.

Her tutor had always been by her side offering his guidance. James Langland had filled her mind with knowledge, encouraged her dreams and embellished them with his own as a natural progression of their relationship. Together, they'd created adventures. Coringal was blessed with a library, and James had brought out the maps so they could travel the world together.

When she was not studying they were out in the countryside. She learned how to trap and skin a rabbit, and how to catch fish with her bare hands. James had taught her to shoot a pistol. One day, when they'd been bored and restless, he'd introduced her to the art of fencing. She'd proved to be an adept pupil, earning the praise of the laconic James.

A hungry ache gathered in her heart. Dearest James, where are you now – and why have you not written to me in all this time?

'*Willow!*' An urgent hiss brought her out of her reverie. Catching a glimpse of a pasty-faced man with a bulbous nose she instinctively followed the older woman's example and dropped a deep curtsy.

King George was older than she expected, at least seventy. She wondered if the rumours she'd heard about his many mistresses were true. He didn't appear all that attractive to her.

'Charming. You may rise.'

'Lady Sommersley, sire. My cousin's ward, and wife to her grandson, Viscount Sommersley.'

'Sommersley?' The King inclined his head towards General Marriot as if trying to remember something and enlisting his aide for the purpose.

'Earl Lytton's heir. Lady Sommersley is the daughter of the Marquess of Lynchcross.'

'Ah, yes. I must exchange a word with him. Bring him and his delightful stepdaughter to me when Lynchcross arrives.' The King's glance washed over her absently. 'So young, and so pretty. Your husband is a lucky man, my dear.'

Her cheeks dimpled into a rosy blush. 'Thank you, your Majesty.' She breathed a sigh of relief when the King turned back to Lady Edwina.

'The general informs me you plan to travel to Dorset shortly. The roads are hazardous these days. Some of our regiment is travelling to Dorchester before too long. We will advise the general to arrange an escort. It will save you the expense of hiring outriders.' One nod and he passed on down the line, their faces and names already forgotten.

'You didn't tell me we were going to the country, Grandmother.' Willow gently fluttered her eyelashes at Hugh Macbride, who was weaving through the crush with a glass of lemonade clutched in each hand. 'It will be nice to leave London.'

'I decided quite recently.' Crossly, Lady Edwina watched the young officer walk towards them. 'You're flirting quite shamefully. Discourage the young man, or I'll box your ears and send him packing myself.'

'I see no harm in it.' Spreading her fan in a graceful arc, Willow applied her gaze to the crowd. A middle-aged man whose paunch hung low over his breeches winked at her. She stared back haughtily.

'Lieutenant Macbride is like all soldiers,' Edwina said softly. 'His manoeuvres have only one purpose away from the battlefield, and that is to conquer the prize a woman holds between her thighs. *That*, my dear, belongs to your husband.'

'Grandmother!' Willow fanned vigorously at the rosy blush that appeared on her cheeks, 'You who cite modesty as a virtue should not speak to me of such pursuits.'

'Bah!' Edwina exclaimed, quite gratified by the shock in Willow's voice. It wasn't often she could get the better of her these days. 'Tell me you do not lie abed and imagine the time when your husband pleasures you in such a way.'

'Indeed, I do not know to what you refer.' Willow blushed even more furiously. 'I'm ignorant of such things.'

'For your own sake, I pray you remain so until your husband returns,' Edwina said tartly.

Further conversation was forestalled by the arrival of Hugh Macbride. He handed them each some lemonade. 'Would you care to stroll amongst the trees, Lady Sommersley?' he said, giving her a dazzling smile. 'You look flushed. I fear the heat in the marquee is too much for you.'

'Lady Sommersley is stronger than she looks.' Edwina glanced over his shoulder and spotted Marquess Lynchcross accompanied by his nephew, Eduard, and Daphne de Vere. She smiled at the misery on Daphne's face. That would teach her for marrying that Lynchcross whelp and making a fool of my grandson.

'Excuse us, Lieutenant,' she purred. 'We have our respects to pay to Lady Sommersley's father.'

Willow began to tremble when Lady Edwina took her arm and led her through the crowd. She'd not met him since her marriage, and had no wish to. 'Please do not make me pay my respects, for truth to tell, I have none.'

Edwina ignored her plea. 'You cannot go through life avoiding the man.' The girl was as white as a spring snowdrop and, had it not been too late, as the marquess had already seen them, she would have had second thoughts.

'You need not say anything more than necessary to him. I'd be obliged, if you would engage Daphne de Vere in conversation. I hear she gave birth to a child within a year of her marriage. You can enquire about the brat whilst I tackle the marquess about your dowry. The negotiations have gone on too long.'

'I want nothing from him.' Willow wished Lady Edwina would drop the matter of a dowry. 'It's bad enough that I inherited his bloodline.'

'Your wants do not come into it. A settlement is due, and I intend to obtain it for my grandson.' Edwina patted her ward's hand. 'And you, my dear child, are entitled to your marriage portion.

25

I intend to be tenacious about the matter. If it's not resolved soon I'll petition His Majesty.'

Several people gave Lady Edwina an interested glance and sidled closer when she neared the marquess. Eyes narrowing, the marquess brushed his lips across the gloved fingers she offered.

The face of the marquess was pitted by pox, his lips twisted into a permanent sneer. A slight deformity in his calf gave the man a twisted gait that added to the legend that he was a dangerous man without conscience.

The legend was not without substance. He'd triumphed on the duelling field, and whispers circulated about certain activities he and his associates indulged in.

Half-hidden by Edwina's larger form, Willow would have stayed there if her cousin Eduard had not taken her hand and dragged her out. She shuddered when he smiled, recoiling from the stale smell of his breath. Daphne de Vere, whom she'd met briefly before their marriages, deserved her sympathy. Daphne shrugged as they exchanged a glance, her lips twitching into an oddly ironic smile.

'My little cousin has grown beautiful, has she not?' Eduard wore a gold waistcoat embroidered all over with green vine leaves. His coat and breeches were scarlet satin. Powder from his high-dressed wig scattered his shoulders.

Brought to the attention of her father, she shrank involuntarily from the scrutiny of his astute pale eyes. She managed a strained smile. He couldn't harm her now, she told herself. She belonged to Gerard, who was honour bound to

26

defend her from hurt and insult. *Yet she did not want her husband to die on her account.* Her smile faded and she briefly curtsied.

'She resembles her mother, does she not?' Edwina's voice adopted a slightly malicious tone. 'Marietta was about the same age when you took her in marriage, if I recall.'

The marquess's tongue flicked at his lips. 'Let's hope the resemblance ends there. The woman dabbled in the black arts.'

Willow took a fearful step backwards at the hatred in his expression.

'I have decided the question of dowry. I'll send round the deeds to Coringal.'

'And her marriage portion?'

'Five hundred guineas.'

'The amount is an insult. Fifteen thousand and her mother's jewellery,' Edwina said firmly.

'We will not quibble in public, madam.' The marquess glanced at the listening bystanders. Recognizing one who was close to the King he capitulated grudgingly. 'There are one or two trinkets the girl can have and I'll agree to ten thousand guineas. I'll probably win it back at the gaming tables over the next month.'

'In gold,' Edwina murmured. 'I do not trust paper.'

His mouth tightened. 'I'll instruct my banker to place both that amount and the deeds to Coringal at your disposal.'

Satisfied, Edwina nodded her head. Willow had told her the Irish estate was unproductive for farming, but that remained to be seen. Given a good manager and the modern farming methods

Gerard had constantly talked about, anything was possible.

Having finished the distasteful business to her satisfaction, she gave Willow an exasperated look and turned to Daphne de Vere herself.

'I hear you have a child, madam.'

Willow caught her breath when love softened Daphne's eyes.

'I have a dear little boy who is nearing his third birthday. His name is Edward George.'

'You name him after his father then?'

A merest hesitation, then Daphne said smoothly, 'And after the King, who was the main sponsor at his christening.'

The King! Edwina gave Daphne a speculative look. The young marchioness moved in high circles these days.

'I would love to see him.' Willow gazed appealingly at Lady Edwina.

'It will not be possible. We're leaving for Dorset within the week and have no time to entertain.'

'Then you must call on *me*. I'd be most grateful for your company. Tomorrow at three?'

Mindful that Daphne de Vere was a marchioness in her own right, and outranked her, Edwina's acceptance was graceful. 'Naturally, we would be delighted.'

Willow's smile bathed her in friendliness. 'Does little Edward resemble you or his father?'

'Neither. He has brown eyes and a headful of dark curls. He is straight of limb and tall for his age. He's a handsome lad and some say he favours the Lytton connection, in that he has my father's looks.'

'Lytton connection?' She gazed at Daphne in complete surprise. 'In what way are you related to the Lyttons, Lady Daphne?'

'My late father was second cousin to Earl Lytton. Our families have always been neighbours and friends and I hope that will continue. I'd like to think my son has neighbours he can respect and trust when he inherits Sheronwood.'

She flicked a faintly damning glance at the marquess, smiling without mirth when he cleared his throat. For a moment her brown eyes conveyed malice.

Edwina warmed to the young marchioness as they took leave of each other. Daphne de Vere had more spirit than she'd first thought. She was unhappy, yet had wit enough to insult her husband in public. She'd probably pay for it, the French fop had a vicious look to him.

Had Daphne known her son would be punished for her remarks with a beating she would not have been so forward.

Later, locked in her room, she could hear his screams become sobs, then the sobs become whimpers. When she finally got him back and tended the bruises on his trembling body with witch hazel, rage filled her heart.

Tenderly, she took her son in her arms and cradled him against her heart. Right then and there she resolved that Eduard Lynchcross would never hurt her son again. Her health had been below par of late. It would give her an excuse to take Edward to Sheronwood to visit his grandmother. She would not return to live with Eduard.

Placing a kiss on her son's bruised cheek she whispered in his ear, 'I will kill him if he does this to you again.'

'All of London is talking about Sapphire.' Daphne offered Lady Edwina another sweetmeat. 'The woman is a mystery. Some say she's of French birth, others that she was lately an inhabitant of a town called New Orleans in the Americas. It's said she has a knack of seeing into the past as well as the future.'

'You would not catch me parting with money to know what's gone before,' Edwina scorned. 'I'm already in possession of that knowledge.'

'Rumour says her face is so hideous she wears a veil to cover it. Sapphire promised to cure Isabelle Penforth of her barrenness. She gave Isabelle a potion to slip into her husband's drink, and has promised her a child within a year.'

'*Bah!*' Edwina said fiercely. 'Her husband can barely mount a horse let alone father a child. He has one foot in the grave. An aphrodisiac will send the other one over the edge. He is too old for such excitement.'

Though she gave a little laugh, Willow blushed. The fact that she'd been married for several years and was still intact was cause of concern to her. Something in her feared her husband's return and the act that would make her his wife. Another part of her longed for a child like Edward to love. She laid her cheek against his silky hair and breathed in the scent of his skin.

'You're lucky to have such a handsome son.'

Daphne gave Willow a sympathetic smile. Her

30

state of virginity and her absent husband was common talk in London circles. Certain sections of society were betting over who would overcome Lady Edwina's tight control, and seduce her.

'Have you heard from Gerard recently?' she enquired of Lady Edwina.

'I received word only yesterday. He intends to return before Christmas.'

Willow's heart gave a nervous jump. Why hadn't she been told? She wished her grandmother would treat her like an adult. Her finger traced a blue mark on Edward's hand. Idly, she pushed back a section of his sleeve and gazed in horror.

'You poor darling,' she gasped. 'You have hurt yourself.'

His lower lip began to tremble. 'Papa beat me with his cane.'

'Oh, my poor love.' Falling to her knees Daphne gathered up her son and hugged him tight. Tears stung her eyes as she gazed from one to the other. 'I beg you to help me. Eduard is insane, and will kill him one day. He's jealous that the marquess favours Edward as his heir. Allow us to travel to Dorset with you.'

Edward began to sob in sympathy with his mother.

All was pandemonium until Edwina took charge in her own indomitable manner. The child was pacified with a sweetmeat, then a maid summoned to clear away the tea things. When they were alone again, she called for Edward's nurse to take him to the nursery to play.

She chose to forget that Daphne de Vere had spurned her dear grandson in favour of the

31

child's father, and therefore deserved all she got. That was water under the bridge. Besides, she'd grown to love the vivacious Willow in a way she'd never thought possible over the past four years.

'Now, my dear,' she said kindly. 'You'll tell me all about it and we'll see what can be done to help.'

'Will this journey never end?'

Lady Edwina had been querulous for the past half-hour. No wonder, Willow thought, sighing as their two hired coaches stuck fast in the mud once again. What should have been a two-day journey had stretched into three when a summer storm had flooded the Piddle River just outside of Dorchester. They'd found overnight lodging at a wayside inn.

'I swear the bed was crawling with lice,' Edwina scratched her neck and sighed. 'And you tossed and turned all night. I didn't get a wink of sleep.'

Nonsense! Willow grinned as she took a deep breath of the country air. The bed had been wonderfully clean and Lady Edwina's snores had practically raised the thatch from the roof.

She bestowed a smile on Edward, pleased that the excitement of having soldiers as an escort had taken his mind from his mother.

Daphne had begged to be allowed to accompany her son to visit her grandmother at Sheronwood. Her husband had agreed the child could go, but had spitefully refused Daphne leave to accompany him.

'It will not be for much longer.' Gazing out of the coach window she smiled as she beckoned to

Hugh Macbride. 'We will take some exercise whilst the men free the coaches.'

'And ruin our complexions?' Lady Edwina grumbled, allowing Hugh Macbride to assist her from the coach to a grassy raised strip. She put out a hand to help Willow herself, bestowing a scowl on the man. 'You may help the child and his nurse.'

'My pleasure, ma'am.' The nurse was a young widow, and handsome enough to turn a few heads. Taking her by the waist, Hugh Macbride lifted her across the gap, his hands still lingering about her waist after he'd set her on her feet.

The smile they exchanged was intercepted by Lady Edwina, who frowned at him. 'About your business, sir. You are here as escort and you neglect your duties.'

'Beware of the soldier, Willow,' she grumbled as he strode away. 'He is too handsome for his own good, and conquest comes easily to him.'

'Are all men so free with their affections?' She laid her cheek against the old lady's arm as they promenaded on the sun-dappled grass. 'I wish I'd been born a man. It would be nice to follow my heart and live a life without restriction.'

'Who says a man has no restrictions?' Edwina smiled at her naivete. 'It's a man's duty to care and provide for his family. As for following his heart—'

'Gerard Lytton would now be married to Daphne de Vere and master of Sheronwood,' Willow interjected bitterly. 'Please do not remind me again, Grandmother. It's hateful to know one's husband loves another, even if that husband has cause to despise his wife. There is no pride in knowing I'm unworthy of his attention.' Tears pricked her eyes. 'Now I'm to meet his family. They will despise me also.'

'I have never heard such nonsense in all my life!' Edwina's severe expression softened as a fleeting memory of herself at that age flashed into her mind.

'The earl and countess will welcome you as a daughter. As for Gerard.' Stopping, she gazed into Willow's upturned face. 'You have it in you to make him forget Daphne de Vere ever existed. Gerard is the type of man who enjoys a challenge. By nature you are not submissive, Willow. No doubt you and he will argue. If you are clever you can win him round to your point of view.'

'And how do I go about that, Grandmother? My intellect cannot be equal to his.' Anxiously she gazed into Lady Edwina's eyes. 'I can read and write, and have learned about the wonders of distant lands, but I've not had his education.'

'Your woman's instinct will show you the way.' Edwina kissed her cheek. She didn't have the heart to tell her intellect wouldn't come into it, only physical attraction. Educated women were frowned upon, and Willow had more education than most, thanks to her tutor's liberated ideas.

'Look, our coach is freed,' she said happily. 'Now we can make speed whilst the soldiers dig the baggage coach from the mire. Sheronwood is only a short distance. We can refresh ourselves there before continuing on to Lytton House.'

But Sheronwood was barred to them. Hugh Macbride cantered back towards the coach with a worried look on his face.

'Some of the Sheronwood servants have small-pox,' he said. 'Lady Rosamond requests you extend hospitality to her great-grandson at Lytton House until she's certain the infection is contained.'

Edwina's lips pursed as she hastily withdrew her head. 'Drive on, coachman,' she cried out. 'We must reach Lytton House before night falls and the highwaymen seek us out.'

Hardly likely, Willow thought. Not with an officer and two soldiers in attendance. Nevertheless, her heart beat a little faster when, two hours later, the procession came to a halt.

It was that time of evening when the sun sent long fingers of gold searching through the trees, and dusk pressed warm and purple against their backs. The air was whirling with all manner of flying insects and the breeze was a dying breath of sound amongst the trees.

On either side of them branches reached out from the dense forest. There was a waiting and watching quality about the forest, as if it had taken a deep breath, then paused to survey the newcomers to its midst.

Willow closed her eyes to its embrace, smiling as she breathed in its earthy aroma. It calmed her senses, cleansing from her nostrils the stale smell of the city she'd left behind.

She thought she could hear the forest's heart pulsing beneath her, in its depths, the rustles and squeaks of the creatures sheltering in its secret ways.

Whatever the future held for her, this forest

would always nurture her soul, she thought. She would never be alone whilst she lived in its shadow. Her eyes held the knowledge when she opened them, and she felt strangely content.

'Why have we stopped?' Lady Edwina demanded as Hugh Macbride reined in his horse beside them and laid his pistol across the saddle.

'A rider approaches.'

CHAPTER TWO

The hoofbeats were coming thick and fast through the undergrowth. Willow grinned at her flight of fancy. The forest's pulsing heart was a horseman.

'The rider makes no effort to conceal himself,' she observed, as the soldiers gathered about them with pistols drawn. 'He intends us no harm.'

'Hallo, the coach,' the rider shouted, bursting from a forest track. 'Jeffrey Lytton greets you.' Dust swirled when he brought his horse to a showy, sliding halt. Whipping his tricorn from his head he leaped to the ground and bowed before them.

The soldiers grinned and moved their startled mounts aside.

No more than a youth of about fifteen, Jeffrey's smile was as wide as it could get without splitting his face in half. His eyes twinkled with merriment as he poked his head over the coach door. 'Grandmother, I have come to escort you in.'

'Then God help us,' Edwina snorted, 'for you make enough noise to alert every highwayman this side of London.'

Willow's dowry had been delivered by messenger just before they'd left London. Convinced it was all a trick and the marquess had planted an army of felons along the highway to steal it back, Edwina had been overly concerned for their safety. She forgot her worries when she surveyed her youngest grandson.

'How tall you've grown. You're the image of Ambrose. You may give me a kiss before I introduce you to your sister-in-law.'

Willow could hardly remember her husband's face. Jeffrey Lytton reminded her of it when he gazed through his pewter-grey eyes and smiled. After he pressed his lips to the hand she offered, he avoided her gaze bashfully and mumbled, 'Welcome, Sister.'

'Thank you, Jeffrey. Lady Edwina has mentioned you so often I feel I already know you.'

Jeffrey's glance settled on Edward, who was gazing at the snorting horse through shining eyes. 'Who are you, young sir?'

'Edward George de Vere.' Edward smiled enthusiastically at him. 'May I ride on the back of your horse?'

'I shall be glad of the company.' Plucking Edward from the coach, Jeffrey placed him on the saddle then mounted behind him.

Noting the nurse's agitation, Edwina said haughtily, 'The Lytton men have horsemanship bred in their bones. Edward will come to no harm.'

Aware she'd be mistress of Lytton House one day, Willow gazed at it with interest as they rolled down a carriageway bordered by various hued shrubs.

The great house rose from the ground as if it had grown amongst the trees that surrounded it. A flight of steps led up to a terrace, then to a set of solid doors curved into the shape of a shield. The windows and French doors were of similar shape, square paned, with patterns of coloured glass set into the upper sections. Creepers rambled upon the stonework, giving the whole place a comfortable air of rapport with its environment.

Just perceived through an avenue of yew trees a pavilion was set in a lake. Joined to the shore by an arched bridge, it seemed to float on glass like a miniature castle.

Fragrance drifted from the garden: roses, lavender, summer stocks, and scents she could not identify. There was something magical about what she felt. She was being embraced, as if she'd lived in this house before and was now being welcomed back to its heart.

Tears came to her eyes and trembled on her lids as she followed Lady Edwina up the curving steps and into a vast hall, which was blazing with light from the many candles lit to welcome them.

After the maids were taken under the wing of the housekeeper, and Edward dispatched with his nanny and a plump young servant girl to the nursery wing, Willow sank into a curtsy before the imposing figure of Earl Ambrose Lytton.

He was a handsome man, still muscular and upright at fifty or so, with the look of the outdoors upon him.

She'd met the earl briefly when he'd visited London shortly after her forced marriage. He'd spent a great deal of time with Lady Edwina, the murmur of their voices barely audible to her.

She'd sat on the staircase chewing her nails to the quick whilst she waited to be summoned into his presence. When the time had finally come her heart had been hammering against her ribs, her stomach queasy with apprehension.

He'd merely smiled at her and asked if she was happy living with Lady Edwina. When she'd nodded dumbly he'd patted her cheek then turned to the old lady.

'If you're happy with the arrangement I'll leave the child in your charge, then, Edwina.'

She'd warmed to the earl, and had just plucked up the courage to ask him how her horse fared when Lady Edwina had dismissed her.

In his presence for the second time she still experienced awe. Bowing her head, she said simply, 'Your daughter-in-law greets you, Lord Lytton. I ask for your blessing.'

One finger lifted her chin; his smile was kindness itself. 'My home is blessed by your presence. Let me look at you.'

Ambrose was shaken by what he saw, but his grey eyes gave away nothing of his thoughts. The girl was no longer the pinched-faced waif he remembered: she was the image of her mother.

Time had faded the memory of Marietta Givanchy, yet part of him still mourned the loss of her innocence, so cruelly destroyed by the Marquess of Lynchcross. Marietta had been a flame in his heart until she'd died shortly after giving birth, then she'd become ashes.

Now her daughter stood before him, as fresh and delicate as a newly opened flower. Fate might have snatched Marietta from him, but her daughter had been sent to heal his hurt.

Stooping a little, he kissed her cheek. 'Lady Caroline is indisposed at the moment and confined to her bed. She begs your indulgence and hopes to be able to greet you herself on the morrow.'

Tearing his eyes away he exchanged a glance with Edwina. 'There's little improvement in Caroline's condition. Perhaps your presence will lift her spirits.'

An exasperated look came over Lady Edwina's face. 'Caroline was always inclined to melancholy. It's about time she stopped indulging herself.' Beckoning to a maid to light her way she lifted up her skirts and headed for the stairs, muttering to herself as she went, 'She should be grateful the child did not survive its first year. Indeed, I cannot understand her at all. First she hates the poor little cripple, then when God sees fit to take her she grieves unnaturally.'

Catching Willow's eye, Ambrose held out his arm to her. 'Come to my study where we can become better acquainted. The housekeeper will attend us later.'

The study's gleaming oak panels and dark-blue velvet curtains conveyed a sense of masculinity. Facing the unlit fireplace were two leather chairs, so old that the hide had worn through to the horsehair in parts, and the sheen completely gone from them.

Willow seated herself in one. Her nostrils quivered with the newness of male-dominated scents of tobacco, perspiration and leather, then attempted to separate them from the more familiar ones of candles and beeswax. The room had an earthy country smell, yet its odour wasn't unpleasant.

'I'd forgotten you were so pretty,' Ambrose murmured, handing her a small glass of Madeira which glowed amber in the candlelight. 'My son is a lucky man.'

'I doubt if he remembers my appearance.' She gazed at the books lining the walls with interest. 'We met only fleetingly, and then I was but a child.'

And am still a child if I know Lady Edwina. Not in the least put out by her candour, Ambrose watched her glance wander across the paintings of hunting scenes. This one brought a smile, that one a frown. The painting of the fourth earl astride a charger, a fierce expression on his face as his sword sliced the air made her giggle. She turned and enchanted him with her smile.

'I cannot imagine why I was awed by you. You are not so fearsome when compared to the gentleman on the charger.'

Ambrose chuckled. 'He was my grandfather. I doubt the artist was kind to him. The portrait was banished to the attic whilst he lived.' He bade enter when a knock sounded on the door.

A middle-aged woman in a brown dress with starched white cuffs, apron and cap, bobbed a curtsy. 'I've prepared the rooms for Lady Som-

41

mersley as the countess instructed, My Lord.'

'Take her to them immediately, she must be tired.' Rising to his feet the earl took her hand and kissed her fingers. 'I hope you will be happy here. If there's anything you need you must tell Mrs Breton. She'll be happy to serve you.'

Mrs Breton looked far from happy to serve as she led her silently up the stairs then along a gallery lined with faces of long dead ancestors.

Willow shivered. Her own face would be staring from a gilt frame one day. They all looked so serious, but then marriage *was* a serious business. Idly, she wondered if any of the faces had ever loved each other.

The air grew musty as they turned into a corridor and traversed its length. Finally, Mrs Breton pushed open a door and stood aside for her to enter.

'I have lit the fire, My Lady.' She crossed to an adjoining door and thrust it open. 'Your bed-chamber is through here. A clothes closet and your maid's room through the other door. I've taken the liberty of instructing one of the foot-men to serve dinner in your chamber tonight. Lord Ambrose thought you'd prefer it after your journey.'

'Thank you, Mrs Breton.' She wrinkled her nose at the musty, damp smell pervading the place. 'Where's my maid?'

Mrs Breton's lips squeezed tightly together. Uneasily, she shifted from one foot to the other. 'In the scullery heating water. She seemed to think My Lady would require a bath.'

'She's right. I'm in the habit of bathing daily,

and have been two days without one.' Removing her cloak she threw it on the bed.

The dim light couldn't disguise a thick coating of dust. The dirty bed hangings were faded and stained with age. The room reeked of a neglect that not even the fire could cheer.

That the countess should choose to allocate her such quarters was an insult that bode badly for their future relationship.

If the rest of the house was any indication, Mrs Breton was an excellent housekeeper who took pride in her work. Aware that no servant could serve two mistresses, and that Mrs Breton could make her life difficult if she so chose, she'd have to step carefully.

She smiled. 'I hope my bathing at this time will not be inconvenient. As I commented to the earl, he's lucky in that his household appears extremely well managed.'

She wanted to laugh when her flattery brought a mollified expression to Mrs Breton's face. Theatrically, she swayed slightly before sinking into an overstuffed armchair. Closing her eyes, she whispered tiredly, 'I'll instruct my maid to consult with you in future. I'm indeed sorry to put you to so much trouble.'

'It's no trouble at all, Lady Sommersley.' The rustle of skirts put Mrs Breton directly in front of her. 'Is there anything I can do to be of help?'

Opening her eyes she gave a wan smile. 'Thank you, Mrs Breton. Kitty will be here shortly to ready me for bed. Be assured, the earl will hear of your devotion to my welfare.'

'I beg of you do not use the bed until I've

changed the straw palliasse for one of down. That one is sure to be damp.' Mrs Breton busied herself pulling the covers off the newly-made bed. 'I must have mistaken the instructions, though why the mistress insisted you be put in this wing when there are better chambers available, is beyond my understanding.'

'No doubt it can be cleaned. I shall ask the earl to recommend a maid of all work.'

The housekeeper appeared flustered when Kitty entered the room. 'I beg your pardon, My Lady. I spoke out of turn.'

'It's quite all right, Mrs Breton.' She gave her a conspiratorial smile. 'I didn't hear any criticism, and neither did my maid.'

'Indeed, I did not.' Kitty placed her burden on the floor and groaned as she straightened her back. ''Tis a long way from the scullery with your bath water. It will be cold before the bath is filled.'

Mrs Breton sniffed at Kitty's familiar tone.

Kitty, an orphaned child of a disgraced Irish maid, had been taken to Coringal Estate to serve Willow by a village woman. They'd both been eleven at the time. She'd become Willow's friend and companion, as well as her maid.

Lady Edwina constantly impressed on her the need to make Kitty aware of her station. From habit, she made allowances for her familiarity – something Mrs Breton would have to learn.

'Perhaps Mrs Breton could suggest a strong girl from the village who will fetch and carry the bathwater, and generally do for us. Sixpence a week should be sufficient wage.'

It was more than sufficient. Mrs Breton nodded her head and smiled in agreement. 'I have a niece who is simple in the head, but strong. Her name is Nellie.'

And she will do the work for threepence, Willow thought. She exchanged a smile with Kitty. It seemed that a deal had been struck. She was well satisfied. Life would be more comfortable from now on.

Caroline, Countess Lytton, was in a bad humour, and didn't bother to conceal it. 'I have no intention of welcoming this upstart who tricked Gerard into marriage.' Petulantly she took a bonbon from a dish and greedily crunched it between her teeth. 'To my mind, she's as bad as her father.'

Beckoning to her maid, she waited until her pillows had been plumped to her satisfaction before continuing her diatribe. 'She must indeed be sly to ingratiate herself into your good grace. Either that, or you're losing your wits in your old age.'

Stung, Edwina gazed at her daughter through narrowed eyes. Caroline had changed much over the past few years.

Her body had turned to fat, due no doubt to her habit of lying abed most of the day and consuming a selection from the dishes of sweetmeats placed about the room. Lines of discontent dragged her mouth down at the corners, giving her a shrewish look.

'If anyone is losing their wits it's you, Caroline.' Edwina stood up, preparing to take her leave. 'Your appearance disgusts me. You need to get some exercise and fresh air.'

'I'm ill.' Caroline lay back on the pillows and closed her eyes. 'My stomach hurts, and my head thumps unceasingly when I rise.' Self-pitying tears flooded her eyes. 'Ambrose rarely visits, and when Jeffrey pays his respects he cannot wait to leave. As for Gerard, he could be dead. I've heard the savages in the New World remove the scalps from their victims.'

She glared at her mother. 'It would have been more honourable for Gerard to have died challenging the marquess. And as for the sly trickery of this girl who duped him into marriage, does she really imagine I'll welcome her?'

'You selfish little fool.'

Caroline shrank into her pillows as her mother leaned over her.

'Your husband and sons are more than you deserve. Nobody thinks Gerard a coward. Indeed, his stature grew in the way he took control of a bad situation and rescued Willow from the cruelty of her father.'

'He should have sent her back. It is what she deserved.'

'You do your son no honour by wishing death upon him, nor by insulting his wife. She is a dear and worthy child, and the daughter of your childhood friend. *Bah!* I have no patience with you.' Running out of breath Edwina strode away from the bed, her back so stiff it resembled the raised hackles of a dog.

'Very well,' Caroline whined as she threw the door open. 'You may bring her this afternoon at three. But do not expect me to like her.'

46

'What you need, my girl, is a stick across your back,' Edwina muttered. Caroline was a stranger to her now, one she didn't much care for. What had happened to the daughter she'd once known and loved? It couldn't be grief for the child after all this time.

She puzzled over it whilst she made her way downstairs. Caroline had hated the poor misshapen mite and had banned the child from her sight. Only Ambrose had shown the child any pity, but his manner towards his wife had cooled after the infant's death.

Dear Ambrose. Edwina's good humour was restored as she thought of her son-in-law. He was a gentleman in every sense of the word, and his sons showed every indication of taking after him.

Gerard had the more fiery temperament of the three, but the quality enhanced, rather than detracted from him, giving his personality a dangerous edge that added an aura of uncertainty. Gerard had a presence others usually respected.

As she made her way to the main guest chambers, Edwina was looking forward to Gerard's return with something akin to eagerness. She'd resolved to live long enough to hold her great-grandchild in her arms, and couldn't wait to see which of its two strong-willed parents the child would resemble.

Five minutes later, she waylaid Mrs Breton on the servants' stairs and informed the hapless housekeeper what she thought of the quarters her ward had been allocated. Had she not realized her interference would only worsen matters, she would have confronted her daughter about it.

47

Personally, she supervised the cleaning, demanding new bed-hangings and fresh flowers. When she was finally satisfied the housekeeper was doing her job properly, she drew Kitty Adams aside.

'Where is your mistress this morning?'

'Out riding, My Lady. Mister Jeffrey is showing her the estate.'

'Humph!' Edwina's gaze fell on Nellie Breton in her tattered skirt. 'Who is *that* creature?'

'My niece, Lady Edwina.' Mrs Breton frowned as Nellie gave a gap-toothed smile. 'She's thick in the head and has been hired to fetch and carry for Lady Sommersley.'

Edwina crossed to Nellie and stared at her in curiosity. She'd never seen an idiot at close quarters before. 'What's your name, girl?' she said loudly.

'Nellie.' Forgetting to curtsy, Nellie fixed her eyes on Lady Edwina. 'I'm a good girl – and strong.'

'I'm sure you are.' Pitying the unfortunate, ugly girl, Edwina's voice softened. 'I will provide you with a new gown. You cannot serve your mistress wearing those rags.'

Eyes shining, Nellie dropped to her knees and kissed her benefactor's hand. 'Thank you, Lady. Nellie never forgets kindness.'

'Get up, get up!' Jerking her hand away, Edwina backed from the room. 'You will see to it Mrs Breton,' she called. 'Something serviceable. Present the bill to me.'

Willow discarded her cumbersome riding skirt to

expose the breeches she wore underneath. She grinned when Jeffrey gasped in shock, and placed a conspiratorial finger over his mouth. 'Swear you will not tell.'

'On my blood,' Jeffrey stammered.

Circe's breath whistled shrilly through her nostrils and she nudged Willow in the back. Willow tumbled into the straw.

Brian O'Shea laughed, his calloused hands reached out to pull her to her feet. 'Circe hasn't forgotten you, girlie.'

She stepped into the stirrup Brian made with his hands. Excitement bubbled through her veins as she was tossed on to the mare's back. She rubbed her face against Circe's silky mane and breathed in her familiar scent. 'Thank you, God,' she whispered. 'I feel I've truly come home now.'

Anxious, Jeffrey watched from his own mount. No amount of coaxing would stop Willow from taking the horse out. Still, he tried again. 'I beg you, Sister. Do not be rash. None but Brian O'Shea rides the mare. At least put a saddle on her.'

'Hush, Jeffrey.' Perched atop the prancing horse she dazzled him with her smile, then exchanged an amused glance with Brian. 'Circe and I have known each other since she was old enough to bear my weight. As for a saddle.' Her smile became wry. 'I know riding astride is frowned upon for women, but I know no other way. Circe may be broken to a saddle now, but I am not.'

'It would be my pleasure to teach you.' He coloured at his boldness. He shouldn't be encouraging his sister-in-law to flout convention.

49

He shrugged, as her violet eyes teased him. Instinct told him she'd flout it anyway, and he was not in the position to insist.

'Then you shall, Jeffrey.' She saw him watch her small hands apply tension to the reins, assessing her level of expertise. She gave a small smile. 'The tuition shall start tomorrow. Today you will escort me round the estate that is to be my home.'

Arrows of happiness aimed themselves at Jeffrey's misgivings, banishing them from his mind. She was the most captivating creature he'd ever set eyes on. He would be her protector, he thought, following the prancing horse and rider from the cobbled yard. Anything she demanded he would give, even his life. At least ... until his brother came home.

He stayed with her until they reached the first meadow. His own mount, infected by the raw excitement of the other horse and rider, neighed and pawed restlessly at the ground.

'This path will take us around the lake, over the rise and into the forest beyond. The clearing with the abandoned cottage is about a mile in.' He hesitated. 'The track into the forest is barred by the trunk of an oak tree which fell during a storm last winter. Usually I put my horse to it but...'

But his companion had gone.

Jeffrey momentarily admired the small figure clinging lightly to Circe's back, and blessed his brother's good luck for procuring such a wife.

Then he thought of the fallen tree and frowned. Her mount was fresh and Willow was without a saddle and stirrups for support. Heart in his mouth, he urged his horse after her in a vain attempt to catch her up. Nothing could match Circe for speed, and Willow had given her her head.

Willow had no such fears as she led Circe along the tree trunk. 'Can you do it, girl?' Circe's ears pricked forward. 'There's a slight downward slope on the other side just like at Coringal. Remember the wall at Coringal, how we used to pretend you had wings like Pegasus and we flew right over the top?'

Cantering the mare back along the track Willow felt Circe's tail flick upright into a plume and knew she remembered.

'*Stop!*'

Knowing she couldn't possibly hear his shout, Jeffrey reined in his horse on the rise and watched horse and rider wheel about. The tiny figure almost lay along Circe's back as the mare pawed the air then, tail erect, began to canter towards the tree trunk. His mouth stretched into a grin of delight. Horse and rider were almost one. They were a wonderful sight.

Excitement mounted in him as the pair picked up speed. He heard himself urging them on.

When they reached the tree trunk, Circe seemed to hesitate, giving him a moment's doubt. Then the mare gathered her muscles together and soared across the barrier with room to spare.

Breath expelled from his mouth with a harsh rattling sound as a figure in red emerged from a stand of trees. It was the lieutenant who'd acted as escort. He took the jump at a gallop and

51

disappeared into the forest after her.

Having observed the officer's familiarity the day before, and Willow's frosty replies, Jeffrey knew this was no assignation. Even if it was, he was duty bound to intercept and protect his sister-in-law's good name.

His heart began to pound as he suddenly realized there was a world of difference between being a protector in his heart and acting on it. Nevertheless, he urged his horse to a gallop and prayed he'd catch up with Willow before the soldier did.

The presence of danger played no part in Willow's thinking that morning. She was enjoying her freedom from the constraints placed on her by Lady Edwina's patronage.

Jeffrey was a pleasant companion, and had proved to be more malleable than she'd expected. Having discovered he could fence, she intended to take advantage of his swordsmanship and practise the skills she'd been forced to abandon over the past four years. When they reached the clearing he'd promised her a match.

Hearing hoofbeats behind her, she leapt from Circe's back and turned to face him. Her smile faded when Hugh Macbride emerged from the trees.

'*You!*'

'Lady Sommersley.' Leaning forward in his saddle, his eyes lingered on her breeches for a few seconds.

She felt uncomfortable when he smiled.

'Very fetching, my dear.' Leaping from his horse

he strolled lazily towards her and gave a little bow. 'I see you ride with no groom. I must warn you, an unescorted woman positively *invites* danger.'

'You're mistaken, Lieutenant,' she retorted. 'I do not ride alone. You need not delay your journey on my account.'

He opened the top button of his tunic. 'I never disengage my duties lightly, madam. I'll keep you company until your escort appears.' He held up a hand when she sought to protest. 'Do not argue. Once I've set my course on a path of action I'm not easily swayed from it. An admirable trait in a soldier, don't you think?'

'I suppose a soldier must possess such a quality if he wishes to conquer rather than be conquered.' She wondered where Jeffrey was. Turning her back on Hugh Macbride she wandered over to the cottage and peered through the grimy window. The cottage was crudely furnished and had the air of not being lived in for a long time.

'Where do you go from here?' she asked, turning back towards him. She gave a startled gasp when his breath fanned against her cheek. 'Step back, sir. You are immodestly close.'

He ignored her demand. 'We're to be stationed at Dorchester until the spring, then on to India.' His eyes bored hotly into hers. 'One kiss and I'll bear the exile a happy man.'

Alarmed by the intimacy of his smile, she prepared to push past him. His arms came up either side of her, trapping her against the building.

'Let me go, sir,' she managed to get out before his mouth cut off her words. She'd often imagined what kissing would feel like, but the rush of bodily pleasure she experienced was unprecedented.

She momentarily froze as his hot mouth explored hers, then gasped in dismay as his hands brushed against her breasts. Placing her hands against his chest she tried to push him away. The action served only to inflame him.

He laughed at her blushing face, then taking her hand, placed it against the swelling mound in his groin. 'You should not tease, My Lady,' he said, pushing himself against her hand and cupping his manhood snugly inside it. 'See what you have done to me?'

'Pray let me go, sir,' she entreated, all too aware of his intention. 'My husband will have no regard for me if he does not find me intact on his return.'

Her naïve remark brought an expression of avarice to his handsome face. The shape in her hand nudged into extra firmness.

'Your husband deserves cuckolding for his neglect of you.' The back of his hand stroked down her face, his fingers lingered on her lips. 'What a trophy,' he gloated. 'One hundred guineas to the man who takes your maidenhood. I'll have a lock of your hair to prove it. I'll be the toast of London.'

Her temper, which had lain dormant for quite some time, suddenly flared into life. 'You will not take it easily, sir.'

Sinking her teeth into his hand she bit down with all her might. At the same time her nails dug into the abomination encased in her hand.

Had her ears been pansies they'd have shrivelled from the heat of the oath Hugh Macbride roared. He caught one of her wrists as she sought to evade him, twisting it until she cried out with pain.

'If you do not give yourself willingly I'll be forced to hurt you. The outcome will be the same.' He smiled as he divested himself of his weapons and accoutrements, and placed his loaded pistol on the window sill to keep it out of the dust. 'Using force will merely add pleasure to the conquest.'

'Is ravishing a defenceless woman part of a soldier's duty?' Her free hand crept towards her dagger and loosened it from its scabbard. She'd kept it sharp since her husband had demonstrated its uselessness.

'Let's say it's one of the more pleasant aspects of soldiering.' He kicked open the door of the cottage. 'Come, madam. I'll see if I can find a soft bed for your initiation. I'm not without skill in these matters and can offer you pleasure in return for your cooperation.'

'Marquess Lynchcross is my father,' she warned, giving him one last chance to change his mind. 'He'll kill you.'

He threw back his head and guffawed with laughter. 'You little fool, it's the marquess who provides the purse for the sport. He's heard that your husband is expected home, and is after his blood.'

Colour drained from her face. Her own father! What manner of man could hate his own daughter enough to fund such a wager? Was he devoid of all conscience? She remembered the savagery of the beating he'd inflicted on her when she'd been fourteen. Her father was a sadist. No wonder her mother had cursed him on her deathbed. The hurt fled, replaced by loathing.

Like a blighted apple, her life would wither and die should Hugh Macbride carry out his vile intention.

The Lytton family would be embroiled in a scandal; she, disgraced. Her husband would be obliged to challenge Hugh Macbride, then meet her father if he survived. She would be cast from the company of those she loved, for even Lady Edwina would be unforgiving should her beloved Gerard perish in defence of her. Life would not be worth living in that event, so she might as well kill herself now.

Her heart leapt in fear as her thumb touched against the blade of the knife. Life surged through her body like sap rising in spring.

Why should I be the one to lose my life? she asked herself. It was the soldier who deserved to be punished.

'My father will not make sport of me, and neither will you,' she hissed. Counting on surprise, her dagger slashed upwards. 'Take this back to London as a message to the marquess.'

'Lucifer's oath!' His startled exclamation ended in a gurgle as blood gushed warmly from his cheek. He'd been expertly sliced from his eye right to his jaw-bone.

He staggered backwards, his hand automatically favouring the wound. *What an adversary!* She was going to be worth pursuing even *without* the price on her head. Women who needed a little taming were always exciting. This one was as wild and as beautiful as the mare she rode.

She was already heading for the mare, a great black beast lacking both saddle and stirrups. He wanted to laugh when she realized she couldn't mount without help. Her eyes scanned the surrounding forest for an escape route. Whatever direction she moved in he could block, and she knew it. Her glance grazed over his sword lying on the ground, then came back to it.

Her predictability was to be expected. He was surprised she would choose to die to preserve her virginity. There was something touchingly old-fashioned about it. Tempted to let her go, he remembered his gambling debts. The one-hundred-guinea purse was as good as his.

'Damn you, girl!' It was a strategy he wouldn't have expected from a woman. A feint towards the sword, then after his foot came down on it he looked up to find himself gazing down the barrel of his own pistol.

'Back away. If you make a move towards your sword I'll shoot you!'

'The pistol is not primed,' he lied, his voice displaying more confidence than he felt.

'I'm familiar with the use of a pistol.'

The fact that neither her hand nor her eyes wavered in their intent, convinced him she was telling the truth. He took a hasty step backward.

Willow had no idea what to do next. Threatening to shoot was one thing, but carrying out the deed in cold blood...? A delicate shudder trickled through her body as she watched the blood seep from his wound.

She had no desire to kill him now she'd gained the upper hand. The scar he'd carry would be punishment enough. When word of the incident got out it would serve as a warning to others who sought to win her father's purse.

But how could she escape? She was unable to mount Circe unaided, and as soon as she turned away he would be upon her. Already, she could see his mind at work, the confidence returning to his eyes. The solution was so simple she wanted to laugh out loud when it occurred to her.

'Remove your breeches, sir.'

Hugh Macbride gazed desperately around him as he realized what her strategy was. 'Let me go, madam. I'll ride away and we'll forget this incident ever happened.'

'You may, but I will not.' Confidence restored, she lowered the gun a fraction, 'Come, Lieutenant, why the modesty? A minute ago you couldn't wait to get them off.'

The position in which the gun was pointed wasn't reassuring. His eyes narrowed. Lady Sommersley had a surprisingly sadistic sense of humour. He just hoped she knew her way around a pistol. 'Isn't the wound revenge enough? Do you seek to shame me in front of my men as well?'

'You shame yourself, sir.' Relief flooded her when Jeffrey came panting into the clearing.

'You are unharmed, Sister?' Rushing to her side, he gazed with astonished eyes at the cocked pistol, then at the wound on Hugh Macbride's face. 'I would have arrived sooner had my horse not become lame. You'll allow me the honour of finishing him off.' Drawing one of the rapiers he

carried from its sheath, he removed the protective tip.

'I'll allow you no such thing,' she snapped. 'The
man is an officer of the King's Own Regiment,
and disarmed. His death would bring you no
honour.' Recognizing Jeffrey's need to prove himself she smiled at him. 'If you could but persuade
him to remove his breeches, we could take his
horse and escape.'

'It would not be seemly to offend your eyes
with such a sight.'

Hugh Macbride's lips twitched at Jeffrey's
words. She wanted to grin herself, and only just
managed to stifle a giggle.

'He will disrobe in the cottage and throw his
clothes out through the door.'

Jeffrey was given to showy gestures, she
realized, when the rapier slashed towards the
officer's discarded coat and neatly severed every
button. As a demonstration of swordsmanship it
was without par: as a warning, it worked.

Hugh Macbride's eyes narrowed warily. 'I'll do
as you ask, but I beg you. Do not leave me without uniform.'

'Your clothing will be left at the edge of the
clearing.' Taking the pistol from her hand Jeffrey
indicated the cottage with it, his eyes flint hard.
'We will leave your horse on the track to the road.
You owe your life to my sister-in-law's indulgence
in this matter, but let me warn you, if you ever set
foot on this estate again you'll draw your last
breath before you leave. Is that understood?'

Hugh bowed his head in defeat. Walking into
the cottage he closed the door behind him, his

eyes smouldering with embarrassment.

Due to his extreme youth, it was inevitable Jeffrey would crow about his part in the rescue of his sister-in-law. Just as inevitable – word reached Hugh Macbride's men before he did.

They said nothing when their bloodied officer rejoined them in a foul humour. But when they reached Dorchester and the officer was taken to a surgeon for attention, the tale was told, then retold with gleeful malice at the tavern. From there the story boarded a coach to London.

By the time Hugh Macbride emerged from the surgeon's house, his face criss-crossed by stitches, his treatment at the hands of a young noblewoman whom he'd sought to seduce was well on the way to becoming public knowledge.

Meanwhile, the hapless victim – having been interviewed by the earl and rigorously interrogated by Lady Edwina – was now subject to the scrutiny of her mother-in-law.

It was a case of instant dislike for both parties.

'She does not have the refinement of her mother,' the mistress of the house said. Her fingers hovered over a dish of tiny almond biscuits. Selecting the largest she popped it into her mouth and flicked Willow a disdainful gaze.

'My mother tells me your accomplishments are indifferent. Marietta had the sweetest singing voice and her embroidery was excellent.'

'She must indeed have been a wonderful woman,' Willow muttered, bored to tears with this litany of perfection with which she was being presented. 'Pray tell me she had faults so I may compare myself to her in, at least, one way.'

'If you insist.' Caroline's mouth tightened into a thin cruel, line. 'Your mother was a flirt. That is ... until your father came into her life. After that, she never flirted again.'

'That's enough!' Edwina got to her feet. 'It does you no credit to speak ill of the dead, Caroline, especially when that ill concerns the innocent child of that person.'

'Innocent indeed,' Caroline scorned, counting Willow's sins off on her fingers 'First she traps the heir to Lytton Estate in marriage. Now she becomes involved in a situation with an officer, which not only causes Jeffrey to risk his life, but brings shame on the family name. I do not consider that to be the action of an innocent child.' A sigh deflated her back into the pillows and reduced her voice to a whine. 'For pity's sake, take the scheming creature from my sight. She's not welcome here.'

'Then I will not inflict my presence upon you any longer.' With all the dignity she could muster, Willow rose to her feet. She had done nothing to be ashamed of. She engaged her mother-in-law's glance coolly. 'My respects, Mother-in-law.' Making a parody of a curtsy she slowly exited the room, her head held high. Only the spots of colour glowing in her cheeks gave indication of her inner turmoil.

Following her, Edwina felt proud of Willow's courage and control.

Once outside, the control deserted her, however. Tears sprang to her eyes and her teeth bit into her trembling bottom lip. 'What have I done

61

to deserve such dislike?' she whispered.

'Nothing, my love.' Edwina pulled her close, and oblivious to the tears staining her dress, she led Willow towards her quarters. 'Caroline despises herself, and she blames others for it. Come, we'll take tea together. You will tell me again exactly what took place this morning. As much as I love my grandson, I fear the young rapscallion has a talent for embroidering the truth.'

Despite her tears, Willow laughed. 'Jeffrey is a fine, brave boy. Already I'm growing fond of him.'

'And he you.' Lady Edwina's dry remark brought consternation to Willow's face. 'Jeffrey is at an impressionable age. Puppy love can be painful. Be careful how you treat him, my dear.'

'I'll try to be considerate of his feelings, Grand-mother.' Willow smiled, grateful for the timely warning. 'My regard for him will be that of a sister.'

The maturity with which she spoke reassured Lady Edwina. She hoped Gerard would be equally solicitous of Willow's feelings when he returned. Unless he'd very much changed, she couldn't see any reason why he wouldn't be.

At Sheronwood, three new cases of smallpox appeared.

Lady Rosamond sent word to Lytton House via a manservant, who stood some distance from the gatekeeper and relayed the message by word of mouth.

'The mistress is putting the place in quarantine. No one's to be allowed in or out.'

'You'd best be getting back there then,' the

gatekeeper said nervously.

'Not bloody likely,' the servant exclaimed. 'I'm not sick and I don't aim to get sick. I'm off to America. I hear tell there's plenty of opportunities there for the likes of me.'

'Not without money, there ain't.'

'The Marquess of Lynchcross will provide the means.' The man gave a sly wink. 'I knows things he wouldn't want to become public knowledge.'

'Such as?' Despite his fear of the disease, the gatekeeper's curiosity got the better of him. He allowed the servant to sidle closer and listened to what he had to say. After a while, the gate-keeper's eyes widened in shocked surprise.

'Does your mistress know about it?'

'Not her. She's as deaf as a post. Anyway, nobody visits that part of the house since the estate manager declared it unsafe, except for that hard-faced cow of a housekeeper.' The servant grinned. 'It took half a bottle of brandy to loosen her up enough to find out what was goin' on, but it's going to be worth it. The marquess will be glad to pay me off. Just you wait and see.'

A week later a boat fished the body of the man from the River Thames. His throat had been cut.

The cadaver was taken to the morgue where it joined two other bodies taken from the river that day. Without identification, the three corpses were piled on a cart and conveyed to Guy's Hospital for dissection.

The morgue-keeper jingled the coins in his pocket as he walked happily towards the tavern. It had proved to be a lucrative day.

CHAPTER THREE

Autumn – 1754 – Winter

Smallpox! Even though she and Kitty had survived a mild case in Ireland, the word sent a thrill of dread through Willow. 'Can it be caught twice?'

Edwina shrugged. 'Doctor Tansy says there's evidence of immunity.'

They were walking in the garden. Autumn had lingered through October and the day was clad in an amber-hued haze. Leaves drifted about their shoulders like russet snowflakes before falling to the ground to be crunched underfoot. The mellow stone walls of Lytton House shone pink, the mullioned windows flaming reflections of sunlight. Willow couldn't believe some of its occupants would be dead before the disease ran its course.

Everything looked so normal. In the orchard, workers were picking the last of the fruit for storage, children gathered baskets of chestnuts in the grounds. Honey was being collected, herbs picked for drying.

To her left, a thin wisp of smoke spiralled towards the sky from a bonfire. She shivered. If the contagion spread, the bonfires would be kept stoked with the soiled bedding and clothing of the infected. Nothing could be left to chance.

'It's essential the servants are given no cause to

panic,' Edwina said. 'Ambrose is going to summon them to the great hall and put into action the plan suggested by Doctor Tansy. The diseased will be isolated in one wing. Those who have survived earlier contact will care for those who succumb.

'A notice of quarantine will be posted on the gate. Deaths must be recorded; the corpses sewn securely into canvas sacks and left at the gate for the cart to pick up.'

'It didn't work at Sheronwood,' Willow pointed out, shuddering at the scenario her Grandmother painted. 'The servants deserted, leaving Lady Rosamond and those already sick to die alone.'

'Sheronwood lacked a master, and Rosamond was too weak to enforce her will.' Edwina sighed. 'Thank God young Edward was with us.'

'But now *we* have the infection the Sheronwood heir is still in danger.'

'Daphne de Vere is young enough to produce another heir should the need arise.' Edwina frowned in distaste as she added absently, 'Though rumour has it her husband practises the French fashion.'

'What is that?'

Sometimes, Edwina forgot Willow was married only in name. She'd be ignorant of such practices. Still, she surmised, what Daphne had managed once with her husband she could manage again. All men could be enticed to do their duty, even those of an effeminate nature.

However, it was not her job to educate Willow in such matters. Gerard would not thank her for it if she did. She must remain pure in mind and body until he decided otherwise.

Edwina wondered where he was at that moment. It had been two months since she'd received his last letter. 'Gerard survived smallpox in his infancy,' she mused. 'He will not be in danger when he arrives home.'

'He's in England? You've heard from him?'

'Not of late. He is *en route* I should imagine.'

'Perhaps he'll decide to stay in London.'

Exasperation gripped Edwina when Willow smiled. The girl revelled in the freedom of country life. Ambrose and Jeffrey adored her.

Most of the household was aware she disguised herself as a boy, rode astride, fenced, hunted for rabbits in the forest and behaved in an unfeminine fashion when she thought she wasn't being observed. The servants talked of little else. All admired her spirit and turned a blind eye to it.

'Your smile is too smug,' Edwina warned. 'Your husband will not be as indulgent with you as his brother and the earl. He'll have your respect.'

'That he'll have to earn.' Willow's eyes snapped with defiance at the thought of being told what to do by a husband she hardly knew. 'I will not be dominated by a man who insults his wife by ignoring her for several years.'

I do not doubt that, Edwina thought. Gerard will have to learn how to compromise. The sparkling confidence in Willow's eyes made her smile. And you will not have things all *your* way missy, and that will do *you* no harm.

Linking arms, Edwina gazed up at the house. 'I pray God spares the Lytton family and all who serve them from this dreadful disease, be they believers or sinners.'

God, it seemed, was not disposed towards granting favours that day – nor for some time to come.

'I forbid you to do this, Willow.' Shocked, Edwina gazed at her ward. More shocking than her actions was the large, white apron worn over a plain servant's gown. 'Nursing the servants is not a fitting occupation for a lady.'

Taking one end of a vinegar-soaked sheet Willow ignored her words, handing the other end to the idiot girl, Nellie. She secured it across a doorway. 'The servants are dropping like flies, Grandmother. If they're to survive they need help, if they're destined to die they need comfort.'

Over the past five weeks, the disease had swiftly cut a swathe through Lytton House. A third of the servants had died. Most of the family had already been exposed to the disease and had some immunity.

The exception was Caroline Lytton, who was locked in her room with her maid. No one was allowed in. Her meals were left outside, the windows kept tightly shut.

Edward de Vere had been mildly infected. Willow had nursed him back to recovery herself after his nurse succumbed to the disease. The boy's fevered body had stirred her to such pity she'd forgotten her own comfort and resolved to relieve the suffering the disease forced on its victims.

She'd swiftly earned the respect of the staff who were suffering extreme fatigue. Knowing the servants could not work indefinitely without rest, she'd developed a rotating system of duties, restricted to those which were strictly necessary.

'When I inform Ambrose of what you are about he'll be as shocked as me.'

'I have the earl's permission,' she said calmly. It wasn't exactly the truth; the earl had merely given her permission to nurse Edward, heir to Sheronwood.

The earl set his own fine example by working as long and as hard as any man on the estate. Jeffrey trod in his father's footsteps. Father and son left before the sun was up, returning exhausted after dark. Although they never discussed it with her, she suspected they shared the more grisly tasks associated with the disease.

Knowing Lady Edwina was at a loose end without her company, Willow kissed her on the cheek. 'It would help me much if you could be company to young Edward during his convalescence, Grandmother. I've left him in the charge of a young scullery maid.' She pressed two fingers against her brow to ease her tiredness. 'I could do with her strong arms.'

Emotion overwhelmed Edwina. She was a useless old woman. Willow was wearing herself out, and she was doing nothing but criticize when she should be helping. 'It was indeed a fortunate day when Gerard brought you to my door,' she choked out. 'Words cannot express how I feel about you.'

'Then do not try.' Willow knew that if she started weeping, nothing would stop her, with the tragedy surrounding her. She couldn't afford to break down.

The hug they exchanged said it all.

Despite her precautions, Caroline succumbed to the disease two days later. Her death was mercifully swift, her high fever causing convulsions which stopped her heart before the disease ran its course.

Summoned by Lady Caroline's terrified maid, Willow did her best to nurse her mother-in-law whilst she comforted Lady Edwina. One lucid moment occurred in the hour before Caroline died, one in which she begged Willow to come closer.

'I'm sorry Marietta,' she whispered, her eyes glazed with fever. 'It was always you Ambrose loved. The marquess ... I did not expect him to compromise you when I enlisted his help.' A cough rattled in her throat.

The glass of water she held to Caroline's lips was pushed away. 'He made me pay. He threatened to inform Ambrose of my part in the affair if I did not ... did not...' Her voice rose to an anguished wail. 'The crippled child was God's punishment.'

'Hush.' Willow exchanged an appalled glance with Edwina. 'Do not fret about the past.'

Caroline seemed desperate to cleanse her soul of guilt. 'Ambrose was unaware the marquess fathered the infant, but I knew he'd eventually suspect.' Her face twisted into a grimace. 'I smothered her with a cloth.'

Edwina gave a shocked cry.

'When Ambrose found out I'd killed the child, he began to pity me. He always loved you.' Her hand clamped around Willow's wrist with surprising strength. *'Forgive me, Marietta!'*

At Edwina's nod, Willow whispered the words Caroline needed to hear. Shortly after, Caroline lapsed into unconsciousness.

'We'd better send word to Ambrose.' Ashen-faced, Edwina rose to her feet. 'Is there no end to my daughter's wickedness?' she whispered. 'Her soul will surely burn in Hell.'

Lady Edwina seemed to have aged ten years in as many minutes. Willow understood the ramifications of Caroline's confession. Made on the deathbed, it was therefore the truth. The earl would have no choice but to call out the marquess.

'Perhaps it would be better if the earl was left in ignorance,' Willow suggested, checking that the maid was not within earshot. 'I see no benefit for any of us in telling him, only grief.'

'You can forgive her for the wrong she did your mother?'

'Her wrong-doing was the catalyst for my existence,' she said simply. 'If the confession is revealed, will it bring the crippled child or my mother back to life? I'd rather carry the burden of her sin than compound it with the downfall of Ambrose. The earl's no match for my father. Let this be our secret.'

'It will be as you say.' Colour returned to Edwina's cheeks. She gazed down at her daughter with more compassion. 'No wonder she was troubled. I will stay and pray until death claims her. It will not be long.'

'May God hear your prayers, Grandmother,'

Willow murmured, stooping to kiss the woman's cheek. 'For I must admit He pays scant regard to mine.'

A sudden cold spell signalled the end of the epidemic. Tired to the marrow, Willow gazed out at the thick frost crusting the grounds. The two servants still confined to bed would be out of quarantine tomorrow. No new cases had been reported.

Caroline's body had been taken away with the rest and buried in the family plot without pomp or ceremony. The earl had shown little emotion. Jeffrey, now accustomed to the sight of death, had accepted the news with a weary resignation that made Willow's heart bleed for him.

The heat had gone from the bonfires, the flickering flames had become a spiral of acrid smoke that coiled upwards to join the clouds.

'Thank God it's over.' Drawing a shawl round her shoulders she gave orders for the house to be scrubbed from top to bottom with vinegar, then made fragrant with bunches of dried lavender and rosemary.

They'd just completed the task, when one of the maids came to fetch her. The girl's eyes were heavy with fatigue. 'Master Jeffrey has the sickness. The master said to come at once.'

A thrill of despair ran through Willow's body. *Dear God*, she prayed, hurrying after the maid. *Do not take Jeffrey from us. He has hardly lived. Take me if Your appetite has not yet been sated, but not Jeffrey. Please, Lord.*

Ambrose looked like death itself. Grey-faced

and hollow-eyed, she had never seen such anguish in a man. It would be useless asking him to get some rest whilst his son needed him.

'You must have had the symptoms for some time,' she scolded, coaxing the youth into swallowing an infusion of meadowsweet. 'The rash is already advanced. Why did you not tell me you were unwell?'

'I did not notice until this morning when I began to itch.' She could have died at the fright in his eyes.

She puzzled over a group of blisters decorating Jeffrey's arm. There was something different about this. The rash of the smallpox victims she'd nursed had started on the trunk; Jeffrey's rash was characterized by a line of blisters. His fever was mild. A smile nudged the corner of her mouth as she turned to Ambrose.

'He survived smallpox in infancy, did he not?'

Ambrose nodded tiredly.

'I believe this is shingles.'

'Shingles!' His breath expelled in one relieved rush. 'You're positive?'

'Almost.' She could have danced upon the spot with relief. She would not take God for granted again. 'I will ask Doctor Tansy to confirm it when he comes to visit.'

Her smile was joyous when she gazed at him. Ambrose was momentarily overcome by dizziness and staggered to a chair. Instantly, she was by his side, concern mirrored on her face.

'Jeffrey is in no danger. I insist you go to bed and rest, dearest Father.' Leaning forward, she kissed the look of uncertainty from his gaunt cheek. 'If need be, I'll call you.'

Ambrose was stumbling when he left. A great lassitude filled his limbs and his tongue seemed too large for his mouth. He felt older than his fifty-six years.

He'd hardly seated himself on the bed when his head seemed to split asunder and he fell sideways. Without the strength to lift himself, he rolled from the bed to the floor.

His valet gazed down at him with fearful eyes.

I'm dying, he tried to say. Summon Gerard to my side. To his horror, he found he was unable to move or utter a word.

Gerard heaved a sigh of relief when he finally set foot on English soil. The journey across the Atlantic Ocean had been made perilous by storms. Both he and Charles had succumbed to the malady of sea-sickness. Dry land was reassuringly solid.

Charles stamped his feet against the cold. 'It looks as though it might snow. Don't tarry too long in London if you intend spending New Year's Eve at Lytton House. The road will become impassable.'

'I leave in the morning.' He fingered his beard. He'd intended to visit a barber before he headed for Dorset. Now he decided against it, it would provide protection from the cold.

Impulsively he turned to his friend. 'Travel down with me, Charles. You're most welcome to spend the New Year celebrations with us.'

'I must pay my respects to my family. Then I intend to find myself some rooms before I apply to become a student surgeon at Guy's Hospital.' He clasped the hand Gerard extended. 'Keep well, friend.'

'And you.'

They'd shared much together, but their brotherhood had reached an end. They'd matured over the past few years and now had different paths to take, different responsibilities to fulfil.

Neither of them looked back when they parted, and neither man admitted that the tears blurring their vision was caused by anything but the biting cold.

Daphne de Vere smiled when the marquess slid a heavy diamond necklace against her throat.

'Black looks well on you,' he said. 'Widowhood will suit you.'

My grandmother is hardly cold in her grave, she thought, and not only does he pursue his own stepdaughter, he hastens death towards his nephew.

'I'm not a widow yet,' she said quietly. 'And I cannot accept such a gift. People will talk.'

'Let them.' The marquess was besotted with Daphne. From a rather plump child who'd learned to please him in many ways, she'd blossomed into a voluptuous woman.

Eduard had been chosen as a spouse for his lack of manly attributes. The bastard son of his dead sister had surprised and thwarted him by getting Daphne with child.

Daphne had become a skilled courtesan since he'd introduced her to the court shortly after her marriage. The King was fond of her, and sought her company on many an occasion.

She led a demanding life, one from which the marquess was beginning to find himself excluded. The strain was beginning to show in the paleness of her face, and the listlessness which beset her when she woke.

Once her maid had carefully applied the white paste, rouge and patches, to her face, she sparkled with a beauty, energy and wit that was the envy of the other court ladies.

Edward was the only bone of contention between them. Daphne was adamant her son would stay in Dorset. Eduard suffered from ever increasing bouts of insanity, and was now permanently restrained. She was scared he would escape and harm her son, as he often threatened.

'Lady Sommersley writes that my son is happy at Lytton House,' she pointed out. 'He's survived smallpox and is making progress with his riding lessons.'

'He could have riding lessons here.'

'The King has indicated he's pleased with his godson's progress. He wishes him to stay there.' Tears pricked her eyes. 'Perhaps I shall find time to visit him in the spring.'

The marquess was not prepared to oppose the King's will, and despite his inclination to see his heir, had no intention of losing face by visiting Lytton House.

If only he'd been able to father a son from his three dead wives. Of his daughters, only one had survived. Willow, the daughter of the witch. He would have killed her in infancy had he not been in fear of her mother.

Marietta had been his ward from a defunct French branch of the family. She'd come to him with a fortune after her mother had been arrested – then executed – for offences against the French throne.

Marietta had been independent by nature. The more he'd tried to beat it out of her the worse she'd become.

When she'd fallen in love with Ambrose Lytton, the empty-headed Caroline Cowan had warned him of the affair. Full of spite, she'd been frightened of losing the earl.

He'd deflowered Marietta when she was fifteen, then married her himself. He'd possessed her body, but had never conquered her mind. She'd hated him with a passion. For years, she'd both excited and repelled him.

Her interest in the occult had bothered him somewhat, but he'd overlooked that at first. When she'd unexpectedly become pregnant a few years after the marriage, his hopes for an heir had been revived. Delivered of a healthy daughter, she laughed at his bitter disappointment.

'You'll never beget a male heir,' she'd prophesied. 'I have cursed your seed.'

In his rage he'd torn the suckling infant from her breast. 'You'll never see the child again,' he'd whispered. 'And you'll never know if she lives or dies.'

'I'll know.' Her eyes had been full of malevolence. 'Willow has God's protection. If your hand brings her death, you'll burn in everlasting fire. Whilst I live I will *always* know. I'm gifted with second sight.'

'You shall not live long enough to use it.'

His rage had known no bounds. That night he'd given her to several of his drunken compatriots for sport. Afterwards, he'd beaten her to pulp and taken her body to the woods.

The moon had sent a beam of silver to touch her face as he'd laid her in her grave. Her eyes, glowing with loathing had flickered open. They'd haunted his dreams ever since.

Shivers raced up his spine as he caught Daphne's glance in the mirror. For a moment, she had the look of one who was enjoying his discomfort. Rational thought took over. Daphne knew nothing, and even if she did she'd say nothing, fearing she'd risk losing her popularity in court circles. She enjoyed her position too much.

Besides, Marietta's curse had not worked, he scoffed. Daphne had provided him with a strong heir who'd just survived smallpox. He slipped his hand inside her bodice and touched the ripe peak of her nipple. His desire was something almost tangible, beating in his breast like a drum.

It was a desire she ignored. Daphne was no longer the sweet, innocent child he'd fondled upon his lap. Unaware then that his fondness for her sprang from the sickness in him, now she punished him for it withholding from him that which he craved most.

She gave a silvery laugh as she slapped his hand away. Her eyes glowed cruelly as she rose from her seat and shook her rustling skirt into place. 'Do not crush my gown. The King requests my company later tonight.'

He bit back a frustrated sigh as he offered

Daphne his arm. Had it been anyone else he would have called him out and killed him. His fingers closed around the necklace, then gently twisted it. Fear came into her eyes as the necklace tightened around her neck.

'He is an old man. He will tire of you soon.'

Loosening his grip, he flicked an imaginary piece of fluff from the cuff of his green brocade coat.

'I invited Sapphire,' Daphne said, as they descended the sweeping marble staircase to the salon below. 'She wrote to say she was honoured by my invitation but was leaving shortly for the country.'

'She should feel honoured,' he growled. 'You're the toast of London, my dear.' Proudly he added, 'If it hadn't been for me you'd be buried in the country breeding brats for the Lytton family. Don't you ever forget that.'

Daphne thought bitterly: no, I'll never forget it!

Snow! The flake on her tongue melted swiftly as Willow drew it into her mouth. Grinning at Brian O'Shea she indicated the track. 'A race?'

Brian was exercising Ambrose's stallion, a muscular grey with an ungainly rapid stride, an ugly nose and an intelligent eye. Most of the horses on the estate were bred from him, but so far Circe had refused to be covered by him.

Brian indicated the hedge Willow was pointed at. 'This old boy can run, but his steeplechasing days are over.' He watched Circe dance delicately on the spot. 'She's frisky this morning. She'll be coming into season again, I reckon. It's a pity we

78

haven't permission to use one of the Sheronwood stallions. The Lytton stables could do with some fresh blood.'

'Sheronwood is deserted, and the horses sold.'

'One of the stallions escaped and is roaming the grounds.' Brian grinned to himself. 'To be sure, he's a handsome fellow, almost as dark as Circe with a white star on his nose.'

'Then we'd be doing them a favour if we stabled the poor creature for the winter.' Willow gazed at Brian with twinkling eyes. 'To be sure, the poor creature will freeze to death if my wily Irish groom doesn't play the Good Samaritan.'

'You're a girl after me own heart, darlin' child.'

'So say you, Brian O'Shea.' She gave a soft laugh. 'If that's the case, why does Kitty spend more time at the stables than she does attending her mistress? Is it teaching her to ride, you're after?'

Brian smiled. 'It's marrying her I'm after, but she won't say yes and she won't say no at the moment. Her first loyalty is to you.' Gloom edged into his voice. 'Even if Kitty said yes we'd need the earl's permission, and he – poor soul – is in no state to grant it. The man would be better off dead.'

'If you dare say that again I'll have you thrown off the estate,' she snapped. 'Doctor Tansy said the earl might regain his faculties and strength, and I have told God that he *must*.'

Unaffected by her imperious flash of temper, Brian grinned. Only Willow would presume to tell God what to do. The Almighty would not think the worst of her for it. He watched as, expertly, she applied her hands to the reins. *Willow is as fine and as mettlesome as the horse she rides. God grant her husband the sensitivity to recognize her wild spirit.*

Patting the earl's stallion on the nose, he watched Circe carry its rider safely over the fence. If she had a fault it was that she never skirted obstacles. She faced them head on with little regard for the consequences, and that wasn't always wise.

Fury snickered in impatience to be off after them.

'Beggin' your pardon, Fury,' he said. 'Circe's like her mistress and no match for a staid old fellow like you. It's a fine mate with Arab blood she'll be havin', and that's what Brian O'Shea's after gettin' for her.'

He brought in the stallion late that afternoon. The horse was young and proud, his coat winter rough, his plumed tail matted with thorny twigs. Gaunt with hunger, his ribs showed plainly through his coat, yet his nostrils flared at the new sights and sounds and he found the energy to squeal a challenge to the stable rafters.

From her stall, Circe watched him perform, then gave a flirtatious little snicker.

'Be patient, me darlin',' he crooned leading the stallion into an adjoining stall. He sent the stableboy scurrying for a grooming comb. 'I'll be building up his strength before he makes your acquaintance. The viscount will be overjoyed with the outcome, so he will. To be sure, it was a lucky day altogether when he met my darlin' Willow.'

Just at that moment the viscount was cursing his luck. He'd been hoping to reach Dorchester before nightfall, but his mount had thrown a shoe. It was nearly dark, the sky bleak. A bitter wind cut through his heavy cloak and numbed him through to the bone.

Gerard's one consolation as he wearily trudged towards the distant lights of an inn, was the thought that only fools would be abroad on such a night.

Which was just as well, because his pack horse was fully laden. He also carried a considerable amount of gold coin and jewellery on his person, including the Lytton betrothal ring which had been returned to his lawyer by Daphne de Vere.

He scowled as he thought of the ring. Its flawless oval diamond was supposed to signify the purity of the wearer. By all accounts, Daphne had forgotten the meaning of purity. She'd become a notorious courtesan in his absence and was well ensconced in court circles.

He counted himself lucky to have escaped the clutches of such a woman, but he mourned the loss of the childhood friend he'd once cared for.

Breath steamed from his body as, with head bowed, he battled against the bite of the wind-driven snow. Cursing it soundly, he kept pushing on. Feet numb, his beard full of icicles, he stumbled through the inn door some twenty minutes later.

'Is there someone to tend my horses? They're nigh on frozen and in need of a feed and a warm stable,' Gerard croaked to the innkeeper. His legs collapsed under him as he sank on to a bench adjacent to the roaring fire.

'The lad will see to it.' The innkeeper, who recognized quality when he saw it, set a tankard of mulled wine in front of his customer.

'Come far?'

'London.'

'My good wife's mutton stew and dumplings will chase the cold from your bones if you've a mind to eat sir.'

'I've a mind to both eat and stay the night,' he muttered, his stomach growling at the mention of food. He eyed his host's ample belly with something akin to awe. 'Your girth is recommendation enough of your lady's cooking abilities.'

The conversation, which had temporarily ceased at his entrance, hummed pleasantly back into life. Loosening his cloak from his shoulders, he shook the melting ice from his beard and removed his hat, setting it in the hearth to dry.

'Begging your pardon, sir,' a voice said at his elbow. 'The hat will be ruined if left to dry in such a way. The brim must be emptied of snow and the inside padded to keep its shape. If you'll allow me, sir?'

The fire hissed as the snow was flicked into the fire. 'My name is Rodgers, sir. I was personal servant to Squire Tupworthy until he was unfortunate enough to die.'

'Tupworthy dead? A pity, he was a decent man.' His gaze flickered over the small, dark-haired man. Although shabbily dressed, he was clean and tidy. His face had the look of a servant who knew his own worth.

'How come you here?' Gerard asked him.

'The new squire had his own man. The inn-keeper offered me bed and sustenance for my labour.' Pride came into his face. 'I intend to go to London when the weather improves and seek more suitable employment.'

Gerard liked what he saw of the man. He'd got used to being without a body servant for most of his time abroad. Now he was back he would need one. 'You have references?'

Rodgers took a crumpled letter from his pocket. 'I have this letter from the late squire's lawyer, who's offered to vouch for me.' Indignation came into his face. 'My employer valued me highly. I confess, I didn't expect to be thrown out in the dead of winter without recompense and reference.'

He remembered the old squire being neatly turned out. Attacking the huge platter of food the innkeeper had set in front of him, Gerard's eyes scanned the contents of the letter. Satisfied, he gazed up at the man.

'Tell me of the new squire.'

'He comes from the north.' Rodgers hesitated, as if wondering how far he should go. 'His lady is a gentle soul, and not deserving of his treatment of her. I confess, his patronage is no great loss. More I cannot say.'

Gerard liked his answer. Rodgers had the superior attitude typical of a good personal servant. There was a definite order amongst the servant class, he mused. The more elevated the master or mistress, the more status the servant had.

He prided himself on being a good judge of

character. If fairly treated, this one would put his master's needs before his own, and take pride in his work.

'You've made it patently obvious you're fussy about whom you work for, so I'll be equally honest with you. Despite my present appearance, I'm also fussy. I'm in need of a man at the moment and am prepared to take you on paid trial for a month. In that time we'll discover the best and the worst each has to offer. You agree to my terms?'

'I'd be honoured to serve you, sir,' Rodgers picked up Gerard's cloak. 'I'll make sure these are dried and your bed is properly aired. You have luggage, sir?'

'On the pack horse. You needn't bother to unpack the bags until we reach my home on the morrow.'

Rodgers cocked an enquiring eyebrow his way.

Gerard smiled at him. 'Our destination is Lytton House. I'm Viscount Sommersley. My father is Earl Lytton.'

'Yes, My Lord.' If Rodgers was surprised he was too well trained to show it. 'Is there anything else you need, My Lord? I can vouch for the apple pie.'

'Thank you, Rodgers. 'He began to relax as the effects of the fire and the wine took over. He'd forgotten how pleasant it was to be fussed over. 'Tell the innkeeper I'll sample his wife's pie in a little while. I'm too full to contemplate it at the moment.'

An hour later, feeling pleasantly warm and full, he nursed a tankard of ale and gazed into the fire.

Apart from the enterprising Rodgers none had approached him.

Most of the inn's patrons were simple country folk, though a group of red-coated officers had burst noisily through the door earlier and established themselves at the far end of the room. He listened to the soft familiar buzz of country dialect with pleasurable nostalgia.

'It ain't the first time lights be seen up at the house. Some say 'tis Lady Rosamond's ghost walking abroad.'

'It weren't right her dying alone in that big house.'

The drowsiness left his eyes. Daphne's grandmother dead? A pity. He'd liked the old lady.

'Baines said he saw a coach go in through the gates the other night. It was glowing all over, and an unholy wailing was coming from inside. The rain was hissing down, that night and the road were mucky. He swears there were no tracks to mark the passing of it.'

'He must have been at the slops.'

Both men laughed, then one of them said loudly, 'I hears tell the regiment is leaving these parts come spring. Our womenfolk will be able to venture out in safety then.'

One of the officers jumped to his feet and raised his tankard on high. 'No offence, but most of the women round here aren't worth pursuing on a dark night. Those who are, queue up at the barracks' gate.'

'That's not what we hear,' one of the locals shouted. ''Tis said that an officer of your regiment was sent packing by a certain young wife of

85

an absent viscount. He escaped with his breeches round his ankles and his face slashed from top to bottom.'

Raucous laughter followed this broadside.

Gerard's eyes snapped open. Tension crept into his limbs as one of the officers lumbered drunkenly to his feet and hauled himself on to the table. A newly healed scar adorned his face.

'I was ambushed by the woman's brother-in-law,' he sneered. 'Lady Sommersley was willing enough. In fact, she was *more* than willing with her husband away.' The soldier drew his sword from its scabbard and slashed at the smoke-thickened air above his head. 'Any who want to argue the fact can answer to Hugh Macbride personally.'

His companions shifted awkwardly as he gazed around him belligerently. What had started as good-natured fun had suddenly got out of hand.

One of the other men stood up to place a restraining hand on the man's arm. 'Come down from there, Hugh. Your tongue is loosened with rum and you discredit your uniform.'

'Well!' he roared, taking one last belligerent look around. 'Any takers amongst you country scum?'

'I'll champion the lady.'

Gerard's voice was icy enough to send a chill through the blood of most of the people present.

'And who the hell are you, sir?'

'The lady's husband.' Rising to his feet he strode across the room, his rage a palpable thing. Ignoring the sabre, he bunched the man's uniform jacket in his fist and dragged him from his perch. 'You are too drunk to deal with now, sir. I suggest your companions sober you up by dawn. We will meet in the meadow at the back of the inn.'

Hugh Macbride paled as his fingers touched the scar on his face. 'I spoke only in jest, sir. Lady Sommersley would have defended herself until death to protect—'

'*Enough!*' he snarled. 'Do not mention my lady with your foul breath. That you've chosen to make advances to her is reason enough for me to challenge you. The fact that you've insulted her name and mine in a public house is reason enough to kill you. Name your weapon. I have duelling pistols in my pack.'

'Swords,' Hugh Macbride said sullenly, choosing a weapon he'd had plenty of practice with.

'I'll act as your second, My Lord.' The officer who'd protested, detached himself from his fellows and stood at Gerard's side. His sense of fair play had been offended by the choice of weapons. 'You may borrow my sabre. If need be, I can instruct you on its use.'

'Your name, sir?'

'Captain Anthony Dowling at your service, My Lord.'

Gerard looked into the man's face and wanted to grin. He could probably *teach* this officer a thing or two about swordsmanship. He nodded his head. 'My thanks.'

From the moment he looked into the hard, grey depths of his protagonist's eyes, Hugh knew his life was forfeit.

It would have been worth it if he could have

attained what his heart had desired most, but the violet-eyed woman had managed to thwart him. He'd oft lain awake at night plotting her downfall and dreaming of the time he'd plumb the depths of passion so plainly written on her face.

He'd expected to die in battle like his father and grandfather, not in ignominious defeat over a woman. He could almost admire the man he fought as his initial thrusts were parried disdainfully.

The fine linen shirt and fitted breeches displayed a man of hard-tempered muscles; his eyes contained a sense of purpose. Whatever the viscount set out to do he'd most surely achieve, and it was obvious he had no intention of dying this morning. He was a fitting mate for the virgin temptress.

There was a sense of inevitability, as, a few seconds later, his adversary flicked the weapon from his hand. He was outclassed. The viscount was not even going to make a pretence of a fight: a clean kill was his aim.

'She will not refuse you,' Hugh whispered, gazing into the eyes of the man about to kill him.

His fingers closed around his shirt front and ripped the linen apart, baring his chest in a gesture of bravado. Silently he asked God to accept his soul as the point of Gerard's weapon pricked cold steel against his skin.

Impressed by the courage the officer displayed in the face of death, Gerard suddenly thought, the man is too young to die, and England needs soldiers of valour.

He gazed at the livid scar inflicted on the lieutenant by his wife. The woman had been savage in defence of the asset she guarded. Amusement surfaced in his eyes. When he claimed his right as her husband he hoped she would part with it more easily.

'I'd not have your mother's grief on my conscience,' he murmured, surprising himself at this moment of weakness. 'Heed my warning: if you seek to slander my wife's name again I'll kill you without compunction.'

Handing Anthony Dowling back his sword, he inclined his head to the small group of observers, then donned the coat and cloak Rodgers held ready for him.

'I wish you good day, gentlemen,' he said, his distaste for the affair clearly mirrored in his eyes as he strode towards the waiting horses. Not a backward glance did he give the stunned tableau he'd left behind.

Whilst the soldiers rode silently back to the regimental barracks, Willow and Jeffrey were leaving for their morning ride. To both, the morning was a miracle.

Jeffrey was pleased to be out of the confines of his room and the quarantine imposed by his dose of shingles. He'd found new joy in just being alive. The horrors of the smallpox epidemic had faded from his mind, though the deep sorrow he carried in his heart at the suffering it had caused added a new maturity to his thinking.

He knew now that life could be snatched away before it had hardly begun. Thoughts of his future prospects as second son had come to intrude uncomfortably on his mind.

Warmly clad in a dark-blue jacket and a pair of woollen breeches Jeffrey had outgrown, Willow smiled at the white vista that spread before them.

The scarf threaded round the crown of her tricorn was the same colour as her eyes, and was tied under her chin to keep her ears warm.

She looked charming, Jeffrey thought, watching the lively sparkle of her eyes.

Her smile bathed him in warmth. 'We must not stay out too long, I'll not have you take chill on your first day out.'

'But, Willow,' he protested, about to tell her he was perfectly fit.

'I'll not listen to any arguments.' She gave a light laugh at the sight of Jeffrey's crestfallen face. 'Brian has set some new jumps up for us in the meadow. If snow begins to fall again we shall not be too far from home.'

There, Gerard came upon them. Taking the short cut through the forest he reined in at the top of the rise.

From here, a glimpse of the rooftops of Lytton House was available beyond the lake. The home meadows and the avenue of oaks that led towards the main gates all fell within his vision. Though the grounds and trees were shrouded in snow, he drank in the sight.

His eyes were drawn by the sound of laughter coming from the meadow. He grinned with pleasure as he watched the riders taking the jumps.

Jeffrey he recognized, despite his brother's growth. He sat easy in the saddle, and appeared to be shouting something at the smaller figure. Scooping some snow from a hedge the smaller figure gave a trill of laughter as he threw it at Jeffrey.

Whoever the youth was, he could ride. Leaning forward, Gerard watched him put his mount over the jumps. The horse was a magnificent beast, the rider so familiar with it that Gerard sensed their rapport from where he sat. He gave a shout of admiration when the pair completed the circuit without a fault.

His brother's sword appeared in his hand. 'Stay where you are, sir,' he shouted. 'State your business on Lytton land.'

Overjoyed to see his brother again, Gerard urged his mount forward. 'Will you not extend a welcome to your brother?'

'*Gerard!*'

The urgent whisper clearly reached his ears.

Immediately, the youth kicked the black mare into motion and took a run at the wall.

'Whoa,' Gerard breathed, recalling where he'd last seen the horse. 'The mare has not the speed to clear such an obstacle.'

The rider knew differently. Gerard's heart seemed to suspend its beating when the pair easily cleared the wall.

'*God's oath!*' He couldn't believe what his eyes had just seen. 'Who's riding that mare?'

Jeffrey, delighted to see his brother again, blushed as he lied. ''Tis one of the stable boys.'

Gerard frowned. 'He dresses well for a stable boy.'

'Some of the clothes I've outgrown.' Jeffrey

91

gazed at his brother's manservant, desperate to change the subject. 'Is Gregson no longer with you?'

'He stayed in America.' Gerard grinned, the black mare forgotten in his pleasure at being home. 'You've no idea how long it seems since I saw you last. You're almost a man, Jeffrey.'

'And you look like a ruffian with that beard.'

'Rodgers will have it off me before I seek my father's blessing.' He eyed his brother fondly. 'Come, we'll ride back to the house together and you can tell me what's been happening in my absence. I've been without news of my family for too long. How is our father and mother?'

It was a grief-stricken Gerard who entered his father's home a little while later. He followed his brother straight to the earl's sickbed and gazed at the unmoving form without speaking.

Frightened by his stony countenance, Jeffrey put a tentative hand on his arm, only to have it shrugged off.

Gerard gazed at his brother for a few seconds, his eyes stunned and unseeing, then he strode downstairs to his father's study.

'Let no one pass that door,' he barked at Rodgers. 'I want to grieve alone. Is that understood?'

'Perfectly, My Lord.' Rodgers sighed, as he saw the guilt-stricken grief etched into his master's face. He had a feeling his month's trial was going to be more than he'd bargained for.

CHAPTER FOUR

1755

Tension stalked the corridors of Lytton House. It communicated itself to the inhabitants and manifested in different ways.

Edwina felt it in a painful contraction of muscles in her neck that caused her head and shoulders to ache abominably. The hot poultices Willow administered did not help, and she was heartily sick of peppermint tea.

The servants whispered and grumbled amongst themselves. They cast surreptitious glances at Willow, who affected not to notice as she waited – somewhat impatiently after a week of waiting – to be summoned into her husband's presence.

She was, at that early hour, attending the doctor in the earl's bedchamber. Convinced he'd improved slightly, she was assuring the doctor of the same.

'His eyes have a knowing look to them now. He blinks, and I swear he gripped my hand the other day. Tell me he's improving.'

'If you'll allow me to finish my examination without interruption, My Lady, I'll endeavour to offer a prognosis.' Doctor Tansy gave her a peevish glance. 'His heart seems stronger,' he murmured a few moments later, then cautioned, 'Apoplexy is unpredictable. Perhaps I should bleed him again.'

'I beg you, do not.' Distraught tears pricked her eyes. 'The earl looked so pale and drawn the last time, and was too exhausted to swallow his broth.' Her hand curled protectively around her patient's. 'You said yourself he cannot afford to lose much more weight, and your leeches already grow fat on his blood.'

The earl was gaunt, his cheeks sunk in dark hollows. Of late, his eyes had drawn life to them, and a small spark smouldered at their core. It was that which convinced her he'd regained the will to live. She was certain the earl now understood everything that went on around him.

'You're still giving him the hawthorn tincture I prescribed?'

She nodded. 'I've added honey to mask the taste, for its bitterness is not to his liking.' She gave her Ambrose a fond smile. 'The earl cannot move nor talk, but his face says much nevertheless.'

'Then we'll leave the bleeding until next time, Lady Sommersley. I can see the earl is in good hands.' Picking up his bag, the doctor smiled, deciding it would do no harm to indulge her. 'You'll be pleased to know your judgement is not misplaced: the earl's condition shows a slight improvement.'

'Thank you, Doctor Tansy.'

After he left, she gazed into the earl's eyes. 'You heard what he said, dear Father.' Conveniently, she interpreted the doctor's prognosis to suit herself. 'You've recovered greatly over the past weeks and he's confident of a full recovery.'

Making a great effort, Ambrose squeezed her hand. If he could have laughed he would have, for she affected his brain like one goblet of wine too many. Now he needed all the strength he could muster. His mouth contorted in effort. Her eyes widened in shock. Swiftly, she lowered her ear towards his mouth to catch the word he uttered.

'Gerard?' She raised her head and watched him blink. 'You know he is home?'

The eyes blinked once again.

In her excitement, she forgot protocol addressing him by his first name. 'Dearest Ambrose. You will answer thus. One blink means yes, two will mean no.'

His eyes blinked again, then closed and stayed shut as though the effort had exhausted him. Gently she kissed his cheek.

'The viscount has been indisposed of late, but the news of your improvement will hearten him. I will suggest...' Her voice strengthened and her chin tilted in determination. 'No, I will *inform* my husband that a visit to his father would be beneficial to both. And I'll do it now whilst he's...' She shrugged. 'I shall catch him before he goes out.'

The word she'd been searching for was, sober, Ambrose thought, watching her leave. Servants' gossip informed him that Gerard rolled up his sleeves and toiled in the fields like a madman by day. At night, he shut himself in the study and drank himself senseless. He spoke to no one, not even the estate steward.

Gerard's conscience was troubling him. His son and heir had arrived home to find his mother

95

dead and his father on the brink of joining her. Unable to obtain the benefit of his father's blessing or counselling, he'd sunk into melancholy.

This was no weakness of character: Gerard had always sought to deny his in-built sensitivity. Eventually, he and his conscience would wrestle with the fact and calculate the right answer. Ambrose had no intention of waiting that long with his life hanging in the balance.

The fact that he hadn't died in the first days of his stroke was due to Willow, who had given him the will to live. Instead of offering prayers for his soul, she'd forbidden him to die, then simply said to the Lord, 'What sort of God gives me a father to love then snatches him away? I know I'm selfish and wilful, as Lady Edwina has pointed out many times, and am therefore undeserving of Your attention. But Ambrose Lytton is a good and honest man and I'm in need of him.' She'd taken a deep breath. 'You've proved to have a hearty appetite for souls of late, Lord. You *must* spare his life. He's done nothing to offend You.'

Ambrose had been humbled to think she'd brave the Almighty's wrath on his behalf. He'd added his own silent prayer, asking God to forgive her presumption and allow him time to welcome his son back home.

Gerard was fast losing respect and Willow would not mince her words once she got his measure. Unless his son had greatly changed, the shock would do him good. His only worry was Gerard's unpredictable temper.

Willow had no such worries as she approached

96

the study. She was intercepted by her husband's servant.

'My master is still sleeping. He gave orders not to be disturbed.'

'Stand aside. I bring him a message from the earl.'

'My master is not fit to receive visitors.' Rodgers drew himself up in a dignified manner when he saw the resolution in her eyes. 'Allow me time to prepare him, My Lady.'

'Most certainly not.' She bestowed a conspiratorial smile on him. 'I'm well aware of the dilemma you're in.' As her fingers closed around the door-handle she beckoned to the burly man who'd accompanied her on her mission. 'Please detain Rodgers until you have permission to release him, Grey. Do not enter the study unless I specifically call you. Is that understood?'

'Yes, My Lady.'

Trusting Grey to carry out her order to the letter she pushed open the study door, slid through the gap and closed it behind her.

The room was dimly lit, the blue window hangings proving an effective barrier against the morning light. Back against the door, she listened to the deep, even sound of breathing and knew her husband still slept.

He'll have a rude awakening and will be in foul humour from the drink, she thought, trying to stifle the instinct to flee. Crossing to the window before she ran out of courage, she drew the hangings aside and gazed dispassionately upon the man slumped in the chair.

Though she'd caught a glimpse of him from a

97

distance, up close the power of his presence was disturbing. In repose he had grace, his muscles smoothly taut against the fabric of his shirt and breeches. His stock had been tossed aside, exposing a hint of dark curls at his throat. One booted leg lay casually across the arm of the chair, his bearded head rested sideways upon his broad shoulder.

Gerard's hands were finely boned for such a large man, but were blistered and calloused, the nails ragged and dirty. He was building a wall, someone had reported, carrying each stone by hand and setting them, one by one, into place.

Overcome by curiosity, yet as alert as a cat, she crept closer.

One hand rested on his chest, the other dangled almost to the floor clutching an empty brandy bottle. Beside him on the table stood a full bottle.

He groaned as the light penetrated his eyelids. Bringing his free arm across his face he muttered, 'Pull those damned hangings across. The light hurts my eyes.'

Her nose wrinkled in disgust at the odour of stale brandy and perspiration. Her husband still wore the clothes he worked in. His hair and beard were matted and unkempt. He seemed to have lost all respect for himself.

Throwing open the French windows she gulped in several mouthfuls of cold fresh air.

'*Shut that!*' he roared. 'It's freezing outside.' The hand containing the bottle came up. He examined it through slitted eyes then threw it across the room, where it shattered against the fireplace. He groped for the full one. 'My mouth is foul. Fetch me some coffee to add to this.'

Without bothering to consider the consequences, she snatched the bottle from his hand and snapped, 'You've had enough!' Angrily, she tossed the full bottle after the empty one. It exploded in a spectacular fashion.

From his perch astride the charger, the fourth earl seemed to bristle approval at her. She took a hasty step back when a pair of startled, pewter eyes turned her way and impaled her.

'Who the hell might you be?'

'Your wife.'

'Wife?' The arm went back over his eyes. 'Get out of here and send Rodgers to me. I'm not fit for company.'

'That I have noticed,' she said drily. 'As for Rodgers ... I've ordered him temporarily detained.' Her heart began to thump when her husband dropped his arm and bestowed the blackest of scowls on her. 'Your servant was not disposed to allow me admittance.'

'On my orders.' Gerard wished she'd go away. He was feeling nauseous and his head was aching abominably. 'Since when have you been in charge of this household, woman?'

'Since your mother died and your father became bedridden.' Planting her hands on her hips, she gazed at him, her mouth curling in disgust. 'We cannot all behave like whipped curs.'

Anger flared in his eyes as the remark hit home, but, much to her relief, he let it pass. His tongue came out to flick at his dry lips.

'I have a raging thirst.'

'I'll order you some coffee,' she said, her hand

moving towards the embroidered bell-pull.

'I don't want coffee!'

He uncoiled so fast from the chair that she only felt the draught as his sword came between her and the wall to slice through the bell-pull. The lower portion dangled uselessly from her hand. Wrapping his hand round her throat he pushed her against the wall, effectively trapping her. His smile contained enough sobriety to make her aware he was in complete control of himself.

Which is just as well, she thought, shaken by the swiftness of his action, else his sword thrust would have sliced through her ear as well as the bell-pull. Instinct told her he had no intention of harming her. Nevertheless, she allowed her hand to creep towards the pocket where she kept her dagger.

'Your breath is exceedingly unpleasant,' she observed, clasping her fingers firmly around the handle of the weapon and partly withdrawing it from the scabbard.

'Is it, by God?' Shame came into his eyes. Dropping his arm he took a step back and surveyed her immaculate blue and white flowered gown. What the hell was he trying to prove? This girl was his wife, and would do as he bade. He didn't have to use force.

She looked as fresh and pretty as a bunch of cornflowers in summer. Her youth made him feel old and weary. 'What do you want of me, Wife? Make your request then leave me in peace. Is it more money? You look as though the allowance I make you is enough to keep you in luxury.'

'It's exceedingly generous, more than I need.'

Moving away from him, she positioned herself within range of the door. 'My request – if that's what it is – is thus: that you cease drinking and take your place as the head of the household until your father recovers.'

'*Lucifer's oath!*' *A* startled look came into his eyes. 'You have the effrontery to come in here and tell your husband what to do, madam?' The sword came up again, its deadly tip resting lightly against her throat.

She experienced a heady rush of exhilaration at the dangerous game they were playing. 'I demand it.'

'Demand?' Voice dangerously soft, his eyes hooded when she tilted her chin upwards to expose the white column of her throat in a sacrificial gesture. His mouth twitched into a faint smile at her bravado. She reminded him of the soldier.

'You seem to have a death wish,' he whispered. 'Hasn't anyone told you a man in his cups can be irrational and dangerous?'

'I chose my time with care.' Sure of herself now, she smiled in return. 'You are no longer in your cups, merely suffering the results of last night's excesses. Besides' – she gave an ironic sigh – 'I seem to know you well.'

'You know me not at all,' he murmured, the sword tip circling a blue bow on her cap. He caught the bow as it fell, handing it to her with a mocking bow. 'I've never been a husband to you.'

Despite the flush that crept across her cheeks, she met mockery with mockery. 'Are you not the bravest and most considerate of men? Or does

Lady Edwina feed me falsehoods?'

An eyebrow arched in disbelief. 'My grand-mother said that?'

The amusement in his eyes when she nodded, encouraged her to continue. 'Are you not the revered son of Ambrose, who's summoning all his strength at this moment to lay his hand on your head in blessing?'

Gerard nodded uncomfortably. This was no longer a game and she had all his attention now.

'I've heard much from Jeffrey of you. His hero is a little tarnished of late, but not too much to redeem himself if he tries. You'll be pleased to know he's acted as friend and protector during your absence.'

'I have no liking for sarcasm,' he warned, his sword now lowered. His eyes mirrored his intense pain.

Relentlessly, she continued, determined not to spare him. 'But you are right of course, Husband. Because your absence has been prolonged, I know you not at all. What I've been led to expect is not what I see before me. It's disappointing when one's expectations turn out to be quite different. Do you not agree?'

'The only thing my brain and I agree on at the moment is that it aches abominably, madam.' Patience beginning to wear thin, it showed in his voice. 'I suspect that's due to the fresh air you've induced me to breathe and the humble pie you've forced me to eat.' He gazed down at her thoughtfully. 'If the nagging was designed to bring me to my senses, you've achieved it. I should thank you for it, but no doubt you've been paid in full by my discomfort.'

'Your discomfort brings me no pleasure. I petition you only on the earl's behalf. The demand for the dubious pleasure of your company is his: I'm merely his messenger.'

Her husband was strolling towards the French windows when he turned and stared at her. 'You have the makings of a shrew, by God.' Giving a laugh when she frowned, he grinned, returning to her in two strides. 'Do you not have a kiss for your husband after his long absence?'

'You stink like a goat,' she hissed, drawing the dagger fully from her pocket.

It took but an instant to twist it from her grasp. Remembering the scar on the soldier's face he stared at its sharply honed edge. 'You will not threaten me with this again,' he muttered, throwing it with some force at the picture of the fourth earl. It buried itself in the earl's heart.

Willow shivered. Her husband was not a man to be trifled with.

His astute grey eyes bored coldly into hers. 'I'm going for a ride to clear my head. Tell Rodgers to prepare my bath.'

'You're wearing only shirt and breeches,' she pointed out. Grabbing his cloak from the chair she threw it to him as he left. 'Put that on lest you catch cold.'

'Thank you, Wife.' For the life of him, he couldn't remember her name. His mocking bow brought colour to her cheeks and he laughed as he strode out into the morning. He'd not expected the child he'd left behind to have grown into such a beauty, nor to possess such spirit.

Halfway towards the stables, he stopped to gaze back at the house. Had she said his father was going to recover and was waiting to give his blessing? The day took on a new meaning.

'Saddle up my father's stallion,' he said to the groom when he reached the stables. When the man had done his bidding he gazed at him soberly. 'You're the Irish groom who came with my wife and her horse, are you not?'

'That I am, My Lord. My name is Brian O'Shea.'

'Lady Sommersley?' About to ask Brian his wife's name, Gerard stopped himself. It was bound to come to him once the brandy fumes had cleared from his brain. Instead, he mumbled as he scratched his beard. 'She is no longer a child.'

Brian allowed himself a small smile at his master's expense. 'That she's not, sir.'

'How long is it since I arrived home?'

'Six days, sir. New Year has come and gone two days since.'

'Six days?' Gerard shook his head as he mounted the frisky stallion. No wonder the woman was out of countenance with him. Despite his aching head, his lips curved into a smile. The wench he'd married had a fiery temper when pushed to it.

'Stop fussing.' Grimly Gerard surveyed himself in his mirror. His black breeches were fashioned from finest wool, the silver knee buckles matched the braided edging of his coat. Rodgers had insisted he wear a pearl-grey watered-silk waistcoat that matched the colour of his hose. His black silver-buckled shoes were polished to perfection. His stock and ruffles were spotlessly white. Running a hand over his strangely naked chin, he grunted in approval. 'You certainly know your job.'

'Thank you, My Lord.' Rodgers gazed despairingly at his master's dark mane of hair. 'If you would just allow me powder it, sir.'

'No powder.' Gerard seated himself. 'The damned stuff makes me sneeze.' Despite the ride, his head still ached. By the time Rodgers had fashioned his pigtail into a black silk sheath, his skull was throbbing like a drum.

'Whoever that is, send them away,' he said as knuckles rapped at his door. 'I see no one until I receive my father's blessing.'

Rodgers returned carrying a tray set with bread, ham and cheese. A jug steaming with an aroma of hot chocolate was set next to a glass containing an opaque liquid. Rodgers immediately set the glass in front of him.

'What's that?' He eyed it suspiciously as he set about his breakfast.

'An infusion of feverfew to relieve your headache.' Rodgers couldn't quite hide his grin. 'Lady Sommersley prepared and brought it herself.'

Aware her ironic action would set the servants' tongues wagging, his gaze narrowed on Rodgers. The grin slid away to nothing. 'Tell me, Rodgers, does the mistress of the house often assume the duties of serving maid?'

'Due to the epidemic the staff is considerably reduced, I believe,' Rodgers murmured, trying not to sound unctuous. 'I understand Lady Sommersley is held in high esteem by the servants and is respected for her compassion.'

'No doubt she is if she's performing their duties.' Gerard sipped cautiously at the infusion his wife had prepared. Although the brew had been made tolerable with the addition of honey it had bitter undertones. He wouldn't put it past her to poison him after the way he'd treated her earlier.

Swallowing it in two gulps, he grimaced before rising to his feet. This wife of his had suddenly become a paradox. He couldn't equate this saintly being with a woman who carried a dagger she was prepared to use.

He shook his head, preferring not to think about it. Despite breakfast and a several cups of chocolate his head wasn't up to it. 'Tell Mrs Breton to review the servant situation with Lady Sommersley, then attend me in my father's study on the morrow. I'll pick up some staff at the next hiring fair in Dorchester.'

His headache began to recede as the infusion began to take effect. There were advantages in having a wife, he thought with some surprise, and wondered where she'd acquired her skill with herbal remedies. 'I don't suppose...?'

He stopped himself asking just in time. There was no need to parade his ignorance in front of a servant. He would visit his grandmother after he'd received his father's blessing. His wife's name was bound to crop up in conversation sooner or later.

When he reached his father's room, he hesitated in the door-way and surveyed the scene. On one side of the sick-bed stood his wife. On the other, a muscular-looking manservant to whom she was issuing instructions. Gerard couldn't recall ever seeing him before.

'You will assist the earl's hand to his son's head for the blessing, Grey. Like thus.' She placed her hand delicately on the recumbent form and smiled down at him. 'You will not mind if I demonstrate the procedure to this oaf, Father?'

A lump in his throat threatened to choke him when he saw his father's eyelids flutter.

His wife's glance came back to Grey. 'First you must impress on my husband the method of communication the earl has developed. Remember? One blink for yes and two for no. You will be careful the earl does not overtire himself.'

'Yes, mistress.' The servant gave an indulgent smile when she bent and kissed the earl's cheek. 'Don't you worry, mistress, the earl won't come to no 'arm with me looking after him.'

The man was too familiar. About to step forward and intervene, he observed his wife frown. 'I appreciate that you wish to repay the debt of your daughter's life by serving the earl, but you must learn some respect.'

'I offer my life as forfeit for yours,' Grey said simply. 'Be that respect enough?'

'Then what use would you be to me or the earl?' Gerard grinned at the asperity in his lady's voice. 'Arguing with you is like arguing with a mule, John Grey, only you are twice as stubborn.'

'Yes, My Lady.'

She turned and wagged a finger at him.

'Make sure you treat my husband with proper deference. He is skilled with the sword. If your

107

tongue detours from its proper place he will most surely slice it off before you can recoil it. Much as that would relieve my ears, I cannot spare the time to sew it on again. Is that settled?'

'Yes, My Lady.'

'Good.' She gazed at the earl again. 'I'm going now, Ambrose. Edward is expecting me this hour. If this travelling pugilist gives you any trouble you will tell me. I'll cut out his liver and feed it to the hounds.'

Gerard chuckled at the thought of this dainty creature performing such an aggressive act.

'Oh.' Her violet eyes widened and colour suffused her cheeks. Sinking to the floor in a whisper of silken skirts she spread her fan across her face to hide her blush. 'I did not expect you so soon, sir.'

Bathed, and shorn of his beard, Gerard was younger and more handsome than Willow had expected. The stern look to his fine, hawkish features made her wish she hadn't been quite so forward with him in the study. His eyes were quite penetrating. A knot of apprehension gathered in her midriff and she lowered her eyes, suddenly shy.

'Get up, madam.' Assisting her to her feet, Gerard brushed the fan aside and scrutinized her lazily. The child was still there, apparent in the air of innocence she presented. Still petite, she'd blossomed into a beauty. The soft swell of her bosom was just hinted at through the lace of her fichu. Her skin was unblemished and unadorned, possessing a pale translucence that others strove to emulate through artifice.

108

Her long silky lashes quivered slightly, then her eyelids slid upwards. She darted him a swift, curious glance before lowering them again. Her eyes were exquisite, like dark amethysts. Aware he was still holding her hand, he brushed her fingers gently with his lips. 'We meet again, Wife. I pray my appearance no longer invites your censure, and my odour no longer offends.'

For a moment she looked as though she was about to run, then amusement flared in her eyes. Disengaging her hand, she whispered, 'My compliments to your servant, sir. He seems to be as skilled with soap and a razor as his master is with a sword.'

'Prettily said, madam.' He made her a small bow. 'I'll not return the compliment to *your* servant. What nature has provided needs no enhancement; you're exquisite just us you are, and your manners show a distinct improvement.'

'Thank you, My Lord. I have no disposition towards fishwifery unless the means are justified.'

Her eyes were sparkling now. He smiled to himself. She had enough vanity to appreciate a pretty compliment, and the wit to throw it back at him. Her next words brought his eyes narrowing in on her.

'You do not mind if I call you Gerard? To do otherwise would be tediously stuffy.'

Head to one side, her eyes appeared innocent of duplicity. Yet lurking in their depths was a tiny core of mockery that rendered him suddenly uncomfortable. He chose his next words carefully. 'If it pleases you to use my baptismal name then do so.'

Her smile came so suddenly it took his breath away. 'It would please me also if you would use mine.'

She had guessed! It wasn't often he felt at a loss with women, but then ... she was not like other women he'd known. *A whipped cur*, she'd called him.

Her opinion still rankled. None of his acquaintance would have dared take him to task as she'd done earlier, and none would venture to mock him like this. Her intelligence went beyond that usually attributed to women. But he wasn't about to play her game, and she had much to learn.

Warily, he returned her smile. 'If such a small favour brings you pleasure, it will please me to grant it.' He stood aside to let her pass. 'You'll excuse me now. My father awaits.'

'I'm glad you're home,' she said simply. 'You're sorely needed here.'

A subtle blend of lavender and roses assailed his nostrils as she swept past. After she'd gone, he slowly let out the breath that had captured her fragrance. Then something he'd overheard her say kept him staring into the hall whilst the echo of her footsteps whispered back to him.

'Who the hell is Edward?' he muttered.

Edwina tried not to appear too eager when Gerard requested permission to attend her in her bedchamber, so she kept him waiting. Willow had already acquainted her with the happenings of the morning, and had invited her involvement in an amusing deception.

Considering his transgressions of late, and

Willow's part in his resurrection, she was only too willing to humour her. Incorrigible as Willow was, he deserved it, she told herself.

'You look ill-used,' she scolded, managing to hide her delight when he was admitted, and sounding as if he'd been away for one night instead of four long years. 'I'd decided you were undeserving of my sympathy, but my mind is changed at the sight of you. Your homecoming was beset with sorrow and shock, but I hope your recent indulgence is not to become a habit. We need your strength.'

The shame Gerard felt at her words was not up for discussion. He offered only a brief, 'I beg your forgiveness, Grandmother.'

'It's yours, Gerard, for you are my beloved grandson.' She smiled at him, noting the lines of maturity the previous few years had marked on his face. 'Come and give your grandmother a kiss. I've missed you.'

'I thought of you often, Grandmother.' Kissing both her cheeks he sat on the side of the bed and took her hands in his. 'I didn't expect to find you bedridden.'

'An attack of the rheumatics.' She made a face. 'If your good lady has her way she'll cast it from my bones without delay. She allows no pessimism in the sick. She's kept your father alive by power of will alone. The doctor is quite out of countenance with her.'

Gerard frowned. 'He wishes my father to perish?'

'Of course not. It's just that he says one thing and she does another.' Her smile was thoughtful.

'Ambrose improves a little each day. It's because he loves her and wishes to please her.'

'I've observed them together. She takes advantage of his helplessness and treats him with no deference.'

Edwina noted the ironic tone of Gerard's voice. 'Do not bore me with high-handedness.'

His mouth tightened at her rebuke.

'Your wife has been the mainstay of this household. Despite her youth she's worked longer hours than the servants, and performed tasks no lady should be expected to do. She's kept the household together and earned the respect and love of everyone in it. Yes, she has faults. Flouting convention is one of them.' Her voice softened. 'You should not find it difficult to forgive such a small imperfection. She has many graces to make up for it.'

'She has indeed.' He gazed somewhere into the distance. 'I cannot recall meeting a woman both pleasing to the eye and intelligent before.'

'That's because you've always looked for the one and discounted the other.' She gave a snort of disbelief. 'Women are forced by circumstance to submit to men, therefore they emphasize the one trait and hide the other. Will–'

Gerard's eyes sharpened. He should have remembered such an unusual name.

Edwina sucked in her breath. 'Your wife is not practised in the art of deception. What she feels is mirrored in her eyes whether it be anger, mischief, or rebellion. She applies herself to life with honesty. Remember that, Gerard. Her happiness means much to me, and it's in your hands.'

'I'll do my best to be a good husband to Willow.' He was amused to discover the old lady indulging in such a childish game. When he chided her with it she gave a hint of a shrug and smiled.

'There is much of the child in her to be indulged.'

'We have much to catch up on, Grandmother.' Drawn by the sound of laughter he crossed to the window. Willow was comforting a small boy. Jeffrey was chasing a grey pony on horseback. He cornered the pony behind a shrub and led it back to the child. The boy had the look of a Lytton. 'Your letters didn't mention that my mother had produced another son.'

'No such event occurred.'

Jeffrey leaned from his saddle to present Willow with a leafy twig from the shrub. They laughed when she struck his booted leg with it. The flirtatious gesture annoyed him, and he frowned when his grandmother explained.

'The boy is the child of Daphne de Vere, and heir to Sheronwood. The King is his godfather. Daphne has requested we keep Edward here, believing he will be safer at Lytton House than in London. She hopes to visit him in the spring if her duties at court allow.'

Instructions were issued to the boy, who kicked the pony's flank and set it trotting across the garden.

Pleased to observe the child's fall had not frightened him, he smiled in approval when the boy managed to turn the pony's head and bring it back to his tutors. Willow hugged the child as she lifted him from the pony, then took his hand

and escorted him towards the house. Jeffrey led the pony away towards the stables.

'Heir to Sheronwood, you say?' His voice was cynical as he turned from the window. 'Offering hospitality to relatives of Marquess Lynchcross is fast becoming a habit. Odd, considering he's suspected of murdering my grandfather.'

'Your grandfather killed his father. It was that which started the feud.'

'A duel, I believe.'

'Aye,' Edwina said softly. 'A duel over his mother. The marquess was only fourteen when he caught them together. He vowed he'd never rest until his father was avenged. Now hate has consumed him, and he's unable to stop.'

Startled, he stared at her.

'Why do you think the earl made you swear an oath not to challenge the man? The feud was caused by a Lytton. Ambrose intends that the Lytton family should not add fuel to the fire.'

'The reason for his chicanery now becomes clear,' he reflected. 'Willow's mother practised the black arts, that's why she was foisted on to me.'

'If you're referring to your marriage, Gerard, I should like to point out that Willow was blameless of any wrong.' Edwina's look was as wintry as the snow-laden sky outside. 'She was offered no choice. You saw the state she was in when she arrived.'

'I saw it.' Shame licked at him. 'Tell me about the child. How did he come to be in our charge?'

'Daphne feared for Edward's life with her husband showing signs of madness, so she sent him

114

to Sheronwood to be in his great-grandmother's care. The boy travelled down with Willow and myself. Smallpox took Rosamond before she could meet her great-grandson, so Edward is now in our charge.' Edwina smiled. 'He's a well-behaved child and, as you've observed, favours the Lytton side of the family. Even so, the Marquess is fond of him.'

And any other child who takes his fancy by all account, Gerard thought. No wonder Daphne de Vere had sent her son to the country. The marquess had been her stepfather for a major part of her childhood. Gerard tried to put aside the uneasy thoughts that skimmed the surface of his mind.

A recollection came to mind, one he didn't really wish to examine at close quarters. He dismissed it, concentrating instead on amusing his grandmother with stories of his years in America. They passed a pleasant morning, his grandmother listening intently when he described the tobacco plantation he'd won on the turn of a card in Virginia.

'My husband would have enjoyed hearing about this,' she said when he'd finished. Her hand covered his. 'Your memory of your grandfather would be vague.'

'I remember him as a kindly man who taught me to play chess with great patience. He will always have my respect.' He stood as a maid entered bearing a tray of food. The delicious aroma made his mouth water.

'Poached trout,' Edwina said, lifting the lid from one of the dishes.

'Begging your pardon, My Lord.' The maid eyed him nervously as she bobbed a curtsy. 'Cook says will you be taking dinner tonight.'

'Of course I require dinner.' The girl was a recipient of a frown. 'Why should the cook need to ask?'

'Cook didn't know whether you was still...' The girl hung her head and muttered, 'She thought you might still be ill.'

Was that how his insobriety had been discussed amongst the staff? His head began to throb again, a reminder of his excesses. He'd been a fool. 'As you can see, I'm not.'

'You'll be wanting a tray then?'

'Why the devil should I need a tray? I'm not indisposed.'

'Calm down, Gerard.' Lady Edwina smiled reassuringly at the maid. 'Because of the epidemic, formal dining was dispensed with.'

'On whose orders?'

'Lady Sommersley's.'

'I see.' He began to burn. Dinner at Lytton House had always been an event he enjoyed. He liked a fine table set with polished silver and crystal, enjoyed the company of family and friends, the leisurely ebb and flow of pleasant conversation. He was beginning to feel like a stranger in his own home. The daughter of the marquess would have to learn that some traditions would resume now he was home. 'Tell Lady Sommersley and my brother I'll expect them in the dining-room for dinner.'

'But, sir—'

It was time he made his authority felt. 'Do not

question my order, girl.' Nodding to his grand-mother he strode from the room.

'My Lady?' The maid turned to Edwina for guidance.

'Do as he said, my dear.' She gave the girl a serene smile. It seemed Gerard was about to learn the hard way that disrupting Willow's routine was not the wisest thing to do.

The meal was quite spoiled. His wife was making a fool of him in front of the servants, Gerard fumed, as he paced the length of the dining-hall. She'd deliberately set out to thwart him, to undermine his authority as her husband. Had he been a different type of man he'd have taken a horsewhip to her. And where was Jeffrey?

He stopped pacing to bark an order at the footman, then seated himself and began to wait, his fingers drumming on the table.

A few minutes later the door burst open. In a flurry of blue silk Willow advanced on him, her eyes glittering in the light from the sconce she held aloft.

'I believe you demand my *immediate* presence.'

'It has always been the custom at Lytton to take dinner in the dining-hall,' he said, before she could draw breath. 'In future you'll be on time, or you'll forfeit the right to eat.'

'Thank you for the advice, Husband.' Her voice trembled with the effort of keeping it calm. 'If that's all you wish to relate I'll go about my business without further delay. Pray, excuse me, sir.'

'*No, I will not!*' He could not believe the

insolence of her tone. 'You will remain until my brother joins us, then we will dine together in a civilized fashion.'

'I have no time to be civil. If I forfeit my dinner by not being here, then so be it.'

'You will stay!' His voice flayed her like a whiplash when she turned to leave. 'It's apparent you've had your own way for too long. You're my wife, and as such will obey me.'

'I shall do no such thing. I have no intention of dining with a man who displays such ill manners and bad humour.'

His glare would have intimidated most people, but Willow ignored it. She'd worked hard to establish an easily managed routine in the house and had no intention of acceding to her husband's bullying. He just didn't understand that a routine had to be followed, or chaos would result.

Jeffrey appeared from the shadows behind her and said in a conciliatory manner, 'There's much to do before we dine, Gerard. It was our intention to ask you to join us–'

'*Our* intention?' Gerard's gaze swept haughtily from one to the other. 'Since when have you been a couple?'

'Pray do not display such tedious arrogance.' Willow gazed at the waiting footman. 'Please make sure the earl's tray is taken upstairs.' Her hand swept in an arc across the table. 'Remove this and find some means of keeping it warm. We'll dine later.' She turned towards her husband who was gazing at her with incredulity etched on his face. 'Let me explain the situation.'

118

'There's no need to explain.' His fist crashed down on the table, setting the cutlery dancing. 'It's obvious you have no intention of paying service to your position as wife, or obeying your husband's lawful commands. You've taken my bread, enjoyed the comfort of my roof over your head, and worn the clothes I've provided on your back. You've been spoiled in my absence, and I'm sorely tempted to send you back to your father. Do not try my patience much further, madam.'

An anguished gasp issued from her mouth and she fell silent. Her eyes became fearful, as if haunted by memories of her past. He began to regret his words, but pride would not let him retract them.

'Do not go on, I beg of you, Gerard.' Jeffrey put a restraining hand on his arm. 'I'll dine with you if that's your wish. It will be like old times.'

'No, Jeffrey. It will never be that again.' The anger drained from him as fast as it had arrived. He gazed silently at Willow. She was wearing an expression of such abject misery he was moved to guilt as he remembered the bloody stripes the marquess had given her as a wedding present.

'I've no intention of sending you back.' She stood perfectly still when he advanced towards her. Her rigidity surrounded her with a barrier of tension. The purple quartz of her eyes was cold and glittering in the candlelight. Abject misery or not, she was not appeased by his about face.

'I would point out that I'm not a servant to be ordered about,' she snapped in a voice as cold as her eyes. 'I *demand* to be treated with respect.'

The smile she sent his brother was troubled.

'Explain to my husband the routine I'm forced to follow. He may condescend to listen to you, Jeffrey. God knows, he's too proud to listen to a woman, whom he seems to regard as some sort of chattel.' Her eyes swept over the table. 'You will excuse me, Husband. Others are more needful and deserving of my time.'

He could only admire her grace and courage as she swept from the room leaving her fragrance to linger about him. Then that too was gone. He turned to find Jeffrey staring at him with disdain in his eyes.

Dear God, what had he done to turn his brother against him? He sighed. 'I cannot bear to have you look at me so. Come, tell me what's on your mind. You can speak the truth without fear of reprisal.'

Jeffrey's eyes were flint hard. 'You've changed, Gerard. You're not worthy enough to be husband to Willow.'

'*What!*' He stared at him in astonished outrage for a moment then seeing the misery in his brother's eyes experienced a rush of sympathy. Jeffrey was in love: Willow the object of that love.

'Nevertheless I am her husband,' he said gently. He threw his arm around Jeffrey's stiff shoulders in brotherly affection, waiting a few short moments until he relaxed. 'Come,' he said, sighing, as he led him to the table. 'I seem to be doing everything wrong of late. You'll give me the benefit of your advice, and I'll tell you all about Virginia whilst we wait for the food to be warmed. Why does Willow not have the time to dine with us?'

'Our beloved father will not eat unless she's

there to coax him. We usually have our meal on a tray afterwards and spend some of the evening in his company. Willow said it's important Father feels needed and loved at this time. We were going to invite you to join us.'

'Why did she not tell me that?' he asked, mortified by his lack of understanding of the situation.

'I believe your pride would not allow her to.'

'You're right,' he muttered. He gave his brother a conspiratorial grin. 'Tell me, would Willow regard an apology with favour?'

Jeffrey returned the grin. 'Unless you'd welcome another flea in your ear, wait until her temper cools.'

Gerard decided to make his apology later. The house was quiet when he slipped from his bed and shrugged into his robe. A grin played around his mouth.

Willow would make a delightful change from the women he usually associated with. Something about her told him she'd be an apt pupil once she got over her initial shyness.

Anticipation roused him into a gentle half-readiness and he felt like laughing. Married four years and his wife still a virgin? No wonder she had such a foul temper.

Candle held aloft, he stepped through the concealed door to the adjoining chamber. He stopped, looking about him in uncertainty. The oath he gave was succinct, and his arousal subsided.

Where the hell did she sleep?

CHAPTER FIVE

When they came into the hall they didn't see him at the top of the stairway. Willow's cheeks glowed with cold, her eyes sparkled with mischief.

She snatched the hat from his brother's head and threw it up in the air, laughing when a shower of snowflakes drifted down. Catching the hat with one hand, Jeffrey grinned as he helped her off with her cloak.

They were just back from a ride. Willow's riding habit was mismatched, the blue coat and hat at odds with the brown skirt. It offended Gerard's aesthetic sense.

'Let's go and warm ourselves up in the ball-room,' she suggested, stamping her feet against the cold on the crest of arms embedded in the marble floor.

Gerard shrank into the shadows when Jeffrey gazed about him.

'What if Gerard's about?'

'Stop being faint-hearted, Jeffrey. After his excesses of the past few days he'll probably sleep until noon.'

The scorn in her voice whipped colour into Gerard's face. *Not so, little lady.* His face was thoughtful as he watched them disappear in the direction of the ballroom. His habit was to rise early, especially in winter when the daylight hours were short.

This morning he intended to breakfast with his father's steward and familiarize himself with estate news. He wanted to discuss the new agricultural system he planned to implement. The commonly used strip system was inadequate. He couldn't understand why his father hadn't already begun to modernize the estate.

First, he'd make it his business to find out exactly what Jeffrey and Willow were up to in the ballroom so early in the morning. A grin tugged at his mouth as he descended the stairs and slipped into the study. Was she teaching Jeffrey to dance at this early hour? The thought amused him while he waited for Rodgers to bring his hot chocolate.

Leaning back in his chair, he stared into the fire crackling in the hearth. Despite his worry over his father's state of health, he experienced a sense of well-being. He was home, had the future of the estate to plan for and a woman to warm his nights when he so wished. And what a woman. His wife was exquisite.

His glance roved to the paintings adorning the walls. Mostly they were of horses and the men who rode them. He'd grown up with them, leaning against his father's knee enthralled by the stories his father told. It was said he resembled the fourth-earl with his hawk-like features and fierce frown.

His eyes moved toward the likeness. For a moment he gazed with puzzlement at the blaze of blue in the centre of the fourth earl's uniform jacket, then, coming upright, stared at it for a few unbelieving moments more. The dagger had been removed. Tucked into the ripped canvas was the blue ribbon he'd cut from Willow's cap.

Deciding the chocolate could wait, he sprang to his feet and strode off towards the ballroom, a grin playing around his mouth.

The clash of steel against steel brought him to an abrupt halt in the doorway.

It took a few seconds to register that the youth fencing with his brother was none other than Willow. They were using foils. Automatically, he checked if the tips were guarded before allowing himself to be mildly shocked at her attire.

Far from a disguise, it only served to accentuate her femininity.

The outline of her hips was rounded, but firm beneath the faded fabric of the breeches she wore. Slender, shapely legs disappeared into a pair of worn riding boots. Fetching though her figure was, he managed to drag his eyes away from her provocatively displayed rear and concentrate on her swordsmanship.

She gave a light laugh as she parried a head cut, then scored a point off Jeffrey's padding with her *riposte*. Someone had taught her well. Light on her feet, she was wary as she circled, her eyes alert on her opponent's movement. It took but a few moments to appreciate her skill. Her coordination was good, her timing perfect, her concentration absolute. He could almost see her planning the strategy that would end the bout to her advantage.

Springing forward, she expertly slipped beneath Jeffrey's guard with a perfect thrust to the body. Her rapier formed a quivering arc as it met the resistance of the padding, then sprang straight when she removed it. Jeffrey clutched his hands to his chest, staggered theatrically backwards then sank to the floor.

'You cannot fool me,' she scolded and, ripping the mask from her face, tried to catch her breath. 'You allowed me to win.'

Jeffrey grinned when she threw her mask at him. With lithe grace, he sprang to his feet and bowed low. 'I confess I gave you a couple of openings, but one needed to be skilled to have observed them.'

Gerard laughed, he couldn't help himself. His brother had a smooth tongue for one so young. He was a fine-looking youth, lacking yet of muscular strength. Women would have to watch out for him before too long.

A look of consternation passed between them before they turned to face him.

'I know what you are about to say, Gerard.' Jeffrey slid protectively in front of Willow. 'If anyone is to be chastised it should be me.'

'Nonsense.' Defiantly, Willow pushed herself forward. 'We've done nothing untoward. I *refuse* to be chastised for nothing.'

'You call dressing immodestly nothing?' Wanting to laugh, he waited with interest to hear her reasoning.

'If you were a woman and forced to wear cumbersome skirts, you would soon discover that being so confined is not comfortable – given certain circumstances.'

The expression in her eyes was deliciously indignant. He could admire her ingeniousness when she appealed: 'How do you expect me to fence under such restrictions?'

He understood her point of view, but his enjoyment of the situation was growing too much to let it pass. 'Perhaps I do not expect you to indulge in such unfeminine pastimes as fencing.'

Her voice rose to a squeak. 'Not fence?'

She was easy to tease. He tried to keep the amusement out of his eyes when Jeffrey turned aside with a grin on his face.

'Women should be modest and gentle.' He exchanged a conspiratorial glance with his brother. 'They should run the household, and only concern themselves with womanly pursuits such as embroidery.' He hesitated slightly before thinking of something guaranteed to raise her ire rise even further. 'Women should be decorative and agreeable for their husbands. Above all,' he said quickly when she drew in a deep breath and opened her delicious mouth to protest, 'a woman should keep her place, and never answer her husband back.'

'Never?'

A conflict of emotion danced in the depths of her eyes. First, a spark of rebellion, then disbelief – subdued by an incredible hurt to dim their flame. Her bottom lip trembled; her eyes filled with tears.

'You'll find me sadly lacking then, Husband. I confess, I've none of the admirable qualities you desire in a woman.'

Damnation, he'd made her cry. 'Indeed you have,' he hastened to reassure her. 'You're the sweetest, and most beautiful woman I've ever

126

come across.'

An embroidered handkerchief was removed from her sleeve, an aroma of perfume tantalizing his nostrils. 'But I'm a most disagreeable person, and I argue with you.'

Eyes quivering with tears were turned his way. Drawn into their depths, he discovered a disturbing gleam of mischief. If her purpose was to test his temper it would do no harm to lull her into a false sense of security, he mused.

'There's nothing quite so boring as a woman who has nothing to say for herself,' he encouraged. 'It does not displease me.'

The handkerchief was applied to her eyes leaving Gerard momentarily bereft by the withdrawal of their regard.

She gave the merest of sighs. 'I hate to be thought immodest. I'll give up fencing and apply myself to embroidery instead. Lady Edwina tells me I'll never be a good needlewoman. Still, it will amuse her to berate me for my lack of skill.'

He couldn't abandon her to such a fate. 'You have my permission to continue to fence if it amuses you.'

'And the breeches?'

'As long as you don't wear them abroad.'

'Thank you, Gerard.' She surprised him by lightly kissing his cheek. There was no trace of tears now.

'A reward for the ingeniousness of your plea.'

Their eyes joined and held. A soft, self-mocking smile curved her lips. 'I had not expected you to be quite so perceptive, nor so indulgent with me.'

'*Touché, madam.*' His eyes narrowed a fraction.

She was young, but she had a strong instinct for survival. He picked up her hand, placing a kiss in the palm as compliment. 'Who taught you to fence?'

Dark, feathery lashes dipped momentarily over her eyes. 'It was my tutor, James Langland.'

'Earl Langland's second son?'

She nodded.

'That accounts for it. He's an expert swordsman, and a crack shot, I believe. Some say he equalled your father's prowess before he dropped out of sight.' A frown creased his brow. 'Rumour has it he was deeply in debt to the Marquess. He must have pledged himself to your father to avoid debtors' prison.'

She scowled at the thought. 'Even if that was the case, he was good to me. He applied himself to my education with diligence.' Her eyes affected amusement. 'Although you may regard it as a liability, James taught me many things. I can read, write, calculate figures and play chess. I could also shoot the eye from a frog if need be.'

He ignored her boast and flicked her a grin. 'If you do not find your education a liability, why should I? I should like to meet this James Langland.'

'I know nothing of his whereabouts.' Sadness filled her eyes. 'I should not like to think him still indebted to my father. I've a little money of my own, and with your permission, would forfeit it to buy his freedom.'

Loyalty was something he understood. If he could offer her this small service he might rise a little in her estimation after their confrontation of the day before. 'Allow me to make enquiries on your behalf, Willow.'

The glance they exchanged was of mutual interest. Colour tinted her cheeks. 'I'd be most grateful.'

Jeffrey might just as well not have been there. Used to her undivided attention, he snatched up his coat and strode towards the doorway.

'Jeffrey?' she cried out in astonishment.

'Let him go. He must come to terms with the situation in his own way,' Gerard said harshly.

'I do not understand,' she whispered. 'What situation?'

'Perhaps you should ask yourself that.' Spanning her waist with his hands, he pulled her against him, gazing down at her speculatively.

Her husband's body was hard, his strong thighs slightly parted. That which lay in the apex nudged against the softness of her stomach, quivering awareness into her groin.

'I've already fought with a man over you, lady.' His eyes brooded over the fact. 'Do not encourage Jeffrey in his regard for you. There's no future in it.'

He cut off her gasp with his mouth, taking possession of it in a way that was both humiliating and exciting. Made aware she belonged to no man but him, her blood pulsed through her veins, leaving her strangely weak. Confused by the sensations soaring through her body, she began to struggle, then hung her head when he released her. Tipping up her chin with one finger, he forced her to look at him.

The mouth that had casually claimed hers was

smiling a little. How odd. The caress had made her acutely alive to herself. She recognized reluctance in her awareness to surrender the freedom she cherished and give herself to another in body and soul – as she must. Her husband seemed tolerable enough, yet she was loath to submit herself to his will whilst he was a stranger to her.

'You have not been kissed often?' he said softly.

'Indeed, not.' She blushed when he grinned. 'I've been kissed only once before, and that was forced upon me.' Her face paled as she thought of the price Hugh Macbride had almost paid for his offence. 'It was a trivial matter, not worthy of your notice.'

'You were savage in your defence of yourself, madam. The soldier wears his scar as a badge of shame. You must share his shame if encouragement was offered.'

His face was so stern she hung her head in embarrassment. 'I have no desire to recall the details. I beg you, do not insist that I relate the incident.'

Gerard sighed. 'The soldier's offence was to pay insult to the Lytton name, which I hold in high esteem. To hear your name disrespectfully uttered in a roadside inn was not a trifling matter. I had no choice but to take up his challenge.'

'I swear I offered him no encouragement. Your compassion in this matter is appreciated. Had you been injured I would not be able to live with my remorse.'

He smiled at her tearful expression when she lifted her head. His eyes lingered on her face. She was exquisite. Her high cheekbones and turned-up nose suited her heart-shaped face. Her violet eyes seemed to mirror her every mood. Her hair was mahogany, polished to a deep lustrous shine; her lips – sensuous in shape and texture. No wonder the soldier had pursued her.

'I believe you.' Gently, he ran the ball of his thumb across her lips. 'You did not seek to lay open *my* face when I forced a kiss upon you.'

'Because...' Small white teeth worried at her bottom lip.

'Because what?' he prompted, determined she'd finish what she knew she'd have to accept.

'You're my husband.' The mouse-like caution in her voice was offset by the annoyance sparkling in her eyes. 'It's my duty to submit myself to your pleasure.'

'I don't want your submission.' He chuckled when her eyes flew open in astonishment, then he kissed the softly rounded mouth until he felt a response of trembling anticipation. 'It will be my pleasure to instruct you, so duty becomes an enjoyable pursuit for us both.'

Already melting with pleasure from his kiss, her mouth dimpled into a relieved smile. 'Kissing is not too onerous a duty. If you'd but care to instruct me again, I shall apply myself most diligently to it.'

Her artless comment reminded him she was a stranger to the ways of love. He couldn't remember the last innocent he'd known. Artless, or *artful?*

An uncomfortable memory of Daphne de Vere came into his mind. Someone had taught her the tricks of pleasuring a man, and taught her well. It

131

could only have been her stepfather. Disgust tempered his good humour. Willow was the daughter of the same man. How could he be certain her innocence was not an act? His eyes hardened as he gazed at her.

'Attend me in my bedchamber tonight.'

Her spine prickled at the predatory chill in the grey eyes. His hands stopped her involuntary recoil. Placing his mouth against her ear, he mocked, 'Remember your duty, madam.'

Face flaming with barely controlled temper, she jerked from his grip and hissed, 'It shall be as you command, My Lord.'

As her palms crept up to cover her face he felt a twinge of conscience.

'I did not expect you to mock me, sir,' she muttered.

He experienced shame, but had no intention of retracting his words. He *had* to know if her innocence was genuine. 'You're my wife, Willow.'

Turning away, she stepped into her skirt, fastening it about her slender waist with trembling fingers. 'I'm aware of that fact.'

'Wait.' His fingers closed about her wrist as she sought to leave. 'Am I to have your anger as companion for the day?'

Deep in her eyes, curiosity flared. 'It seems to me you provoked it.'

'Gloom will be my cloak until I see you smile again,' he coaxed.

Pleasure chased the shadows from her face. 'Your tongue has a smooth persuasion. A man has never suffered for my smile before.' Cocking her head to one side, she regarded him much like a curious bird would. 'You have the air of one who easily obtains what his heart desires. It will not hurt you to suffer a little.'

'If that's My Lady's command.' Lifting her hand to his lips he placed a kiss on the fingers. 'Until I see you smile, then.'

'At supper perhaps.' Her voice was shy as he walked away. 'The earl would welcome your presence.'

'And you?' He turned to gaze at her. 'The assumption I made yesterday was wrong; that's a matter for which I beg your forgiveness.'

'You were not to know of my domestic arrangements.' Dimples pulled at the edges of her mouth. 'Leave me now, Gerard. I have an irresistible urge to smile.'

Laughter bubbled up inside him as he continued his stride. When he reached the ornately decorated doors, he turned and grinned at her.

Face hidden in her hands she was trying not to laugh. Their eyes met when she spread her fingers.

He couldn't resist a wink. Her giggle was delightful. He was still grinning when he reached his father's study and found the steward waiting for him.

'The peasantry will not like it,' Bascombe said after Gerard explained the plan.

'And the yeoman farmers will like it even less.' He devoured the last mouthful of ham then, finding himself replete, indicated to the servant that the table be cleared.

His father's steward had been in their employ

since he'd been a boy. Bascombe's son Robert had been a playmate. The man was set in his ways. Gerard wondered if he fully grasped the situation. 'Nevertheless,' he said firmly, 'the strip system is inefficient and will be abandoned.'

He waited until the table was cleared then spread the map of the estate across the surface. 'Walls and hedges will go where indicated, small farms be combined, and rents raised accordingly.' His forefinger stabbed downwards. 'I've already made a start there. Those farmers who are not conversant with the new system will be instructed in its use.'

'Yes, My Lord.' Bascombe hesitated. 'If I may say something, sir.'

'Say it,' he encouraged with a faint smile.

'Respectfully, sir. You've been away for some time. Trouble has risen over this system in other parts of the country.'

'I'm aware of that.' Rising to his feet he gazed out at the falling snow. 'There's always trouble when things change. However, the ranks of the local population have been thinned by the recent smallpox epidemic. Labourers are hard to come by. Those farmers who've proven to be unproductive in the past must go. They'll be recompensed of course, but go they will.' He surprised a look of resignation on Bascombe's face when he turned.

'Come, Bascombe, things won't be too bad. I'll address the meeting of tenants myself. If there be dissent I'll take it upon my own head. You *are* aware of the system's benefits?'

'Yes, sir. My son is one of its firmest advocates.

He's often sought to convince me of its advantages.' Bascombe managed a smile. 'Robert informs me the growing population needs a more productive and efficient farming system. The system achieves that, I believe.'

'How is Robert these days?' he asked, reckoning that Robert's line of thinking was more compatible with his own than that of Bascombe senior. 'Wasn't he apprenticed to a counting house in Dorchester?'

Bascombe's face grew long. 'Gambling has put my son's employer deeply in debt. Robert's worried about the future of his family and is seeking a position elsewhere.'

'Perhaps we could use him here if he's conversant with the enclosure system,' he suggested. 'The estate needs a secretary, and I a clerk.' He smiled reassuringly when concern registered on the steward's face. 'He'd not object to working under his own father, I hope?'

Bascombe smiled. 'No, sir, and there's a cottage on the estate which goes with the position.'

'Fine, fine ... it's settled then.' Dismissing the man, Gerard summoned Rodgers to bring him his warmest cloak and hat, then set off towards the stables.

Brian O'Shea was grooming an emaciated stallion when Gerard entered. The man was crooning softly to it whilst he worked. Eyes half-closed, his ears pricked towards the sound, the stallion appeared to be dozing.

He crossed to the pair as he waited for the stable boy to saddle his gelding.

First, he ran his hand over the stallion's gaunt rib-cage, then walked along its length. 'Hmm,' he muttered, taking the stallion's head between his hands. 'It's got nice lines, but why is the beast in such poor condition?'

'It's a Sheronwood stallion. It escaped when the horses were sold and the poor beastie has been running wild. I brought it in just a few days ago.' Brian gave him a knowing look. 'To be sure, he would make a fitting mate for Circe.'

'She's not produced a foal yet?' He glanced at Circe, who was watching proceedings from her stall.

'She's a proud creature, sir.' He chuckled. 'She's too spirited for old Fury. Last time he tried to cover her she nigh on bit off his ear.'

Gerard grinned. Despite its thinness, the stallion's Arab blood was evident in its lines and movement. 'A Sheronwood stallion, you say?'

'The agent in Dorchester has the papers,' Brian offered, exchanging a glance of mutual understanding with his master. 'The Sheronwood stable was sold at market. I should imagine he'd accept any offer just to get his books in order.'

He led the stallion into a stall. 'Circe will be coming into season again shortly, sir.'

'You don't need to convince me any further. I'll ride in to Dorchester and see the agent now.' Mounting his horse, he smiled at the stable boy. 'You ride Circe well.'

'Circe?' The boy scratched his head and appeared puzzled.

'I thought I saw you riding the mare on my return to Lytton House.'

'No, My Lord. None but Brian O'Shea and–'

His gelding gave a high-pitched whinny when Brian knocked over a metal pail. It danced under him nervously.

'Sorry, My Lord,' Brian muttered, when he managed to get the surging beast under control. 'He's skittish this morning. He needs a good run after being rested yesterday.'

Gerard said nothing more, but his eyes narrowed thoughtfully as he urged his mount into a walk and headed off. The groom had deliberately kicked the pail over. But why would he want to shut the stable boy up? Did it matter who exercised Circe?

The landscape was white with frost, the trees stark shapes against a grey sky. Snow lightly powdered the ground and swirled about him.

He forgot about Circe as the pleasure of being home drifted into thoughts of his childhood. The estate had a sense of timelessness about it. His father had shaped him for stewardship of the land since childhood, involving him in the day-to-day events so it would come to him naturally. Then, it had seemed a long way off; now it was almost upon him, he felt unprepared.

The earldom was not about position or power, it was about responsibility. He would be the keeper of the land for future generations. It was up to him whether it survived into the future. He was not blessed with the patience of his father, but perhaps that was all to the good.

He chuckled when a bird attempted to land on the frozen lake and skittered, squawking with fright, across its surface. When Jeffrey had been small he'd taught him to slide along its frozen edge. In the summer they'd built a raft and played at being pirates.

Once, his mother and a guest had discovered them naked. He'd been sixteen, Jeffrey six. The earl had been in London on business. Gerard had been teaching his brother to swim.

There had been a haze just above the surface of the lake. Dragonflies danced across the water, their iridescent wings flashing like jewels. He'd made a cave in the reeds to hide them from prying eyes. The sound of their laughter had given them away. The image of that day had been brought abruptly to a halt, when...?

The guest had been Marquess Lynchcross! He frowned. Odd that he should suddenly remember the unpleasant memory of that day.

He thought he'd eradicated from his mind the way the marquess had looked at his naked body and the shame of being seen thus by his mother. The marquess had flicked his hastily snatched up clothes aside. Left with only his hands to cover himself – the man's laughter had been doubly humiliating.

His mother had said nothing at the time; that in itself had given him a sense of betrayal. Upon her return, she'd called him into the drawing-room and made him promise not to tell his father about the marquess being on the estate. She'd bought his silence with a gold piece to spend on a saddle he'd coveted. His mother hadn't often had much time for her children, and her anguish had caused dubiety in him even then.

He spurred his mount into a canter as if to

leave the sour taste of the memory behind, but niggling thoughts lingered on. She'd given birth to his sister the following May, rejecting the deformed child as would a cat the runt of the litter.

As he tried to recall the face of the child, all that came to mind was the sneering face of the marquess.

The face haunted him as his mount's hoofs covered the miles into Dorchester. It wasn't until his deal was satisfactorily concluded and he was half-way home, that an ugly suspicion took root. His dislike for the marquess grew into loathing.

To make matters worse, his children would carry the legacy of Lynchcross blood. He understood Willow was not responsible for her father's transgressions, was in fact a victim of them, yet the thought was repugnant to him.

And what of her mother? Marietta Givanchy was supposed to have died shortly after giving birth to Willow. Rumour remained about her ungodly practices. If Willow had inherited her traits, would their children be afflicted by strangeness?

He cast his uneasy thoughts aside when the snow began to fall in earnest, spurring his mount forward. The way before him was hardly visible, so he stuck to the safety of the road.

Nearing the gates to Lytton House, he cursed when a figure stumbled in front of him, causing his horse to rear in fright. Bringing it under control, he slid from its back when he saw the predicament the young black maid was in. A coach had slid on a patch of ice, coming to rest on its side in a ditch. Of the horses and driver there was no sign.

'Where's your driver?'

The maid indicated she was dumb, and wrote upon the snow with a stick.

'He's taken the horses and gone for help these past two hours?'

To the nearest inn no doubt, he thought sourly, as the maid applied her stick once more to the snow.

'Your mistress is ill with cold, and you fear she will perish?'

The girl's head bobbed frantically up and down.

Frozen to the bone himself, he took a brandy flask from his pocket and glanced at the black-veiled figure visible against the cushions. He had no choice but to offer them hospitality. 'Give some of this to your mistress, and take a nip yourself. If you support her on my horse I'll help you to shelter.'

A short while later the woman and her maid were being attended to by Willow in one of the guest rooms.

'You were lucky my husband came that way,' she said, trying not to stare at the black girl. Her eyes fell on the veiled woman who was unconscious with cold. 'The maids will be here shortly with warming pans for your mistress's bed. The fire will soon heat the room, and I'll send up some broth.' Her eyes strove to see through the veil and failed. 'Acquaint me with your mistress's name, girl.'

The girl took her hand and traced letters in her palm. 'It is Sapphire, My Lady. I am Bella.'

'*Sapphire!*' A thrill of pleasurable unease ran

through Willow. 'I've heard tell of her. A most celebrated name in London, I believe?'

Bella's smile was warm as she regarded the mistress of the house. Her eyes rivalled those of Sapphire. Softer and more innocent, they had just a hint of mischief.

'Your slippers are wet, Bella,' she said. 'We look to be about the same size. I'll send my maid with a dry pair. You need not return them.'

'But I could not, madam,' Bella wrote upon her palm, aghast at the thought that the mistress of the house would be so generous. 'It would not be seemly.'

She smiled. 'Then we'll keep it a secret.'

Having supervised lifting Sapphire into the bed, Willow couldn't contain her curiosity any longer. 'Why does your mistress wear a veil?'

Bella's smile faded as her mistress groaned. Anxiously, she bent over her.

'Where are we, Bella?' Even in her distressed state, her voice was softly melodious, containing traces of a French accent.

Willow answered for Bella. 'You're safe at Lytton House.'

'And you are?'

'Lady Sommersley. My father-in-law is the Earl of Lytton.'

She had the uncomfortable feeling she was being thoroughly scrutinized. Then the woman half sat up, whispering faintly, 'I'm acquainted with Ambrose Lytton. I have heard he's at death's door.'

'Death cannot claim him yet,' Willow said vehemently. 'I've made a bargain with God.'

Under the veil, Sapphire's eyes glistened with tears. She saw before her the one person she'd never imagined to see again, the child she'd borne those many years ago. Beauty and goodness spun a cloak of protective light around her.

My daughter is blessed with the gift of love, she thought. It will encompass all who seek it and sustain them through life. She began to wonder if she'd been wise to follow the dark side of her heart. Perhaps she should never have come here.

Giving a groan of despair she closed her eyes. 'Thank you for your kindness, Lady Sommersley. I beg you, leave me to my maid now, for I am tired.'

'Of course.'

The concern in her voice nearly drove Sapphire to tears. Her own dear daughter, after all this time. She could never reveal herself. Hearing her slippered feet whisper towards the door she experienced a strong urge to call her back and embrace her, like any normal mother. But she wasn't normal, and had to deny her impulse.

Later, when she was warm and rested, and the firelight glowed comfortingly on the red and gold embossed walls, Sapphire had Bella bring her crystal.

Sapphire experienced fear. Its depths revealed two paths: one led downhill into darkness, the other upwards into light. The light gave her pain, and the way was strewn with obstacles. Instinctively, she knew which path she must take. With a cry of despair, she buried her face in her hands and wept.

'Will my husband find me desirable, Kitty?'

Already Willow had prevaricated too long. Kitty had arranged to meet Brian O'Shea, and would be late if she didn't go soon. She tried to keep the impatience from her voice. 'If he doesn't, there must be something wrong with him.'

Willow's filmy chemise was edged with pink taffeta ribbons fashioned into rosebuds. Over it, she wore a robe of pale pink velvet edged with white fur. Her hair hung in shining dark ripples to her waist. Held back by two thin braids threaded with rosebuds, they were tied at the nape of her neck with a pink ribbon. She was trembling.

Kitty suddenly felt sorry for her. She couldn't imagine being touched by a man she hardly knew and didn't love. She did her best to allay her mistress's fears, blushing as she confessed, 'It ain't so bad. Me and Brian – *ouch!*'

'How dare you talk to me of such matters, Kitty Adams!' Willow hadn't meant to slap her, but not only had her maid's words shocked her, they reminded her mockingly of her intact state.

Her voice softened when tears filled Kitty's eyes. 'I'll ask the earl's permission for you to marry. I'd not wish to see you unwed and with child.'

Kitty's mouth tightened. Willow had never slapped her before. The reminder of her status came as a shock. It was obvious that the free and easy relationship they'd enjoyed in the past had come to an end. She bobbed a resentful curtsy. 'Thank you, My Lady.'

The spat served to stiffen Willow's resolve. If Kitty had survived the ordeal of being bedded,

then so would she. Taking comfort in the fact that
Gerard was far superior in looks and breeding
than Brian could ever be, she took up her candle
and headed confidently towards the door. 'You
may retire,' she called over her shoulder to Kitty
as she left. 'I do not expect to return tonight.'

As soon as the door closed behind her, Kitty
drew a cloak around her shoulders and headed
down the servants' stairs. She had no intention of
sleeping in draughty, haunted isolation by herself
tonight.

The candle fluttered from face to face as Willow
made her way along the gallery of Lyttons. It
appeared as if the eyes of each were watching her.
The men's eyes seemed lascivious, the women's,
faintly malicious.

She stopped in front of the fourth earl. The
portrait showed him in a different light to the one
in the study. Here, he had a steady intellectual
gaze, and a mouth curving upwards in a gentle
smile. His eyes were grey, his nose rather large
and hooked, and his lean face had an aesthetic
quality. She couldn't imagine him being as fierce
as he looked in the picture in the study. He bore
a striking resemblance to her husband.

Nerves fluttered in her midriff. 'If a son comes
of this night,' she whispered, 'I'll give him your
name as well as that of his father and grandfather. He shall be Radford Ambrose Gerard.'

Having said that, her mind returned to the
begetting of that son. Prickles quivered along her
spine. Taking a deep breath she continued towards her husband's bedchamber. Like every-

thing unpleasant in life, it was best to get it over and done with.

Rodgers had been dismissed for the night. Clad only in breeches, his shirt open to the waist, Gerard sprawled on his back across his bed. The warmth of the room had made him pleasantly drowsy, and he'd discarded the book he'd been poring over.

Life had a certain continuity at Lytton, he was thinking. Despite the current shortage of staff the house was run well and the atmosphere happier than he'd ever known it.

His father had the best of care. The earl's bodily comfort was taken care of by John Grey, who lifted him as easily as if he were a baby. His sustenance was managed by Willow, who alternatively coaxed then scolded his father into swallowing just one more mouthful.

They'd dined together in his father's room this evening, with Jeffrey – still smarting at losing Willow's exclusive attention – silent. After she'd excused herself Gerard had challenged Jeffrey to a game of cards, allowing him to win a gold piece. Throwing the money in the air, Jeffrey had crowed with youthful triumph, his sulks banished.

Choosing that moment to glance at his father, he'd surprised an expression of pleasure in the man's eyes. He realized then that his father's mental faculties had remained unimpaired. Willow seemed to have an instinct about these matters. He resolved to listen to her more carefully in the future.

About to resume his reading, his fingers curled into a fist as the door to his bedchamber creaked open. He relaxed when he saw who it was and, through lowered lids, gazed with enjoyment at the vision in white fur and pink rosebuds standing hesitantly in the doorway.

What the devil was she doing here? His earlier reasoning came to his mind. She was here at his command. He'd determined to discover whether her innocence was soiled by her father's debauched ways.

He resisted the urge to move. Staying perfectly still, he watched her through lowered lids, despising himself for doubting her yet compelled to discover the truth.

The hand that held the candle trembled, ignoring her silent plea to be still. Her husband was sprawled across the bed, asleep, his chest rising and falling with an even rhythm.

Tempted to leave straight away, curiosity caused her to creep closer and gaze down at him. His hands were thrown above his head, the palms curled upwards like autumn leaves. Asleep, he had a vulnerability that made her smile.

Her perusal of him avoided the springy dark hair that peeped from the gap in his shirt. It disturbed her, as did his abandoned pose.

Her cheeks warmed as she found her eyes were drawn to his body. The way he sprawled on his back caused every muscle and bulge to strain against the material covering them. Every time she looked away she was drawn back, and every time she looked she felt a little weaker as if she were bewitched.

Torn between relief and irritation at finding him asleep, Willow was in a quandary. What did one do in such circumstances? Would her husband expect her to waken him? The thought made her quake. The immodesty of such an act would most surely displease him. Then an idea occurred to her.

'I have no experience to guide me in matters such as this,' she whispered, tearing a pink ribbon from her chemise. 'Perhaps you'll not recall summoning me to your bed; if you do, I'd not have you think I disobeyed you.'

What the devil was she about? Stifling an elated rush of amusement, Gerard wanted to laugh out loud. She was as innocent as a newly born lamb. A woman of experience would have wakened him, not stood there blushing and trembling. Now she was leaving her calling card, a pink ribbon looped over his toe.

Tender feelings rioted through his chest. Her fear was almost tangible. She had guts, he'd grant her that. She'd come at his command despite not knowing what to expect – or at the least – expecting to be violated in a most painful manner.

She had reason to be afraid. He'd heard men boast of the sport their virginal brides provided, and no doubt women related their experiences to one another.

She need not worry. He intended to treat her most gently. When she grew used to his attention he'd teach her ways of pleasuring guaranteed to satisfy them both. Unexpectedly, his body experienced a swift arousal. His grunt of annoyance brought a swift, fearful intake of breath from Willow.

She hadn't meant to flee. She'd seen his body change and experienced disgust. Not for her husband – Gerard was a man of undoubted refinement, and not responsible for the ways of a man's body. Her disgust stemmed from the desire to reach out and touch his growing manhood. Added to this, was a shameful feeling inside her that caused a flush of damp heat between her thighs. Her thoughts had been improper. As a result, her body suffered from lust. Both were sins, if the sermons she'd listened to as a child were to be believed.

The noise he'd made had broken her tightly stretched nerves. Snatching up her candle she ran from the room, reaching her quarters with a rapidly beating heart.

'Kitty?' The fire was almost out and the room freezing. 'Damn the girl! She should have built up the fire before she retired.'

Temper rising, she stalked into Kitty's room to rouse her. The bed was empty. She was visiting Brian, no doubt. Drawing her robe around her, she shivered as she experienced the discomfort of abandonment. Miserably, she returned to her chamber, creeping under the covers of her bed.

The noises of the house seemed louder and more menacing tonight. There was a scratching sound from the wall and the floor creaked, as if someone was creeping across it. Now and again came a crack. Somewhere, a door creaked open.

Ears strained, and breath bated, she waited for it to close. Prickles raced up her spine when it banged shut.

Perhaps Gerard had awakened and was seeking her out? Her heart began to race against her reason. He would beat her for disobeying him. When he saw the pink bow tied to his toe he was bound to misinterpret its meaning, would think she mocked him. She was wide awake now. Shivering with cold, her nerves ragged, she wished she had someone to talk to.

'Grandmother!' Relief flooded her as she whispered the name. Lady Edwina always stayed awake until midnight. Gerard would not seek her there. Scrambling from the bed, she wrapped herself warmly in her cloak and headed silently towards the comfort of the old lady's bedchamber.

'Willow?' Edwina smiled as the dejected figure slid silently into her bed-chamber and seated herself on the edge of the bed. She was trembling with cold. She laid her wrinkled hand over the younger, softer one. 'You're troubled about something?'

'I'm cold and in need of counsel.'

'And some hot chocolate, no doubt. My maid is just making me a cup before retiring.' She drew back the bedclothes. 'Come, my dear, join me. We might as well be comfortable.'

Throwing off her cloak, Willow snuggled up to Lady Edwina and said forlornly, 'I'm a failure as a wife. My husband will most surely be displeased with me.'

CHAPTER SIX

It was not like Jeffrey to still be in bed, Willow thought, glancing back at the house.

Their mounts were saddled and waiting, Jeffrey's hound quivered at her heels in anticipation of his morning run. Circe's forelegs pawed at the cobbles with impatience. Now and again, she arched her neck trying to jerk the reins out of the boy's hands. She was unsettling the rest of the stable.

Today, Willow needed to ride. Edgy and impatient, a deep restlessness rode her body, infusing her with energy.

Already, her wrath had fallen on the hapless Kitty, whose dereliction of her duties would have been rewarded with instant dismissal had she been servant to another. Knowing such an act would force her to admit that the anticipated union with her husband had been a failure, she'd been loath to charge her maid with disobedience.

She'd been equally short with Brian. To her chagrin, the groom had chosen something else to do rather than pass the time of day. Now tight-lipped with anger, she decided if Jeffrey was too lazy to rise on time, she'd ride alone.

Slapping her whip against her boot she turned towards her horse. Seconds later she gazed down at the stable boy from Circe's back. 'When my

150

brother-in-law arrives, tell him I've taken the cliff path.'

They rarely went that way. The cliff edge had been undercut by storms. Aware of the areas of danger, she decided to simply avoid them.

She'd not counted on the path being nearly obliterated.

Reining in, she gazed across the sloping expanse of cliff top. The path was barely discernible, an indentation amongst the snow-covered tufts of coarse coastal grass that bound the chalky cliff face to the land. The sky threatened more snow.

To her right was the sea, its sound oddly muffled, the surface heaving sluggishly. A thick mist vaporized from the water, suspended above the surface like a cold grey, writhing shroud. The horizon was hidden from view. She shivered, wondering if she should turn back.

The hound had no such qualms. Bounding along the pathway, he sniffed this way and that, pausing only to gaze at her with bright inquisitive eyes, as if to reassure himself of her companionship.

She smiled, her temper forgotten. 'All right, I'm coming.' She gave a fleeting thought to the fact her actions might be considered reckless, then dismissed it. If she followed the dog's footprints no harm would befall her.

Halfway across the bluff, she gasped with surprise when the mist momentarily lifted. Anchored beyond the entrance to the sandy cove bordering the Sheronwood estate, was a ship. A boat lay at an angle on the shore, beached by a tide that had

151

ebbed, leaving a curved line of seaweed in the sand. Above the line, the sand was disturbed.

Smugglers? A delicious thrill of terror raced through her.

There was a cave in the cliff, and tunnels running directly to the cellars of Sheronwood. The tunnels had been walled up for many years. During storms, or when the tides ran high, the cave and tunnels flooded. Jeffrey had told her the sounds of the sea echoed through the walls of Sheronwood House, if one pressed an ear to them.

A movement caught her eye. Two men emerged from the cave and dragged the boat towards the sea. When one of them beckoned, a woman and man emerged from the cave, leading some half-a-dozen children of various ages. They were ill-dressed for the bitter winter weather.

Her heart went out to them. She wondered if they were children left orphaned after the small-pox epidemic. She'd found homes for some of the orphans with local families. The parish couldn't afford to pay much for their keep. Often, they were taken in on sufferance then abandoned on the steps of the workhouse. Her dream was to fund a small orphanage in the village, so they could be cared for.

The children were shepherded into the boat and rowed towards the ship. The woman and man turned back towards the cave.

The hound suddenly spotted them. He gave a great baying bark, attracting the attention of the man. Raising his head, he gazed into her eyes for a few seconds. Then a gust of wind and a spatter of snowflakes obliterated the landscape. Everything disappeared into a maelstrom of white.

Aware she'd placed herself in danger by her impetuous behaviour, she gazed about her in despair. The blinding snow had a disorientating effect.

Her eyes sought out the dog's footprints. They were almost gone. Sliding from Circe's back she called the hound to heel. He seemed to have found a more interesting pursuit for the faint echo of frenzied barking was borne upon the wind.

Carefully she trudged across, growing colder by the minute. She'd wished she'd waited for Jeffrey instead of being so hasty.

She sighed with relief when the snow thinned. The frenzied bark of the hound reached her ears. He sounded quite close. Once again, he ignored her command.

'Damn the dog,' she muttered, 'he must have cornered a rabbit.' The noise gave her direction, and she trudged numbly towards it.

'*What the devil!*' The animal's front legs were bound together. It struggled on its side, unable to get itself upright. Drawing her knife, she slashed through the leather thong.

A hand descended on her shoulder and spun her round. Eyes widening, she stared into mean, hazel-coloured eyes. Her immediate reaction was to defend herself. The man uttered an obscenity as her knife sliced across his fingers. Blood spurted as he dashed the knife from her hand and raised a clenched fist on high. Circe whinnied with fear and jerked out of her grasp. The dog saw a game in the offing and chased after the horse, snapping at her heels.

Willow followed suit before the fist could descend. Her breath panted in terrified gasps as she scrambled up the slope on all fours. Gaining the summit, her legs refused to carry her any further and she sank to the ground with a frustrated cry.

Seconds later the man loomed menacingly into her vision. She just had enough energy left to sink her teeth into her assailant's hand when he reached out for her. If she was to be raped or murdered, she'd not leave the perpetrator of the crime unscathed.

'Lucifer's oath!'

A hand roughly grasped her collar. Hauled to her feet she was shaken like a rat in the jaws of a dog. Her teeth sank deeper in protest. When the shaking stopped, her nose was pincered in a painful tweak. Forced to release her grip in order to breathe, she lashed out with her foot, managing to connect with a shin-bone.

'*Ouch!* Calm down you little savage. You've drawn blood.'

'*Gerard?*' His voice was furious, but so welcome she threw herself against him and clung on tight, near to hysterics. 'Thank God! I thought you were *him.*'

'Him?' His hands gripped her shoulders, thrusting her away from him. Suspicious eyes gazed down at her. 'You were with a man?'

'*Hah!*' she cried indignantly, thinking it was in character for Gerard to misinterpret the situation. 'Do you imagine I'd brave such weather for an assignation with some man? I was accosted a short time ago.' Aware that the end of her nose was

154

throbbing, she scowled as she gently caressed it. 'Are you always so rough with women, sir?'

The short bark of laughter he gave held no humour. 'Only when I'm in danger of being bitten through to the bone. Your jaws have the grip of a terrier.' He displayed her handiwork to her. Bright beads of blood oozed from the indentation her teeth had made. 'I hope you do not suffer from mad-dog disease.'

'I trust not, also.' She pulled the scarf from her hat. 'I'm truly sorry. Allow me to bind the wound.'

'There's really no need,' he grumbled, allowing her to do it anyway. When she'd finished, he drew his gauntlet over her handiwork.

Despite his tense smile, his expression was grim as he gazed at her. 'Why do you ride unescorted on the cliff face in such foul weather, and why do you feel the need to wear unfeminine dress abroad? Also, I'm interested in the man you mention. Who is he? Why were you running from him?'

'So many questions,' she countered lightly, needing time to consider her answers. 'Can this interrogation wait until we reach Lytton House? I'm numb with cold.'

'Do not attempt to play on my sympathy.' His gaze was not friendly. 'I'll keep you here all day if necessary. I demand to know who the man is.'

She sighed. 'I have no idea.' Biting her bottom lip to keep her teeth from chattering she slapped her arms against her body. The only thing warm about her was the tip of her abused nose, and even that was beginning to cool. 'He was on the beach by the cave with a woman. They brought some children from the cave, then rowed them out to the ship.'

'What nonsense is this?' His voice was sharp with disbelief.

'It's not nonsense.' Stamping her feet to get some warmth into them, she frowned. 'The man saw me, then the snow began to fall.' Reaction to her narrow escape made her tremble. 'The man lay in wait for me at the bottom of the slope. I ... cut him on the hand to get away.'

'You cut him?' Seizing her by the wrist he dragged her towards the slope. 'If this is the truth, there will be evidence.'

'Pray do not make me go down there again,' she cried, digging her heels into the snow. 'My legs will not carry me back up again.'

'Then I'll do it for them.'

'What if he's still there?' Carried forward by his impetus she stumbled after him.

Grim-faced, he drew his sword from its scabbard. 'I'll ask him what fate he intended for my wife and bring him to account for it.'

He slid to a halt at the bottom. Willow's breath grunted from her body as she collided into his back.

'It seems you were telling the truth.' Retrieving her knife, he handed it to her before examining the marks of a scuffle in the snow. A blood-spotted trail of footprints led towards Sheron-wood. He gazed out to sea, but the snow was swirling thickly now. 'Come,' he grunted, holding out a hand to her. 'You can save your explanation until we return home.'

'I must find Circe.' Slipping her hand into his she was drawn close to his side. His arm slid around her body, supporting her as they made their way to the top.

'Jeffrey's in pursuit of her.'

'He'll be in pursuit all day,' she said giving a laugh. 'Circe will respond to no one but Brian O'Shea and myself.'

Gerard had already discovered that for himself. The mare had more quirks than a Jesuit priest. But then, so had he. 'What about the stable boy?'

'What stable boy?'

Her eyes flew open when he gave a grim smile. His voice assumed a silky edge that made her want to groan. One unguarded moment and she was undone.

'I thought as much. Jeffrey lied to me. It was you riding Circe on the day I arrived home.'

She hung her head for a moment. 'If he lied it was only to protect me from your wrath.' She glanced at his eyes to see if they contained anger. They were as grey as the sky above, and devoid of expression. She felt unaccountably nervous. 'I trust he will not get into trouble on my account.'

'Very laudable.'

His dry tone brought flags of colour to her cheeks. 'He was teaching me to use a saddle,' she said a little desperately. 'I'd always ridden bare-back before. You startled us, and we thought you'd disapprove.'

'Bare-back?' Disbelief replaced the blandness. 'Do you ask me to believe Circe can be ridden bare-back by a woman? You haven't the strength to control her.'

Taking her by the waist he lifted her side-on to the saddle and mounted behind her. 'Take care, madam,' he whispered in her ear. 'Your tales begin to assume an aura of incredibility. You'll try my patience too far one of these days.'

'As you try mine,' she seethed, resenting his assumption that because she was female she could not ride as well as him. 'Why should I boast about such a trifling matter? Circe is *my* horse. I should know whether or not she can be ridden that way. Brian O'Shea gave the filly to me after her mother died. I raised her myself.'

'Which accounts for her capricious nature no doubt,' he said grimly.

She bit her tongue. There was no sense in arguing with someone so mulish.

The snow was not so thick away from the cliff edge. The air was considerably warmer. Picking up the tracks of horses they headed towards the forest path.

Willow noticed the ribbons on Gerard's hat, one blue, the other pink. He wore them like a cockade, as if to remind both himself and her of the relationship binding them. He owned her body and soul.

Colour raced to her face. She turned her head against his chest, grateful for his warmth. It was hard to maintain anger when the very gait of the horse forced her to keep her arms around his waist for support. His body was hard and muscular, his thighs firmly moulded to the horse, his hands strong and sensitive in their guidance. His masculine smell and closeness brought a disturbing weakness to her limbs, yet there was nothing

158

threatening about it.

Her ear lay against his chest, absorbing every beat of his heart. It quickened when they spotted Jeffrey in the distance. Circe was circling him with long, stiff-legged strides, her tail plumed up high. Willow laughed with delight.

'She is playing games with him. I beg you watch for a few moments, Gerard. Her antics will put you in good humour again.'

Gerard was chuckling a few minutes later when he urged his mount into a canter. As she clung tighter, she was drawn hard against his body and matched her movements to his. Anger dissipated, they began to enjoy the chase and were both laughing when they caught Jeffrey up.

Jeffrey grinned when Circe high-stepped towards Willow. Giving a high-pitched snicker that sounded suspiciously like a laugh, she tossed her head up and down.

'I'll be damned,' Gerard breathed. 'I've never seen the like of such a creature.'

'Circe was raised in the Irish countryside.' Willow's eyes grew distant. 'She loves it here as much as I do.'

Her voice lapsed into a soft lilt as she held out her hands to the horse. 'She's a wild and lovely creature to be sure, and the country suits her well. Come to me, Circe. We'll fly together you and I, like we did at Coringal.'

Nervously, because she didn't trust Gerard, Circe edged forward to Willow's urging. 'Come, girl,' she whispered, 'he'll not harm you.' She slid from the horse when Circe held back, using Gerard's arm to swing herself down. She landed lightly on the balls of her feet, the movement unconsciously graceful.

Gerard glanced at his brother, and was transfixed by the expression in his eyes. A lump came into his throat. Jeffrey would always love her, and nothing would change that.

He decided to gift Jeffrey the plantation in Virginia when the time was right. Distance would make the situation easier for all of them. Eventually, another woman would fulfil his dreams and needs.

So intent was he in watching the play of emotion on his brother's face, he missed what Willow was doing. Jeffrey dismounted, and making a stirrup with his hands tossed her lightly on to Circe's back. Fear sprang like a tiger into his breast when he saw the discarded saddle.

'I forbid you to do this,' he shouted, as horse and rider moved away from him. 'Stop! I command you.'

'She cannot hear you.' Jeffrey's eyes were calm as he watched Gerard take off after Willow. He smiled sadly to himself. 'No one will tame her wild spirit, not even you.'

Gerard intended to tame her. Angry at her recklessness, his pride took a beating when his attempts to catch her failed. She seemed to be one with the horse as she cleared obstacles he found daunting himself. She appeared to have no regard for either herself or the mare.

It seemed nothing short of a miracle that they both escaped injury. Willow must have realized it too. She'd prudently made herself scarce by the time he rode in, leaving her horse to the ministrations of the groom.

'Lady Sommersley is no longer allowed to ride that mare,' he ground out.

'But, sir,' Brian protested. 'Circe has been ridden by the mistress since she could take her weight.'

'Enough!' Gerard snapped, his anger born from his fear for Willow's safety, and fuelled by her refusal to heed him. That the fear seemed groundless now was of no consequence, yet the accusation in the groom's eyes pricked his conscience.

The woman was making a fool of him, he told himself, his pride inflated by his need to exert his authority. He intended to make her suffer by withdrawing from her that which she loved most. 'You will exercise the mare yourself. Is that understood?'

'It is.' Brian's voice was just within the range of civil. 'Will there be anything else, My Lord?'

'No.' Ignoring the man's surly tone, and not bothering to wait for Jeffrey, he strode off towards the house at a blistering pace, determined to take Willow to task when time allowed.

'Oh!' Willow's advance into the earl's room was temporarily stilled when she saw Sapphire sitting by the bedside. 'Forgive my intrusion. I didn't realize you were visiting.'

'Ambrose and I are old acquaintances.' Sapphire removed her hand from that of Ambrose when Willow advanced. 'He has been gravely ill, has he not?'

'Yes, but he's recovering.' Giving her father-in-law a smile of greeting, she said, 'I intended to

161

read you another chapter from *Robinson Crusoe*, but as you have a visitor...'

'Pray, do not let that prevent you.'

The woman's faintly accented voice made Willow curious. 'Are you French, madam?'

'I'm French born.' There was a slight hesitation. 'I was young when I left France, and have not been back since.'

'My mother was French.' She smiled at Sapphire. 'Her name was Marietta Givanchy. She was very beautiful, I'm told. Perhaps you've heard of her?'

'*Willow?*'

Ambrose spoke her name so clearly that she could hardly believe her own ears. She was even more astonished when Ambrose raised a shaking hand from the bed to indicate the decanter on the table.

'*A drink please.*'

'Ambrose, you're able to move and speak today.' After informing him of the obvious she hastened to do his bidding, spilling most of it on the table in her excitement. 'I must go and inform your sons as soon as I've finished reading to you. They'll be overjoyed.'

Her daughter was radiating such light as she held the wine against Ambrose's lips, that Sapphire's energy was drained by it. Unaccustomed to using her powers for good, she had, in fact, journeyed to Lytton to expose Caroline for instigating her downfall.

Ambrose had made that impossible. Recognizing his one and only true love at once, such joy had filled his eyes she'd been powerless before him. All she'd felt for Ambrose had returned to smite her anew. Her desire to slander his late wife had shrivelled inside her.

Taking his hands in hers she'd used her long dormant power for healing, giving him her strength, despite knowing she'd taken a step on the path to her own destruction.

Closing her eyes, she listened to Willow reading from Daniel Defoe's adventure story, and smiled to herself. The trauma of her life had been worth this one precious moment, of being with the two people she'd loved and lost.

The affection existing between Ambrose and Willow was almost tangible. Sapphire rejoiced in the fact. If death took her tomorrow instead of the appointed hour, then every dark moment of her life would have been worth just this one of contentment.

'Your reputation preceded you here,' Willow whispered, when she finished reading and noticed Ambrose had fallen into a doze. Her awe for the woman was evident in her voice, and there were tears in her eyes when she knelt and kissed Sapphire's hand. 'God must surely have guided you to our door. I believe you've woven some spell about the earl, and I thank you from the bottom of my heart. If there's anything you would ask of me in return?'

'I'd like you to call me Sapphire, my dear.' Longing to take her in her arms, Sapphire bade her rise. 'If Ambrose recovers it's because he's surrounded with love. Love is the most powerful force on earth.'

Something drained from her heart, an old,

embittered anger that had sustained her through her years of darkness. It left her feeling light-headed and close to tears. She couldn't remember the last time she'd allowed herself the luxury of tears, and now was not the time to weaken.

Excusing herself, she rose to her feet and left the room.

'Bring me my crystal,' she said to Bella as soon as she reached her chamber. 'I must see what time has been granted, and how best to use it.'

But Sapphire had been weakened. The crystal remained as dark as the revelation of her own destruction.

Gerard was annoyed when Willow disturbed his meeting with Bascombe and his son Robert. Brow furrowed in a frown, he nodded curtly towards a chair and bade her wait. He'd been trying to catch her alone since her escapade on Circe, and had no intention of allowing her to escape.

Her very presence proved to be a distraction. She brought with her a subtle fragrance, and the silky fabric of her peach-tinted gown whispered seductively every time she moved.

The aura of excitement surrounding her affected everyone. Bascombe and son seemed unable to concentrate, and he glanced her way on more than one occasion himself.

One brocaded slipper tapped in impatient silence on the carpet, her violet eyes gleaming with inner radiance as they consciously studied the paintings.

His annoyance fled when their eyes met. The

firm curve of his mouth softened when she smiled. He'd found it was impossible to remain annoyed with her for long. She was a delectable creature, he mused, experiencing a sense of unreality when he realized, once again, she was his for the taking.

He slowed as his glance slipped to the pale rise of her breasts, almost tasting the luscious buds of her nipples as they would swell into ripeness under the ministration of his tongue. He imagined her tiny waist spanned by his hands, his mouth pressed against the taut stomach, then sliding down into the dark silky beard that guarded the precious gift of her maidenhood. I'll make you beg me to take your gift, little lady, he promised silently. You'll enjoy my assault.

His pleasurable reverie was shattered when Bascombe coughed, bringing him back to the present. He tore his eyes away from the charms of his temptress and tried to gather his wits together. What the hell had they been talking about? He gazed at the steward, expression bemused.

'Sheep, sir. You indicated the meat yield can be improved by inbreeding.'

'That's right, Bascombe.' He ran a tongue over dry lips. 'Robert Blakewell advocated the method, and has achieved excellent results. I want ours to be equally as good.'

Beset by a sudden desire to be alone with his wife, he rose to his feet and indicated the meeting was at an end. The door had hardly closed behind the two men when she captured his glance.

'You'll never guess what's happened, Gerard?' She paused, unconsciously heightening the

165

suspense by making a game out of the news. 'No, you'll never guess in a thousand years.'

He tried not to smile at the quivering excitement in her voice. 'Then you'd better tell me. One thousand years is too long to be kept in suspense.'

'You make fun of me.' Her attempt to pout failed when she smiled again. Rising gracefully from her chair she crossed to where he stood, her eyes shining with happiness. 'Ambrose spoke quite clearly today, and he moved his hand without any help.'

Her eyes drew Gerard's into their jewel bright depths, enchanting him. So bedazzled was he, her words hardly registered in his ears. Nevertheless, he managed to murmur what he hoped was the correct response.

'You're sure?'

'Of course I'm sure.' Puzzlement flirted in the depths of her eyes. 'You do not sound very interested, Gerard.'

How could he take the bearer of such glad tidings to task? 'Of course I'm interested.' Taking her hand he raised it to his lips and murmured, 'Your beauty robs me of coherent thought. My interest is concentrated on your appearance, and not your words.'

Her eyes sparkled at his compliment, her cheeks dimpled in a most comely manner as she caressed the lace at her wrists, softly inviting further comment. 'You like this gown?'

'The gown is pretty enough.' How naïve she was, he thought, his fingertips lightly caressing the curve of her bottom lip. He smiled when she

166

hung her head and blushed. 'Its wearer puts it in the shade, however. You're just as beautiful in pink velvet and rosebuds.'

He watched her blush deepen. Her eyes touched against his in modest confusion before her lashes shaded their beauty again. So soft was her voice, he only just caught her words.

'You were awake?'

Tipping her chin up, he forced her to look at him. 'Why did you run away?'

'I thought you slept and did not wish to disturb you.' She looked a trifle desperate when he smiled. 'I was scared. I'm not used to being married.'

Her expression contained such a plea for understanding, it moved him.

'You're a stranger to me, Gerard. I ... I do not feel married to you.'

'I admit, ours was a short courtship.'

The irony in his voice caused pain to flare in her eyes. He wished he'd never spoken. She'd not been a willing party to the marriage either. *The lesser of two evils*, she'd said at the time.

'Perhaps I should give you time to get used to me. I'm loath to embark on a relationship with a reluctant wife.'

'That's exactly what Grandmother thought you would say.'

A frown knotted his brow, until he remembered there was no other married female available to advise her. If his grandmother was Willow's *confidante*, he'd better make sure the act of union was pleasing.

Inwardly, he cursed. Willow was a fetching little thing, and his physical response to her healthily

167

normal. He'd have to proceed with extreme caution though. He smiled, his mind already planning her slow seduction. He could find relief in Dorchester, should the need become urgent.

Bending to the sensuous curves of her mouth he kissed it into trembling awareness. His voice was husky with desire when he released her. 'You'll be all the sweeter for the seduction.'

Drawing from his pocket the betrothal ring, he slid it on to her finger. 'This is the Lytton betrothal ring. The stone signifies the purity of the wearer, and will remind you of the promise between us.'

Despite the diamond's great beauty, Willow's heart sank like a stone. The last time she'd seen the ring it had graced the finger of Daphne de Vere, the woman her husband loved.

With no pomp, and hardly any ceremony, Daphne de Vere buried her husband in the grounds of St James. Few braved the bitterly cold weather to pay their respects. Those who had were indebted to the marquess in some way, and feared reprisal if they didn't put in an appearance.

Daphne's eyes were glassy with fever under her mourning veil. She'd been plagued by a chest complaint since the onset of winter, and the previous week her handkerchief had come away spotted with blood after she'd suffered a fit of coughing.

Aware the signs augured ill, she'd taken to her bed, but not before sending to Eduard the drug he'd grown addicted to since being afflicted by madness. She'd mixed the dose herself, almost double the usual quantity.

The servants assigned to watch over Eduard had reported he'd been raving and violent the previous night. The apothecary recommended by the marquess had sent her a new prescription.

Playing nursemaid to the mad husband of Daphne de Vere had offered both sport and comfort to the servants set to watch over him. Their last duty had been to seal him unceremoniously in his coffin. They'd left him in his soiled clothes, a green velvet jacket and breeches, and a red brocade waistcoat that matched the heavily rouged cheeks. Even in his madness, Eduard had been a flamboyant dresser.

The mourners at the funeral didn't stay long, it was too cold. Daphne leaned heavily on the marquess's arm as they left the scene, and was borne away in a carriage displaying the Lynch-cross crest before the coffin had been covered with earth.

The grave diggers grumbled as they watched the mourners depart. They'd worked hard digging the hole in the frozen earth. Although they'd been paid by the parish, it was usual for the family of the departed to offer some small recompense. The elder of the two wiped his nose on the back of his hand.

'This one's a toff. Sometimes, they buries them in their clothes.' Scraping the earth from the coffin he applied the edge of his shovel to the lid. 'There might be a silk 'andkerchief or something we can sell.'

'God, he's a tawdry-looking cove,' said the

169

younger one gazing at the half-open eyes of the corpse a little nervously. He drew closer, observing the richness of the clothes. 'They buried him in a hurry, he's still got his wig and shoes on. Look at them buckles. If they ain't silver, my name's not Jack Dodson.'

Within a few minutes Eduard Lynchcross was naked, his coffin sealed, and the earth being shovelled swiftly over his grave.

Later that evening, Jack Dodson laboriously studied a letter he'd taken from the pocket of the corpse's coat. He was not skilled at letters. Even if he had been, the missive was written in a foreign language. He couldn't even make out the name of the person it was addressed to.

Perhaps it was a letter to the man's mistress. It might be worth something to the widow's crippled father. His glance softened as it went to his ten-year-old daughter. A man wouldn't want his daughter to suffer more grief than she had to.

Wrapping the letter in a piece of cloth, he concealed it in the hollow of his armpit, binding it in place with a piece of rag. There it would stay until the bargain had been struck, and the money safely deposited in his pocket.

He draped a shawl around his daughter's shoulders and took her hand in his. They'd dine on more than turnip soup tonight if all went well.

The marquess left Dodson to Simon Carsewell to deal with. His friend had a deadly efficient way of dealing with those who sought to extort money from him.

Of more interest to him was the child. She was a pretty little thing. Awed by the luxurious surroundings, she'd been quite willing to accompany him to the cellars below his house to take part in the games he would teach her.

Bathed in perfumed soap, gowned in silk, her face rouged – the child's eyes were round with wonder as she snuggled against him and ate the sweetmeats he placed in her mouth.

Presently, she grew drowsy. He laid her on a velvet-covered divan and stared down at her from under hooded lids.

His lips twisted in a smile when she drowsily asked for her papa.

'He's dead. I'm your papa now.' His tongue flicked over his dry lips and his eyes began to gleam. 'You must do exactly what Papa tells you, my dear. If not, I'll be forced to beat you.'

The letter was still in Jack Dodson's armpit when the morgue-keeper took his body to Guy's Hospital for dissection by a student surgeon.

The surgeon was Charles Addison. Charles could speak tolerable French but had never learned to read or write it. That made no difference when he found the letter: Gerard Lytton's name was instantly recognizable to him.

'My husband has forbidden me to ride Circe?' Bewildered by the turn of events Willow could only stare at Brian. 'Why did he not tell me himself?' Anger and hurt churned rancidly inside her. What had she done to deserve such treatment? 'Are you sure you're not mistaken?' she

171

asked brokenly.

Brian's lean, dark face mirrored the anguish in Willow's. 'To be sure. When I gave Circe to my own darlin' girl, I thought the pair of you would never be apart.'

'What you thought then is immaterial.' Gerard's face was dark with anger as he strode into the stable yard. 'On this occasion I intend to overlook your familiarity of speech with my wife, but let me warn you ... from this day on you'll address her with the respect due to her position. Is that understood, O'Shea?'

'Yes, My Lord.'

'But, Gerard...' Willow's voice trailed off when she saw the thunderous expression on her husband's face. The shrug she gave seemed to incense him even more, for his eyes raked her from head to toe.

'You're indecently dressed, madam. Go and change into your riding habit.' He pointed to a docile-looking gelding. 'Put a lady's saddle on that, in the meantime, groom.'

'Do not put a lady's saddle on anything, not even the stable door!' Stamping her foot at her husband's high-handed tone, Willow rounded on him. 'That horse is so lazy he cannot walk to the end of the lane. I *demand* to know why you forbid me to ride Circe.'

'You're in no position to demand anything,' he said silkily. 'And if you do not go and change into appropriate clothing, I'll be forced to help you into it, myself.'

'You would not dare!' Scornfully tossing her head, she turned her back on him.

That was a mistake. Seized by the waist she was spun around and roughly tossed over Gerard's shoulder like a sack of potatoes.

'Put me down this instant!' Her dangling fists beat ineffectually at his buttocks as he strode towards the house with her. 'If you do not, I'll scream for help.'

'And who will come to your aid?' Gerard muttered grimly. 'You may think you have the servants in the palm of your hand, but I wager they'd not risk dismissal by interfering.' The laugh he gave contained derision. 'Should I choose to beat you to death in front of their eyes, they'd turn their heads aside.'

'You would not do that.' Her hat jolted loose and her hair fell in gleaming disarray to the snow. 'My hair is getting dirty, Gerard.'

Resignation filled her voice when he took no notice. It was difficult to shrug when hanging upside-down, but she managed it. 'I suppose the condition of my hair matters not if you intend to beat me.'

'Your appearance makes no difference to the outcome.' His gruff voice brought terror to Willow's soul as she remembered the cruel flogging she'd received from her father. The pain had been almost unbearable. She began to tremble.

'I understand that I've angered you, Gerard. I'm bad-tempered and headstrong, and my manners would put the roughest peasant to shame.' A panicky sob caught in her throat and tears scalded her eyes. 'I know I'm an ungrateful wretch, but please do not subject me to another beating. My body still bears the scars my father

173

inflicted on me.'

Gerard's temper turned to ashes in his mouth. Gradually, his footsteps slowed to a stop and he lowered her to the ground. His eyes were bleak as they noted her tearstained cheeks. Taking out his handkerchief, he gently dried them.

'The marquess permanently marked you?'

'It's of no consequence.' Although the scars were small, she hoped Gerard would not think her ugly when he saw them. 'They are very tiny scars. One is like a crescent moon and is quite fetching.' Her mouth twitched into a tentative smile. 'At least, that's what my maid tells me. I cannot see it myself.' Her smile faded when he didn't respond. 'I'm sorry I angered you, Gerard.'

'It was not your fault.' His eyes softened as he reached out and touched her hair. 'My conduct was less than that of a gentleman. Be assured, you'll never receive a beating from me.'

'I'm mightily relieved,' she said candidly, and wondered if it would be safe to broach the subject of Circe once again. She couldn't understand why she'd been banned from riding the mare.

'May I ask you something, Gerard?' When one dark eyebrow raised in assent, she took a deep breath. 'What have I done to be deprived of Circe?'

He bound one of her dark silky locks about his hand whilst his eyes brooded on the question. She'd done nothing but affront his pride. She'd out-ridden him on a horse he'd coveted as soon as he'd set eyes on it, a horse he could not ride himself. Nothing he could do or say would make the mare his. She hadn't been in danger. He'd used it as an excuse, and had handled the situation all wrong.

Even her dress did not shock him now he was used to it. Unconsciously, he noted her trim figure in its ill-assorted garb, and toyed with the idea of having a riding outfit designed for her. He'd not allow her to wear such clothing off the estate, of course, it would set scandalous tongues wagging.

Gerard had actually been on his way to the stables to rescind the instructions about the horse. He'd intended to invite her to accompany him on his ride.

When he'd overheard the familiarity with which the groom had addressed her, he'd been mightily displeased. Servants, no matter how long they'd served a family, should be deferential. He gave a rueful smile. It was time to make peace between them.

'I spoke out of ill-temper yesterday. Your riding is of such excellence it brought envy to my breast. In the heat of the moment I used the power of my position to cause you distress. I ask your forgiveness.' Satisfaction flowed through his body when her eyes lightened. 'If that's forthcoming, I'd like you to do me the favour of accompanying me this morning.'

'A pretty speech, Gerard.'

He grinned as merriment filled her eyes. Thank God she was not disposed to sulk.

'First you take away my horse, then you throw me across your shoulders and threaten to beat me to pulp. Are you a gentleman, or one of the savages you came across in Virginia? *La, sir!* Answer this truthfully: can I trust you to behave like a gentleman?'

Raising her hair to his lips he breathed in an aroma of camomile and lavender before letting it fall in a shimmering cascade over one shoulder. Her unconscious flirting made him smile. 'I can only promise to be a gentleman for one day.'

'Then I shall take advantage of that and be thankful.' Taking him by surprise, she lightly kissed him on the cheek. 'I must go and ask my maid to tidy my hair.'

'Leave it, I beg you.' His eyes touched admiringly on her lustrous, dark tresses as he took her hand in his. 'We'll forget convention this morning and just enjoy our ride together.'

'Can you forget convention?' Her laughter rang in the crisp cold air. He relaxed, laughing with her as they walked back from whence they'd come.

'You'd be surprised just how unconventional I can be on occasion.'

'On what occasion?'

The smile he slanted her way had an enigmatic quality to it. 'That you have yet to discover,' he murmured.

She couldn't understand why her cheeks chose exactly that moment to take on a rosy hue. Thinking about it afterwards, she came to the conclusion it must have been the cold.

From her window, Edwina watched them return to the stable. Observing what had taken place, she'd feared for Willow's welfare but knew better

176

than to try and intervene between husband and wife. She'd soon realized her fears were groundless.

Gerard would not ill-treat a woman, she assured herself. She smiled with satisfaction. Willow was a clever little minx, despite her youth. Aware of her femininity, she did not hesitate to use it to her own advantage.

When Willow had confided her fears about her marriage duties, Edwina had noticed an element of mortification in her voice. The thought that her husband would prefer to fall asleep rather than await her presence, had not sat well with the girl.

That she'd been genuinely scared of the union was also apparent. Edwina could not blame her for that. The thought of losing one's virginity when one had been taught to hold on to it at all costs was daunting. She sighed as she moved away from the window. For all that, the secrets of the bedroom could be extremely pleasurable with the right man. That much she'd told Willow.

'If you ask your husband to teach you the ways of love he'll never seek another,' she'd said.

'But what *are* the ways of love?' Asperity had stung her voice. 'Tell me, Grandmother.'

Edwina had seen the way Gerard looked at Willow, and had observed her response. The awareness was obvious. She would not be left innocent, nor kept in ignorance for much longer.

Humming to herself, she moved to the door. She was feeling much better of late, and the news that Ambrose had also improved considerably had cheered her.

Accosting his personal servant in the hall, she discovered Ambrose was awake and ready to receive visitors. The door was ajar, so she knocked and stepped inside his bedchamber. Transfixed by shock, she stared at the woman by his bed.

'You!' she breathed, unable to quite believe her own eyes. 'How can this be?'

The woman's veil was drawn so swiftly over her face that Edwina wondered if she'd actually seen who she'd thought she'd seen.

Rapid strides took her towards the bed. She gazed down at the small figure in black. Dear God in Heaven, she thought. It is her! She wears the small sapphire ring I gave her for her fifteenth birthday.

Heart full to bursting, Edwina held out her hands in welcome. 'My dearest Marietta. I once loved you as my own, as I do your daughter. Do not hide yourself from me. I know not how you come to be alive, but I thank the Lord that it's so.'

For a moment, Sapphire hesitated. A tiny shudder ran through her.

Then she took a deep steadying breath, and placed both of her hands in those held out to her in friendship. Fate had taken her destiny firmly in hand, and she had not the will to change it.

CHAPTER SEVEN

Gerard had planned the meeting of farmers and labourers carefully, choosing a popular local inn for the gathering.

The gathering passed without incident, the new farming system explained simply by Robert Bascombe. On hand was Anthony Dowling, the officer who'd acted as second in his recent duel, and a couple of soldiers who'd braved the cold for the shilling the duty offered. They were not needed. The ale he provided flowed freely, encouraging a sense of amiability amongst even the most dubious of relationships.

Gerard addressed the men after Robert had spoken, then answered the few questions put by those brave enough to voice their doubts. Afterwards, the landlord provided a meal of bread, cheese and pickles at Gerard's expense.

The inn was thick with smoke, and the odour of sweat permeated every corner of the room. Some of the men had imbibed too freely and were becoming raucous. Gerard drew Anthony Dowling aside. 'I need to speak to you about a small matter. Perhaps there's a private room we can use.'

'You're welcome to join me at my lodgings, sir. 'Tis but a few minutes' ride.' Anthony cast an eye over the increasingly noisy crowd. 'There are dissenters in the crowd. It will take only one to turn this crowd into a mob once they are in their cups.'

'You may be right.' Gerard beckoned to Robert, and the three of them ducked through a back door. Ten minutes later, they were comfortably settled in Anthony's rooms and being served with cake and Madeira by the daughter of his landlady.

She was a buxom creature with bold dark eyes, and breasts that bounced invitingly against her bodice. She giggled when Anthony slapped a hand against her backside and fluttered long, dark eyelashes in Gerard's direction, her eyes loaded with invitation.

His loins tightened. It was a while since he'd lain with a woman, and this was a comely wench.

Anthony grinned as he intercepted the look. 'Be off with you, Mary. I'll call you if we have need of you.'

'Glad to be of service, sir.' Her hips swayed seductively as she left the room.

Anthony gazed at his guests, a faint smile on his lips as he raised his glass. 'As you can see, gentlemen, my lodgings come with all accommodations. Your good health, sirs.'

Pleasantries over, Gerard brought up the matter that had been occupying his mind for the past few days.

'Lady Sommersley was attacked?' Anthony leaned forward, frowning. 'This is indeed a serious matter. Was she injured?'

'Fortunately, my wife managed to defend herself and escape. The man you're looking for bears knife wounds across the fingers of his hand.'

Remembering Hugh Macbride, he grinned

180

when Anthony studied the ceiling for a while. The officer's face was admirably composed when he finally engaged Gerard's gaze, though his eyes looked suspiciously bright.

'There was a ship at anchor, you say?'

Gerard related exactly what Willow had told him she'd seen, adding, 'There were signs of a scuffle and spots of blood leading towards Sheronwood.'

Anthony's forehead furrowed in a frown. 'I've heard rumours of activity there.'

'The locals think the place haunted. Lights have been sighted, and crying heard.' Robert shrugged when Gerard gave a faint smile. 'Rosamond de Vere was deserted by her staff, and died with stinking corpses for company. It's said the stench of the dead still lingers, and her soul cries out for release.'

'Superstitious rubbish,' Gerard said, his voice a trifle louder than normal to keep his unease at bay.

Country folklore had been ingrained in him since birth. His nurse and tutor had been firm believers in the supernatural. The horrifying tales they'd told him had kept him huddled in his bed at night, and the punishment he'd expected to receive from the Devil if he didn't behave had been truly terrifying.

He'd been about fourteen when he'd realized the stories and threats had been their way of controlling him. Though logic told him otherwise, he couldn't quite shake off the feeling he was tempting fate by denying the existence of the supernatural.

The reputation of Willow's mother stole into his thoughts. Was supernatural power hereditary? He chided himself as he brought his attention back to the present company. Willow showed no inclination towards things occult. He grinned. She busied herself with household matters, her appearance, and nagging him about the orphanage.

'You're right, of course,' Robert grinned sheepishly. 'The locals are inclined to exaggerate these things. I have no qualms about the place myself.'

'Nevertheless, from what you've told me, Sheronwood warrants further investigation.' Anthony looked thoughtful. 'I might ride over and take a look in the morning.'

'I'll join you.' Gerard rose to his feet and picked up his hat in preparation for leaving. 'The heir to Sheronwood is under my guardianship. I should like to assure myself his inheritance is safe. I intend to write to Lady Daphne, advising her that a new steward needs to be appointed if the land is to be kept productive.'

Anthony rose, stretching his long frame almost to the ceiling. 'A dispatch rider is leaving for London the day after tomorrow. He'll be pleased to deliver it, and any other missive you might wish to send.'

Remembering he'd offered to enquire about the fate of James Langland on behalf of his wife, he voiced his thanks. He'd include a letter to his lawyer at the same time.

On the way out, they were intercepted by Mary, who watched them descend the narrow stairway with a smile on her face. She leaned back against an open doorway, her breasts thrust forward into tempting peaks, her smile almost cat-like. Behind her, a tousled bed issued its own invitation.

The girl was so willing he could smell the lust rising from her. He was tempted as she swayed towards him, her closeness inciting the most primitive of urges. Idly, he wondered if she was clean and free of disease.

Instantly, an image of Willow came to mind. Her fresh fragrance of lavender and roses, the innocence of her eyes, and most of all, her maidenly blushes. She reacted to his gallantries as predictably as any maid.

The process of courtship was tedious. He grinned to himself. Willow was transparent, and her naïvete kept him constantly amused. When she desired something she didn't rest until she achieved it. He intended she would desire *him*. When she did...? His grin became slightly wolf-ish. He intended to keep her waiting until every inhibiting thought was driven away by her urge for pleasure.

He glanced again at Mary, noting the coarse-ness in her face. It would be unfair to place his innocent wife at risk by lying with a soldier's whore.

An ironic smile flirted at his lips as the heat left his groin. A few short weeks ago, he wouldn't have hesitated.

The girl pouted as he neatly side-stepped, and followed the others into the street. Returning Anthony's questioning grin with a rueful shrug, he mounted and turned his horse towards home.

'I can only see my reflection.' Disappointed, Willow turned to Sapphire and shrugged. 'Perhaps you were mistaken in thinking I have the ability to see into the crystal.'

'I'm not mistaken.' Returning the crystal ball to its velvet-lined box, Sapphire placed it in her daughter's hands. 'You're self-conscious at the moment. What your inner vision detects, your eyes deny. Accept the crystal as a gift.' She smiled when Willow protested. 'I have another, my dear. Meditate as I have shown you. Eventually, answers to your questions will be revealed.'

'I'll endeavour to do as you say.'

Sapphire shifted. Light from the window behind her turned the veil into a filmy mist, revealing the outline of her profile. Willow's breath caught in her throat. Something familiar about the woman made her wonder if they'd met before.

Sapphire was watching her, the scrutiny intense, as if she was memorizing every feature. An overwhelming sense of loss seemed to hang in the air. Willow experienced a deep well of despair that seemed to cry out for something she'd never had.

Emotion overcame her as she recognized the same need in Sapphire. She reached out and, closing her eyes, allowed it to flow like a current between them.

A hand gently touched her cheek, like that of a mother to her newly born infant. She nestled against the soft caress, filled with a deep sense of joy. Her hand closed over Sapphire's; her voice trembled with the strange emotion she experienced.

'You're in pain. I pray your soul finds harmony.'

Sapphire found it hard to restrain her surprise. Her daughter's intuition was stronger than she'd realized. Their souls had touched in a tentative recognition of the other.

It was a strangely moving moment for her. She'd thought her soul beyond redemption, yet some tiny portion had remained unscathed, and struggled to be free from its prison of darkness.

It had been drawn towards her daughter, as if Willow was the mother, she the child in need of nurturing. A tiny seed of hope took root in her heart as she watched Willow depart.

The gift from Gerard was delivered late that afternoon. It arrived in a box covered with red patterned brocade, the dressmaker's name embossed in gold on the lid.

Fingers trembling with anticipation, Willow carefully loosened the gold satin bow and eased off the lid. Her exclamation of delight when she pulled the garments from the box brought Kitty hurrying through from the maid's room.

'Look, Kitty!' Thrusting a plum-coloured frock coat into Kitty's hands, she drew the matching breeches from the box. They were made of the softest wool and lined with silk.

The jacket was trimmed with silver buttons and braid, as was the matching tricorn. There was a black cloak lined with plum silk, black leather riding boots and a cream silk shirt with lace at the cuffs and throat. A pair of black kid gauntlets had the Lytton crest delicately embroidered in silver thread.

'Quickly, Kitty. Help me out of this gown so I can see if it fits.'

I'd be surprised if it didn't, Kitty thought, smiling to herself. The viscount has got your measure, My Lady, and no mistake.

For the second time that day, Kitty helped her mistress dress, and watched her parade in front of the burnished metal mirror.

Nellie came in to throw some logs on the fire. Sparks flew up the chimney. It was never allowed to go out, because there always seemed to be a chill in the room.

Kitty couldn't understand why they stayed in this wing when they could have their pick of accommodations. The last time she'd brought up the matter, Willow had given an enigmatic smile. Kitty frowned when Nellie sidled up to the discarded ribbon. 'Keep your hands off that,' she snapped. 'They be dirty.'

'Pretty,' Nellie crooned, staring at the ribbon's shiny length with fascinated eyes. 'Pretty ribbon for Nellie's hair. Nellie's a good girl.'

'Of course you are, Nellie,' Willow said, before her maid could snap at the idiot again.

She was annoyed with Kitty at the moment. For the past week or two the girl had been late rising. She'd made a mistake by substituting Kitty's wooden pallet for a more comfortable bed. On a couple of occasions, she'd heard her retching into the closed stool. If that wasn't bad enough, every now and then Kitty's manner bordered on insolence.

Although she'd been her childhood companion and friend, Kitty had to come to terms with the changed circumstances. They were adults now. She couldn't be allowed to indulge in such familiarity.

As Gerard had pointed out, it displayed a lack of respect. She stared, without seeing, at her reflection. If Kitty was sick she should have told her, not risked passing on the malady.

Willow usually gave Kitty any discarded ribbons, but this time a perverse little voice in her head urged her say, 'You may have the ribbon, Nellie. Kitty will make a nice bow in your hair with it.'

'I certainly will not!' Kitty quaked as her mistress turned a warning glance her way.

'You will do as you told, Kitty Adams!'

To her consternation, Kitty burst into copious tears and fled from the room. Something ailed her, and Willow intended to find out exactly what it was.

She tied the bow herself to the hair of a delighted Nellie, then sent her to Mrs Breton. Although the staff shortage had been relieved by an infusion of new servants who'd defected from Squire Tupworthy's household, Mrs Breton liked to keep Nellie below stairs and out of sight as much as possible.

Kitty was whey-faced when she finally responded to her summons. Willow had intended to give the girl a piece of her mind, but she looked so woebegone, Willow's heart softened.

'You'd better tell me what ails you,' she said kindly. 'I'm fast running out of patience with your moods.' Seeing the hesitation in her, she smiled in encouragement. 'Has Brian given his

187

heart to another?' She frowned at the thought. 'I'd not have thought him fickle-hearted.'

'He's not.' Kitty replied hotly, then remembering her place, hung her head. 'I have sinned.'

'Oh?' Kitty was of the Catholic faith. Even so, Willow couldn't understand why a small sin would have upset her so. 'Did you confess your sin to the priest?'

'He said I must wed, or my soul will be in peril.' Kitty fell to her knees. 'You promised to seek the earl's permission for us to wed; so far, you've not said yea or nay.'

'I'd forgotten.' A tiny knot of suspicion surfaced. She knew little about the bearing of children, but stored in her mind were half-forgotten snippets she'd overheard whilst she was growing up. 'This sickness you've been having, are you ... with child?'

'Aye, my lady.' Bursting into a fresh lot of weeping, Kitty prostrated herself on the floor. 'I did not mean to sin, but nature has a powerful way of going against the Lord's teachings. Do not beat me or cast me from your door; I've no one else to turn to.'

She didn't know, whether to laugh or cry at the opinion Kitty had formed of her character. 'Get up,' she said with some asperity. 'I'll go and ask the earl's permission now.'

She thought about it for a few seconds. 'I'll also ask him about the orphanage I wish to establish in the village. There are children whose parents died in the smallpox epidemic, and although they're fostered to families who would take them in, their lot is not happy. Some have already been sent to the workhouse. Did you think I'd subject you and your child to the same fate, you silly goose?'

'Thank you, My Lady.' Kitty's face shone with happiness as she got to her feet.

Excitement bubbled up in Willow as she hurried to the door. 'It's about time we had something to celebrate. I'll arrange things with Mrs Breton after I've seen the earl.'

She was smiling when she entered the earl's room. Ambrose was asleep in a chair by the fire. Opposite, Gerard lounged in a matching chair, staring reflectively into the flames.

The atmosphere was contented, the candles not yet lit. Firelight made the shadows leap and dance, highlighting the firmly contoured angles of his face. It was not a restful face even when relaxed, but handsome, nevertheless.

Whatever her father's reasoning, his choice of a husband for her suited her. Had she been given to Simon Carsewell, life would not be worth living.

Alerted to her presence, Gerard's mouth twitched into a smile and his head turned towards her. Lazily, his glance roved over her outfit. 'It fits you well, but surely you don't intend to ride at this hour, it's almost dusk.'

'It looked so beautiful I just *had* to try it on.' She couldn't keep the excitement from her voice. 'It's a thoughtful gift. I thank you from the depths of my heart.'

'A kiss would be better accepted,' he remarked, uncoiling from the chair and drawing her into his arms.

The warmth of the dimly lit room lent sudden intimacy to their relationship. Her awareness of him increased, her heart began to thump in a most alarming manner and her throat suffered from dryness.

Her husband's caresses and sweetly worded compliments had increased of late. Although she looked forward to them – even put herself in the position of inviting them on occasion they had a strangely weakening effect upon her body. Her legs turned to warm wax at the very sight of him sometimes.

'The earl may wake up,' she whispered, overcome by shyness.

'He will not wake just yet.'

His lips, which were slightly austere when he wasn't smiling, softened when they took advantage of her upturned mouth. She was just beginning to enjoy the sensations his kiss evoked, when he began to withdraw. Murmuring a protest deep in her throat, and praying he did not think her wanton, she slid her arms around his neck.

'Pray, kiss me once more, Gerard. I find it most enjoyable.'

There was a moment when time could be measured by a heartbeat. Their lips were so close their breath mingled in scented confusion, their eyes so tangled, each experience the recognition of mutual pleasure. Her lips parted slightly in surprise and Gerard took advantage of them again, this time more ardently.

She had never imagined there could be so much pleasure from a man's kiss. His tongue explored the contours of her lips before making tiny, flickering assaults into the moist parting she inadvertently provided. Trembling and weak from a rush of heat through her veins, she allowed his plundering tongue to probe deeper, until the response of her own was to flirt with his in a most delicious manner.

It seemed to be a lifetime later that the mantel clock chimed four, but only a minute had passed. Her lips were strangely sated when he gazed down at her. She blushed at the expression in his eyes. They were predatory, like that of a falcon about to swoop on its prey.

She shivered slightly. The look was replaced by amusement when Ambrose stirred in the chair.

'Look who's come to visit you,' Gerard drawled, as though nothing untoward had occurred between them. Drawing her forward, he paraded her in front of the earl. 'She's come to show us how becoming her new riding outfit looks.'

'That's not so.' Still all blushes, and tingling deliciously, Willow felt completely defenceless as she tried to remember why she was there at all. 'I have two favours to ask of the earl.' She gazed at Ambrose and smiled with great fondness. 'I'd not bother you with this if it were not of the greatest importance, sir.'

'Speak, Willow. You know I can refuse you nothing.'

Ambrose's voice was much stronger now, the slurring almost eliminated. He was slowly regaining strength in his body. John Grey had devised a way of exercising the earl's muscles, so he'd find it easier to support himself when he learned to walk again.

'The favour is not for me, it's for my maid, Kitty Adams. She seeks permission to marry the groom.' She hesitated, wondering how to broach the delicacy of the matter. Taking a deep breath, she said slowly, 'The priest has advised Kitty it's imperative she weds soon, or her soul will be in mortal peril.'

'You mean the girl has got herself with child?' Gerard's harsh query caused her to jump. 'If your maid has loose morals, she must not remain in your employ.'

'She's been led astray.' She did not see why Kitty should take all the blame, and jumped to her defence immediately. 'I hope you'll see fit to reprimand the man, Gerard. He's not without culpability in the matter.'

'And if he does not wish to marry the girl?'

'That's not possible.' Uneasily, she stared at her husband. 'Brian holds her in great affection. He'd not let her bear this burden alone.'

'Then I'll ascertain the truth of this from his own lips.' He headed towards the door. 'Brian O'Shea is the best groom we've ever had; I'll not have him trapped into marriage against his will.'

'And what of the child?' she snapped, understanding his sudden resentment all too well, and experiencing guilt at her involvement in the trapping of *him* as her husband. Yet, if her father had beaten her to death as he'd threatened? She shuddered. It did not bear thinking about. Anger made her forget the earl was in the room, as she cried out in an impassioned voice, 'Does the child count for naught? Would you cast a mother and her infant into a workhouse, whilst the man responsible seeks another maid to spoil?'

'The child could belong to any man unfortunate enough to have–'

'Enough, Gerard!'

The earl only raised his voice a little, but Gerard immediately fell silent. His body was one stiff column of tension as he turned back towards his father.

Sadly, Ambrose reminded his eldest son, 'You treat both me and your wife with much disrespect. It was my advice Willow sought, not yours.'

'I most humbly beg your pardon, Father.' Gerard neither sounded, nor looked, in the least bit humble as he stood by the door, tensely waiting permission to leave.

Ambrose left him waiting and turned his gaze back to her. 'What's your second request?'

'I've been thinking about the village orphans. If, in your generosity, you could let me have a vacant cottage, I should like to provide for them with the money from my dowry. They could be trained to work for the estate.'

'I'd be willing to donate a cottage for such a cause, but as for your dowry' – Ambrose was regretful, but firm – 'that's for Gerard to decide, my dear.'

Gerard was not disposed to grant any favours at that moment. 'Your dowry is little enough considering the circumstances of our marriage. Such a scheme will bring every beggar child to our door. Permission is not given.' Receiving a dismissive nod from the earl, he gave a stiff bow. Leaving Willow bewildered and hurt by his reference to their hasty marriage, he strode away without another word.

Wounded by his thrust, she turned to the earl, close to tears. 'I've been the cause of discord between you,' she whispered. 'I'm sorry.'

The earl indicated the chair opposite him and she settled herself in its comfortable depths.

'Gerard is proud and his masculine arrogance takes precedence over his good sense at times. However, you must learn not to argue with him in my company. It's demeaning for us both when I'm forced to rebuke him.'

Her tears spilled over as she accepted the earl's censorship. She fumbled for her handkerchief. 'I would not have him stripped of his pride. It will be as you say.'

Ambrose gazed at Willow and blessed all that she was. She had all the qualities of her mother, yet her character had more resilience. He'd have liked to give her the security of knowing she had her mother's love, but unfortunately, Marietta had sworn both he and Lady Edwina to secrecy.

Although Marietta's downfall had not been her fault, she did not want her daughter to assume the burden of it. Her story was so horrifying that, reluctantly, he'd agreed Willow was better kept in ignorance of it.

Marietta's marriage to the marquess had been violent in the extreme. Although it was accepted she'd died shortly after childbirth, Marietta had been beaten by the marquess, then left for dead in a shallow grave in the forest.

Some gypsies who'd witnessed the crime, had dug up her body for the clothes. When they'd discovered her alive, she'd been nursed back to health, then sold into slavery and shipped to America.

Her extraordinary powers had saved her from a life of complete degradation. She'd become the property of a shaman, who'd nurtured her darker powers. When he'd died, she'd returned to England to plan her revenge.

Despite her horrifying past, Ambrose loved Marietta all the more for her courage. He smiled to himself. Even his formidable mother-in-law had been moved to tears over her fate once she'd recovered from her initial horror. Edwina had not demurred when he'd offered Marietta the protection of his home for as long as she wished to stay.

'You can tell your maid permission to wed is granted,' he said, as John Grey quietly entered the room and busied himself lighting the candle sconces. 'She may continue in your service for the time being, if you so wish.'

'I do so wish.' Rising to her feet, she kissed the earl's cheek. 'You're a good man, Earl Lytton. I pray your full recovery is not too far off.'

'I could not wish for a better daughter-in-law.' Ambrose's eyes twinkled suddenly. 'I must tell Gerard to stop his procrastination: kissing will not beget me a grandson.'

'*Oh!*' Mortified, her face turned the same colour as her new riding outfit. The earl had been feigning sleep. 'You'll excuse me, Father,' she whispered faintly. 'I'll go and tell Kitty the good news.'

Ambrose smiled as she fled from the room. He

was pleased Gerard had the sense to take things slowly. Willow needed love like a thirsty plant needed rain in the summer. Love made her bloom, and like a flower, she gave back beauty and love in abundance. Beckoning to John Grey he gave a determined smile, reckoning it was time he stopped skulking in his room.

'Lift me to my feet. I'm of a mind to walk.' Supported by the man's strong arm he took a few shuffling steps. Making it to the other chair he collapsed with a crow of triumph. 'Fetch a bottle and two glasses, John. We'll drink a toast to my damned legs. They've finally realized they're attached for a purpose.'

Gerard's bad humour didn't last long. His temper improved further when his father sent word that the family would resume the habit of formal dining that night.

He instructed Rodgers to take extra care with his grooming, donning a blue velvet jacket over breeches and waistcoat of pearl-grey brocade. His grandmother was a martinet about dressing correctly for the occasion, and he'd no desire to suffer another put down that day.

Except for Sapphire, they were all assembled when he presented himself. John Grey stood behind his father's chair, his face expressionless, waiting to attend to the earl's every need.

'I seem to be late.'

'No: it's we who are early.' The earl indicated the chair next to him and smiled. 'Sit next to me, my son.'

Gerard caught his father's eye and though he'd

rather have done it in private, felt no embarrassment as he offered an apology for attempting to
usurp his authority.

'I ask your forgiveness first, Father. I spoke without thought earlier.' He turned to Willow, whose
place at the table adjoined his. He gave her an easy
smile. 'I also beg your indulgence, madam.'

'And I yours. I spoke too boldly.'

Anxiously, she glanced at his father, smiling
when he inclined his head and indicated the chair
once again.

Gerard had hardly seated himself when Willow's
hand slid into his. Not knowing whether she
sought comfort or offered sympathy, he gently entwined her fingers, then, without thinking, raised
her hand to his lips and kissed it.

When he looked around the table every pair of
eyes was looking at him with interest. Dis-
concerted, he dropped the hand back in her lap
and fussed with his napkin.

The watching eyes had reminded him of his
sixteenth birthday. He'd been on his way to
Sheronwood to show Daphne de Vere the horse
his father had given him as a gift.

He'd come across a woman in the stables. Not
recognizing her as a servant, he'd stopped to
enquire her business on Lytton land.

She'd been about twenty, beautiful to his ado-
lescent eyes, with a luscious ripeness and a knowing manner. It hadn't taken her long to show him
what her business was all about. He'd enjoyed a
delightful hour being initiated into the rites of
love.

When their lovemaking had concluded, a cheer

had rung out. It was then he'd discovered they were being watched by several of the male servants, who'd clubbed together to hire the whore's services for his birthday.

He grinned as he remembered his embarrassment, though he had to admit now, it was the best birthday present he'd ever had.

'Whatever is the matter with you, Gerard?' his grandmother said, her voice as acid as vinegar. 'Did you not hear your father? Stop grinning in that obnoxious fashion and please say grace before we all starve to death.'

The snow had almost cleared. A cold wind swept in from the sea as the two men set off for Sheronwood. Dawn had arrived barely an hour ago; Anthony Dowling a short time after to join him for breakfast.

Gerard had been reluctant to rise from his bed. Sleep had been hard come by. His mind had been unduly active, his thoughts straying to past pleasures. Moreover, his body had sought to remind him, in no uncertain fashion, that he was a man who needed release.

He'd almost been tempted to forget his gentlemanly promise, and seek the comfort of his wife's body. Then he'd remembered her bedchamber was situated in the chilly north wing. The combination of freezing cold and distance had dampened his desire as soon as he set a foot out of bed, causing him to withdraw it hastily.

He intended to have her moved to the convenience of an adjoining chamber, and had secretly ordered pretty new window and bed hangings to

198

surprise her.

He'd gone to sleep planning her seduction. So strong had been the sensuality of it that his body had sought release in its sleep, something that hadn't happened to him since his youth.

He tried not to think of her now, but the fascination of her violet eyes seemed to haunt him. Sometimes they were soft and anxious, sometimes sparkling with innocent, childish mischief, or furious like summer storm clouds.

He envied the affection she reserved for his father and brother. She did not bestow that favour upon him, regarding him with a certain amount of shy wariness. Yet sometimes, when he caught her unawares, something stirred deep in the violet depths, a glimpse of dormant passion, as if she recognized the growing attraction between them.

Realizing Anthony had spoken, he jerked his mind back to the present. They were about to enter one of the tracks leading directly to the Sheronwood Estate. Not used of late, the track was overgrown with nettles and brambles, and pockmarked with rabbit holes. They'd have to pick their way carefully.

Anthony drew up beside him when he slowed his horse to a walk. 'A man's body was found floating in the village pond last night.'

'Some drunk who stumbled and fell?' he quizzed. It had happened before, and would happen again.

'Possibly.' Anthony ducked to avoid an overhanging bough. 'One thing might interest you, My Lord. The dead man had recent knife wounds across the back of his hands.'

'Did he, by God?' Gerard's eyebrow arched in surprise. 'That bears witness to the episode on the cliff top.' He pondered on what Willow had told him as they continued their journey. Why would there be children at Sheronwood? And why would they be taken on board a ship?

Presently, the forest began to thin. They entered a stand of birches stripped bare for winter, their slender silver trunks decorated with lichen. Visible between the trunks, was Sheronwood, the house of Daphne de Vere. Had they wed, as planned, the house would now be his, he mused.

It had been a long time since he'd last set eyes on it. Apart from the general air of neglect, the sturdy brick residence seemed exactly the same. But not quite... They were approaching from the back of the house, and something seemed out of place.

Leaning forward, he gazed with such intensity at the place that Anthony wondered if the viscount was still aware of his existence.

'The outside door to the cellar has been boarded up,' he said eventually. 'I wonder why?'

'To stop intruders getting in, I'd imagine.'

'They've not boarded up the other doors, nor the windows. Access could easily be gained.'

'Perhaps whoever did it, thinks the rumours will be enough to keep looters out.' Anthony jumped as a twig snapped under his horse's hoof.

'Why should anyone want to, unless there's something to hide?' Gerard threw the man a grin. 'I'm of a mind to look around. There's a way in if you're game.' He didn't wait for an answer, but when he dismounted and set off towards the house on foot, Anthony followed suit.

They gained entrance by means of a sturdy tree limb, and a faulty catch to the window of a maid's room attached to a guest chamber on the second floor.

Anthony grinned as they clambered over the sill. 'May one enquire if the maid was willing?'

Gerard returned the grin. 'Almost any maid is willing, if one goes about it the right way.'

Sheronwood had an air of neglect. Cobwebs hung in corners and festooned the chandeliers, dust coated the fine, gilt furniture Rosamond de Vere had been so fond of. Saddened to think so fine a lady had died here unattended and alone, he made a small, silent prayer for her soul.

It occurred to him that his own family could have suffered exactly the same fate, had it not been for Willow. Somehow, she'd found the strength to keep his father's house together and contain the disease. Although she could not save all, she'd kept him a home to come back to. Had she not taken the burden of the epidemic upon her shoulders, his father and Jeffrey might have perished also. If they had perished, his conscience would have been too full of remorse to bear.

'Listen.'

The whisper of sound drifting through the house raised the hairs on the back of his neck. Rising to a high keening sound, it was like a wail of despair coming from the depths of hell, before it sank to a subdued sobbing murmur. It ceased abruptly, leaving an eerie silence in its wake.

'What the hell was that?' Steel whispered against scabbards as two swords were drawn as one. 'Is the house inhabited by dead souls, after all?'

'I'll wager no apparition uttered that sound.' By voicing it aloud, Gerard was able to convince himself of the fact. 'The sound came from below us. That's where we must look for the source.'

The source proved to be elusive. Sheronwood appeared to be uninhabited. The air was musty and stale, the dust undisturbed. As far as Gerard could see, the contents of the house seemed to be intact. The boarding of the outside cellar door was satisfactorily explained when inside access was discovered to be similarly treated.

'The cellars are extensive.' Gerard's foot kicked against the boards. 'This must have been done to discourage looters. I think the sound might have been a freak wind in the tunnels below.'

A scuffling sound came from the other side of the boards, then a soft thud. Though they listened, the sound was not repeated.

'Rats,' Anthony grunted and, sheathing his sword, gave a self-deprecating smile. 'It seems our excursion was a wasted exercise. My theory is, the attack on Lady Sommersley was an isolated incident. It's possible she disturbed the ship's crew picking up illegal passengers.'

'My wife said they were children.'

'The adults may have already been ferried to the ship,' he pointed out. 'Obviously, the captain thought the passage money better in his pocket than that of the ship's owner. I doubt if he'll risk using this place again, especially now his partner is dead.'

'What of the woman my wife mentioned?'

'Gone, I should imagine. She wouldn't wait here to be caught and hauled before a magistrate.'

The explanation seemed feasible to Gerard. After checking the doors and windows were securely fastened, they unbolted the front door and started to make their way around the house.

A skinny ginger kitten wandered from the garden bed into his path. Picking it up by the scruff of the neck, Gerard was about to put it out of its misery when he hesitated. Willow would enjoy having a kitten to fuss over. It might take her mind from the village orphans.

Stuffing the kitten inside his coat, he returned Anthony's grin with a shrug, and strode towards the horses before the kitten's siblings arrived and demanded the same treatment.

Sapphire reclined against the velvet cushions, trying to piece together the last remnants of her waning energy. She'd spent an exhausting afternoon visiting orphaned children in the district with her daughter.

Willow seemed to be well thought of, but her own presence had been regarded with uncomfortable suspicion. A couple of women had crossed themselves against her, eyes had been averted and someone had spat upon the ground after she'd passed.

The sullen attitude of the villagers had gone unnoticed by Willow, and had been reserved for her alone. The accumulation of uneasy dislike had generated tension in her, resulting in a headache.

She smiled wanly when Bella anxiously bathed the perspiration from her face and took her hand. 'Don't worry about me, Bella. I've seen what the future holds, and am not afraid. The joy of being in my daughter's presence is reward enough for the unhappiness of the past. What think you of her?'

A husky sound came from Bella's throat. Her eyes lit up and her mouth curved into a broad smile.

'I'm pleased you like her, because one day–'

Knuckles rapped lightly at the door. Sapphire just managed to replace her veil before her daughter entered, carrying a glass of liquid on a tray.

'I've brought something to ease your headache.'

Had Willow stopped to wonder how she'd known about the headache? She hadn't mentioned it to her, but the more time they spent in each other's company the more she instinctively picked up her thoughts and feelings.

Sapphire hadn't expected that, and for once was at a loss. Nevertheless, she was pleased the girl was thoughtful of her welfare. Then Willow did something that surprised her even more. Reaching out her hand, she placed it against her forehead.

'Your malady is caused by tension. I'll massage it away.' She held out the glass of opaque liquid. 'This is made from feverfew and honey and will relax you.'

Thoughtfully, she surveyed Sapphire's chest with its many bottles, its jars of herbs, and the mortar and pestle. 'I daresay you consider me a fool when it's usual for people to come to you for such cures. Please forgive the intrusion. Grandmother has often said my interest in people could cause them embarrassment. She says I'm too inquisitive for my own good.'

'Wait.' Sapphire was unable to suppress a laugh at Willow's candid confession. It was a novelty to be treated as a normal being when people usually regarded her with too much awe, or recoiled from her altogether. 'I've not tried a headache cure such as you offer.'

Willow smiled in gratification. 'I'll tell you how to make it. It's quite easy to prepare, and has a soothing effect as well as curative properties. I learned the secret of this when I was growing up in Ireland. There was a woman in the village near Coringal who taught me about herbs, and how to prepare different medicinal potions. Her name was...'

Siobhan! Sapphire couldn't help but smile as Willow told her of her life in Ireland. Her daughter's sense of humour embellished the tale with a gentle and delightful irony, whilst her fingers soothed the tension from her scalp.

Brian O'Shea was Siobhan's nephew. He'd been a child the first time they'd met, but had accepted, as had they all, that he'd play a small part in Sapphire's destiny.

She'd met Siobhan only once, when she'd been forced to accompany the marquess on a visit to his dying mother at Coringal. Each had recognized the other's gift, had known their paths had crossed for a purpose. Siobhan had not said anything when she'd handed her an amulet, but Sapphire had known her life would not be happy. She'd never felt the ring had been meant for her to wear, and now she knew why.

Brian had looked up at her when she'd been given the amulet, and had said in his serious, child's voice, 'When your child comes to Coringal, I'll be the friend and protector of her spirit. Another, who's not of the sight, will be the guardian of her mind and body, and will hold her welfare close to his heart.'

'She will be as resilient as a Willow in the wind,' Siobhan had said.

Sapphire had remembered his words when her daughter had been born. Superstitiously, she'd given her child the name chosen for her by the forces of fate. She'd spent only a precious few weeks with the child, but was content with the knowledge she'd be protected. She'd not expected to see Willow again when she'd been snatched from her arms.

'Fetch that small pouch from my jewellery chest, Bella,' Sapphire instructed, after she'd dutifully swallowed her daughter's simple preparation. 'There's something I wish to give to Willow.'

Willow glowed with pleasure when Sapphire drew an exquisite enamelled ring from the pouch and slid it on her finger. The blood red background had an intertwining design of a silver bird on it.

Extending her hand to admire its effect, she stared at it in silence for a moment, then said quietly, 'How can this be?'

Sapphire started when she followed the girl's

glance to the ring.

The bird was a silver hawk poised to descend on its prey. She recognized it now as the hawk decorating the seal of Lytton House, and wondered how she'd failed to notice the significance of it before.

CHAPTER EIGHT

Annie Tupworthy badly wanted to give birth to a son. She'd carried six children in as many years: all had been female, all except one had died at birth.

Once she provided her husband with a male heir, he'd continue to frequent the bawdy houses, but he'd leave her alone. She was weary from the constant pregnancies, and the beatings he inflicted on her.

The despair she felt didn't show in her eyes as she set a jug of ale in front of the squire and his guest, the Wesleyan preacher, Reverend Pollock.

The two men had spent the last hour discussing Earl Lytton's illness, Viscount Sommersley's modernization of the estate and, most of all, the woman called Sapphire. Neither had a good word to say about anyone, especially Sapphire, whose mystic powers were well known.

When her husband brusquely dismissed her, Annie hurried to get her cloak. If he found out she'd arranged a rendezvous with Sapphire in a secluded cottage on the outskirts of the village he'd beat her senseless. She caressed her swollen stomach. She was willing to risk it if the outcome was a son.

The tenant had been eager to rent the accommodation for a small sum of money, though her eyes had widened with fear and she'd hurriedly crossed herself when she'd heard who Annie was meeting with that day.

Sapphire hadn't intended to make herself available for consultation again. When Annie Tupworthy's plea for help had arrived, she'd sensed the aura of despair.

She'd lived with such a man as Squire Tupworthy, and had suffered similar brutality. If the woman had asked for something to end her husband's life – as others in her position had – she would have refused.

Of late, she'd come to the conclusion life was ordained, with death arriving at its appointed hour. To interfere with divine law was dangerous to the soul. Annie Tupworthy's plea was born of desperation. The woman considered ending her own life. Having experienced the despair that drove a woman to contemplate such an act, it had touched her heart.

Consultation with her crystal had revealed an abrupt end to Annie's misery, and augured happiness in her future. *That* she could tell her.

There had also been an omen of evil in the crystal, a shadowy dark shape fluttering in the periphery of the glass. It had appeared thrice, and its presence worried her.

Accompanied by Bella, she slipped unseen from

208

the house and made her way to the stables. The afternoon was mild for winter, with a blustery wind carrying the salty tang of the ocean to her nostrils. Three horses were saddled and ready. She raised an eyebrow in surprise as she glanced at Brian.

'You accompany us?'

'That I do, lady. A need for caution surrounds you.'

So, Brian had picked up on that, too. 'You're not frightened I'll enchant you?' Sapphire smiled behind her veil when Brian gave a twisted little grin.

'I know you, lady.' His gypsy eyes touched on the veil and saw through it. 'Your daughter has brought your soul forth from the dark place.'

'She's made me weak.'

'Nay, lady.' Brian's face was grave as he helped the two women on to their mounts. 'You're vulnerable, and it frightens you. Love is resilient, bringing power to both the giver and receiver. Men sacrifice themselves for love.'

'And women also.' A chill settled around her heart as she murmured, 'The path I tread is not easy.'

'Your choice was made when you set foot on Lytton soil.' A shiver raced up Brian's spine when a glossy black raven set down upon a fence post and stared silently at them. Hastily, he crossed himself as the bird flew off towards the road. God grant this woman strength for the trial ahead, he thought.

'Tell the officer exactly how it happened, Biggs.'

209

Still angry from his encounter with Squire Tupworthy, Gerard's voice was terse as he bade his gatekeeper speak. 'Damn it all, man, it happened just outside the gate. You must have seen something.'

'It's a bit hard to explain, My Lord.' A worried frown furrowed Biggs's forehead and he chewed nervously on a straw clutched between his teeth.

'The squire arrived unannounced, and demanded to see the earl,' Gerard prompted impatiently.

That much was the truth. A footman requested the man's card and the squire had become belligerent. Striding from the study, Gerard had advised Tupworthy to depart. The squire had insulted him. When he persisted in his quest to see the earl, Gerard had called some footmen to eject the man before he succumbed to the temptation to run him through.

'That he did, My Lord,' the gate-man answered. 'He seemed to be in his cups, and was shouting something about farming systems when he came back.' Biggs gazed at the sky. 'He was uncomplimentary about Lady Sommersley.'

Gerard's ire rose at the thought. 'Exactly what did he say?'

'I'd rather not repeat it, sir.'

'Come, man, you needn't be afraid.' His cane tapped impatiently against the side of his boot. 'The man is dead. I'll not hold you accountable for another's remark.'

'And I'll not repeat an ill word spoken against the mistress in company,' Biggs said doggedly, his eyes sliding towards Anthony Dowling, who

210

obligingly walked out of earshot.

'Well, man?'

Biggs's cheeks turned a dull red. 'He said the mistress be tainted by the Lynchcross blood. He said the Givanchy curse applied to her too, and she'll most likely prove to be barren. I was tempted to close his foul mouth with my fist, that I was. A finer lady–'

'That will do, Biggs.' He squashed the spurt of anger Biggs's words brought, but was tight-lipped when he beckoned to Anthony Dowling. 'Tell Captain Dowling how the squire's accident occurred.'

Biggs paled suddenly. 'A raven flew at the horse and startled it. It reared, and the squire was unseated. His neck fell across that boulder over there. I heard a crack, and he just went limp.'

They all gazed at the body lying huddled under its cloak.

'The raven flew off towards the stables,' Biggs offered, looking about him fearfully. 'Some say the raven is a bringer of evil. It were seen in the village just before that man drowned.'

Gerard patted Biggs's shoulder. 'Talk of super-natural intervention is both tedious and dangerous. Just two days ago, Captain Dowling and I were forced to visit Sheronwood on such rumour. I'll tell you, Biggs, the rumours of supernatural events were without foundation. The house was undisturbed and there was not an apparition in sight. You understand what I'm saying?'

'Yes, My Lord.' Biggs wondered if he should tell the viscount what he'd heard about the children at Sheronwood.

'Good man.' The viscount flipped him a coin. 'I know I can rely on you to keep your mouth shut. The cart should be here to take the body back to the Manor House, shortly. The rider I sent spoke to the preacher who's staying there. He's taken it upon himself to inform and comfort Mrs Tupworthy.'

Biggs shrugged, as Gerard turned back towards the house. If the viscount had been to Sheronwood and found nothing, why should he risk a reprimand by repeating what the Sheronwood servant had told him? It had obviously been all lies.

The raven was huddled with the rooks amongst the trees when the riders passed below. It didn't belong to the rookery, and the smaller birds grumbled uneasily amongst themselves. Suddenly, it gave a harsh caw and flew up into the air.

Startled, the rooks rose and flew in a noisy circle. When they settled, the outsider had gone. High in the sky, the raven followed the three riders, coming to rest on the warm brick chimney stack of a cottage on the outskirts of the village.

Inside the cottage, Annie Tupworthy was doubled up in agony. Her membrane had broken twenty minutes earlier, and her labour had commenced straight away. The birth was almost imminent. She gazed at Sapphire in mute appeal as she came through the door.

'My dear woman!' Taking one look at her, Sapphire turned her maid. 'Quickly, Bella. Help her to the bed and loosen her clothing, then see if you can find some clean rags. Her baby seems to be in somewhat of a hurry.' She gazed over her shoulder at Brian, who hovered awkwardly just inside the door. 'Make haste to the Manor House and fetch a carriage.'

'Shall I inform the squire, Lady?'

She hesitated, presentiment settling round her shoulders like a dark shroud. Evil was abroad. 'He'll not be there. Bring the lady's maid and the children's nurse. Tell the nurse to bring swaddling clothes for the infant and a blanket to wrap him in.'

'Him?' Annie clutched Sapphire's wrist. 'My child will be a boy?'

'Yes, my dear,' she said soothingly, whilst she drew aside her skirts and prepared her for the birthing. 'He'll be strong of limb and clever of mind, and will have the look of your father.'

'He'll not have a nature like his own father?' Annie shuddered as a spasm of pain gripped her. 'I'd not have him inflicted thus.'

'I promise you a son you'll be proud of. When he's a man he'll distinguish himself in the service of the king, and will achieve high rank and estate. This, I know.'

Perspiration beaded Annie's face as Sapphire removed her veil. Observing the bruises on the woman's legs, it was hard to hide her pity and anger. There was one consolation: Annie Tupworthy would never suffer another beating from her husband.

Annie's gaze widened at the sight of Sapphire's face. She bore an astounding resemblance to the young mistress of Lytton, whom she'd once seen from a distance. Then she saw the beauty of Sapphire's eyes and lost herself in the purple mist of their depths.

Her body became as light as air and she seemed to float on a sea of pale blue, her body cradled in its gentle waves. There was neither pain nor discomfort, and she could hear nothing but the sound of Sapphire's voice.

It was soft, like a moonbeam touching the furled flower of a lily. Little by little, the flower began to open, its satiny interior pure and lovely. Deep in the heart of the flower was a tiny, curled-up creature.

Annie's love reached out and surrounded it. The creature opened its eyes and gazed at her. Tears trembled in her eyes, but she couldn't understand why because she was surrounded by beauty and felt so happy. Her tears fell into the lily and the creature was washed gently into her waiting arms.

Opening her eyes, she gazed at the child Sapphire had placed in her arms, then up at the woman who'd safely delivered him. She was wearing her veil. Annie couldn't recollect what her face had looked like. She had no record of time passing. Possessed of a sense of tranquillity she hadn't experienced for a long time, she smiled through her tears.

'I cannot thank you enough.' Her eyes slid back to her child, who nestled comfortably against her breast. 'I'd be honoured if you'd choose a name for him. It must be a secret name, for my husband will not countenance any but his own for our son.'

'Call him, Carlisle.'

'That was my father's name,' Annie said in astonishment.

'Then it's a fitting name for your son. Let him wear it with pride.'

Sapphire stood when she heard the sound of a carriage coming to a halt. Bad news travelled fast it seemed, for the Wesleyan preacher was with the servants, his face grave.

'My dear Mrs Tupworthy.' The words slipped unctuously from his mouth, as if they'd been anointed with oil. 'There has been an accident.'

He looked down at the child, spread his tiny legs apart with his thumbs and examined his gender. 'It's fortunate you've birthed a son. The Tupworthy name will survive.' He gazed at her for a moment, saw his words had been understood and added, as if it were a foregone conclusion, 'You'll name your son after his father, of course?'

Annie felt like smiling, but under the circumstances didn't dare. Glancing at Sapphire, she said almost defiantly, 'My son shall be called Carlisle, after his grandfather.'

The reverend's glance became speculative. 'A handsome name for a handsome child. I'll give him my blessing before I deliver my sermon to the villagers.'

The reverend fell to his knees and his voice took on a dramatic cadence. 'All in this dwelling shall bow before the Lord, and thank Him for the child's safe deliverance.'

All in the dwelling did, except for Sapphire and her maid. Everyone saw them leave except Annie, whose sense of freedom at hearing the squire was dead was so overwhelming it caused her to burst into tears.

The reverend was not surprised when Sapphire left. Her reputation had preceded her from London. Her presence in the district had become the stuff of gossip.

It was *she* who caused the butter to become rancid; *she* who stopped hens from laying and incited fermentation in the udders of cows. John Wesley's teachings had alerted the reverend that the Devil took different guises. He'd convinced himself, and most of the villagers, that Sapphire was a witch.

Up on the chimney stack, the raven cocked its head to one side and gazed with bead-bright eyes at the departing horses. It settled down to wait. From its vantage point, it could see the ivy-covered stone cross on the village green and the stream that fed the village pond.

Two children sat upon the stone that supported the ducking stool. People came from their homes. Dressed in their Sunday best they congregated upon the green with an air of expectancy.

Presently, the door of the cottage opened and the Reverend Pollock came out and mounted his horse. The green was but a short way, but he rode through the crowd, aware of the awe his appearance brought. He was a big man, handsome, with a deep resonant voice that commanded attention.

Reverend Pollock was thinking of Annie Tupworthy. It was unfortunate her infant had been

216

delivered by the sorceress. The boy would need the help of the Lord, and strong discipline to keep the Devil at bay. A strap across the buttocks at regular intervals would soon whip the Devil from his soul, and infuse him with a healthy respect for the Lord's anger.

He'd long been seeking a wife of piety and means. Annie Tupworthy was comfortably off; she and her children would need a strong man to guide them.

When he reached his appointed place beneath the cross, he smiled expansively at the crowd, then waited until the murmuring voices died to an expectant hush. He threw out his arms in a dramatic gesture – knowing he resembled a crucifix – and sent a fierce gaze searching amongst the crowd.

'The Devil has sent his agent among you,' he began, his glance settling on a raw-boned girl with a vacant smile. 'The agent arrived in a carriage of fire, her nostrils smoking with the brimstone of Hell. She's sheltered amongst a nest of vipers – and that nest is called Lytton House.'

As a shocked murmur raced through the crowd, Nellie gazed at the raven on the roof of a cottage. She gave a slack-mouthed smile.

The raven cocked its head to one side in a listening attitude, its eyes fixed on the figure addressing the crowd.

Willow was keeping the earl company in the drawing-room when Gerard returned to the house. She'd just finished reading the last chapter of *Robinson Crusoe* when Ambrose murmured,

'Edwina tells me you play the harp. Would you play something for me?'

Sending a servant to fetch her harp, she smiled at him. 'Do not expect too much, dearest Father. I was taught by a peasant woman who lived near Coringal, and can play only a few Irish tunes.'

Ambrose took her hand in his. 'Tell me about Coringal. Was life hard for you there?'

'Indeed no.' Astonishment came into her eyes. 'Coringal is a beautiful house, smaller than Lytton and a trifle dilapidated, but just as welcoming. It's situated in wild country, with towering hills behind, and mists so dense some mistake it for rain.'

A soft smile touched her lips. 'Each morning was a miracle, as it is here. Sometimes, the grass was so green and the air so soft, it made me want to cry. James Langland, who was my tutor, said it was because I had an affinity with the ethereal things of life.'

Taking her harp from the servant she ran her fingers gently over the strings. 'Often the sound of the harp touches my heart in exactly the same way. It reminds me of Coringal, and can make me cry. I'll endeavour not to do so today.'

The note she coaxed from the instrument reminded her of a song about a soldier. 'A soldier is dying...' she murmured, 'and he's remembering the love he left behind.'

It was a sad song, the soldier beseeching God to let him live long enough to say goodbye to his true love. Eventually, she appeared to him in a dream, and the soldier died with a smile on his lips. Her eyes were damp when she finished, her smile tremulous.

'James always teased me about that song. He said the girl probably married someone else, and forgot all about the soldier.' She gave a light, lilting laugh. 'James said I was a romantic, and destined to fall in love with a man who showed me tenderness.'

Her voice trailed off when Gerard came into the room and smiled at her.

Though he'd heard her words, and noted the yearning in her voice, he didn't intend to tease her with them. 'I heard a little of your song as I came along the corridor.'

She looked lovely in a gown of pale lilac over a darker flounced petticoat. Her lace cap was tied under her pointed chin, and was decorated with ribbons and flowers. He longed to pull it from her head and watch her glorious hair tumble about her shoulders in perfumed disarray as her face dimpled into a smile.

The ginger kitten he'd given her the week before, its neck adorned with a lilac ribbon, played at her feet. If his father hadn't been with her, he would have drawn her gently towards him and kissed her sweet mouth into a murmuring honeyed response.

'It was a charming song,' he murmured, trying to hide the desire in his eyes. 'If you'd humour me by singing it again, I'll give you some news concerning James Langland.'

'You'd make me sing for the news?'

He enjoyed the flirtatious little pout she gave when her fingers plucked a shimmering note from the harp, and decided to step up his campaign to win her heart. The trouble was, he rarely seemed to find her alone, as if everyone else in the house conspired to monopolize her time. Her incredibly beautiful eyes gazed at him now through seductively long lashes.

'The song is too sad to sing again. I shall choose another.' The grin she gave him was captivating. 'This a song about a man who loved his sweetheart's voice so much, he confined her within a cage and made her sing all day. She turned into a lark, escaped, and flew away from her prison of love.' Mischief coloured her eyes. 'I'll expect you to join in the chorus.'

The song had a happy sound, and a fast rhythm that set their feet tapping. The chorus, a tongue-twister, was picked up by Gerard. It then became a contest as it was repeated at a faster pace by Willow. Eventually, breathless and laughing they both admitted defeat.

'It's a wonder the lady had enough breath left to fly,' Ambrose remarked. Gerard had surprised him by joining Willow in song. His eldest son was usually bored by simple drawing-room pleasures. Could it be that Willow's personality was beginning to exert an influence over him? He hoped so. It wouldn't hurt Gerard to relax a little in private.

'I have news,' Gerard said, when his breathing returned to normal.

'Of James Langland?' Setting the harp on a table, Willow drew the kitten into her lap and edged forward in her seat, gazing at Gerard with eager expectancy. 'You've discovered his where-abouts? He's well?'

'I have news of the day's events for my father first.' He'd also received information of a different sort, a perturbing document Charles Addison had found on the body of a murdered man. The letter was written by the deceased husband of Daphne de Vere, containing an accusation. Even if its truth was verified, it must remain his secret. With the greatest difficulty, he put it from his mind and concentrated on the matter at hand.

He couldn't resist the urge to tease Willow a little. 'James Langland's affairs occupy only a small part of it. As he's of such little importance, I shall leave him until last.'

'Of course, Gerard. I just thought...' Giving a small sigh, she settled disconsolately back in her chair and plucked at a lace-edged handkerchief. 'Your own news must take precedence.'

He'd not expected such a reaction. The disappointment in her eyes, and the dejected slump to her shoulders nudged immediately at his conscience. 'Do not take my words to heart, Willow. I sought only to tease...'

'No, no.' The handkerchief was applied daintily to the corner of each eye. 'It was presumptuous of me to expect my curiosity to be appeased, even though you exacted payment beforehand.'

Exacted payment! The song, of course. He clapped the heel of his hand against his forehead. She'd regarded it as an obligation he would honour. How insecure she was.

'With my father's permission, I will tell you of James Langland first. I had intended—'

'Pray, do not.' Her voice quavered slightly, as if she were about to cry. 'The affairs of men must

221

surely be of more importance than that of a mere woman.' The handkerchief covered her mouth and a small choking noise came from her.

Afraid she was about to burst into tears, he produced a letter from his pocket and waved it hurriedly in the air. 'I *insist* on giving you news of your tutor first.'

His father gave a great guffaw of laughter, alerting him to the fact his wife's tears were actually giggles. The immediate jolt to his pride brought a sensation of affront before he admitted to himself his attitude was stuffy in the extreme. The fact that he felt a fool, was nothing to the fool he'd look if he stood on his dignity. His grin was ironic as he allowed himself to relax.

'You owe me a ribbon, I believe. If I'm to be made a fool of, I would have the world know it.'

'That doesn't seem fair.' She handed over her handkerchief instead. 'You do not wear fur-belows. Were you to make a fool of me, I'd have no means of letting the world know.'

'As the game seems one-sided, it matters not.'

He slid the token inside his waistcoat, close to his heart. Engaging her eyes in a more personal manner, he saw the merriment replaced by a shy awareness. She was not resisting her seduction, had just recognized its inevitability, and had decided to enjoy it.

A thrill of anticipation raced through him when he saw the opportunity to spend some time alone with Willow. 'I go to London soon on business,' he murmured. 'I'd be happy if you'd accompany me?'

'I do not overly like London.' Flattered by the

222

disappointment flaring in his eyes, she smiled a trifle smugly. 'However, if you desire my company...?'

It wasn't her company he desired, and the minx knew it. His mouth widened into a rueful grin when she gave a breathless giggle. She was going to make him work for his conquest of her, and was telling him. For that, he'd keep her in suspense about James Langland a little longer.

'The roads will be impassable if it rains heavily,' Ambrose warned. 'It's not a journey to be undertaken lightly at this time of year.'

'We'll take horses,' Gerard said, unfolding the lawyer's letter. 'Willow can ride as well as any man, and better than most.'

It was the greatest compliment he could have paid her. Watching her glow with happiness at the praise, Ambrose caught his son's glance and smiled. Gerard had more skill with women than he'd imagined, and the patience of a hunter. Leaning back in his chair, Ambrose closed his eyes and listened to what he had to say.

He learned of the squire's untimely death, of the birth of Annie Tupworthy's son and Sapphire's involvement in it. The news of James Langland's incarceration in debtors' prison on charges brought by the marquess, prompted an outraged gasp from Willow.

Her indignation at her tutor's ill-treatment was jumbled up with her gratitude to Gerard for getting him released. She had the child-like innocence her mother had once had, and Ambrose hoped she'd never be forced to lose it. He grew drowsy as he often did of late. Closing his eyes he drifted into a contented state of half-wakefulness, then opened his eyes and smiled when he heard his younger son come into the room. Jeffrey is growing into manhood fast, he thought. I must consult with Gerard about his future. It seems like only yesterday the lad was born and already his voice deepens with maturity.

'Captain Dowling is in the study, Gerard. He wishes to see you most urgently.' Jeffrey's face lit up when he saw Willow. 'Brian O'Shea is going to allow me to put the new stallion through his paces in the morning. You'll come and watch?'

'Nothing on earth will prevent me, Jeffrey. I'll bring Edward to watch. He idolizes you, and will be most upset if he misses seeing his riding master in action.'

'Then I'd best make sure I stay on the beast's back.' Jeffrey's grin indicated he wasn't at all displeased with the notion of being idolized.

'Am I to be included as a spectator of this event?' Ambrose had a sudden urge to see his younger son break the new stallion to the saddle. He'd taught both of his sons to ride and took pride in their ability. He smiled at the astonished eyes that gazed at him. 'I'm heartily sick of being confined to the house, Willow.'

'Of course you are, dearest Father.' Willow blinked away her tears at the imagined reprimand. 'I've been selfish. First, I bully you because you do not improve as quickly as I'd like, then, when you do improve, I fuss like an overprotective hen with a chick. Why did you not advise me of my shortcomings sooner?'

Gerard chuckled at the notion she put forward.

'Because you have no shortcomings in his eyes, only perfections.'

She smiled as Gerard bent over her hand, then curled her fingers around the warm imprint his kiss left there. Had she possessed the courage, she'd have placed a kiss of her own in the indentation between his eye and the dark line of hair. She experienced a flutter of breathless anticipation at the thought. 'Will you attend also, Gerard? If Jeffrey's going to show off his riding skills he must have a worthy audience.'

'I'd not miss it for the world.' He grinned as he slapped his brother on the shoulder. 'You must excuse me. The matter Captain Dowling wishes to discuss must be urgent if he disturbs me at this hour. It's almost dusk.'

'The matter is thus,' Anthony said, as soon as Gerard stepped into the study. 'This afternoon, Reverend Pollock named your household in his sermon. He said you were harbouring a sorceress in your midst, a woman called Sapphire.'

Gerard gave him a startled glance. 'The man must be mad to try and incite fear amongst the peasantry. He must be stopped.'

'He *has* been stopped,' Anthony said grimly. 'He's just been reported dead.' The officer spread his hands in a gesture of helplessness. 'A witness said a raven flew at his horse and it threw him. His neck was broken.'

'A coincidence,' Gerard said, with more confidence than he felt.

Anthony shrugged. 'It's rumoured your guest has the evil eye, and the raven is her familiar. Your family could be in great danger.'

'From the villagers, you mean?' It was not uncommon for the poorer classes to join forces. All it took was a general feeling of discontent, and someone, or *something*, to incite them.

The peasantry in this part of the country were superstitious. Gerard surmised they'd stay safely at home whilst they imagined evil stalked the countryside looking for victims. 'I do not think we're in immediate danger. They'll lack leadership if Pollock is dead.'

Well aware of Sapphire's reputation, Gerard had not observed her as anything out of the ordinary. She was unobtrusive in her ways, well liked by those who had contact with her. Willow had formed a friendship with her. Even his grandmother – a lady of good sense – seemed approving of her presence.

Because of Sapphire's acquaintance with his father, she'd been given the protection of the house. Gerard was duty bound to honour that.

Crossing to the window, he stared out at the fading light. 'If you wish to speak to our guest and put your fears at rest I'll ask if she'll be good enough to attend you in the study.'

There was a mist coming off the sea. Though he'd watched it roll in many times before in the familiar surrounds of his home, his heightened imagination found it somewhat sinister. Goosebumps prickled up his spine. Something unexplainable was going on and he was unhappy about it. The fact was, the occurrences had only started after Sapphire had arrived.

'I cannot see what the woman has done to be

vilified by the preacher,' he mused. 'The only time she left the estate without my wife as companion was to give aid to a woman suffering in childbirth today. If that's casting an evil eye, every midwife in the county must be guilty of it.'

The eyes that sought Anthony's were half-amused and half-serious. 'The child was not born with cloven feet and horns upon his forehead, I wager?'

'Not to my knowledge.' The officer smiled nervously. 'I do not see the need to question your guest. It's a rum business. I'm uncertain of how to proceed with the investigation.'

'As am I,' Gerard said grimly. 'The matter may die down now there's no fuel to feed it.' Crossing to the bell rope, he rang for a servant. 'You'll accept the hospitality of my house and stay the night, Captain?' His lips twisted in a wry grin as he turned to face the officer. 'I must request that you do not discuss this matter outside this room. I would not have the ladies alarmed.'

'Of course not, My Lord.' Anthony gave a relieved smile. 'Thank you, sir. I admit I was not looking forward to the return journey with no moon to light the way.'

After giving instructions to the servant he'd summoned, Gerard turned back to the man and inspected him from head to toe. 'My servant will clean the dust from your uniform before we go to the drawing-room.'

Later, as Gerard sprawled on his back on the vast bed he occupied, he sought to isolate the quality that drew men to Willow. Anthony Dowling had been instantly smitten by her. He'd become so tongue-tied, that Lady Edwina had fixed him with a stare and asked him if all his family suffered from stammering.

In his father's eyes, Willow could do no wrong, as if she were a favoured daughter. He enjoyed seeing the rapport between his wife and his father. Her affection for the earl was genuine, and his father responded to it.

Jeffrey would lay down his life for her, he'd wager. The thought brought a frown to his face. How far Jeffrey would go to defend her against himself was a matter for speculation, and one he did not wish to put to the test.

His brother was at an age when the hot blood of youth took precedence over rational thought. What the lad needed... He grinned as an image of the girl at Anthony Dowling's lodging came into his mind. She was exactly what Jeffrey needed!

As for himself? Although he considered himself lucky Willow was pleasing to the eye, he was too experienced a campaigner to fall under her spell. She was his wife for one reason only, to provide the estate with heirs. The words of the gate-keeper came to his mind and he scowled.

Was the Lynchcross blood tainted? What if she did prove to be barren? What if the accusation contained in the letter from Eduard Lynchcross was true, and not the ramblings of an insane mind? Could he have fathered young Edward?

Grabbing up a candle, he slipped from his room and strode resolutely along the carpeted corridor and up the stairs to the top of the house.

A night-light burned on the nursery table. From the vicinity of the maid's room came the sound of snoring. He crept into the room that held the sleeping form of Edward, and gazed down at the boy with troubled eyes.

It was several minutes before he retraced his steps. The house was quiet and dark. Only the eyes of his ancestors in the portrait gallery watched his progress. Reflecting the gleam of candlelight, their eyes seemed to follow him. Old friends, they bothered Gerard not a bit. Pausing in front of the fourth earl, he whispered, 'What would you do if Edward was *your* bastard?'

The fourth earl remained silent. Clearly, Gerard heard a door close. It came from the north wing where Willow slept. Why she'd chosen to accommodate herself in such miserable quarters was beyond his comprehension.

The wing was supposed to be haunted by the ghosts of a manservant and that of his lover, who'd been the wife of one of the earls. Legend had it the lovers had been locked in a secret room, concealed behind a tapestry, and left to starve to death.

Uneasily, he wondered if Willow had inherited an interest in the occult. Was that why she'd isolated herself, so she could remain unobserved whilst practising the unholy rites? His mouth stretched in a tight grin as he realized his imagination was getting the better of him.

He was about to return to his chamber when the sound of slippered feet whispered along the corridor. The hairs lifted on the back of his neck.

It proved to be no ghostly visitation, however.

Candle snuffed, he drew back into the shadows and observed the cloaked figure of Kitty Adams glide silently past. Off to meet Brian O'Shea no doubt, leaving her mistress alone and unattended.

Devilment came into his eyes as he wondered how Willow would react to a surprise visit from her husband.

The corridor was long, the bedchambers too numerous to count as he set about his task of finding her. This will take me all night, he fretted, opening another door to no avail.

About to turn back in defeat, his nostrils were teased by a fleeting fragrance. A tiny flicker of firelight danced beneath the last door at the end of the corridor. He hastened towards it.

His breath hissed audibly in his throat as he approached her bed. Asleep, she lay on her back, her innocence and vulnerability achingly apparent to him. Her hair spread like ripples of dark water across the sheets. Childlike, one small hand curled against the cheek that turned against it. Her mouth was slightly parted, her breath whispered evenly with each rise and fall of her breast.

Her beauty was breathtaking. As he gazed at the recumbent form, a lump formed in his throat. 'I hardly know you,' he whispered. 'Yet my desire for you grows each time I see you.' Relighting his candle from the fire, he carefully placed it on her dressing-table and positioned himself at the side of her bed.

Being married was proving to be more difficult than he'd imagined. With as much dispassion as he could muster he gazed down at his wife's slender body. Had she been a drab, the bedding of her would have been simple.

The bedding would be simple now, an insidious voice inside his head whispered, and his body responded excitingly to the thought. *She's yours. All you need do is take her. She'll not be expecting pleasure from the act. Thrust her legs apart and slake your appetite upon her. It's your right as her husband. She'll struggle and cry whilst you break her to your will and sow your seed inside her. Think how powerful you'll feel. You've been a long time without bodily comfort and release.*

'No,' he murmured regretfully. 'I'll not act like some crude oaf. She has dreams and feelings, as she revealed in her conversation with my father today. I'll not be the instrument of her misery.'

Tenderly, he kissed her softly parted mouth. She whispered his name. How sweet it sounded when whispered thus. He kissed her again, relishing the soft, seductive swell of her lips. *Sweet Jesus!* he prayed, let her wake. She's so relaxed she'll be amenable to my attention now.

The delicious, scented hollows at the base of her throat succumbed to the fluttering probe of his tongue and she gave a tiny sigh.

Two soft breasts were outlined under the bed linen, just a finger's length away. He gently brushed them into erectness. This time, the sigh she gave had an ecstatic sound. Yet she still slept. It didn't seem possible. A quiet desperation grew in him as he slid the covers from her body and gently shook her.

'Willow?' He explored the silky contours of her body, breathing her name over and over again.

What could be more natural than this night should see a consummation of their marriage?

She stretched like a languorous cat, moist and ripe for the taking. He took her gently shuddering over the peak, then shook her again, firmer this time, but she was like a rag doll in his hands and curled into a protective ball when he released her.

Body on fire, it took all of his strength not to turn her on her back, and take his joy of her whilst she lay unconscious.

A mockery of a grin laced his mouth as he tore a small trophy from her bodice. His eyes searched the perimeters of the room. She'd managed to enchant him without any sorcerer's symbols to aid her. Placing a parting kiss against her ear, he whispered, 'Sleep, My Lady.'

This night was not for him, but her dreams would be haunted by the exquisite pleasure his touch had surely given her. His own release, by necessity, would come in another way.

Noticing some vials, he realized she'd taken a sleeping draught. He couldn't think of any reason why she'd have trouble sleeping. His eyes narrowed. It was more likely she'd been *given* some sort of sleeping draught.

Pulling the covers over her body he picked up a half-empty cup of chocolate and sniffed. Balm and valerian! He'd learned enough from Charles Addison to know balm was a mild sedative used for women's problems. Valerian was a sleeping draught. A combination of the two would knock out a horse, as he'd learned to his cost four years previously.

He scowled as he remembered Kitty Adams gliding towards the stairs. Had she drugged Willow, and cheated him out of his comfort as a result? He intended to make it his business to find out.

Willow had never had a dream so pleasurable. When she half woke in the morning – and was in the lethargic state before real awakening – her mind and body re-experienced it.

It had been almost real, Gerard coming to her. She hoped the dream was an omen that her marriage union would be a pleasant one.

'Kitty!' she shouted. Leaping from the bed, she stripped the chemise from her body, noticing a rip on the bodice where a length of lace had come off. No doubt Kitty would find it amongst the sheets and sew it back on. She threw the chemise over a chair. 'Bring me a bowl of water to wash with and my tooth sponge.'

'Kitty?' Hurrying to the maid's room she cursed when she saw the bed hadn't been slept in. She'd expressly forbidden her permission to visit Brian before their marriage. Couldn't the girl wait?

She dragged the pitcher of water from the dresser, splashed some into a bowl and hurriedly made her toilet before pulling on her riding outfit. About to attack her tangled locks with the hair brush, she impatiently gave permission to enter when a knock sounded on the door.

'Have you seen Kitty?' she asked, when the housekeeper set a tray of tea on the table.

'She has been dismissed from her position and assigned to the scullery, My Lady.' Mrs Breton took the brush from her hand. 'If you'll allow me.'

'My maid has been dismissed?' Incredulous, she gazed at Mrs Breton. 'On whose order?'

'The viscount's, My Lady.' Mrs Breton looked uncomfortable as she began to dress Willow's hair. 'I understand Kitty abandoned her duties last night. The viscount was extremely annoyed when he caught her trying to sneak in this morning. She got a good dressing down, and was lucky not to have been dismissed.'

'Was she indeed?'

Choosing to forget that she'd been unsatisfied with Kitty's attitude herself, of late, her temper began to rise. Whatever Kitty had done, Gerard had no right to dismiss her without consultation. She glanced at the way Mrs Breton was fashioning her hair and snatched the brush from her hand.

'This will not do. Go and tell Kitty to come to me at once.'

'Do not ask me to do that, My Lady.' Mrs Breton looked most unhappy. 'She'll have no choice but to obey you, and I'll have no choice other than to dismiss her, and have her escorted from the estate. The viscount has given me specific orders concerning this matter.'

'I see.' She rose to her feet. 'Where's my husband now?'

'In the study.' Mrs Breton followed her out to the hall. 'You cannot go down with your hair undressed, My Lady,' she said, her voice shocked.

'I can do whatever I please, Mrs Breton.'

She didn't bother knocking, just opened the study door and walked straight in.

Gerard looked up from the desk and frowned ominously. 'Am I to understand you wish to see me?'

'You are.' Her voice rose a notch as she uttered a deliberate falsehood. 'Kitty had my permission to be absent last night. You had no right to dismiss her. I *insist* on having her back.'

Gerard rose to his feet and came to stand in front of her, his eyes silver bright as they probed the depths of hers. 'Did she also have permission to drug you senseless with a sleeping draught last night?'

'I don't know what you're talking about.' Her insides quaked at the deceptively silky tone of her husband's voice. In contrast, his eyes were as cold as polished metal. She had an uncomfortable feeling he'd seen through her lie. Her voice trembled with tension. 'Even if she was knowledgeable about medication, she'd not do such a thing.'

'No?' His hand went to his pocket and pulled out the missing lace from her chemise. His smile was cruelly mocking as he dangled it in front of her eyes. 'Tell me, Wife: were your dreams pleasant last night?'

Her mouth became dry as she remembered the caress of lips and hands teasing her body into exquisite fulfilment, of her own half-remembered abandonment. The recollection caused a dewy aching awareness in the secret depths of her body. A deep, painful flush of embarrassment swept over her.

'You are no gentleman, sir.' Her fury boiled over when she saw the laughter in his eyes.

Snatching the lace from his grasp she lashed out with the other hand and caught him a stinging blow across his cheek. 'I hate you, Gerard,' she hissed.

The laughter faded from his eyes as he stared at her in shock. There was a hot patch on his face where her hand had marked it. She took a step backwards when he moved.

He gave a tight smile as he jerked the bell-pull. There was menace in his whisper. 'Be thankful I've promised never to beat you, because you're closer to it now than you've ever been.

'Accompany Lady Sommersley to her bed-chamber and make her presentable,' he said quietly when Mrs Breton appeared. 'If she refuses to co-operate you may lock her in her room and inform me. Is that understood?'

'Yes, My Lord.'

He ignored the sympathetic glance Mrs Breton gave Willow. 'Have my wife's belongings moved to the chamber adjoining mine. The one she resides in now is barely habitable. I cannot understand why she chose such accommodations.'

Willow seethed at being spoken of as if she wasn't there, but she sensed Mrs Breton's sympathy, and blessed the woman when she dared to say, 'Lady Sommersley was assigned the chambers by your late mother, My Lord.'

'My mother?' His expression contained a mixture of shame and disbelief. 'My mother was inhospitable towards my wife?'

'Yes, My Lord,' Mrs Breton's tone was firm. 'And though I should not say it, for no good reason I could see.'

'Mrs Breton,' Willow implored, twisting the situation to her advantage, despite the fact she was close to tears. 'It does not matter now. I was grateful for the roof over my head. We must not speak ill of the dead.'

'That will be all.' Unable to gaze at his wife's wounded expression without capitulating, Gerard picked up a paper from the desk and scrutinized it with more than his usual intensity.

When he heard the study door shut, he thumped his hand on the desk and swore in frustration. He should have known his mother would have found some way to exercise her spite against Willow. She'd set her heart on Daphne de Vere and Sheronwood for him.

'You fool!' he muttered. 'You'll never win Willow's heart by being cruel. She has suffered enough.'

CHAPTER NINE

'Well done,' Willow cried out in admiration. The stallion had done its best to unseat its rider and now responded to Jeffrey's handling. Flanks slicked with foam, it cantered obediently under his guidance. Jeffrey's grin was wide as he slid from its back and handed the reins to Brian.

'Did you see the fight he put up, father? I never thought I'd stay in the saddle.'

The earl looked tired. The short walk from the house had exhausted him, despite having John to

237

lean on. Nevertheless, he smiled with great love at his youngest son, lavishing praise on him before whispering something to John. John picked the earl up and carried him back towards the house.

Waiting until the hubbub had died down, Willow kissed Edward and handed him over to his nurse before strolling off towards the stable building.

Gerard was occupied with Anthony Dowling. She was pleased he had a guest. It meant he would not ride with her today. He'd outraged her sensibilities with his behaviour of the previous night.

'Willow?' Catching her up at a run, Jeffrey smiled an apology. 'Captain Dowling has offered to show me the regimental horses being put through their paces, so I'll be unable to escort you today. Gerard bids you wait while he changes. He'll accompany you on your ride.'

Out of the corner of her eye, she saw he was watching them. She threw him frosty look. 'Tell my husband he need not bother to change on my account. I'm more than happy with the company of the groom.'

'You will wait,' Gerard snapped, striding off towards the house without a backward glance. She simmered with resentment at being issued an order in front of a guest.

Jeffrey stared thoughtfully towards his brother's retreating back. 'He seems out of countenance this morning.'

'We've crossed swords,' she said carelessly. 'He can be a most aggravating man on occasion. I was compelled to point this out to him.' En-

238

couraged by Jeffrey's grin, she whispered, 'I've got no intention of obeying his order like some servant girl. If he's not back in a few minutes, he can chase my tail.'

The awe in Jeffrey's eyes spurred her on. After a few minutes, she decided Gerard's time had run out and turned her face to the cold kiss of the wind. Eyeing the ragged streamers of clouds, she wondered if it would rain.

Spring was almost upon them. Buds had swelled to bursting point, and there seemed to be an air of expectancy about everything – including the horses! Such a cacophony of squeals and snickers came from the stables she could hardly hear herself think as she walked towards Circe's stall.

Circe was so full of nervous energy Brian advised she should not be ridden. Knowing why, she tried to hide her excitement.

Brian had changed since Gerard had taken him to task. As with Kitty, the difference in their status was becoming more and more apparent, and the easiness between them had gone.

Propriety forbade discussion of the mating of her horse. Once, she would have discussed Circe's coupling and the likely outcome. Now she held her tongue. The subject had become men's business.

The stallion had been broken that morning for a reason. When he was taken to cover her mare, much of his energy would be spent and he'd treat his mate more kindly.

Brian saddled up a mettlesome chestnut mare. It would give her a good ride.

She ran her hand over the rippling flanks to quiet it and said to Brian, 'I daresay you've heard Kitty no longer works as my maid.'

'That I have, My Lady.' Brian straightened up from what he was doing and gave her a direct gaze. 'Kitty was wrong to endanger your life; the viscount showed remarkable restraint in the matter.'

'I did not think you would take his side.' Tossing her head, she took the reins from his hand and mounted in her usual manner. 'Where does your loyalty lie?'

Anger came into Brian's eyes, but his voice remained even. 'Have I given you reason to question it, My Lady?'

'You give me reason by siding with my husband against Kitty. What am I to do without a maid?'

'That's not a question the groom need answer,' Gerard said harshly, as he strode into the stable. Leading his horse from the stall, he set the saddle on its back himself. 'About your business, O'Shea, I wish to speak to my wife alone.'

Alarmed by his furious tone, she edged the chestnut away from him. Even Brian hesitated about carrying out his order.

'Get out!' Gerard hissed, causing Brian to scurry off.

'I've no wish to speak to you, Gerard.' She took a deep breath to control the apprehensive quaver in her voice. 'What I said to you this morning still applies. You are no gentleman, and I ... I despise you.'

Tension seared between them and communicated itself to her mount. It stamped upon the

240

ground and attempted to jerk the reins from her hands.

'Do you indeed?' Gerard forgot his resolve about winning Willow's heart. He intended to bring her to heel, and now was a good time to start. Expression grim, he impaled her with one hard stare. 'Despise me or not, you're my wife. It's time you started to act like one. A lady does not question her husband's lawful orders, nor does she gossip about him like some common washerwoman.'

Willow gasped. 'I was only—'

'Do not interrupt!' Gerard thundered. 'You placed O'Shea in an untenable position. You presumed on past friendship to encourage a man in the division of his loyalty.'

'I did no such thing.' Outrage overcame her earlier timidity and manifested itself as stubbornness. 'If I did, you drove me to it with your high-handed attitude. You had no right to dismiss my maid without consultation, and less right to make me look a fool in front of Mrs Breton.'

Indignation and hurt pride made her voice rise an octave. 'How dare you tell her to imprison me in my room if I refused to co-operate? Do not take me to task over the lack of propriety I learned from you.'

'Take care, woman,' Gerard snarled. 'You're going too far.'

Her grip tightened round her whip and she was hard pressed not to strike him with it. 'Stand aside, Gerard, or I'll run you down. I'd rather ride alone than put up with another minute of your company.'

The chestnut surged forward when she gently dug her heels into its side. Gerard flung himself sideways into a pile of straw. The chestnut's reaction was unexpected. Willow fought to bring it under control when it reared in the confined space.

Unseated, she tumbled from its back and landed on top of her husband in a tangle of arms and legs. Immediately, his arms closed around her like bands of steel.

It was no use struggling against his superior strength as she glared into eyes as furious as her own.

'You deserve a good beating, woman.'

'So do you,' she hissed, her voice equally threatening. 'If I were a man I'd give you one.'

'If you were a man I'd run you through.' He gave a short, mirthless bark of laughter. 'I've never known another woman quite so obdurate, unreasoning and disagreeable.'

'Do not let the fact I'm a woman stop you,' she taunted, showing her displeasure by scorching him with the fury of her eyes and voice. She wished her hands were free so she could strike him. 'I will quite willingly engage you in a duel if you'd but let me go.'

She tried to wriggle from his grasp, but found herself pulled closer until she could hardly breathe. He was using his strength unfairly. 'I may suffer defeat,' she gasped, 'but it would give me great pleasure to slice your ears from your head first.'

'My ears?'

When laughter came into his eyes she scowled

ferociously at him. 'I daresay you would not find it so funny when it occurred.'

'Indeed not. My hat would fall over my eyes without their support.'

Up close, Gerard's eyes had little black smudges in the grey, the irises were dark and deep. His firm chin contained a small dimple, and the sides of his mouth crinkled most attractively when he grinned.

She would not allow herself to return his grin. His face smelled deliciously of the soap his servant had shaved him with, his dark hair was neatly dressed into a silk-encased pigtail. She was glad he didn't wear a wig, though if she cut off his ears...? Despite her intention to the contrary, she smiled at the ludicrous picture his words conjured up.

'That would cause you no end of inconvenience, would it not?'

'Indeed.'

The amusement in her eyes matched his own now. Her pulse gave an elated little leap. 'Would you relax your arms just a little,' she murmured. 'I can hardly breathe, and your buttons are exceedingly uncomfortable.' She discovered she had no desire to leave the comfort of his arms altogether. Now her anger-tensed body had relaxed, he was most accommodating to lie against.

Unbidden, what had taken place the night before came into her mind. Blood raced to her cheeks. This man, who'd been a stranger to her until just recently, had touched her body most intimately, her reaction...

His touch had been wonderful, she thought

dreamily. Quivers of ecstasy raced through her flesh and she became moist with anticipation. She'd seen the desire she evoked in his eyes, and guessed she craved the same thing – the union of the flesh. He would have experienced this mysterious union already. Men lived by their own rules and needs, it seemed. She'd heard there were women who took coin to cater to them.

She enjoyed his pursuit of her. She'd heard he'd refurbished the room next to his for her comfort. It was being prepared for her initiation into womanhood. His sensitivity had endeared him to her. Now she was unsure. Had she been left intact last night? Would he consider it forward if she asked?

His grey eyes seemed to be reading her most intimate thoughts. Lowering her eyes from the knowing light in his, she blushed. The fiery centre of each breast thrust against the cool silk of her shirt as she half-remembered a caress of fingers upon them. The awakening of her body had been ecstatic, with a promise of untapped pleasures.

'Why do you blush, Wife?' His arms had relaxed slightly, his voice was soft and teasing. 'Is the closeness of my body uncomfortable?'

'Indeed, no.' Her voice was so hesitant she could hardly hear it herself 'If I blush it's because...' She hesitated, out of her depth. 'I was wondering, Gerard.' She took a deep breath before she ran out of courage under his half-amused scrutiny. 'Last night ... I remember only ... pleasurable feelings. Did we ... you...?' She could not go on. Gasping at her own temerity, she buried her face

244

against the warmth of his neck.

'We did not.' Gerard smiled, finding her naïvete refreshing. At the same time he recognized his pride had been stroked by her words. 'What you experienced was only a small part of lovemaking. I'm delighted you were pleasured by my attention, but would rather you experienced it when fully conscious.'

'It's natural to feel thus?'

The eyes gazing up at him were overflowing with shy innocence. Tenderness rioted through his body, the power of it nearly overwhelming him. Thank God he hadn't given in to his baser instincts.

'My sweeting, it's natural to experience so much pleasure in lovemaking that it drives every other thought from your mind.'

Her heart beat faster at the endearment. She remembered Lady Edwina's advice on the subject of relationships between husband and wife. 'Will you teach me these pleasurable ways of love, Gerard?'

He would have most willingly set about teaching her then and there, had they not been lying in a pile of straw. A stable, with the smell and sound of horses all around – not to mention a strong likelihood of being disturbed without notice – was not a fitting place to initiate his lady.

'We'll reach paradise together,' he promised.

He kissed her most lovingly before they rose from the straw, appeased when her lips clung to his. She'd be easy to teach.

Willow had already learned her first lesson: her husband's temper could be deflected if she went about it the right way. That her husband was thinking exactly the same thing about her, didn't enter her head.

They returned from their ride to find her new chamber prepared. Her delight in it was evident in her eyes.

'There's a separate bathing chamber through that door; beyond it, the maid's room,' Gerard said, enjoying her pleasure.

'It's so pretty.' She touched the delicate hangings of the white and gold gilded bed, then gazed at a plump, trumpeting cherub. Her fingers strummed across the strings of her harp and the room was filled with a shivering, exuberant sound. 'You did this for me, did you not?'

The joy he found in her reaction made his voice unaccountably gruff. 'I can think of no other I'd be inclined to go to all this trouble for.'

'How can I thank you?'

Did she need to ask? He grinned, saying to Mrs Breton, 'I'll attend My Lady until her bath is prepared. We need to ready ourselves to pay our respects to Mrs Tupworthy.'

'But I have no maid.' Seizing the opportunity to trade on his improved disposition, her eyes widened. 'Mrs Breton has not the skill to dress my hair properly. May I not make use of Kitty until we hire another maid?'

Her eyes were luminous as they gazed with helpless innocence into his. Her dark lashes had separated into entrancing, feathery spikes where a light shower of rain had dampened her face.

Although captivated, Gerard found it hard to

keep a straight face. She was a consummate flirt. He enjoyed the way her lashes dipped over her eyes then fluttered upwards, to reveal them again.

He pulled a handkerchief from his pocket and dabbed a few raindrops from her nose before handing it to her. He smiled, letting her know he was not fooled. She was not beyond laughing at herself if her amused expression was anything to go by, but would the amusement stay there when she couldn't get her own way in this?

'You may not.' There was enough firmness in his voice to let her know she would not win on this issue. 'There must be someone who can act as a maid.'

'Bella is skilled, and can be spared for most of the day by her mistress,' Mrs Breton said.

'Then fetch her.'

Willow pouted prettily when the housekeeper went about her business. It was obvious he would not be swayed on this matter.

She'd accepted his ruling, Gerard thought, but grudgingly, if the way she shredded the handkerchief between her fingers was any indication.

Suddenly, her shoulders stiffened. Stabbing him with an anguished look, she gave a cry of rage, and dashing the flimsy piece of material to the floor, ground it under the heel of her boot.

What the devil! As he stooped to picked up the square of muslin, he noticed the name embroidered in the corner. He gazed at his smouldering wife with instant awareness. Affairs had progressed swifter than he'd imagined: she was jealous.

A wickedly sensual smile curved at his mouth. Two steps took him to her side. Taking her face between his hands, he gazed down at her for long moments. Gradually, the tension left her, the corners of her mouth crinkled into a smile. He kissed her then, with enough passion to tease a response, but not enough to endanger his own comfort.

'Honor is the name of my overseer's daughter on the plantation in Virginia,' he explained, a little later. He watched her inspect her hair in the small silver-backed mirror Bella held up for her. 'I don't know how I came to have the hand-kerchief. She must have slipped it in my pocket as a keepsake before I left.'

His hand slid inside his waistcoat and explored the tiny inside pocket. 'It's yours I keep close to my heart.'

It had been a long time since he'd observed the ritual of a woman at her dressing-table. Willow had been self-conscious at first, but had found it hard to maintain her disapproving countenance whilst he paid her pretty compliments. Her vanity would not allow it.

'She's but a child of fourteen,' he added.

Her eyes met his squarely in the mirror and her mouth curved into a faintly contemptuous smile as she reminded him, 'I was but fourteen when we married.' Smiling with approval at Bella, she dismissed her.

Gerard considered his answer. 'You were also a child.' His finger stroked along the creamy skin of her shoulder, bringing a delicate shiver to the surface. 'My absence allowed you the time to grow up.'

'And what of this Honor, the girl who gave you a token of her regard? Is she pretty?'

The violet of her eyes deepened, drew him into their azure depths.

She has the most damnable effect on me, he thought, his mouth twisting in wry acknowledgement of the fact. 'No doubt Honor will grow into a handsome woman, but you've gone beyond mere beauty now, you're exquisite. The most glittering gem you own would pale into insignificance when placed against your skin.'

'The effect would not be hard to achieve.' Her laugh was silver bright as she flipped open a small jewellery casket and drew out a string of red glass beads.

They did not enhance the soft blue gown she wore. Gerard frowned. Upending the casket, he spread its meagre contents across her dressing-table. 'This is all the jewellery you own?'

'This is what my father sent with my dowry. It's all that's left of that which belonged to my mother.' Her dainty fingers caressed a gold brooch in the shape of a flower, exploring the indentations where gems had once been set. 'Lady Edwina said this had a diamond at its centre, and the petals were covered in tiny sapphires. It was given to my French grandmother by her lover, she believes.'

Dropping the brooch, she selected a silver pendant and flipped it open. 'I prefer this. See, there's a likeness of my mother.' Shyly, she held it out for his inspection. 'I resemble her, I think.'

There was certainly a likeness. He smiled, detecting in her a need to relate to the woman pictured in the locket.

'The resemblance is remarkable.' He watched her face light up in a smile. A dark tendril of hair curled against the creamy nape of her neck and he experienced an irresistible urge to press his lips against the spot. He found a perfect excuse. Taking his leave, he returned within a minute and placed a circlet of pearls around her neck.

'You bought these for me?'

The happiness of her smile made him feel guilty. He'd paid scant attention to Willow in his absence, and had bought the pearls as a gift for his mother. To save answering with a lie, he inclined his head and kissed the curl against her neck. He enjoyed the delicate little shiver she gave and the way she arched her neck to accommodate his caress.

She moved with a show of reluctance from his embrace, and rising from her seat, turned to face him in a slither of pale blue silk, embroidered lace and the delicate fragrance of her perfume. 'I'm ready. Do I meet with your approval?'

'You're too perfect,' he growled. 'I prefer you in a chemise with your hair about your waist.'

Colour crept under her skin. A self-conscious smile flitted across her lips, then faded when her eyes engaged his. 'I've not thanked you for the gift, Gerard.'

Placing a perfumed hand each side of his face, she guided it down to hers to be kissed. Surprisingly, she made a thorough job of it. She learned fast.

Annie Tupworthy was appreciative of the visit by the viscount and his wife, but embarrassed that her shortage of staff meant she was unable to entertain them properly.

'We're not here to be entertained,' Gerard said, noticing her distress. 'We're here to enquire after your welfare and that of your son. The loss of your husband must have come as a shock. If there's anything I can do to help, please feel free to ask. I'll put my clerk at your disposal and he can sort out your husband's business affairs, perhaps?'

'Thank you, My Lord. I'd be most grateful for the help.'

'Carlisle is so handsome.' Willow was bending over the crib making soft, cooing sounds. 'Gerard, do come and see him.'

The daughter of the house was a pretty child of about five. Her quiet demeanour and good manners were a credit to her mother. She gave him a shy smile, then giggled when Gerard tickled her under the chin. He grinned at her, enchanted by her petite perfection. Having a daughter would not be too bad, if this little maid was anything to go by.

He made the appropriate noises whilst he did what was expected of him. The infant boy resembled a skinned rabbit. Milk dribbled from the corner of his pursed-up mouth and his blotchy face seemed screwed into a permanent frown. No wonder the child frowned, he thought, feeling sympathy for him. He was bound from shoulders to toe in a piece of linen, and couldn't

251

move anything except his head.

Willow seemed enamoured by the infant. When the nurse gave in to her pleading and placed the infant in her arms, she promptly cuddled him against her breast and covered his face in kisses.

He pictured their own son snuggled against her, and experienced a strange contentment. She would be a good mother. He must get her with child as soon as possible. It might take her mind off the village orphans.

The issue was fast becoming a bone of contention between them. She refused to admit her scheme to fund an orphanage was unworkable. Her capital could not support it long term, and he wasn't prepared to squander any of the Lytton funds until the estate was making a profit again. That could take several years.

'Is there anything you need?' she enquired, before they took their leave. She'd brought a basket of preserves and some early daffodils she'd picked from the garden.

'I'm in need of a young woman who can act as both maid and companion to my daughter. If you hear of one I should be most obliged.' Annie hesitated before adding, 'I would also be honoured if you would stand as godparents to Carlisle. We are quite alone in the world, so I have no relatives to sponsor him.' There was a quiet resignation in her tone, as though she expected to be turned down.

'We would be honoured.'

Willow tried to keep the astonishment from showing in her face.

'You must call on my wife when you're fully

recovered and bring your charming daughter to visit. No doubt our ward would enjoy having someone his own age for company.'

Edward! On the way back to Lytton, Willow couldn't help wondering why he'd suddenly mentioned Edward. He'd hardly acknowledged the boy's existence up until now, except to tell her that Daphne had written to say she was unwell, and had requested he be kept at Lytton indefinitely.

Edward rarely asked about his mother now. He'd become part of the family, and was kept so busy with his various activities he didn't have time to fret. The country air had brought a healthy bloom to his cheeks, and he was growing into a sturdy, outgoing child.

She was pleased Edward was staying at Lytton, but wondered at an illness so debilitating as to keep a mother from her child. Only death would part her and her children when she had them. She'd recently captured a likeness of Edward on paper, and intended to send it to Daphne when the opportunity presented itself.

About to ask him what ailed Daphne, she caught Gerard's glance on her face. His eyes were lazily soft. When he smiled, she was acutely aware of how sensuous the curves of his mouth were. She took a quick intake of breath, overcome by a sudden craving to be kissed by that mouth. Her craving seemed to be reciprocated, for he growled deep in his throat.

'Come here, Wife.'

He was still kissing her when the coachman guided the carriage to a halt outside the entrance to Lytton.

'Edward is renounced as your heir!' Daphne stared at the marquess in disbelief. 'Are you mad?'

'On the contrary, my dear.' The voice of the marquess was silky smooth. 'I have lodged an official disclaimer with my lawyer stating my reasons. You will countersign this paper, acknowledging the validity of my action.'

'But why...?' A spasm of coughing racked Daphne. Her voice was weaker when she'd finished. She gave the man she loathed a tenuous smile. 'There's no one else who bears your name. This is one of your cruel jests, yes? You said you loved me, asked me to become your wife.'

'And you refused.' The marquess yawned, but his eyes glinted meanly in their sockets as he gave a carelessly callous smile. 'I admit your games kept me amused longer than most. When you were young and willing to please I'd have given you anything. Yet it pleased you to spurn the protection I offered you. I will not ask again.'

'I ceased to be young the day you married my mother.' Daphne's voice was bitter. 'Did you really think I'd place Sheronwood and the welfare of my son in your grasping hands?'

Leaning forward, the marquess breathed in her ear, 'You attempted to cheat me. Edward has no Lynchcross blood in his veins.'

Daphne gave a shocked start. So he knew? How had he found out? 'You'll need proof before you can disinherit Edward.' Her smile became mocking as she stared up at him. 'People will say you're piqued because your effeminate nephew achieved what you could not.' She choked out a laugh. 'I'll tell them the marquess can only satisfy himself with children.' Her voice was cut off when a hand slid round her throat and tightened about her windpipe.

'They will not take the word of a diseased courtesan like you.' His eyes had glazed over. Fear struck her like a poisoned arrow when he whispered almost to himself. 'I have signed confessions from the apothecary and two male servants formerly in your employ. They've sworn you poisoned your husband with belladonna, madam.'

He thrust a parchment on to the table and placed a quill in her trembling fingers. 'Sign it, else you'll be charged with murdering your husband.'

'Eduard was made insane by disease,' she whispered, staring at him with fearful eyes. 'It was you who instructed the apothecary to prescribe the fatal dose.'

'You'll never be able prove it.'

When his fingers tightened, she scrambled to comply with his demand. He twisted her neck towards him when her signature was scrawled across the document and, tearing the pen from her hand, flung it aside.

'Eduard kept a journal, which has lately come into my possession.' The pale, pitiless eyes focusing on hers were full of hate. 'Eduard was incapable of being a husband to you. He suspected your child was fathered by Gerard Lytton. For that, I'll have the life of your son.'

'It's not true,' she managed to rasp against the throttling hand. Fear leaped into her throat, bringing a salty taste. 'Do not kill Edward, I beg you. He's protected by the King.'

'I have another fate in mind for your son, madam.' Placing his mouth close to her ear, he poured into it his vile plan for Edward.

Her eyes snapped open in horror before he closed off her air completely. A welcoming blackness descended on her.

'After that, I'll slit the throat of the man who planted his vile seed in your womb and plotted to take what's mine,' the marquess muttered, throwing her body aside.

Daphne's maid gave a squeal of fright when she entered the chamber and saw her mistress lying on the floor.

'Your mistress has collapsed,' he snapped. Picking up the paper he strutted to the door. 'Attend to her.'

In the depths of her crystal, Willow could see nothing but a reflection of her face. She'd concentrated on the shining sphere for what seemed like hours. Her eyes were tired, her head beginning to ache.

Sapphire had been convinced she had the gift to see in the crystal, but the effort fatigued her. She allowed her mind to drift to other thoughts. She enjoyed the company of Sapphire, for apart from Lady Edwina, no woman had ever taken an interest in her before. With Sapphire, she could relax.

She'd found herself telling Sapphire about her upbringing at Coringal, and her treatment at the hands of her father. Then she'd told her of her forced marriage to Gerard, her love for Lytton House, and the happiness and sense of belonging she'd found within its walls.

Sapphire offered understanding without censorship. Relaxed in her presence, it had become a habit to confide the little things that worried her, and those which brought her pleasure. Some inner part of her seemed to have always known the woman.

A faint ringing sound from the crystal drew her attention. The glass became so clear she saw it was bigger inside than outside. 'How can this be?' she whispered, intrigued by the phenomenon.

In the depths of the crystal, the shape of a great house appeared. The house was of French design, with formal gardens interspaced with neat pathways. There was a fountain below a terrace, a naked nymph with water gushing from an urn held above its head. She could hear the water cascading into the bowl.

On a seat by the fountain, sat a girl of about twelve. She had a wooden doll in her hand and was attended by a governess. As she watched, a woman came through the opened windows of the house and ran towards the child. She was being pursued by three men and was crying out in terror.

Bella slipped unseen from the room and hurried to her mistress, her eyes wide with excitement.

Two of the men dragged the woman away, knocking the governess to the ground. The girl was crying when the third man took her hand and led her away. She kept turning to look at her mother, who was struggling in the grip of the other two men.

Willow could feel the child's terror, and her breath came in short anguished gasps. There was something familiar about the people. She leaned closer. One man was her father, though of more youthful appearance. The girl...? Her face became thoughtful when the scene abruptly became mist.

She'd only caught a glimpse of the child's face, but she could have sworn it was Sapphire ... or herself?

Turning her face to the mirror, she gazed at her own reflection before that of the child faded from her mind, then drew her sketching pad towards her. When she'd finished recording the scene she'd witnessed, she rose to her feet and made her way to Lady Edwina's room.

'What is it, child?' Edwina was just about to take tea, and sent her maid to fetch another cup. 'You look as though you've seen a ghost.'

'You think I need a reason to visit you, Grand-mother?'

'Undoubtedly.' Edwina chuckled. 'Your husband seems to demand more of your presence every day.' The delicate blush staining Willow's cheeks didn't escape her notice. 'You find Gerard an agreeable husband, yes?'

'He's not offensive to me.'

The casual shrug Willow gave brought up Edwina's ire. *Not offensive?* The chit was hard to please if that was all she could find to say about her husband. 'Stop twitching, child,' she snapped. 'A lady must appear elegant at all times.'

'Pray do not chastise me, Grandmother,' she pleaded. 'I'm troubled. I need your advice, not your condemnation.'

'Troubled, my dear?' Taking Willow's hands in hers, she dismissed her maid. 'I'll do what I can to advise you, but if it is a marital problem I cannot interfere.'

'Marital problem?' She gazed at Edwina uncomprehendingly. 'I have no marital problems.' She thrust the drawing into her hands. 'Something strange is happening, which concerns my mother. It's imperative I discover the circumstances of her childhood.'

Edwina glanced at the drawing, but made no sense of it. Was Willow sensitive, like her mother? Had she picked up something from Marietta's past? With sinking heart, she stammered, 'I'm afraid I cannot help you, child.'

'I'm no longer a child.' Willow's chin lifted in the determined manner Edwina knew so well as she retrieved the sketch. 'If you cannot help, I'll be forced to write to my father. She was his ward before their marriage.'

'Wait!' Edwina cried out, as Willow rose from the chair and prepared to leave. She knew the marquess would only seek to slander Marietta, if he condescended to answer at all. 'You'll give me a little time to think about this?'

'Of course.' Bending to kiss the woman, Willow turned the kiss into a hug and whispered with great emotion and longing in her voice, 'I suspect my mother is still alive.'

Edwina's heart lunged in dismay. How long had she harboured this suspicion, and had she any inkling who her mother was? Hands shaking, she untangled herself from Willow's hug and poured tea from the ornate silver teapot.

She waited until Willow had composed herself, then handed her a dainty porcelain cup and saucer edged with gold. It was part of a Meissen tea service, a birthday gift from Gerard several years before. Edwina was exceedingly fond of it and used it only on special occasions.

'Some stones are best left unturned,' was the only counsel she could think to give Willow. As she watched her take a sip of the tea she endeavoured to draw the subject away from Marietta. 'Be careful with that cup, Willow dear. This tea service was a gift from Gerard. I only use it on special occasions.'

Willow gazed at it in silence, then back at her with a query in her eyes.

'It would be my daughter's birthday, had she lived.'

Willow had almost forgotten the existence of the woman whose place she had taken as mistress. She found it hard to relate the embittered Lady Caroline to either of her sons, or to Lady Edwina as her mother.

Caroline Lytton had been mistress of this house, she'd breathed the same air, had been wife to the earl and suffered in childbirth to bear him sons. Her portrait hung in the gallery with the other countesses. A portrait of Ambrose hung next to her. Whether by accident or design, they'd been hung with their faces gazing away from each other.

'Did Caroline love the earl?' she asked, suddenly feeling sorry for her predecessor.

Edwina smiled slightly, wondering if Willow

would ever lose her romantic streak, or her inquisitive nature. 'Aye, child, Caroline loved him to distraction. That's why I cannot understand...' She did not need to voice her thought. Willow shared with her the burden of Caroline's confession and it strengthened the bond between them.

'Should we tell Sapphire about Caroline's deathbed confession?' Willow murmured, mouth suddenly dry with tension. 'Caroline wanted her forgiveness.'

The cup dropped from Edwina's suddenly nerveless fingers, spilling its contents on to the Aubusson rug. Had she read her thoughts? Lifting her eyes to those of the younger woman, she gave her an awed glance, before saying with as much dignity as she could muster, 'I will not countenance trickery. Please leave, and have some respect for my feelings. I'm no longer desirous of your company.'

Although she flushed with shame, and tears stung her eyes, Willow's mouth tightened in rebellion. Rising to her feet, she swept haughtily from the room without a backward glance or another word.

For once, Edwina was at a loss. Ringing for her maid, she instructed her to clean up the mess, then after determining her precious cup and saucer was still intact, sent the woman to request Sapphire to attend her.

The two were closeted together for an hour. When Sapphire left, they were still no closer to resolving the matter.

It was only a matter of time before Willow begged Lady Edwina's forgiveness, for she knew she'd be miserable until it was gained.

'I know not what came over me,' she whispered, laying her cheek against the old woman's parchment-like hand. 'The potion Kitty gave me must have addled my brain, for I suffered a hallucination before I came to you, and the sketch was a result of that.'

Relieved that she'd found a convincing reason for her suspicions concerning her mother, Edwina accepted her apology without further comment.

They were friends again when they descended together to the dining-room, but Willow was wondering why Lady Edwina hadn't seized the opportunity to lecture her on her shortcomings again.

It was out of character for her to accept an excuse so hastily, or forgive rudeness so easily. It was almost as if...? As if Lady Edwina wished to forget the whole episode.

The problem deserted her mind entirely, and her eyes began to sparkle when they encountered the beguiling smile of her husband. She savoured the thrill of elation that chased through her body.

Tonight, she surmised, he intends to make me his wife in the flesh. She was eager to experience the delights he'd promised. Such thrilling anticipation built up in her, she could hardly eat all through dinner, and trembled with bliss every time he glanced her way.

Gerard's thoughts were running along the same lines. Willow had responded most favourably to his attention today. The gift of the pearls, such a small token on his part, had obviously thrilled her. She was easy to please. Her fingers stroked the satiny smoothness of the pearls every time she glanced his way. Whether she knew it or not, there was a wealth of invitation in her eyes.

Jeffrey's absence from the table caused Gerard little concern. Time passed without notice when one was involved in sensual pursuits. An untried youth such as his brother would be regarded as a conquest by the buxom whore. He doubted she'd let Jeffrey escape too easily from her bed. The moon was bright enough to light the lad's way home, and a side door would be left open for his return.

Only his grandmother commented on Jeffrey's absence. It was Willow who answered her with such sweet innocence he was hard put not to laugh as he exchanged an amused glance with his father.

'Jeffrey was invited to watch the regimental horses being drilled. In all likelihood, he's persuaded the soldiers to let him join in the manoeuvres, and has been in the saddle all day.'

'As long as he does not come home dressed in uniform, announcing he's going off to fight a war.' Edwina gazed fiercely down her long nose at Ambrose. 'I refuse to let my grandsons become soldiers, and so must you.'

Jeffrey's return had no such glory attached to it. The hands on the study clock had reached quarter past the hour of ten when Gerard's thoughts strayed to his wife.

No doubt she was readying herself that very moment for his visit. He had no intention of disappointing her maidenly heart, nor sparing her blushes this night.

He'd just stood up when the thud of hoofbeats came to his ears. The hound at his feet growled softly in its throat. The hound would have recognized Jeffrey's horse, he thought, crossing to the window. Besides which, his brother would have used the short cut and gone straight to the stable.

Picking up the loaded pistol he kept on the desk, he snuffed the candle and rang for a manservant before gazing out into the brilliant, moonlit grounds.

'Hallo, the house.' A tall, thin man dismounted, and stood in full view of the darkened study window, making no attempt to conceal himself. Gerard relaxed his guard slightly. A sorry-looking nag stood quietly next to the man, its head hanging down.

Opening the window a chink, he slid halfway through the aperture. 'State your business, sir, and keep your hands where I can see them.'

'My business is with Viscount Sommersley.' The man held his palms outward as his gaze sought for Gerard in the shadows. 'I come unarmed. My weapons are in my pack.'

'I'm the man you seek.' He stepped into the garden. 'Why come you to my door at this time of night?'

The man's head jerked towards his horse. 'You are the brother of this unfortunate youth, I believe.'

Dear, God! Jeffrey was slung like a sack of turnips over the saddle! Heart in his mouth, he stuck the pistol in his belt and hurried towards the pack horse.

'La, sir! You'll blow your tackle to smithereens if you're not careful.' 'The pistol was flipped from his belt and rendered safe before he had time to turn. The man handed it to him with a bow and a sardonic smile. 'Your brother is not harmed except for a few bruises. He's the worse for drink I'm afraid, and will be afflicted with a headache come morning.'

His eyes flew open in shock. 'Good God, he's naked!' Jeffrey was wrapped in the man's cloak, and his dirty bare feet dangled from beneath it.

'He was set upon by vagabonds, and would have chased them into the forest on foot had I not prevented him by tying his ankle to a stake.'

'I'm in your debt.' Hauling Jeffrey from the horse, the two of them carried him into the study.

The man gazed down at him and grinned. 'The lad was most indignant about the matter and insisted I apprehend the thieves. His clothes are in the bundle attached to my saddle. Unfortunately, he was unable to stand still long enough for me to put them on his back. The activity caused the drink to ferment in his head and he ran in circles until he got so dizzy he dropped unconscious.' Cocking his head to one side, he measured Gerard with his eyes. 'He proved easier to handle that way.'

'I cannot thank you enough, sir.' Grinning to himself, he turned to the servants who'd appeared at his side. 'Carry my brother to his chamber and make him comfortable. Be discreet. I'll expect you to have regard for his pride, and forget this happened. Return to the study when you've finished.'

'Your name, sir?' he asked, when his brother had been carted away.

'James Langland at your service, My Lord.'

The man was about forty, the flesh sparse upon his bones. Apart from his nose, which curved hugely from his face like a beak, he was personable. An astute pair of light-brown eyes gazed at him with interest. Gerard took an instant liking to James Langland.

'I've heard much of you. You were Willow's tutor, were you not?'

'The same.' James smiled. 'If nothing else, I pride myself on the fact I taught her to defend herself. She's the best shot I've ever come across, and a quick study.'

'She boasted once she could shoot the eye from a frog,' Gerard said drily. 'I've yet to see any evidence of it. The frogs around here seem to have remained intact.'

'You seem to doubt her, My Lord.' The languid edge to the man's voice was at odds with his penetrating eyes. 'Willow may be a skinny child with a wild imagination and a tendency to dramatize, but I tell you this, sir: if my pupil says she can shoot the eye from a frog, she's quite capable of doing it.'

'I believe you.' Willow would have been indignant had she heard her tutor's description of her. The thought made him want to laugh.

'You do, eh!' James Langland uncoiled from his chair and prowled restlessly around the room. 'You seem a reasonable man, sir. By now you must know I'm not here by chance. I heard that

Willow was under the protection of your house. I came here to satisfy myself she is well cared for. I grew uncommonly fond of the child, and came to regard her as a daughter.'

'You can satisfy yourself on that account in the morning if you wish.' He glanced at one of the servants, who'd returned with James's cloak folded neatly over his arm. 'Bring our guest some supper, rouse one of the stable lads to see to his horse, then find him a bed for the night.'

'By the way,' James said casually, when all had been done and they were about to retire. 'The rogues who set about your brother are tied to a tree in the forest. I was unable to catch his horse.'

The man was more capable than most. 'I'm in your debt,' he said, reckoning the horse would find its own way home.

'A refreshing change, indeed.' James Langland's smile was ironic in the extreme. 'Where I'm concerned, it's usually the other way round.'

The candlewick flickered in a pool of molten tallow. All that remained of the fire was a few warm embers.

Gerard gazed down at the supine form of his wife, enjoying the innocent beauty of her as she slept. He was about to rob her of that innocence, but by doing so he'd disclose the mystery of her femininity to her. She would become all the more precious for the gift she gave him.

He was still dressed in his shirt and breeches. Quickly discarding them, he slid on to the bed beside her and gently kissed her awake.

'Gerard?' Her eyelids fluttered open, and she

gazed at him so anxiously his heart seemed to melt. 'I have something to tell you.'

'And I you. But let it wait until morning, my love. I've long awaited this moment.' He was as amorous as a tom-cat and eager to claim what was his. His mouth sought her sweet, pointed nipples through the material of her chemise.

'Please stop, Gerard.' He frowned as her hands found his shoulders and pushed him away. 'I am indisposed.'

The candle went out in a hiss of hot wax. What cursed luck, he thought, inhaling the rancid odour of smoke lingering in the air.

Her voice was hardly audible, so ashamed did she sound. 'The potion Kitty gave me last night was for women's problems as well as sleeping. It has...' She gave a slight sniff. 'It has caused my moon cycle to arrive prematurely.'

He wondered if she were crying. If that proved to be the case, he thought he might join her.

'You do not mind waiting a little longer?' she said anxiously.

'I don't mind,' he lied, minding like hell. His romancing of her had built his desires to fever pitch and he was suffering an agony of craving. He cursed the fact that sweet words and lies meant more to women than the truth, on occasion. After that, he cursed the instinct that had made him act the gentleman when he should have demanded she fulfil her marital duties earlier.

Shyly she asked, 'Will you stay with me a while? You can join me if you would like. I would enjoy it if you held me.'

Join her? *Sweet Jesus!* He felt like laughing as

the funny side of the situation occurred to him.

What sort of torment had this virgin wife of his planned? he asked himself, sliding his naked body under the sheets.

And what could be worse than holding a woman who smelled as sweet as this one in his arms, who snuggled almost naked against his chest and breathed gently into his ear?

The answer was not long in coming; having that woman enquire in a sleepy voice before drifting into sleep. 'You are comfortable, Gerard?'

CHAPTER TEN

Spring 1755

'James Langland!'

Willow would have thrown herself on the man if Gerard hadn't physically restrained her. He laughed, enjoying the astonishment on their faces.

'Willow?' Head inclined, James walked around her, gazing quizzically through his eye-glass all the while. Finally, he said in an accusatory tone, 'You've become a woman while my back was turned.'

'And you've neglected me shamefully,' she reproached softly. 'Not one letter in all this time have you sent me.'

'You are wrong there, cherub.' James became suddenly sober. 'My letters were intercepted by

269

your father and returned. Then, when I pounded on his door and demanded he let me see you–' He shrugged, biting off his words as he took her hands. 'Well, never mind that, my dear. Now I've seen you I can go on my way a happy man.'

Tears immediately sprang to her eyes. She was glad Gerard had arranged to have him released from prison anonymously. He'd not have been able to face her otherwise. Gazing at his thin body and the pallor of his skin, she knew he was in need of sustenance.

'Go...? With you looking so scrawny a starving fox would pity you?'

Her scornful remark reminded Gerard of his grandmother. He was grinning when she turned to him and implored, 'Please convince James to stay for a while, Gerard.'

James's glance took in the array of dishes being carried into the dining-room. His nose twitched hungrily. 'I need to find employment, cherub. I intend to offer myself as a tutor at the spring hiring fair.'

'That's not for another fortnight.' Sliding his arm around Willow's waist Gerard pulled her close. His grin became a smile as he sprang his own surprise. 'If my wife wishes you to stay then you're doubly welcome.'

'Your wife?'

Out came the eye-glass again. This time Gerard was subjected to a thorough head-to-toe scrutiny. Finally, James nodded his approval.

'I cannot decide whether to offer congratulations or commiserations, My Lord.' His eyes twinkled with sudden mirth when Willow made an exasperated sound deep in her throat. 'She was ever a contrary child, but interesting nonetheless.'

'I agree. Her company does not bore a man.' Gerard chuckled, prepared to indulge in a small amount of banter at her expense. 'I'd not thought to marry so unconventional a woman.'

Blushing furiously, she turned her face into his sleeve.

James gave a satisfied chuckle now he'd bested his erstwhile pupil. 'In return for your hospitality, I'll give your brother fencing tuition of the calibre he will not find outside the academy in Paris.'

Gerard remembered James was reputed to be one of the best swordsmen in England, and certainly the finest shot. 'I could do with a little practice myself.'

'I'll instruct you in the use of a pistol also.' James's voice was dry in the extreme. 'But first I'll discover if you're worth the effort.' He grinned at the proud flare of his host's nostrils and the narrowing of his eyes. 'A contest, sir. You and your brother against myself' – his eyes flicked to Willow – 'and a partner of my choice.'

Coaxed from its hiding place, her face was as alert as a cat who'd just seen a mouse emerge from the wainscot. He had no need to ask who Langland's partner would be. He could feel the excitement quivering through her body.

'Allow me to place a wager on my sons, sir.' Catching the end of the conversation, Ambrose smiled as he was escorted into the room on the arm of John Grey. 'Twenty guineas.'

'You'll lose it, My Lord,' James advised the earl

271

after introductions had been affected. 'My partner can out-shoot any man alive, with a couple of exceptions. I include myself in those.'

'Then you should not be afraid to take me up on it.' Ambrose's eyes narrowed. 'Methink you are full of conceit, sir.'

James shrugged off the barb. 'Undeniably. And I can offer only my note.'

'It's not my usual policy to accept notes, sir.'

'Then I cannot accept your wager.' James bowed. 'You see before you an impoverished man, recently released from debtors' prison.'

'I'll stake the wager,' Willow offered, eager to provide James with the opportunity to win himself a purse in the most acceptable way possible. She blushed when every pair of eyes turned her way.

'You?' The earl's eyes were displeased. 'You'd lay money against your husband?'

'And why should she not, Father?' Gerard's thumb stroked reassuringly against her waist. 'If I'm not mistaken, she'll be partnering James.'

The earl looked shaken. 'She's but a woman. You must forbid it, Gerard.'

When her body became rigid beside him, he experienced a sudden empathy with her. The marquess had paid scant thought to Willow when he'd banished her with James Langland to Ireland. It was only luck that the man had been of honourable intent and morals. It was apparent James had taken his avocation seriously under duress. He'd sought to give value for the notes once held by the marquess, and had been wrongfully imprisoned for his pains. He could not

272

blame the man for endowing her with male skills. He'd have known no other way.

'I see no harm in it.' He grinned when her breath left her body in a rush. 'Jeffrey tells me she's a passable shot. I'm curious to measure her ability for myself. It's not as if it's a public shooting contest.'

When the earl still looked dubious, Willow crossed to his side.

'I will not enter this contest if it upsets you, dearest Father.' Her voice was sincere despite the disappointment in it. 'James was as much a father to me when I was growing up, as you are now. He'd not encourage me in anything to bring shame upon you.' Tears rendered her eyes luminous and emphasized their sadness. 'I'll not be able to bear it if you look upon me with censure.'

'Nothing you do shames me, Daughter.'

She was adept at gaining her own way, Gerard thought, watching his father's hand close around hers.

A small invisible knife twisted in his heart as he recalled his baby sister. If his suspicions were correct, the child would have been half-sister to both himself and Willow. Gall twisted his gut and the brightness fled from the day. He was not the pacifist his father was.

Remembering the oath he'd been obliged to swear, he experienced a flare of rebellion against the restraint. Lynchcross had a lot to answer for. One day, he'd bring him to account for his crimes against the Lyttons, and to hell with who'd started the feuding!

He promptly forgot about it when Jeffrey came

into the room. His brother took one look at the food, stared at James for a moment with a puzzled expression, then turned an ashen countenance upon the company to state unnecessarily, 'I have an uncommonly foul headache this morning; I think I'll return to my bed.'

Gerard winked at James, who was tucking heartily into a platter of bread and butter, fried ham, and boiled eggs. 'Will you ride with me this morning?' he enquired, sliding into the seat beside him. 'There are a couple of problems needing my attention.'

'Delighted, dear sir,' said James with a grin.

Gerard had taken such a liking to the man, he surprised even himself, after such a short acquaintance. 'I would prefer it if you addressed me as Gerard,' he said, and basked in the glow of Willow's approval.

The shooting contest had been scheduled for ten days hence, a few days after Kitty and Brian's wedding.

To Willow's surprise, Gerard offered no objection to her attending the wedding ceremony, but insisted on accompanying her, advising they'd stay only long enough to toast the couple's health and extend their best wishes.

'Arrangements for the nuptials are well in hand,' Mrs Breton informed her when she waylaid her in the hall the day before the event. 'The celebration will go ahead with as little disruption to the household as possible.'

The door to the study opened. Gerard stuck his head through the gap and caught her eye. 'When you've a moment to spare, Willow.'

'My business with Mrs Breton is finished.' They exchanged a smile as the housekeeper bobbed a curtsy and moved towards the kitchen.

She experienced elation when Gerard's long legs covered the distance between them. His black coat and breeches gave him a dangerous appearance as he towered over her.

Grinning, he stooped to steal a kiss. 'Walk around the lake with me.' Guessing her indisposition must be nearing its end, he'd decided to step up his campaign. He twisted the small silky tendril of hair escaping from under her cap around his finger. 'It's not often I can enjoy your company alone.'

His finger left the curl and stroked along the creamy skin of her jaw-bone until it found the niche under her chin. She almost purred like a kitten when he tipped up her chin and kissed her again. 'This morning I saw some ducklings amongst the reeds. We can sit in the pavilion and see if they venture out.'

Obviously enchanted by the prospect, she spread her fan and gazed at him over it. Her eyes were slumberous, her voice low and husky. 'I'd very much like to see them.'

And would very much like to tease me in the pavilion with your kisses, madam. A pulse in his temple leaped into life at the promise in her eyes. She was too quick a study, and had fast learned the power of her femininity.

His grey eyes hid his thoughts. This wife of his was driving him to distraction. His courtship of her had turned into a self-inflicted punishment.

He could think of little else but the act that would make her truly his. His mind was filled with her, every breath he took was perfumed with her being. He lusted for her like a starving man for sustenance. When she took his arm, his skin was alive and singing to her touch, as though there were no layer of cloth between.

The air was alive with the promise of spring as they skirted the lake. Blue and yellow irises flirted at the edge of the water, spiders spun delicate lace to sparkle invitingly amongst the reeds. Clumps of daffodils bobbed and curtsied to each other, like courtiers clothed in green and gold.

The breeze had an April softness and a suggestion of rain over the next hill. As soon as the thought left his mind, the lake became pocked with circles of ripples that widened one into the other. She started to laugh when he took her hand and urged her to sprint across the bridge towards the pavilion.

'La, sir!' she cried, shaking the raindrops from the cornflower-blue ruffles of her petticoat and turning laughter-bright eyes towards him. 'You were in a devil of a hurry to get me here.'

He drew her impatiently into his arms. 'If you'd sooner be drenched than kissed I'll gladly throw you into the lake.'

Her breath caught in her throat when she saw the expression in her husband's eyes. Beneath the laughter was a raw, hungry desire that set her heart beating like an erratic drum. It was daunting to think she evoked such emotion in a man. What was up to then a pleasant game, no longer seemed quite so funny.

'I'd sooner be thrown in the lake than be the cause of the suffering I see in your eyes.' She continued to speak, despite the glimmer of a smile he gave. 'I truly wish to be a good wife in my duty to you. If I seem to tease, it's because I have no instruction in the propriety of relationships between husband and wife.' She bowed her head in demure obedience. 'It's your right to chastise me if you wish.'

'And what is your preference in the matter?' The time was past to play such games, and his voice had an edge of sobriety to it.

She gave him a quick glance. The smile had left his eyes, his austere mouth and face seemed strangely taut.

'I've seen marriages aplenty where the wife is martyr to her duty. Is that the chastisement you'd have me inflict on you?'

'Indeed, no.' Her chin tilted in determination at the thought. 'I do not wish for that. Indeed ... I wish I'd not raised the matter.' Out of her depth, she sought desperately for words to help her from the trap she'd set for herself. 'You're not the type of man to treat a woman with contempt.'

'I'm a man like any other.' Tipping up her chin, he gazed into her eyes and smiled. 'The fact that you tease, leads me to believe you're as eager as I for our union.'

'I have feelings that I do not yet understand.' She could not tear her eyes away from his, and the breathless anticipation in her voice was all too apparent to her. 'Is that wrong?'

When she would have hung her head again, he

277

prevented her. A tiny narrowing of his eyes made her head spin. Then, when a tender smile creased the corners of his mouth, she was attacked by a profusion of blushes.

Drawing her down upon a wooden bench he took her hand and traced along the sensitive creases of her palm. 'Such feelings are natural when a man and woman are each attracted to the other. The eventual outcome is the greatest ecstasy they can experience together. Those feelings are born of the need to procreate, as nature intended.'

Her lips found his and she whispered against them. 'I'd have us experience that ecstasy together soon.'

Sweet Jesus! His tongue flickered into her mouth and tasted of its sweetness before he set her from him. 'You seek to push me beyond endurance.' His eyes reflected the vulnerability of his position. 'Such familiarity must be reserved for the privacy of the boudoir from now on. You will inform me when your indisposition is resolved.'

'You're very prudish at times.' Rising to her feet, she walked to the water's edge. Her face was impish with laughter when she slanted him a glance over her shoulder. 'Perhaps I'll forget to inform you.' Such consternation came into his face that she couldn't help but giggle. 'What if my feelings desert me altogether?'

He gazed threateningly at her when she giggled again, then said with a tightly controlled grin, 'Perhaps I'll beat you after all. Today seems a good day for it.'

Picking up her skirts, she fled when he made a threatening move towards her. It didn't take him long to catch her up. His hands spanned her waist and she was effortlessly lifted off her feet and twirled around until she was breathless with laughter.

'You, madam, deserve to be punished.' His eyes darkened with passion as he slid her down his body and set her on her feet. Softly, he informed her, 'One day I'll bind you to the bed with silken cords, and you'll beg for release before I'm finished with you.'

She shivered at the silky possessiveness of his voice, but it was a shiver of rapture. Her body responded most favourably to the threat, informing her it was impatient to experience this journey into the unknown.

'Is that a promise, Husband?' she murmured, her eyes flirting deliciously with his.

'Most definitely.' Well pleased with her response, he gently captured her mouth and sealed the promise with a kiss.

Kitty and Brian's wedding was solemnized by the Catholic priest in an arbour decorated with almond blossoms.

Willow had not seen Kitty since she'd been dismissed as her maid, and her eyes pricked with unshed tears when Kitty studiously avoided her eyes. She was polite when Willow offered her congratulations after the ceremony, and dropped her a curtsy.

Their relationship had irrevocably changed and she'd never been more aware of the gulf between

279

mistress and servant.

She was quiet when she left on Gerard's arm, realizing something of her childhood had died. She experienced a few moments of insecurity, then put it behind her as she gazed at the house she'd grown to love. Her future had never been more clear to her.

Her destiny was to live her life within its walls, warm the bed of the man who was her husband and bear his children. She would grow old and die here. Her portrait and Gerard's would join the others in the gallery, and be forgotten in time.

The first son they produced from their union, and all the Lytton first-born sons who followed after, would perpetuate the process. Life was short when measured in portraits, so she'd better get on with it.

'Gerard,' she asked, 'where are the family records kept?'

'In the library.' He slanted her a questioning glance. 'Why do you ask?'

'I thought I might like to learn a little about your ancestors.' Spreading her fan to hide her nervousness, she gazed at him, her eyes seductively innocent. 'I do not wish to appear ignorant when our children ask about them.'

A smile lifted the corners of his mouth when he realized she was being delicate. 'You're no longer indisposed?'

'No.' Her voice was softly shy and a faint pink tint dawned on the creamy skin above the spread of the fan. 'Gerard...?' There was a tiny pleading note in her voice. 'I'm not as bold as I appeared yesterday. I cannot be other than apprehensive.'

'Your apprehension will be short-lived,' he promised, captivated by her guilelessness. 'My intention is to make your initiation a delight for you.' Brushing her fan aside, he gently kissed her, then unwittingly revealed his eagerness for the consummation by murmuring, 'If you'd care to accompany me to my chamber, I have a gift for you.'

'I cannot.' Her laugh made him aware she'd seen through his ruse. 'Edward is recovering from quinsy. Although his fever is abating and the soreness almost gone from his throat, I've promised his nurse I'll sit with him for a short time whilst she attends the wedding feast. Your gift must wait until later.'

'Perhaps I can read him a story.'

'It's strange this sudden interest you have in Edward.' She gave him a teasing grin. 'Does the thought of fatherhood appeal to you?'

'The thought of begetting that child has more priority at the moment,' he whispered, keeping his voice as teasing as hers. 'You're a fetching creature, my Lady Sommersley, and shall be properly brought to bed tonight. Then we shall discover who's the greater tease.'

Daphne de Vere, dying! Gerard gazed at the travel-weary messenger and tried to gauge his feelings. He was sorry for Daphne, of course. They'd been childhood playmates and once betrothed. Despite that, it was difficult for him to clearly recall her face. His eyes went back to the note.

281

Come on receipt of this note, Gerard. I have inform-
ation of the greatest importance to impart to you, and
little time left in which to do it. Daphne.

This could only be to tell him what he already
knew, that Edward was the product of his barely
remembered coupling with her on the night of
his wedding.

The note couldn't have arrived at a worst time.
About to retire, and having looked forward all
afternoon to sampling the delights of his wife's
flesh – he was now called at short notice to the
deathbed of a woman he'd come to despise.

Yet, it was imperative she confirmed his
relationship with Edward. If the child was about
to inherit Sheronwood, he intended to seek legal
guardianship. Having Daphne's signature on the
petition would greatly enhance his chances. It
would give him control of the Sheronwood
Estate until the boy came of age, and prevent the
marquess from plundering it.

'I'll leave within the hour,' he said, realizing he
had very little choice.

Neither the messenger nor his beast were in a
fit state to accompany him. He'd take the stallion. The horse was sound of wind, and able to
cover long distances at fast speed. He'd proved to
be most manageable now he'd been broken.
'Stable your horse, then find yourself a bed in the
servants' quarters.'

Breaking the news to Willow would be the hard
part. He only hoped his gift would mollify any
disappointment she might experience. She could
not fail to admire the finely wrought gold chain.

At intervals along its length, tiny diamonds twinkled like stars. The pearly clasp represented the moon.

Dangling it from his finger so it sparkled in the candle light, he made his way to her chamber, an apology framed on his lips.

'It's indeed a handsome gift,' she exclaimed. Clad only in a gauzy chemise, her hair was agleam with perfumed ripples.

Her face had been in shadow when he'd told her he could not stay, but she did not sound at all distressed when she murmured in a low voice, 'You will secure your gift about my person before you leave? I'd keep it close to me until your return.'

Touched by the sentiment, he fumbled the clasp open, and was about to place it around her neck when she whispered, 'I would have it about my waist.'

He experienced a sense of wonder when she undid the ribbons at her shoulders and shrugged the chemise free. It pooled around her ankles like a silken mist.

She still wore her hose, tied about her thighs with pale-pink ribbons. Her body was small-waisted, exquisitely formed, and tempting enough to rouse any red-blooded male.

He was no exception. His fingers trembled when he clasped the chain around her waist. The clasp fell naturally into the enclave of her navel. His eyes travelled downwards to her silky pelt, his throat drying at the sensuous picture she presented in her stockings and waist chain.

'Thank you, Husband,' she whispered, her

smile so virginal and pure that he had a primitive urge to throw her to the floor like some conquering soldier and ravish her until she screamed for mercy.

Did she really imagine he'd leave her yet? He could spare her an hour, at least. She belonged to him. He was ready for her, and she for him. Daphne could wait.

Sliding his hands over the bones of her hips to her softly rounded buttocks, he fell to his knees, drew her towards him and kissed the dusky citadel at the junction of her thighs in sweet assault.

Willow's eyes flew open in shocked surprise. She'd not imagined the sight of her naked body would incite such response from him. She tried not to panic at this excitingly intimate gesture.

His intention to rush to Daphne's side had brought such a tumult of jealousy into her heart she'd determined to stop him before she succumbed to the urge to shred the skin from his face with her bare hands. Instinctively, she'd used the only weapon she had to keep him at her side.

His reaction to her seemingly innocent overtures was exciting, her shock, an erotic urge that almost compelled her to open herself to his seeking tongue. Before she could, his hands slid up her body and gently pulled her forward until her breasts almost brushed his lips. It seemed her breasts anticipated his onslaught, for each nipple thrust towards the dewy curl of his tongue with an unbearable, erotic eagerness.

Even as a moan of protest left her lips her body reacted with thrilling abandonment, then the moan became a long drawn-out groan of pleasure. Her head arched backwards, then slowly came forward, her hair cascading about her husband's head.

All her inhibitions fled. This ecstasy of feeling was totally unexpected. Even as she wondered if it were normal to feel such joy in her nakedness, she revelled in it. Taking his face in her palms, she tilted it upwards and gazed into the passionate depths of his eyes.

'Is it shameful to feel such ... desire?'

He quivered. Half his face was in shadow, the other half etched with candle-glow. The dark hollows of his eyes reflected the flame and burned with white light. A pulse leaped against the restraint of her palm. He could have easily broken the barrier of her hands, but he just smiled. 'Nothing is shameful between husband and wife.'

'I wish to please you.' She hesitated, then giving a shy smile, added earnestly, 'I also wish to please myself. I did not think to find a man's body so attractive. I confess to having urges which may be immodest. If I touch you in the ways you touch me would that be too forward? I have no wish to shock you.' When his mouth curved into a smile, her face heated. 'Do not laugh at me,' she implored, lowering her eyes in confusion.

His lips gently brushed against each closed eyelid, as he whispered with great tenderness, 'I'm not laughing, my love.' His palms slid with sensuous warmth over each silken buttock when he pulled her on to his lap. 'I was smiling at your impatience. You're hardly a wife, yet you seek to experience everything at once.'

His words contained no censure, only dry amusement.

She giggled. 'That's true, Gerard.' Her fingers busied themselves with the fastenings at his throat, whilst his amused themselves exploring that which she usually sat upon. 'Will you not make yourself a little more comfortable?' she invited, wriggling a little when he tickled her. 'The state of nakedness is very pleasant.'

He gave a throaty chuckle. His hands cupped her buttocks as he lifted her against him and effortlessly rose to his feet in one fluid motion. He brushed his fingers lightly against the soft skin of her inner thighs, so near to the centre of her desire she felt exposed and helpless.

Resisting the urge to lift her legs and anchor herself around his waist she tensed slightly. That would put her most private part directly upon the very obvious swelling contained within his breeches.

Her newly found courage fled, and she stammered blushingly, 'You're causing me much confusion in this matter, Gerard.'

Dipping his head, he found her lips and murmured against them, 'For that I'm grateful my love. I'd not have the initiative taken from me on this occasion.' His hands made further invasion, and she seemed to have no choice when he lifted her a little higher, but to circle his body with her legs.

The power of his maleness was shockingly apparent, his strength pulsing against her, waiting to be unleashed upon her soft female body. A great lassitude filled her limbs and a trembling urge to be possessed rendered her weakly submissive.

Gerard would fill her, she thought. He would make her submit to his needs from this day forward. She knew she belonged to him, knew he could do with her as he wished. Perspiration dewed her as her body reacted with primitive joy to the knowledge. Her heart began to race so fast she thought it might fly from her chest. Laying her head against his shoulder in supplication, she whispered quietly, 'Pray be gentle. My courage has all but deserted me.'

The possessive kiss he gave her left her gasping for breath, and did nothing to reassure her. She was trembling when he lowered her to the bed. Half mesmerized by the glance that raked her body, yet feeling immodest, she sought to escape from the abandoned position he'd placed her in by drawing up her knees.

'Stay like that,' he growled, his glance slowly caressing her.

Her limbs seemed suspended in honey as she watched him deftly strip the clothes from his body. His skin was smooth and golden in the firelight, lightly furred across the chest and stomach, darkening to a wiry nest from whence his manhood sprouted in proud defiance of gravity.

He would hurt her, she decided, quivering a little. Her body could not support incursion from such a mighty weapon. Yet the part that would receive it, seemed to pulsate with its own invitation, and delighted in the prospect.

She'd expected him to enter her straight away, but he did not. Joining her on the bed he laid his thigh across her parted legs and lowered his lips to her nipples.

'*Ah ... sweet agony*,' she cried, as her tortured nipples swelled into his mouth. A soft, triumphant chuckle reached her ears. Then she experienced an insidious fluttering sensation between her thighs, like butterflies. First, she arched towards it seeking it out, then when she realized it was his soft exploration she blushed, and sought to bring her legs together.

'Enjoy it, My Lady,' he coaxed against her ear. 'I've no intention of letting you escape me now.'

Everything was sensation. His lips whispered loving words of intent, his hands and mouth carried it out. She began to anticipate him, her mouth opening to him, her tongue flirting with his, her breasts unashamedly competing for his touch, and her most private place...? He'd made it his own possession. She surrendered it willingly, arching the secret spring of her desire against his fingers in feverish symphony to his rhythm. Full of wild longings, she gasped out his name.

Willow was proving to be more passionate than Gerard had thought possible. Hardly able to contain himself, he watched her neck curve in abandoned ecstasy. 'Who's the tease now, My Lady?' he whispered against her ear. The breathless gasp she gave in reply, served only to inflame him more.

Dipping his head, he slid his tongue along the length of her body and made unerringly for the erectly sensitive tongue that nestled amongst the silk. She gave a long shuddering moan and tried to bring her thighs together.

He wanted her moist. When he felt her on the brink of shuddering dampness, he straddled her and gazed down upon her. His passion was like a wild beast captured inside him. It was time to unleash it.

Willow's eyes were closed, her head arched back, her hands abandoned on the pillow. She was panting from a partially opened mouth, and her tumbled hair lay in wild ringlets about her. He covered her hands with his own. She opened her eyes, imploring him in a purple, glistening blaze of sensuality as she gazed back at him.

'Gerard, my husband, take me unto you as wife.'

The whispered supplication shivered erotically in the air between them. Locking her eyes into his, he guided his arousal into her velvet citadel and nudged himself just inside her. She whimpered slightly when he encountered resistance. Closing his mouth over hers he pushed a little harder.

Then something totally unexpected happened. Her stockinged legs clasped around his waist and she deliberately arched herself against him. The resistance gave, he slid into her and felt her muscles close around him.

'*Sweet Jesus!* he whispered, momentarily wondering if he'd ever experienced such a sensuous woman. She was trembling beneath him, utterly abandoned to the pleasure she experienced. Gently murmuring his name, she gripped him when he slid away from her, as if determined to keep him inside her.

He'd meant to take his time, but her action excited him beyond endurance. He moved against her, into her, aware she was encouraging him with small cries.

Then she was rising against him, moving with him, faster and faster, into a chaos created by their peaking passions. They reached an explosive climactic fulfilment together, her long shuddering gasp matched by his cry of triumph when she captured the hot flood of his passion deep inside her.

He collapsed against her, his heart racing like a wild creature, and booming within the cavern of his chest. Her fingers began stroking his hair in a most loving manner, gentling him, like she did her horse. The soft arches of her feet caressed against his buttocks, then came to rest upon his calves in the hollows behind his knees.

It was several seconds before his breathing quietened enough to raise himself up and look at her. Her face had the sultry softness of a woman who'd been loved well. He smiled, pleased with both her and himself. 'That was not too onerous a duty, was it?'

'Indeed, not.' She'd not forgotten how to blush, for her cheeks stained a delicate rose. 'You're pleased with me, Gerard?'

Pleased with her? It was an understatement of the highest order. Rolling, over on to his back he playfully took her with him. 'I'll tell you that a little later.'

'You've decided not to go to London, then.' She tried to keep the note of triumph from her voice, then wished she'd not spoken at all when he gazed at her with regret. It was too soon to leave her after such loving, but Gerard had no choice. Pushing her from him, he rolled from the bed and picked up his clothes. 'I must.' He leaned over, gently kissing her lips before heading towards the connecting door.

'Rodgers?' he called, closing it behind him

His servant was asleep in a chair, but sprang awake when Gerard nudged him with his foot. 'Go and tell one of the stable boys to saddle the stallion. I'm called urgently to London and will not be back for a few days. You're not required to accompany me.'

Rodgers didn't turn a hair at his naked form. Taking the clothes from his master's hands, he placed them tidily over a chair then laid out his riding attire before hurrying to do his bidding.

Nellie, who sometimes wandered when the moon was full, watched Gerard leave. Her eyes glinted with tears. Drawn by her mistress's cries, she'd watched through a crack in the door whilst the viscount had inflicted his vile punishment on her.

Crooning softly to herself, she swore she would find some way to avenge her.

Gerard was thankful for the moonlight. Showers had dampened the road, keeping the dust to a minimum. There had not been enough rain to churn it into mire, and the going was easy. The stallion was fresh, and wanted to gallop. Keeping him down to a canter, they covered the miles effortlessly.

He'd been on the road for an hour before he suspected he was being followed. It was nothing he could put his finger on. The stallion's ears kept pricking towards the rear, as if he heard another horse. Now and again, Gerard thought he heard a muffled snicker, but the sound of his creaking leathers drowned it out.

Remembering his brother's assault, he decided to take no chances. He pulled into the shadow of a tree, drew his sword and waited. Sure enough, the sound of hoofbeats came to his ears. The horse and rider had been keeping pace with him and was travelling at a fast canter, its rider making no attempt at concealment.

Nevertheless, he intended to challenge the rider. If he was about legitimate business he might prove a suitable companion for the road. He waited until the rider was a few yards away, then came out from behind the tree. 'Rein in your horse so I can take a look at you,' he said harshly.

He cursed as a yelp of fright reached his ears. Drawn to a sudden stop, the rider's horse reared, slashed at the air with its front legs and whinnied so loudly his own mount gave a few stiff-legged bucks before settling down again.

'You addle-brained wolf-hound,' Willow hissed, still trying to control her prancing horse. 'I thought you were a highwayman.'

'Lucky for you I was not.' Rattled by her sudden appearance, he retreated into anger. 'What the hell are you doing here?'

'I should imagine it's perfectly obvious.' She sounded as angry as he. 'I'm coming with you.'

His mouth drew into a thin line. 'Are you, indeed?'

In the moonlight, Willow saw the haughty lines of her husband's jaw tighten and his nostrils flare with anger.

'I think not, madam. You'll return to Lytton at once.'

'By myself?'

'You got here by yourself,' he pointed out.

'But I was not alone. You were within shouting distance, Gerard.'

Her twisted reasoning did nothing to improve his mood. She'd presented him with a quandary. If he took her back, there was no guarantee she'd not follow him again, and he'd waste valuable time. On the other hand, to insist she return by herself would put her in peril. She'd known that before she started out.

'It seems you have the winning hand.' He gave an exasperated sigh. 'Why did you not stay in bed where I left you?'

'And languish like a love-sick mistress who awaits your favour? I refuse to be treated like some scullery maid you've just tumbled.'

Her words shocked him, as did the watery shadow of her smile. Her vulnerability was all too apparent to him when she drew in a shuddering breath and said in quiet desperation, 'I'm well aware that you love Daphne de Vere, but I'll not stand meekly by and allow you to go from my bed to hers whenever she crooks her little finger.'

'Daphne de Vere is dying.'

'Oh!'

She looked so stricken, he instantly regretted his bald statement. 'I should have told you the reason for Daphne's note. I need her signature to gain legal guardianship of Edward. He'll inherit Sheronwood and its title before too long. He must be protected from your father until he comes of age. That's her wish.'

'I'll return to Lytton immediately.' If Daphne, was dying, there was no need to fear she'd come between them. 'I'm so sorry, Gerard. The situation cannot be easy for you.'

'You cannot return to Lytton alone.' He gave her clothing a wry grin. 'Keep yourself well covered, and do not speak unless you have to. We'll pass you off as a boy should the need arise.'

'Thank you, Gerard.'

'Save your thanks until we reach London and the blisters on your rear are the size of hens' eggs.' He grinned at her. 'You're the one who's addle-brained if you think I love Daphne de Vere.' Closing the distance between them, he leaned across and kissed her. 'Let us go, Wife. Keep pace with me and we'll be in London by noon.' He could have made the distance faster by himself, but didn't bother telling her that. The ride would be punishment enough.

Willow's thighs ached, her spine felt as if it was about to snap, and her hands would not uncurl from the reins. She was so fatigued she couldn't summon the energy to dismount. Giving Gerard a glance of mute appeal, she groaned as he lifted her from her horse.

He bore evidence of strain himself. Circe and the stallion displayed none of their usual spirit when they were led away to be cooled down.

'La, Gerard. You're a hard taskmaster. You pushed me to the limit.'

Her attempt at humour brought a tender smile

to his lips. He'd never met anyone quite so game, nor quite so stubborn. Carrying his weary burden into the house, he ordered a bath to be filled, then gave instructions to the housekeeper to find someone to act as maid to his lady.

He stripped the garments from her body himself, then, when her bath was prepared, lowered her into the warm water. She smelled of perspiration, horse, and the stale aftermath of their loving. Her face was caked in dust. He grinned when he noted the chain of diamonds still clasped around her waist, and tried to ignore his erotic thoughts as he kneaded the knots from her shoulders and listened to her blissful sighs.

He kissed her briefly when an elderly maid came into the room, chuckling to himself when she gave him a shocked look.

'Get some sleep, my love,' he advised, kissing her a second time for good measure. 'I'll see you at dinner.'

Gerard didn't take long over his toilet. He'd been accustomed to fend for himself in Virginia, and within the hour headed out on foot, washed, shaved and cleanly – though not richly – attired. The streets were teeming with footpads and pickpockets, and he didn't intend to attract attention.

His first stop was at St James's coffee house, where he acquainted himself with the latest gossip. Then on to Daphne's house, situated half a mile away.

There was a sense of familiarity about the streets for him. A circle of people shouted encouragement at two bloodied cocks fighting to the death. A chained bear was being prodded with sticks, the street urchins darting within inches of its lethal claws and maddened glare for coins. Outside an inn, two men were exchanging blows in a makeshift ring. The rotting carcass of a dead dog was sprawled nearby, its belly bloated, rats cannibalizing its flesh. The stench was awful. He placed a handkerchief over his nose as he made his way through it all.

He was shocked by Daphne's appearance. The once robust girl had become a shadow. Her unhealthy appearance was not enhanced by the thick layer of white lead paint, heavily rouged cheeks and outlandish black patches. Dark bruises were evident against the slack, dry skin of her neck.

He wondered what sort of animal her current lover was to inflict such tokens of love upon an ailing woman. She looked grotesque as she reclined against the pillows. He experienced an involuntary recoil.

'Madam.' He managed to smile as he waved her attendants away.

'Gerard?' Daphne's voice was so weak he had to bend forward to hear her. 'I knew you'd come.' Her effort to speak brought a spasm of coughing. The handkerchief she held to her mouth came away frothed with blood. 'You must stop him, Gerard.'

'Stop him?' Pity engulfed him as he saw her fever-bright eyes. 'Of whom do you speak, Daphne?'

'The marquess.' As she sipped at the water and brandy mixture he held to her lips, her voice grew stronger. 'The papers for custodianship of both Sheronwood and Edward are lodged with the King. They'll be returned to my lawyer for your signature on the morrow.'

How had she managed to get priority on such a matter? 'Come closer,' she whispered, before he could ponder on it further. 'I've much of importance to tell you, and little time left to do it in.'

Her voice had a dry rustling sound, like fallen leaves stirred by the wind. He tried not to be shocked at what he heard, and was half inclined to disbelieve the litany of accusations she made against the marquess.

Daphne vacillated between past and present, sometimes referring to times when they were children, then in the same breath describing the abuse to which the marquess had subjected her. How much of it was the imagination of a fevered brain, he could not ascertain. Despite his disgust, he could not hide his fascination.

Anger burned in him when she told him of the price on Willow's virtue. 'He's tripled the purse since you returned from America. She will be game for every rake in town should you bring her back to London. Be careful, Gerard. The marquess has no conscience, and seeks to provoke a duel.'

'He'll not succeed in making me challenge,' he said drily. 'I'm under a sacred oath to my father.' But that does not mean I cannot accept a challenge from him, he was thinking.

'He may push the issue. He's under the impression you fathered Edward. He's forced me to sign a document validating his suspicion and has

297

used it to disinherit Edward.'

He started. 'I received a letter from your husband intimating the same thing.' He gazed at her with dispassionate eyes. 'I'll have the truth from you before you die, Daphne. If Edward is my son, I need to know it.'

She managed a smile. 'Damn your arrogance, Gerard. How can Edward be your son? His natal day is eleven months after my marriage. Besides...' The scornful laugh tripping from her tongue, induced another coughing fit. 'The drug you were fed rendered you impotent.'

Relief took precedence over the pique his pride momentarily suffered. 'Then Edward is truly a child of your marriage?'

Daphne shuddered. 'Truly, he is not. My husband preferred to slake his appetites with men. It was only his temper he expended on me.' The disgust on his face drove Daphne to laughter, and another spell of coughing racked her body. This time it took her longer to recover.

'You are a decent and honest man, Gerard, and I thank God for it. If I was free to tell you who fathered Edward I would.' Her voice became a sigh. 'I can only tell you this: Edward's sire holds high office, and cannot place him under his direct protection. You understand?'

'Only too well.' Supporting his head in his hands, he was too stunned to think of anything else to say.

Her hand covered his. 'I hope you're happy with the child you were forced to wed?'

'She is no child.' There was something slightly obscene about Daphne discussing his marriage, but he knew she had not the breath to waste on idle conversation. 'What's your interest in the matter, Daphne?' he asked more gently.

'The marriage was of my doing.' She placed a wasted hand upon his sleeve when he gave an incredulous gasp. 'It was the only thing I could think of to save her from the fate her father had in store for her. She was to be broken by Simon Carsewell, then sent to France. There, she would have become the plaything of the highest bidder.'

His face paled at the thought of Willow as a victim of such licentious company. A violent shudder racked him.

'Willow was such a wild and innocent little thing,' Daphne, continued. 'She was starved of affection. Her expectations of her father were cruelly shattered when she met him.' Her eyes fluttered shut. 'The marquess saw her marriage to you as sport once I convinced him she carried her mother's dark powers in her blood. For me, it was a fitting way to punish him for what he'd taken from me. Willow is his blood; she'll inherit everything when he dies. His fortune will end up in Lytton hands, now.' Her voice faded away to a sigh. 'I loved you, Gerard, but it was too late for me. I knew you'd come to care for her.'

'I'm beginning to,' he admitted gruffly. 'But she's set my notion of womanly attributes on its heels.'

He remembered the sketch Willow had given him to deliver and pressed it into Daphne's hands. Her face lit up with tearful pleasure when she examined it. Once again, he was forced to consider if Willow's blood could possibly be contaminated. So far, she'd shown no signs of being possessed – a satisfied grin came and went – except by himself!

Daphne was lying against the pillows, exhausted now, the sketch held against her cheek. For the first time, he realized she was a victim of circumstance. She'd never deserved his condemnation. Thinking she slept, he was moved to kiss the painted parchment of her cheek.

'Guard Edward well,' she whispered. 'He'll never be safe whilst the marquess lives.' Tears began to course down her cheeks. 'Leave me now. Tell my nurse to return and make me comfortable. I wish to rest.'

When he was outside and gulping in a lungful of air, he realized the odour of imminent death lingered about Daphne.

'You did not tell me your father made sport of your virginity?'

Willow looked beautiful in a pale-green embroidered petticoat, the frilled overskirt gathered into bows. They were playing chess, and had reached a position where neither could escape without placing themselves in great peril.

'I assumed that was why you duelled with the officer from the King's Regiment.' She grinned and made her move. 'Check.'

'And mate.' Gerard watched her small white teeth bite upon her bottom lip. 'The marquess has tripled the purse.'

The laughter left her eyes. 'That's ridiculous. You've already claimed your rights as my husband. Besides' – her eyelashes fluttered gently, and the amusement returned – 'I know I'm unworldly, but surely my favours cannot be worth so much.'

'They are priceless to me.' He gave her a grin, then frowned when he saw the error he'd made on the board. 'He has convinced himself you would be repugnant to me. I don't like the thought of you being subject to the attention of every rake in town, but I cannot challenge them all.'

'If you claim the purse, you will not have to.'

Her queen found an unassailable opening and he capitulated. The notion was so startling it robbed him of breath. A grin flirted at the corner of his mouth as the idea took root. 'You have a devious mind, My Lady.'

'Not as devious as yours, I hope.' Her smile was seductive as her eyes drifted up to meet his, her voice breathless with anticipation.

'Oh?' He met her mischievous gaze with feigned puzzlement.

'A pedlar came to the door when you were out. I ... I bought you a gift.' Her composure cracked and she blushed. 'I've placed it behind your cushion.'

Two seconds later he gazed at the silk cords in his hands, grinning as he remembered the episode in the pavilion and the promise he'd made that day.

Never dreaming she'd be so compliant to his wishes, he gazed at her in delighted surprise, made a couple of loops, then leaned forward and placed them around her wrists.

'Come, madam,' he whispered, tightening them as, with a show of delightful reluctance, she rose to her feet. 'I'll teach you what desire is all about. You'll enjoy this lesson.'

'You will not hurt me,' she whispered, laying her head against his shoulder in sudden confusion.

It was all part of the game.

'Not if you submit to my wishes,' he assured her.

She would submit, and enjoy her submission. He had no intention of allowing her to do otherwise, and she didn't expect it.

CHAPTER ELEVEN

The marquess had not heard that his daughter and her husband were in London, nor had he issued an invitation for them to attend his assembly. When they advanced into the salon his eyes narrowed speculatively and the momentary lull in the conversation was followed by an excited buzz of talk.

Pocketing his winnings, Charles Addison detached himself from the gaming tables and hurried forward to greet his friend.

'Had I known you were in London I would have called upon you.' His glance swept admiringly over Willow. 'Your bride is exquisite. Her bone structure's superb.'

'Ever the doctor, Charles.' Though he laughed, Gerard's eyes were watchful. 'Can you never look at a woman without commenting on some part of her anatomy?'

'You know I can, but with this one, I have the feeling you'd call me out.'

'You could be right.' His glance lazily roved around the salon to search for people he was acquainted with. There were several who could be counted on as friends.

His glance sharpened on Simon Carsewell, who was staring openly at Willow. His exploits included the drunken rape of a young seamstress in France, and the murder of the father who'd tried to defend her. His companion was a cur of a man who feasted on his leftovers. Both were in debt to the marquess, and hung about him like fawning dogs.

'I've heard rumours, Charles. Are they true?'

Charles knew exactly to what he referred. He gazed warningly at him.

Gerard's mouth creased in a suggestion of a smile. 'Lady Sommersley's aware her father makes sport of her.'

'You do not intend to call him out? He's shot to death three men in the last six months.'

Gerard smiled reassuringly at Willow when she anxiously entwined her fingers through his and whispered, 'You'll remember your oath to your father?'

'I promise you'll not become a widow just yet, my love.' His eyes filled with contempt when they met those of the marquess. The room held a collective breath when he spoke loudly enough for the man to hear. 'I believe there's a wager concerning my wife. Would anyone care to tell me about it?'

303

Simon Carsewell swaggered forward. 'My pleasure, dear Viscount. The marquess has set a purse of three hundred guineas upon her virtue.' He leered at Willow. 'I'd gladly pay five hundred for the privilege.'

Shocked whispers followed the insult. Contempt flamed in Willow's eyes and Carsewell took a hasty step backward when she hissed, 'I will cut your eyes from your poxy head and grind them under my heel if you come one step closer.'

Gerard's fingers locked round hers as she made an involuntary movement towards her pocket for her dagger, though he was tempted to allow her to carry out her threat. 'You may save your money, Carsewell.' He didn't move so much as an inch, but the muscles tightened along his arm, and Willow knew how much it cost him to keep his temper under control. 'We're not here to sell, we're here to collect.'

Someone laughed, a derisive guffaw that was picked up by the crowd.

Charles grinned at the easing of tension in the room. It was inconceivable his friend would have left such a prize intact.

'You were not invited here.' Dislike glittered in the eyes of the marquess. 'Take the she-devil's spawn, Lytton. Get out, before I have you both thrown into the gutter.'

There were a couple of hisses, then the room erupted in a cacophony of stamping feet. When the noise died down somebody shouted, 'Shame on you, Lynchcross. Pay the Viscount.'

'I'll see the son of a whore in hell first.'

Charles sucked in his breath. The bounds of

acceptable behaviour had been breached, and his friend was not noted for his restraint.

But Gerard merely said to the room at large, 'I'm here to collect a debt. We all suspect of course, that the marquess is the lowest of creatures. I hadn't realized he was also a cheat, and without honour.'

The marquess flushed. 'Take care, sir. I'll not be insulted in my own home.'

'Your home?' Though he smiled, the tone of his voice echoed the contempt he felt. 'I understand it was paid for dearly.' He gazed round at the mesmerized crowd. 'The marquess earns his funds, and takes his pleasures, from the children he kidnaps to amuse his depraved companions abroad.'

He picked up a glass and sniffed its contents as a shocked murmur came from the company. 'The wine you enjoy is stolen from the inheritance of a four-year-old boy whose mother is dying. He is the son of Daphne de Vere.'

'Shame!' someone cried out. One or two people drifted towards the door. Scenting a juicy scandal, most stayed to see what the outcome would be. Without exception, every one of them hoped to see the marquess bested.

'Take back what you said, or I'll call you out.'

Willow made a tiny, anguished sound in her throat when she realized what he was about.

A dangerous grin slid across Gerard's face. 'I'll see you in hell first.'

The marquess looked bored. 'Have it your own way, Lytton. Pistols at dawn.'

'The choice of weapons is mine, I believe.' He smiled as the marquess's head jerked up. 'My

305

preference is swords.'

Behind him, Charles cursed. 'I'll act as your second. Mayhap my stitching skills will come in handy.'

Wariness came into the marquess's eyes. Raising his cuff, he made an aside to Simon Carsewell, who nodded.

'Please, Gerard,' Willow whispered, trembling against him with fear. 'Retract your words. None can beat my father in a duel.'

'Hush, angel,' he said tenderly. 'I know what I'm doing.'

'Swords it is.' The marquess feigned a yawn. 'We'll meet in my stable-yard on the morrow. Now that's settled, you may leave.'

'You owe me three hundred guineas, I believe.' Gerard's expression was lethal now. 'I hope you've no intention of refusing to honour the debt.'

Taking a purse from his belt, the marquess threw it at Gerard's feet. 'I hope the slut was worth it,' he sneered.

'That's not a topic for discussion.' Taking her hand, Gerard pressed the purse into her palm and closed her fingers round it.

His eyes smiled into hers, but the icy fury in their depths made her shiver when he said, 'This should support your orphans for some time to come.'

The assembly applauded when they made a dignified exit from the room. Behind them, the crowd began to lambast the marquess. Gerard grinned. The marquess would not be welcome in society drawing-rooms after tonight.

Rising slowly to his feet, the marquess pushed

through the crowd of jeering people, looking neither to left or right. Rage fermented in his heart as one or two of his guests cuffed him from the safety of the crowd. Apart from Simon Carsewell, who followed him like the mongrel dog he was, he hadn't a friend left in London. Gerard Lytton would pay dearly for what he'd done this night.

Charles followed his friend out, and was just in time to see Willow buckle at the knees.

'Hell!' Such alarm coloured Gerard's voice that Charles stepped forward and opened the carriage door before the driver could descend from his seat.

'It's just a faint,' he reassured him, after checking Willow's pulse and propping her neatly turned ankles on Gerard's lap so the blood would reach her head. 'What do you expect after what you put her through? Are you mad, Gerard? If you intend to commit suicide, a ball through the heart is the easier way to go.'

'Quite possibly. I cannot hope to out-shoot him, but word has it the marquess has lost his edge when it comes to sword-play. Did you see his eyes? He was plotting something. I've a feeling he'll send his dogs to murder me in my bed tonight.'

'Then your lady must be protected.' Charles grinned. 'I know someone who would give her sanctuary, but I must warn you, she and her sister entertain ... in a discreet sort of way.'

Gazing down at Willow, who seemed to be regaining her wits, Gerard gave a wry smile. 'Placing her in a house of ill-repute is better than jeopardizing her life, but I'll never hear the last of it.'

'She need never find out if you're quick.' Charles took a bottle from his pocket. 'A harmless, but strong sleeping draught. Your good lady will be back in her own bed before she wakes.'

Simon Carsewell was thinking of the woman with the violet eyes, as he and his companion gained entrance to the Lytton residence.

His tongue slid over his lips. After they'd slit the throat of her husband he'd have free rein with her. Her debauchery would be sweeter had Lytton been allowed to live long enough to witness it, but he dare not risk it.

'Fool,' he hissed, when his companion stumbled against some furniture. But all remained quiet, except for the sound of snoring coming from the upper regions.

'Lytton is an uncommonly loud sleeper,' the other man said with a quiet laugh. 'It's civil of him to guide us to his chamber.'

Not only was it civil, they found the door invitingly ajar and a candle left burning to light their way. There was an outline of two figures under the sheets. One turned over on its back when a floorboard creaked. Momentarily, the snoring stopped, then started again, louder than ever.

'The viscount is yours,' Carsewell whispered to his companion, removing the sock from about his neck to use as a gag. 'If you make it quick I'll let you take a turn with the woman.'

Cold steel pressed against Carsewell's neck. He

froze, as a laconic voice drawled, 'I'd drop your weapon if I were you, friend.'

As the other man spun towards the door, someone stepped from behind it and pressed a pistol against his temple. He swore, then opening his hand, allowed his dagger to thud to the floor.

Two figures rose from the bed. One was General Robert Marriot, cousin to Lady Edwina, the other a young subaltern. The subaltern was wearing one of Lady Edwina's voluminous night robes, and a lacy cap.

'I'll mention your brave deed at the regimental dinner, Oswald,' the general said with a perfectly straight face.

'I'd rather it didn't get out, General.' The subaltern almost panicked in his haste to divest himself of the garments. 'I'll never live it down.'

'Personally, I thought you looked quite fetching.' The general's voice was dry as he gazed at Gerard and Charles. 'What say you, gentlemen?'

'I prefer my women with fewer whiskers,' Charles drawled, the point of his knife etching a thin red line into Carsewell's neck when he dared to move.

'Go and tell the escort we're bringing the prisoners down, Oswald. Tell them to shoot to kill if either of them tries to escape.' Robert Marriot gazed with scorn at the two men. 'I'm taking you cowards back to the barracks for questioning. The answers you give will determine whether your punishment be imprisonment or hanging. Is that understood?'

The general was pleased with the outcome of affair. He'd been embarrassed by the Hugh

309

Macbride episode. Although he'd transferred the young man to a posting abroad, he needed to redeem himself in Earl Lytton's eyes.

Willow showed no sign of restlessness when Gerard went to fetch her from her place of safety.

Later, when he'd clumsily acted as maid to his lady, and successfully removed every item of clothing from her body except her chemise, he flopped her on to the bed and stared down at her.

She was invitingly relaxed, her breasts thrusting ripely against the material of the chemise. His arousal came, hot and strong. A grin played around his mouth.

Charles had promised she'd sleep until dawn, and he was glad she'd not be awake to worry about the duel until it was over. But if he'd misjudged the marquess he'd not live to enjoy her charms again. It didn't seem fair to leave her unloved. Perhaps he could give her an infant to remember him by this night – an heir for Lytton.

The hastily contrived excuse banished any twinge of conscience he may have entertained. Shrugging out of his clothes, he pulled the chemise up over her head and bent his lips to her breasts. Her reaction was drowsily sensual, and he smiled.

'Sweet dreams, angel,' he whispered.

The sun was high when she woke. Her limbs felt strangely lethargic as she stretched her naked body against the sheets. Where was her chemise? A memory of delicious lovemaking flitted into her mind, then slipped elusively away.

Aware of a tender sensation between her thighs, she guessed Gerard had taken his enjoyment of her. Strange how she could not clearly remember it. She must have fallen soundly asleep after the ride to London, because all she could remember was coming out of her father's house and...?

'*Gerard!*'

Screaming his name as her memory returned, she scrambled from the bed, pulled her robe around her body and rushed to the partially open window.

The scene below was so normal she couldn't believe it.

A cart trundled by, piled high with household goods of every type for sale. A woman hurried past, a basket of silvery fish balanced on her head. Several honking geese were driven past by a grubby-looking boy with a stick. Glancing up at the window, he gave her a cheeky smile.

She wanted to scream at them all to go home – tell them her husband was, in all likelihood, lying dead at that very minute in the stable-yard of the marquess. She did not want life to go on without him.

A sob gathered in her throat. Turning from the window, she was about to throw herself on the bed and weep in despair when she saw him leaning nonchalantly against the doorway.

'You're alive,' she scolded, her relief a palpable thing. A smile eclipsed her frown. 'What miracle is this, Gerard? You're still alive.'

'So it seems.' His voice was drily amused. 'Half of London turned out to witness my demise. They were sadly disappointed. Your father set sail for France last night.'

'He fled?' She scowled again. 'I knew he'd be a craven coward when put to the test.'

'You'd rather I'd fought him and died?' he teased.

'Indeed not.' Closing the gap between them she slid into his arms and laid her head against his warmly beating heart. 'I had no qualms you'd best him in a fair fight.'

'Then it was not you I heard shout my name with such fright?'

She plucked from the air what seemed a perfectly feasible excuse. 'My father is full of trickery. I slept so soundly, I thought he may have drugged me somehow, and killed you while you slept.'

Though shaken, he grinned at her ingenious tale. She'd never know how close to the truth she'd come. 'Then who do you think took possession of your senses and made your dreams so sweet?'

'Indeed? I had no dreams worthy of note.' Her eyes flirted with his most outrageously. 'Are you sure it was not you who were dreaming?'

'Perhaps I should refresh your memory, wench,' he said with a grin. 'I have ten minutes to tumble you on the bed before I need go out.'

'Ten minutes?'

Gliding to the door she turned the key in the lock then, with unerring aim, hurled it through the open window into the strip of garden below. Dropping her robe to the floor, she smiled so seductively through her sleep-tumbled hair, every thought was erased from his mind except his need to love her.

'It seems you're my prisoner, Gerard.'

If half of London had turned up to see him slain by the marquess, it seemed the other half had gathered beneath the window to watch him climb down the front of the house to retrieve the key.

Knowing it would be common gossip in the coffee houses by noon, he decided to give them their money's worth. Urged on by the violet-eyed woman laughing at him from the window, and the cheers of the small crowd gathered below, he climbed back up again.

Daphne de Vere had died during the night, her lawyer informed Gerard when the documents were signed and exchanged. As the guardian of the young Marquess de Vere, what were his instructions regarding the London property?

The house had been built by Christopher Wren for Daphne's father. Daphne had been fond of it, and he knew she'd want it kept for her son.

'Arrange for everything except the furniture to be packed and conveyed to Sheronwood. The house can be leased, the income invested until Edward is of age. I will give you the name of my lawyer.'

He leaned forward and smiled when the lawyer's face adopted a resigned expression. 'Actually, I see no reason why you should not continue to manage the estate. If the marchioness trusted you with it, that's good enough for me. It will ensure there's no conflict of interest.'

'His Majesty the King, who sponsored the child at his christening, wishes to provide for the boy's education. His Majesty has placed a sum of gold at your disposal. He would be assured of your utmost discretion in the matter.'

'I suggest the gold be inventoried as part of the estate,' Gerard murmured. 'It can then be drawn upon without inviting comment.'

There was approval in the lawyer's eyes when the business was concluded. 'The marchioness showed good sense in her choice of wardship for her son. She always spoke warmly of you, and would have been glad you survived to attend this meeting.'

'You had your doubts?' Remembering how fast news travelled in London, Gerard gave a rueful grin.

'The duel was mentioned at Child's coffee house this morning.'

'Then you will know my opponent did not put in an appearance,' he growled. 'He fled to France.'

'I believe there's a warrant issued for his arrest.' The lawyer held out his hand. 'Be vigilant whilst he's still at large. He does not forget a grudge.'

Gerard didn't need the man's warning. There was an uneasy feeling gnawing at his gut, as if he'd forgotten something important. He puzzled over it in vain, then realized what it was as soon as he reached the house and read General Marriot's note.

The ship on which the marquess sailed intended docking at Poole to pick up cargo. He remembered the sobbing voice echoing through the walls of Sheronwood, and the boarded-up cellar. Everything clicked into place.

314

'Willow!' he shouted. 'I leave for Lytton as soon as possible. Edward is in grave danger.'

He was thankful she was not the type of woman who was subject to the vapours. Appearing at the top of the stairs she said simply, 'I'm coming with you.'

This time, it was Willow who urged them on when Gerard would have stopped to let her rest. She knew her sore muscles would stiffen if she stopped and she'd be unable to mount again.

Lytton House came into sight at the break of day. A mist was rising from the lake. The sun spread its light across the land, shimmering on the dew with red and gold flashes. Beyond the house, the hills gently sloped towards the sky, retaining their mysterious shadows.

Their minds found a certain synergy as they gazed at each other. Lytton had a timelessness about it, and together they experienced the pull of its presence.

'It never fails to awe me,' Gerard murmured, entwining her fingers with his.

The sun gradually banished the shadows. Like a carpet, the day unrolled over the land, marching over the drab shadows to push them away.

The grey slate roof of Lytton warmed to blue, the hills came alive with sheep and cattle. Dew-drenched grass gave up moisture in vapours of mist that writhed upwards to disappear into the clouds. It seemed no time before daisies, primroses, and buttercups opened to make the day golden-hued, as if they'd been painted on by the sun.

Two familiar figures detached themselves from the stables. Willow smiled, feeling as though she were truly home at last. 'Look,' she whispered. 'There's Jeffrey with James.'

They rode forward to greet them. Instead of a smile of welcome, Jeffrey took one look at her and scowled fiercely at his brother.

'Look at the state of your lady and feel ashamed,' he said in a cold voice. 'She and her mount have been pushed past exhaustion.'

'Nay Jeffrey,' she whispered. 'It's unfair to blame Gerard when I set the pace. Edward is in danger. His mother is dead, and my father means to harm him.'

The colour ebbed from Jeffrey's face, leaving it ashen. 'Thank God I didn't let the marquess's servant take him.'

'He's here?' Her heart began to thump alarmingly. 'My father sent an envoy for Edward?'

'The servant arrived yesterday at dusk. He showed me a letter from the marquess claiming guardianship. It demanded he be released into the servant's care.'

'And you refused?' Despite his exhaustion, Gerard grinned with new vigour.

'Of course.' Jeffrey's voice had a new maturity to it. 'Edward is ill, a recurrence of the quinsy. Doctor Tansy said he may not be moved until the fever subsides.'

'Thank God you're of good sense.' Gerard's smile was ignored by his brother. 'A lot is going on of which you're unaware.'

'Then perhaps you'd care to enlighten me.' Jeffrey's voice softened when he looked at Willow.

'If you do not take her home to rest, I'll do it for you, Brother.'

'We'll talk on your return,' he promised, exchanging a glance with James. 'Keep vigilant if the marquess is abroad in these parts. He's not fussy which of the Lyttons he kills.'

'I most certainly will,' Jeffrey said agreeably. 'There's a great deal I wish to say to you, and twenty men of his ilk will not be allowed to prevent me.'

'And none of it good, I imagine,' Gerard muttered with a sigh as they moved off.

'Why is he so annoyed with you?' Willow puzzled. 'His rudeness is out of character.' Anxiously, she gazed at him. 'He must be ailing. Perhaps Edward's quinsy is contagious. You'll forgive him, Gerard?'

'How can I *not* forgive him?' He managed a weary grin. 'Not only is he my brother, his emotions towards you are complicated by his youth. He'll think better of his outburst before long, and apologize.'

'I was hoping you'd overlooked his continuing regard for me.' Her voice was low. 'Though I've seen little of him these days, I've tried to treat him only with sisterly affection.'

'I know.' His smile warmed her heart. 'First love is painful, especially when that love is not reciprocated. You'll occupy a special niche in his heart for the rest of his life.'

And what of your heart, Husband? Will I ever occupy a special niche there? she wanted to ask.

She thought of Caroline's unrequited love for Ambrose. She understood now why her predecessor had risked everything to plot her rival's down-fall. She would do exactly the same to win the regard of Gerard, whom she'd come to love with all her heart.

Gerard should have guessed the marquess wouldn't have quietly taken no for an answer. Edward's nurse was discovered two hours later by the footman who'd been sent to the nursery to find out why breakfast hadn't been collected.

The nurse and nursery maid were bound and gagged. They were almost hysterical when released. He had to speak sharply to get any sense out of them. He blessed Willow for keeping calm. It was good to have someone by his side who did not panic in a crisis.

He was thankful to find Edward hadn't even woken – he'd been dosed with laudanum to soothe his throat and help him sleep – but of the boy there was no sign.

He left the nursery staff to their weeping and called the family together. After informing them of the situation regarding Edward, he sent a messenger to Dorchester to call in the regiment.

He was disturbed to learn from his father of another death involving a raven: the priest who'd officiated at Kitty and Brian's wedding. He considered it prudent to inform the family of the similar deaths, and warn them to be on guard.

He didn't consider it necessary to tell Sapphire she'd been named by the Wesleyan preacher; it would serve no good. But he recalled Willow's link with the occult through her mother, and shivered.

Later, when he intended to talk to his father alone, he found Sapphire in attendance. Usually, she'd rise and leave with no more than a greeting when he came in. On this occasion, she turned to him and said quietly, 'You're worried about the raven. Rest assured, Willow is not the cause of its manifestation.'

It struck him then, that her voice, though French accented, had the same lilting timbre as Willow's. 'How did you know of my suspicions?'

'I picked up your thoughts.'

It was the first time she'd addressed him directly. His senses were assaulted with a strange quiver of familiarity. She brought Willow into his mind, and he had a strong urge to look upon her face.

'A coincidence,' he said lightly.

Sapphire exchanged a glance with his father that left him feeling excluded. They had the familiarity of lovers, and it shocked him.

'You doubt me?' She laid a small hand lightly on his sleeve. 'You were thinking you'd like to see my face. I remind you of Willow, do I not?'

'You remind me very much of her.' The smile he'd been about to give, faded, as his gaze absently took in her form. The woman was petite, and neatly made like Willow. She even walked like Willow. His eyes narrowed suspiciously. 'Who are you?'

She drew the veil back from her face. 'Look upon my countenance and you'll see the truth written on it.'

The huge, violet eyes and small turned-up nose left him in no doubt. 'Why do you hide your face from the world?' he observed. Then he frowned, and in a voice suddenly harsh, 'And why did you feign death and desert your baby daughter? She deserved better than to be left at the mercy of the marquess.'

'I had no choice.' Sapphire indicated a chair. 'Spare me five minutes and I'll tell you my story.'

Sapphire spared him nothing, yet there was no self-pity in her voice.'

His father's hand slid over her hand in support when she finished the shocking tale. Gerard frowned again. The intimacy between them appeared to be more than just friendship.

He engaged his father's eyes and took a deep breath. 'Forgive me if I cross the bounds between father and son. There's a question I wish to ask you, as one man to another.'

'If you are going to ask if I love Marietta, the answer is yes,' Ambrose said simply. 'I've always loved her.'

'Then why did you not–'

'I was betrothed to your mother.'

'And she wouldn't release you?'

'He didn't have time to ask,' Sapphire said dully. 'I was compelled to wed the marquess, and thus began my misery. I've often railed against the forces of fate that kept us apart, but realize now that destiny shaped my fortune to ensure my daughter's happiness.'

An awful suspicion began to form in his mind. He stood up. He had no wish to accuse his late mother of such complicity, not even in his mind. 'Why are you telling me this?'

'Because Willow suspects I'm her mother.' In

an unguarded moment, her love for her daughter showed as raw, naked pain upon the canvas of her face. 'I would die having her ignorant, rather than reveal how unworthy I am to be called mother by her.'

'You are dramatizing the importance of your status, and underestimating your daughter, madam.' He gazed at her with unfriendly eyes. 'You seek to play upon my sympathy. I suspect your accident was one of convenience, and that fate and destiny had nothing to do with it. You deliberately sought out your daughter so you could play some small part in her life. That I can understand, but do me the justice of honesty, and that I'll give you in return. I've never met a woman with so much courage and strength as Willow. If you chose to deny her this knowledge then you *will* be unworthy of her.'

'*Gerard!*' Ambrose warned, as storm clouds gathered in his son's eyes. 'Your remarks are insulting, and uncalled for.'

'No, Ambrose. He's partly right and I deserved them.' Rising to her feet, Sapphire kissed Gerard lightly on the cheek. 'I sought only revenge when I came here. Willow was an unexpected bonus. Whether you believe it or not, destiny has given my daughter a husband to be proud of. For that, I'm thankful.'

Without another word she tripped lightly from the room, leaving him stunned. He gazed reflectively at his father, who, now Sapphire had gone, appeared vulnerable and exhausted.

'It does not take much to figure out what happened,' his father said quietly. 'Caroline was never the same after Marietta was reported dead. I'd thought the birth of her daughter would bring her joy, but it did not. She was already dead inside.'

It was almost as if he was talking to himself.

'Caroline became bitter after her daughter was born. I felt sorry for the poor little thing, but I did not think...?'

'Think what?' Gerard asked, when his father opened his eyes.

Ambrose could not bring himself to soil the memory of Caroline to her son. What would it achieve to tell him? Caroline had probably been forced into it. He should have had the courage to call out the marquess for his efforts at peace-making had come to naught.

'Oh, nothing of importance.' He uttered a heavy sigh, realizing his cowardice had weighed heavily on his conscience all these years. 'It's too late to change the past. I could have been a better husband, perhaps.'

His father's unspoken words confirmed what Gerard had only suspected: his sister had been fathered by the marquess, and his father knew it.

'That may be true.' Tears in his eyes, he stooped to hug the earl. 'But you couldn't have been a better father to your sons. No man could.'

The images faded from the crystal and, despite her worry about Edward, Willow smiled. Taking up her drawing tablet she quickly sketched a series of scenes. Adding them to her previous sketch, she rolled them up and secured them with a violet ribbon.

She handed the roll of drawings to Bella, instructing her to take them to Sapphire.

Ten minutes later, there was a knock at the door. Heart beating nervously, she bade her mother enter.

Sapphire had discarded her plain black dress for one of soft grey. She was unveiled, her eyes unguarded as they gazed at her. Troubled and unsure, Willow knew they mirrored her own.

'You have the ability to tune into my thoughts,' Sapphire said slowly.

It was the admission she'd sought. My mother has suffered so much that she is afraid to allow herself to love, she was thinking. What if she's too proud to allow me to love her?

Pain suddenly rioted through her body. Not her own pain, she realized, it was her mother's she experienced. Something dark haunted her depths. She was putting a protective force between them.

She took a tentative step forward, nearly crying out with the agony of her mother's soul. Sapphire was retreating into herself, retreating behind the barrier between them. Tension quivered like menace waiting to strike, warning her to keep the distance between them intact. It was the power binding Sapphire to the old ways.

Don't try and repel me, her heart cried out. Let me love you.

You have chosen your path, Sapphire told herself in the face of Willow's appeal. You must find the courage to see it through to the end. The thread began to unravel as Willow reached out her hands.

'Take them,' her daughter entreated. 'I'm of

your flesh, and will help make you whole.'

Something in Sapphire snapped. Then her daughter was in her arms. As each experienced the love of the other, tears ran unashamedly down their faces.

'Oh, my dear,' she said softly. 'I'd sacrifice the rest of my life for just this one moment of joy.'

It took only a moment to realize it was exactly what she had done.

Sheronwood looked as deserted as the last time they'd been there. Although the soldiers searched the house from top to bottom it was of no avail. There was no sign of Edward, and the view from the upper windows revealed the cove was empty of shipping.

The tide was in. Seawater surged through the entrance to the cove and smashed against the cliff face in clouds of white spray.

Despairingly, Gerard concluded that they were too late. Nevertheless, they prised the boards from the cellar door and descended into the depths of the house. The entrance to the tunnels was boarded up, as they'd been for several years. Dredging a memory from his childhood, he remembered a series of steps led steeply downwards.

Earlier generations of the de Vere family had used Sheronwood for smuggling. There was a labyrinth of tunnels, most of which came to a dead end. Some joined one to another in case an escape route was needed. One ended behind a secret door in the ballroom panelling, another led to the cave on the beach. A branch tunnel terminated in a chamber with a small window-like aperture set just above high tide in the cliff face. It had been a look-out. When the tide was exceptionally high, most of the tunnel network flooded.

Aided by the smugglers' map on display in the library, he had explored them once. He'd been five, and had clung tightly to the hand of Daphne's father, scared he'd lose contact and be left alone in the dark. Not long afterwards, the tunnels had been blocked by a fall and the cellar entrance boarded up.

He grinned as he looked around. He'd been allowed to make a copy of the map, and that exercise was still imprinted on his brain. When Jeffrey was growing up he'd impressed his brother with highly embellished tales of his adventures in the caves.

A shout from Anthony chased the nostalgia from his eyes.

'The boards are on a pivot and move to one side.'

Gerard was the first down the steps, followed closely by Anthony. They carried lanterns. The soldiers were quite content to keep watch. He briefly wondered how many bottles of Sheronwood wine would be opened in the barracks that night, then decided it would be worth it if he could get Edward back.

'Be careful,' he warned Anthony. 'The tunnels are blocked, and there may have been more falls.'

'If the tunnels are blocked, where's the draught coming from?'

'Listen!' The officer ran into his back when he suddenly stopped and held up his hand. He could have sworn he'd heard a child sobbing above the roar of the waves.

'I hear nothing but the sea.' Anthony sounded nervous. 'How far into the tunnels does the water intrude? It sounds extremely close, and high tide is yet an hour away.'

'An hour? Are you sure?' Gerard turned and gazed at him doubtfully. 'The tide was high when we came in.'

'It will be exceptionally high today. We had a full moon a couple of nights ago and can expect a spring tide.'

A roaring sound filled his ears, and it was not the sea. Suddenly, he knew where Edward was. The marquess was diabolical. Even as he wondered how a man could be so lacking in compassion as to leave a child to drown, he was deciding to kill him. He'd follow his enemy to France, if need be.

'Stay here,' he said to Anthony. 'I know where the child is. If I fail to return, tell my wife–'

A cry of fright clearly reached his ears, then another from a different source, as if one had infected another. It was joined by a third.

'It sounds as though you'll need me, friend.' Anthony poked him in the back. 'Lead on. I hope you've a nose for direction and speed. I have the feeling we'll need it.'

A sour odour of damp seaweed lingered in the tunnels. The flickering lanterns gave a glimpse of a line on the wall that denoted an ominously high tide at some time in the past. The wind that howled up the tunnel at the approach of each breaker was cold, and smelt of salt. It struck

Gerard that he and Anthony would be drowned in the tunnels if he took a wrong turn. When they were forced to struggle through swirling, knee-high water, he was tempted to turn back.

Then he heard Edward call Willow's name. There was such desperation in the child's voice he knew he must not fail him. At the very least, he owed Daphne the life of her son.

Spray from the sea was crashing through the aperture when they finally found the chamber. The children were huddled together in a corner, water sucking at their feet.

'Jesus help us!' Anthony exclaimed.

'We've no time for praying, man.' Gerard picked up the nearest child and swung her on to his shoulders. 'Hold tight,' he instructed. Edward's eyes were fever bright, his body hot and shaking when he grabbed him up and cuddled him against his body.

Edward gave a cry of recognition as he clung for safety against his chest. An unaccustomed warmth spread through him when he gazed down at the child, but he had no time to analyse it.

'I hope you can manage the other two,' he muttered, wishing the child on his shoulders had not taken his order quite so literally when her fingers wound tightly in his hair.

They barely had time to clear the chamber when a wave crashed through the aperture and set it awash. Water pursued them halfway up the tunnel and swirled chest high before it receded with a menacing hiss.

The children's terrified screams were nerve racking. Gerard barked at them for silence.

'That was close.' The *sangfroid* in Anthony's voice was at odds with his earlier nervousness, as if he'd put his courage to the test and come out intact. 'I admit I'm not overly fond of confined spaces, so let's make haste before your lantern extinguishes itself. I dropped mine in the scramble up the tunnel.'

The soldiers looked astonished when their saturated figures emerged from the tunnel.

'God's truth!' one of them exclaimed, scratching his head. 'I thought we was looking for the young marquess. Where did all them brats come from?'

Once the children had been transported to Lytton House, fed on chicken broth and made tidy, they were interviewed by Anthony Dowling.

A soldier was dispatched to seek out the woman hired as the children's gaoler, who had fled into the surrounding countryside when she'd heard them arrive.

The two boys, aged about nine and ten, were brothers, and had lived for the past two years in a London workhouse.

The girl said she'd been taken to a toff's house in London by her father, who was a grave-digger. She was able to recall recognizable features of the house, then more falteringly, and with Willow's tearful encouragement, told of her father's death before describing the man who'd abused her.

Except for Edward, the children had been subject to depravity of the basest sort. Each one implicated Marquess Lynchcross.

'I'll send a dispatch rider with my report to General Marriot at the break of dawn,' Anthony said with satisfaction. 'The activities of the

328

marquess are now over. I'm at a loss at what to do with the children, though.'

'If we adopted my plan to start a village orphanage...?' Willow's voice trailed off when Gerard frowned at her. He'd already explained there was not the funds for the purpose at this time, though the fact that he'd given her the 300-guinea purse for the purpose had heartened her.

'It's for you to decide, of course.' She smiled at Anthony, reducing him to a speechless wreck. 'You'll excuse me, Captain. I must go and see Edward. He's still distressed.' Her eyes sent Gerard an entreaty before the door closed behind her.

After she'd gone, Gerard crossed to the window and stared at the grounds of his home. If not for an accident of birth, both he and Jeffrey might be in the same position as these children. He did not have it in him to send them back to be abused all over again by unscrupulous men like the marquess.

'I'll see if the boys would prefer to stay and be trained into employment here,' he said with a shrug. 'At least they'll be fed and clothed. As for the girl, she seems a bright little thing, and polite. Mrs Tupworthy is looking for a companion for her daughter. No doubt she'll offer her a home.'

Later, in the privacy of their chambers, he told Willow what he'd arranged for the children. He was the recipient of a loving look, and a hug as reward.

Delighted as she was with his news, he could see she was bursting with news of her own as she crossed to the chair he occupied.

'I have need to confide something to you, Gerard.' The sparkling excitement in her eyes belied the gravity in her voice. 'I can hardly believe what has happened.'

'What is it, my love?' He guessed what it was, but didn't have the heart to take the joy of her telling it away from her.

'It's Sapphire. She's not Sapphire – she's Marietta Givanchy.'

'First she is Sapphire, then she's not.' He raised a quizzical eyebrow. 'Then you tell me she's somebody else.' Tempted to laugh, he managed to keep his face blank. He tipped up her chin and tenderly kissed her. 'What enigma is this, my sweeting?'

'No enigma.' He loved the way her lips clung to his and the small flare of desire in her eyes. Then impatience replaced it. 'Do you not see? Sapphire is my mother. She did not die after all, and came to Lytton to find me. Is that not wonderful?'

'It's wonderful indeed.' He noticed she was wearing the pink velvet robe with the fur trim, under it the chemise trimmed with pink rosebuds.

He pulled her on to his lap. 'Tell me how you came to discover Sapphire was your mother.'

'It began when she gave me a small crystal ball...'

The fur began to tickle his nose. He begged her remove the robe before he sneezed.

'I did not see anything at first...'

Her breasts were level with his mouth whilst he listened to her talk. He amused himself breathing

330

on them, watching the nipples harden like sweet, ripe berries.

'If you're to listen to my tale we'll be more comfortable on the bed,' she said huskily, as she rose to her feet. 'My rear end is painful from riding ... you would be good enough to inspect it for blisters before I continue my tale?'

Gerard *would* be good enough. When he'd finished his inspection he pronounced her free of blemish, except for a small crescent shaped scar adorning the curve of her waist.

Pressing his lips against it, he felt her shudder, and remembered how she'd come about the blemish. Hands curving around her buttocks, he brought her – legs astride – back down to his lap.

'Do you think you could ride another mile with me?' he whispered, tracing the perimeters of her luscious mouth with his tongue.

'A mile?' Her eyes widened with desire. A provocative smile curved her lips and she said a trifle wickedly, 'It's for you to command, and me to obey, Husband...'

CHAPTER TWELVE

Spring – 1755 – Summer

'Gerard must speak to the gardeners.' Edwina decapitated a flower bloom with her cane. 'Look at these weeds, they're a disgrace.'

'It's a marguerite, Grandmother.'

'Nonsense.' Giving Willow a disapproving look, Edwina settled back in her chair. 'I know a dandelion when I see one.'

'Don't be cross with me,' Willow implored, laying her head against the older woman's shoulder. 'I've been so happy of late.'

'I doubt that not at all.' There was no relenting in Edwina's voice. 'Your husband indulges your every whim.' If the truth be told, she was annoyed that Willow spared her so little time these days. She turned, staring at the girl with indignant eyes. 'A shooting match? What can Gerard be thinking of?'

Willow's eyes sparkled with mischief. 'No doubt he's thinking he and Jeffrey will outshoot James and myself, and win the purse.'

'Do not confound me by stating the obvious. You knew very well what I meant.' Her glance swept over the two Lytton males to settle on the figure of James Langland, who was squinting down the barrel of one of his pistols. 'You cannot fool me, nor wrap me around your little finger like some I could mention.'

'I would not try.' Kissing Lady Edwina's cheek, Willow sighed. 'Gerard is very handsome.'

Edwina couldn't quite succeed in keeping the smugness from her smile. It had been obvious to her for some time: Gerard had a self-satisfied look about him. When his eyes strayed to Willow, they contained an intimacy that spoke of knowledge.

'He's tolerably well set-up,' she agreed, pleased her prediction had come to fruition, and running her eye over Willow's waist for signs of thickening.

'I think he resembles you,' Willow whispered. 'But do not tell Ambrose I said so. He's quite sure Gerard resembles him.'

She grinned to herself as a pleased look came into Lady Edwina's eyes.

'You may be right, my dear.' Mollified, the old lady cast a fond eye at her eldest grandson. 'He's intelligent as well as handsome, as my dear husband was.' She gazed down her nose at James. 'A good bloodline always shows. Compared to Gerard, that man is a bag of bones.' She ignored Willow's giggle as she warmed to her theme. 'I knew his grandmother, of course.'

Quite agreeable to indulge in a little gossip, Willow gave Lady Edwina a smile of encouragement.

Spreading her fan across her lips, Edwina began to elaborate at length. 'Eugenia was a nonentity, one of the Gloucester Herberts. They were all puny creatures. Eugenia was all skin and bone, and had teeth like a horse. She was so conceited she couldn't see her faults as anything but virtues. She bore thirteen children for her husband, and out-lived him by fifteen years. James Langland is very much like her.'

Giving birth to thirteen children and out-living a husband by fifteen years didn't sound like the actions of a puny person to Willow. She smothered another giggle. 'James is not in the least bit conceited, Grandmother.'

'Don't argue with me, girl. If I say he's conceited, he's conceited. I can guarantee my grandsons will out-shoot him, then you'll not be so smug.'

'If you'd care to place a wager on the outcome...?'

'Ladies do not gamble.' Edwina gave a loud sniff, then glanced around to see if anyone was watching. 'You'll not out-smart me,' she hissed. 'I'll have five guineas on my grandsons' skills.'

James strolled to where they sat. He nodded to Lady Edwina, then smiled and whispered in Willow's ear as he offered her his arm. 'There's a gusty cross wind. It comes across the lake from the right. Shoot when the ripples are least active.'

It seemed as though everyone in the house had turned out to watch the contest. Tables and chairs had been set upon the lawn. Servants walked amongst them with tea in delicate china cups, lemonade, and trays of sweetmeats.

Edward was there with his nurse, his adoring glance alternating between Jeffrey, and his new hero, Gerard.

The day was warm, the wind fitful but cool enough to remind them it was not quite May.

Gerard smiled when they reached him. Flipping open the lid of a flat box, he said, 'These were given to me for my coming of age. I'd like you to have them.'

The two pistols had highly polished wooden grips with embossed silver trim. Gerard's initials were carved into the handle where her fingers would curve underneath. He smiled at her a trifle quizzically when she weighed them in her hands expertly. 'They were always a little on the light side for me.'

Her eyes caught his as he spoke, and a surge of desire left her breathless. A mocking little smile crossed his lips as he leaned forward and kissed her. 'Good luck, angel.'

'You'll allow her time to get the feel of these pistols.' James took them from her hands, checked them and nodded his approval before proceeding to load them. He gave her a wicked grin as he caught her eye. 'I'll set two stones on the top of the bench, cherub.'

Willow's eyes sparkled when Gerard gave an indulgent chuckle. He was not chuckling a minute or so later when the stones disintegrated into grit.

'*Holy priest!*' The exclamation came from Lady Edwina. She was discomfited when both Gerard and Jeffrey grinned at her. The chit had outsmarted her after all.

A crowd of rooks took to the air and circled around in noisy confusion above the trees. Detaching itself from the smaller birds, a raven soared across the meadow to circle the people in the garden. It came to rest on a gargoyle decorating a corner of the roof of Lytton House.

From the attic window below, Nellie crooned softly to it.

The raven's bright stare surveyed the heads below, then settled on the dark pigtailed head of the tallest of the shooters. Tilting its head to one side, it made a harsh guttural noise in its throat and settled into its feathers.

Half an hour later, Willow and James were three points up. The two teams had only one shot each left when Jeffrey stepped forward. His aim had been consistent. He'd benefited greatly from James's tuition.

Jeffrey hit the target just off centre, bringing a spatter of applause from the spectators. Even the servants had stopped to watch now. The air was charged with tension. Jeffrey's eyes sought his father's for approval and they exchanged a grin.

James brought up his gun and fired. Distracted by a sudden shout from Edward, his shot went wide. He shrugged and stepped back. 'The best of the next two shots decides the match.'

Willow didn't look at Gerard when he took his stance, knowing it didn't matter where his shot went. What mattered, was that hers hit the target dead centre. All her focus was on that one thought.

She frowned as a distraction came into the corner of her vision. There was a raven soaring above them. A bad omen? She shivered as the sun lost its warmth.

For some reason, she exchanged an alarmed glance with her mother. Sapphire half rose, shielding the sun from her eyes with her hands.

There was a click as Gerard's gun cocked.

Dear God! What was the raven about? The bird hurtled downwards, its neck outstretched, its beak glinting like a deadly weapon. Straight at her husband!

Everything happened in a split second. Cocking her pistol, Willow took aim and fired in one fluid motion.

There was a scream from Sapphire. Gerard half-turned, his eyes flared and he dropped to one knee when he saw the gun pointed in his direction. His pistol automatically turned towards her, his finger tightened on the trigger. The expression in his eyes was as lethal as the gun in his hand.

'No!' Jeffrey's shout had hardly registered on Willow's ears when the raven hit Gerard's shoulder. His gun discharged, the ball wrenching the pistol from her hand. It spun into the grass, the barrel shattered.

Silence pressed in on them, suffocating the sounds of the day. Her throbbing hand cradled by the other, she gazed at Gerard in horror, and he at her. He glanced at the dead raven, a mixture of revulsion and awe painted on his face as feathers drifted around him like black snow. When he looked at her again, there was pain and anger in his eyes.

'You could have killed me.'

'Impossible, my friend.' The usual laconic tone was missing from James's voice as he placed a restraining hand on Gerard's sleeve. 'She was aiming at the bird.'

The hand was cast aside as horror took

precedence over the other emotions. 'What is worse, I could have killed you.' Colour drained from Gerard's face at the thought.

How angry he sounded. There was a roaring sound in Willow's ears and she experienced nausea. What he'd omitted to mention was he would have killed her had the raven not thrown him off balance. Choking on a sob, she turned and fled towards the house.

Damnation! The anguish in her eyes brought guilt flooding through Gerard. Didn't she realize his anger was directed against himself? Dropping his pistol to the table he started out after her.

When he entered her bedchamber she was curled in a chair by the window, a handkerchief pressed to her eyes. Her tears came as a surprise. This was no pretty appeal on her part, her handkerchief was sodden, her eyes swollen and red. The heartbroken sound of weeping wrenched at his heart.

'You've taken this too much to heart, my love.' His attempt to take her in his arms met with resistance as she stiffened and pushed him away. He dropped to his knees. 'You had a fright, that's all. There was no harm done.'

'How can you say that?' Her voice was tragic. 'You were about to shoot me through the heart. I saw it in your eyes.'

She trembled when he reached out and touched her hand. The pain had diminished slightly. There was no swelling apparent so the bones were still intact. She winced when he probed it carefully.

'It's but a mild sprain, and should soon mend.' He feathered kisses upon the site of the pain as if to heal the hurt. 'What you saw was merely a re-action, my love.'

A reaction that had frightened even himself. He'd been thinking of the marquess each time he discharged his gun at the target. The man had become an obsession, and Gerard's anger burned like fire whenever he thought of him.

When her shot had whistled over his head, he'd automatically turned and aimed. It had taken a split-second to register that she was not the marquess. The other half of the second did not bear thinking about.

His explanation did not drive the wary look from her eyes. Gently, he caressed the palms of her hands with his thumbs, his heart aching for her pain and insecurity.

'You remembered I was his blood,' she accused. 'If Jeffrey hadn't shouted–'

He shook his head in denial. 'The gun discharged when the raven hit me.'

Gradually, she relaxed. Taking advantage, he leaned forward and stole her breath from her mouth with a kiss, coaxing softly, 'I beg you to forgive me.'

His tone was as honeyed as his kiss had been. The beginning of a smile trembled upon her lips. 'If you would but kiss me again, I'll consider it.'

He was in the middle of obliging her when the door opened and his grandmother walked in. She didn't look in the least bit apologetic at interrupting what was so obviously a private moment. Annoyed, he sprang to his feet and retreated to the window.

'Ambrose has declared the match won by Willow

and that Langland creature,' Edwina grumbled. 'I've come to pay the five guineas I owe.' Her glance lit on Willow's tear-stained face and she gave a long drawn out, 'Hurrumph! That will teach you to play with fire, young lady. Perhaps you'll think twice before challenging my grandsons again.' Throwing some coins on the bed she threw them a scowl and stalked from the room.

Despite his embarrassment, he found it hard to keep a straight face when Willow gazed at him. Eyes alight with merriment, her lips trembled with the effort of keeping it in. A quaver of laughter escaped her half-kissed mouth. 'You're indeed a dangerous man, Gerard. You ignite at the least provocation.'

'You should have listened to her warning, angel,' he growled, advancing on her with intent in his eyes and laughter on his lips. 'Didn't I just hear her tell you to think twice before challenging me?'

Her eyes embraced his with a smouldering passion.

'Lock the door, Gerard.' Her mouth blew shivering erotic kisses gently into his ear as he took her into his arms. Her voice had the husky, seductive tone he'd grown to love. 'We'll discover just how fiery you are.'

Sapphire was walking arm in arm with Willow in the garden. Deep in conversation, their intimacy was apparent for everyone to see.

Watching from the study window, Gerard gave an ironic smile. He tried not to resent the time she spent with her mother, but because he worried about Sapphire's reputation, he couldn't bring himself to really like the woman.

She seemed to have taken over both his father, and wife, of late, and he felt excluded. He turned and smiled at the man sprawled in one of the battered leather chairs.

'So you've decided to take the post Annie Tupworthy has offered. A wise choice, James.'

'I wonder,' James said. 'Sometimes, it's wiser to make a clean break from ties of the past.'

The meaning of the man's words were not lost on him. 'She would be broken-hearted if you left. Besides, she's convinced herself that you and Annie Tupworthy are a good match.'

James grinned self-consciously. 'If she has romance on her mind she can forget it. I have nothing to offer a woman.'

Handing James a glass of Madeira, Gerard took the opposite chair. 'It was Willow who recommended you for the position. You were always more than a tutor to her, James. She speaks of you with great fondness.'

'Fondness I do not deserve, for I lied to her all those years.' He contemplated the liquid in his glass. 'I've never told this to anyone before, but you are her husband, and one day she might discover the truth. I'd not have her think too badly of me.'

'What is it, man?' he urged, when James hesitated.

'I was sent to Coringal to be her gaoler. My instructions were to keep her in isolation until the marquess sent for her. She was to be denied help if she became sick. If she died, she was to be

341

buried in an unmarked grave. The marquess intimated if she was to die suddenly, my notes would be paid off that much sooner.'

'And you agreed to that?' Gerard was on his feet, his eyes hot with furious accusation. 'Why did you not challenge the man? You were the only swordsman in England who could have beaten him.'

'Sit down, my hot-blooded friend.' James cast weary eyes his way. 'I had no reason to call him out. I owed him a great deal of money, and because of my gambling debts my family had cast me out. I had no other way of honouring the debt. Be thankful it was me, and not some villain like Simon Carsewell who was given charge of her. She'd not have lived to see her first birthday.'

'My apologies.' Gerard shuddered as he subsided back into his chair. 'I cannot bear to think of her suffering. I was hasty in my judgement.'

A grin curled his way. 'You're often hasty.' Draining his glass, James rose from the chair and casually held it out to be refilled. 'If you intend to kill the marquess in a duel with swords, you must develop a thicker skin.

'Although you're now as skilled as he with the sword, you're easily goaded into anger. It expends itself in energy, and you lose the edge over your opponent. The marquess has no such failing: he's calculating; he's quick to find an opponent's weakness to exploit, and fights to kill. Remember that.'

'He sent his dogs to murder me whilst I slept, then scuttled off abroad.' Gerard grimaced in disgust. 'That sounds more like a coward's way than that of a man who's confident he can beat me at sword-play.'

'I admit he has not fought with swords for some time, preferring the pistol of late. I should imagine he'll be honing his skills at the Paris Academy. Remember, Gerard, the man is full of trickery.' James poked a bony finger into his chest. 'You made him look a fool in public, he'll never forgive you that.'

James grinned as, lazily, he scrutinized Gerard from head to toe. 'At the risk of sounding indelicate, I've noticed Willow occupies much of your time. Far be it for me to interfere between husband and wife, but you have the look of a man whose balls are pickled in perfume at the moment.'

Gerard nearly choked on his drink.

'Spend your afternoons indulging in another type of swordplay unless you intend to make her a widow. I guarantee, it will be time well spent.'

She would not like it. Hearing the rustle of her silken skirts as she paraded past the open study window, Gerard allowed his glance to linger on her charms for a brief moment.

She was clad in a pale-grey pleated gown over a blue quilted petticoat and stomacher. Her straw hat was adorned with a posy of striking red poppies. Matching ribbons fluttered in the breeze. She'd have red ribbons tied around her stockings, he guessed.

A smile played around his mouth. She might invite him to undo them with his teeth, like she had the day before. Then again, she might leave her stockings on. His mouth grew dry at the thought

343

and his groin tightened. She became more innovative each day, and he was fast becoming besotted with her.

It would be hard to forgo the sensual delights of their afternoons together, but if that's what it took...

He regarded James's advice with the seriousness it deserved, having a great respect for his skill. If there were faults in his temperament – faults that would rob him of the edge with the marquess – they must be eliminated.

'When do we start to work?'

'Sunday's as good a day as any.' He dashed his glass of Madeira into Gerard's face.

Incensed by the action, Gerard's hand shook with rage as he reached for his short sword. It had hardly cleared its scabbard when he froze. The tip of James's sword, which had been safely sheathed a moment before, pricked blood from the centre of his chest.

James's eyes were deadly and unwavering, leaving him under no illusion that he was staring death in the face. Opening his hand, he let his sword fall to the floor.

Although James grinned, his eyes remained lethal. 'That was wise,' he said softly. 'Never allow temper to push you to a rash action. A little wine in the face does not kill: a sword does. If you draw your sword, make sure you have the advantage. You may not be given a second chance.'

The sword was removed and returned to its scabbard, the voice became laconic, the eyes faintly amused. 'Thus endeth your first lesson.'

Gerard had gone to Sheronwood with Robert Bascombe; Jeffrey and James were out riding along the beach; Lady Edwina was resting; and Sapphire was cloistered with Ambrose in the drawing-room.

Gerard had been most apologetic when he'd left, explaining that he'd offered Robert Bascombe the management of the Sheronwood Estate, and he needed to be made familiar with the house and grounds before the Saturday hiring fare.

Apologetic, but firm. Her soft, lingering kiss had drawn a response from her husband, but not the response she'd wanted.

'Tonight,' he'd whispered, his mouth drawing from her depths a promise of passion, and leaving it trembling on the brink of discovery. 'I'll come to you tonight, my love.'

'He no longer finds me attractive,' she said disconsolately to the kitten, who opened one eye then went back to sleep. 'If I could have found my red beads to complete this ensemble, the outcome may have been different.' Knowing she was being selfish and vain, she forgot her beads and gazed through the open window at the soft May day.

The scent of lilac drifted in the air, and all manner of flying insects and birds were abroad. Dragonflies skimmed above the ducks on the lake, and two red squirrels – looking like marionettes with their jerkily controlled movements – chased each other around the lawn. If there was ever a more perfect day, she'd never seen it. Her heart lifted.

When she'd wed Gerard, she'd never expected to live in such a perfect place. She loved it here and, what was more important, loved her husband. But, would he ever love her?

Fetching the crystal, she focused into its depths and gradually blotted out all extraneous thought. To her disappointment, she couldn't bring him into the sphere. Instead, an image of her mother appeared. She was surrounded with dappled jade light, like sunlight on water. Her hair floated out behind her, her eyes gazed through the green shades to shadowy figures above her She turned towards her, her movements graceful as if she floated on air, her eyes...? Her eyes had no expression. They were lacking life!

Giving a frightened cry, she dashed the crystal to the floor and watched it shatter into gleaming shards. What had she seen?

Bella came running at the sound, staring at her with round, sorrowful eyes.

'What was it?' She crossed to the maid and took her by the shoulders. 'What manner of evil did I see in that devil's plaything?'

Tears gathered in Bella's eyes and slowly trickled down her cheek.

'Speak to me, Bella,' she said, gently shaking her. 'My mother said you could, if you'd but try.'

'It ... is ... the end of Sapphire's journey. That is what you saw.'

Sapphire's journey? Her eyes suddenly widened in horror. 'I saw her death? If that's the future one sees in the crystal, I vow to God, I'll never cast my eyes upon one again.'

Unease gripped her when the sound of voices

raised in anger reached her ears. Releasing her grip on Bella's shoulders, she rushed to the window.

Coming down the carriageway was a group of villagers brandishing cudgels and hay forks. She picked up the remaining pistol of the pair Gerard had given her, hastily loaded it and hurried downstairs.

'There's a mob,' she said, when Lady Edwina poked her head inquisitively out of her room, when she passed. 'Lock your chamber door and stay inside.' The old lady obeyed with such alacrity, under different circumstances she'd have laughed to think she'd accept an order from her without so much as a murmur.

Sending the first servant she saw to the stables to tell Brian to alert her husband, and with no time to secure the house, she sauntered casually through the front door and stood at the top of the steps, her pistol concealed by her skirts. Lodged in her heart, was a forlorn hope that she might be able to keep the mob at bay until the men returned. Logic told her otherwise.

'What's the meaning of this intrusion?'

The mob became quiet at the sight of the lone woman standing at the top of the steps.

'Speak up,' she said sharply. 'You were making enough noise a few seconds ago to raise the dead.' She fixed her gaze on a large, ruddy-faced man at the front of the group. 'You! What's your name?'

'Bellows, missus.' The man snatched his hat from his head and automatically held it against his chest in a sign of respect.

347

'State your business with the earl. He's resting at the moment and cannot be disturbed.' She thanked God that Ambrose was in the drawing-room. The noise would not reach there to alert him to the danger.

'Go on, Bellows,' someone shouted from the back. 'You was making the threats and doing all the cussing at the meeting.'

Bellows' expression became belligerent when someone laughed. The hat was jammed back over his bald pate.

'Our business ain't with the earl,' he said loudly, 'it's with the sorceress. Hand the woman over to us, and we'll go quietly.'

'Sorceress?' Under no illusion to whom the man was referring, her heart began to race. 'Who amongst you accuses the Lyttons of harbouring a sorceress?'

'Nellie Breton denounces the woman called Sapphire.'

There was some pushing and shoving from the back of the crowd. Grinning self-consciously, Nellie came forward to stand next to the man.

'Nellie is a poor idiot who knows no better.' Willow gave Nellie a smile. 'You didn't mean to accuse Sapphire of sorcery, did you, Nellie?'

Nellie's head jerked up and down in assent.

'You mustn't tell lies,' Willow scolded.

'Nellie doesn't lie.' She raised her fist on high. 'The preacher said she brought the raven. It tells Nellie to do bad things.'

A chill ran down Willow's spine as her mother joined her on the step.

Bellows cried out, 'There's the witch. Let her

undergo trial by water.' He waved a wicked look-ing sickle in the air. 'I'll deal with the mistress of the house; her husband ain't going to put me off my farm with his newfangled notions.'

'Stand back.' She brought up her pistol as a precautionary measure. It was snatched from her fingers by her mother as Bellows took a step forward.

'Don't you hurt my mistress.'

The pistol discharged just as Nellie threw her-self at the man. She took the shot in the head and dropped like a stone.

Imbued with false courage from the ale he'd consumed, Bellows shouted belligerently before he could be deprived of his sport, 'She's killed poor Nellie. Take her, let's get it over with before she kills our children. If she survives trial by water, we'll know who lied.'

'Nobody survives the ducking stool.' Willow's voice was desperate. 'Pray, do not do this.'

'Do not waste your breath, Daughter.' When her mother gazed deeply into her eyes, a great feeling of love and peace stole through her body. 'I unwittingly brought evil into your life and it will leave with me. I chose this path and must see it through to the end before I find peace with God.'

She took her in a loving embrace. 'The trial's not yet over, but you'll triumph and your life will be happy. Know that I love you, Willow. Keep me always in your heart.' Her mother pushed her away. 'Quickly now, child. Go to Ambrose. He must not be alone at this moment.'

There was a surge of bodies up the steps.

Propelled into a wall, a terrible pain exploded in Willow's head. The sky became obscured by mist, and the sun faded into darkness.

The garden was quiet when she drifted back into consciousness. For a few hazy moments she thought nothing had happened, until she saw the body of Nellie lying beneath the steps. A circle of red beads glinted on her neck looking like bright drops of blood. Her heart mourned for the simple servant who'd given her life to save her from harm.

'Help me up,' she said to a servant who was bending anxiously over her. 'Then send someone to move Nellie's body.'

Ambrose was sitting by the open window gazing into the garden when she made her way into the drawing-room. She tried to hide her agitation when he smiled lovingly at her. Perhaps Gerard would arrive in time to stop the villagers drowning her mother, despite the horrifying prediction in the crystal.

'Did you see Marietta?' Ambrose smiled when she didn't answer. 'She promised to come for me after her walk in the garden, my dear.'

Thank God he didn't suspect! She managed a smile, even though her head throbbed abominably. Pouring herself a small glass of brandy and water, she slowly sipped it to compose herself, then crossed to where he sat.

He patted the chair next to him. 'Come sit with me awhile, Daughter. I have a gift for you.'

She kissed his cheek. 'You've already given me everything I need and value – your love.'

'You return it twofold.' His smile brought tears to her eyes. 'The gift is from your mother.' He took the small sapphire ring her mother usually wore from his pocket, and slid it on to her finger. 'She bade me give it to you before she went out.'

His hand closed around hers. She left it there for the comfort it offered. Prickles teased up her back as she realized her mother had known what was coming.

Dear God! She couldn't break the news to Ambrose, not until she was sure. She tried to keep normality in her voice, but choked on it when she asked unnecessarily, 'How long has she been gone?'

'Just for a moment. Marietta wouldn't leave me alone for long. We've vowed never to be apart again.'

His eyes had been shut. Now he opened them. They were filled with such love and joy that she felt humbled by it. 'Here she is now.'

Relieved beyond belief, she turned towards the window. The mob must have thought better of their actions and released her, but there was nothing beyond the terrace but an empty garden bathed in sunlight. She turned towards Ambrose with a puzzled expression on her face. The hand holding hers had relaxed.

He was leaning back in his chair, the smile still on his lips. His eyes gazed into the garden, but the earthly light was gone from them. They saw nothing but that which was beyond life.

She gazed at him with great reverence, rejoicing that the strain of his illness had fled his face.

'I did not think you would leave when my back

was turned, Ambrose,' she whispered, a trifle indignantly. 'You were a good man, and I truly loved you.' Gently smoothing the eyelids over his dimmed eyes, she gazed into his dear face. It was relaxed in death, each tiny line of tension erased.

'Go with God, Ambrose,' she whispered, kissing him gently on the cheek. She did not cry. After saying a short prayer for his soul, she rose from her knees and went to fetch John Grey.

There was much to do before she could allow herself the luxury of grieving.

Ambrose was buried in the family crypt a few days later. The tiny village church was packed, for he'd been much loved in the district.

Sapphire had been afforded no such luxury. As far as the church was concerned she'd been proved a heretic by the nature of her death. It mattered not that she'd been denounced by the village idiot, nor that the mob had been stirred to hatred beyond reason by the Wesleyan preacher.

It was strange, they all said afterwards. The witch had seemed to be expecting them. She'd neither struggled nor cried out when they'd dragged her to the ducking stool, but she'd murmured a prayer of repentance.

Although no one in the village would admit it, her death brought no satisfaction. In his cups, Bellows wandered under a London-bound coach that same night, and was crushed.

The estate workers turned up for work the next day, and tried to ignore the small procession following a coffin which was buried in an isolated corner of a field.

The following week, the site was enclosed by a low stone wall and a headstone erected. Those who could read, and were curious enough, waited until the flowers died before they drifted over to read the epitaph on the headstone.

Marietta Givanchy 1709-1755.
Beloved mother of Willow,
Countess of Lytton.

The stinking French fishing boat the marquess was on was nearing the coast of England. His arrangement with the fishermen was to be put ashore at the Sheronwood cove just before dawn, then the boat would wait beyond the cove for his signal fire before sending back the dinghy to pick him up.

He was taking a risk returning to England knowing there was a warrant issued to arrest him on sight. It was of small consequence. He had no intention of being apprehended and could live out his life quite comfortably abroad.

He had investments in France, including his château, which had once been the childhood home of Marietta Givanchy. It had been given to him years ago by a French duke for services rendered. Situated discreetly in the countryside, there he provided a source of amusement that was much in demand amongst the more dissolute of the French aristocracy.

Of late, the marquess had undertaken practice with the finest swordsmen France had to offer. Now he was going to kill Gerard Lytton. Once he'd gone, it would be a simple matter to dispose of the earl and the younger son.

Four years previously, the marquess had decided to take his daughter to France and auction her to the highest bidder. His sneer became a scowl. It wasn't too late to revive his plan.

His eyes narrowed into cruel little slits as he thought of Willow. She was a feisty little thing, just like her mother. The marriage had been a mistake. Either Gerard Lytton had managed to tame her, or he'd fallen under her spell. Whichever, it would be his pleasure to inform Lytton of her fate before he killed him.

Wrapping his cloak around his body, he glowered as he balanced himself on the slimy deck. The girl was shaped in Marietta's image. For all he knew, she could have been fathered by the Prince of Darkness himself.

He paled at the truth of the thought. That's exactly what must have happened: Marietta had been impregnated with Satan's evil spawn.

'Willow is the Daughter of Darkness!' he said out loud, and wondered why he hadn't guessed the truth before.

Willow would not allow herself to cry. She'd borne grief of her mother's loss alone, the results of the mob's action forbidden by her husband to be mentioned again.

It seemed unfair for fate to have restored her mother to her, only to snatch her away again. Even more unfair was the realization she'd been allowed to experience a husband's love, and would never experience it again.

The Lytton household had been stunned by the

events that had taken place. The house no longer had a mistress, for she'd been denied the authority by her husband. The house was full of tension. Quarrels erupted as the servants debated the issues; all felt sorrow for their young mistress. Though thinking she was being treated unfairly, none dare speak against her husband.

Willow had risen early, driven from her bed by her resolve to end the conflict in the only way she could think of. Gerard slept alone in the adjoining room, as he'd done since that terrible day in May.

The day was young, the birds who chorused the dawn from the tree outside her window, still mute. The sounds of daybreak had made no inroads on the faint sputtering hiss of the incoming tide against the rocks.

Good, she thought, buckling her riding boots around her calves. If I drown, the ebbing tide will wash me out to sea, and Jeffrey will not be able to look upon my battered body and blame the earl. She choked back a sob. It's not Gerard's fault he cannot bring himself to love me. Everything he'd said to her was true, and she couldn't fault his reasoning.

'Your parents have brought death upon my home.' So remote had his face been he might have been talking to a stranger. 'I cannot forget their blood runs in your veins. You leave for Coringal within the week, madam. I do not wish to set eyes on you again.'

In vain she'd argued with him. 'What of the Lytton name? You need heirs.'

'Jeffrey and his children will be heir to Lytton

after me.'

'He wants to go to Virginia, you know he does. For God's sake, Gerard, listen to reason. I'm your wife. You cannot banish me without good cause.'

His eyes had bored into hers, implacable and devoid of emotion. He did not raise his voice. 'I can do exactly as I please with you. As for Jeffrey, he's his father's son and will do what is expected of him. You'll go back from whence you came.'

Lady Edwina was sympathetic, but dared not plead her case. Even Jeffrey had been unable to move his brother to reason. The ensuing argument had been terrible to hear, and had driven a gulf between the two brothers.

Gerard's grief was buried in a deep, dark place, and kept alive by the rage that burned within his soul. She'd been the catalyst that had turned his ordered world into chaos. He did not hate her; he just wanted her out of his sight so he could forget what had happened, and heal in his own time.

If he'd been thinking straight, he'd have known that by blaming her, he sought to abrogate himself of guilt. His mind was not ready for that. He'd reacted to the first solution that came into his head.

Willow had no such thoughts. Her reaction was more simple: she loved him, and she loved Lytton House. She'd not leave either of them willingly. She'd rather die, as she'd explained to Gerard in her letter. If by chance she perished, he'd be free to marry again, and his heirs would take their rightful place in the line of succession.

Placing a blood-red rose on the letter as a symbol of her love, she crept into his room to lay it on the pillow next to his cheek. Gently, she kissed him, then giving his dear face one last, loving glance, quietly made her way downstairs and out to the stables.

Circe snickered softly to her when she mounted. It had been a long time since she'd ridden bare-back. It had lost its novelty for her now. The predawn had a velvety texture to it, the air was moist. A pale moon rode low on the horizon, and the canopy of stars was dimming.

She shivered when she reached the cliff path and a cold breeze sent her dark hair whipping in tendrils against her face. Dismounting, she stood looking into the darkness below. The waves crashed against the rocks, warning her the path was dangerous. She turned to her mare.

'Go back, my darling Circe. I'd not have you hurt.' The mare shivered when she ran her hand along its side. Tears pricked her eyes.

'That's a fine-looking foal you'll be having there,' she whispered. 'Didn't Brian find you a dandy for a mate.' She slapped her hand hard against Circe's rump. It was no use prolonging the parting.

As the mare's footfalls faded into the distance, she gazed towards the water. Fear touched her eyes, and she prayed she'd picked the right spot.

Removing her fine leather boots, she folded her cloak neatly on top, took a deep breath, then launched herself into the dark menacing void below.

CHAPTER THIRTEEN

'That damned woman and her absurd logic!' Gerard had never felt so angry. 'What does she think I'm going to do, rush to the cliff top and search for her body?'

That's exactly what he was about to do. Despite his conviction this was an attempt to catch his attention, he was deeply worried.

What if she couldn't swim well enough to get back to shore? Logic grappled with his fears. She'd once told him she could swim like an otter. On the other hand...? She had a vivid imagination, and was prone to embellishment.

He stood still long enough to shrug into the jacket Rodgers held out for him. Why shouldn't her wild tales be believed? He grasped at the one tale he'd discounted, her boast that she could shoot the eye from a frog. That had proved to be true, only the frog had become a raven in reality.

His mouth twisted in wry appreciation of her skill. She was a paradox. No woman should be able to shoot a moving target like that. But if she had not, he thought, his anger lessening a little, I'd most probably be dead, and she'd not be making a fool out of me again.

The thought restored his ire. 'Haven't I had enough grief of late?' he lamented. 'I'll put her over my knee when I find her and teach her a lesson she's long deserved.' His mouth stretched into a mirthless grin at the thought of her smooth white buttocks flinching under his hands. 'The woman has pushed me too far this time, *by God, she has!*'

'Yes, sir.' Rodgers grinned to himself. It was about time his master regained the substance of his true nature. The young countess could be trusted to find some way to prod her husband out of his depression. The staff had made wagers on it. As a result, his pocket would be fatter by nightfall. 'Your hat, My Lord.'

'Thank you, Rodgers.' Absently he pinned the rosebud to the brim. 'Not a word to my grandmother about this. I'm in no mood to be nagged, and I don't want her alarmed unnecessarily.'

'Certainly not, sir. You're having breakfast before you go out?'

'Good God, man, what sort of rogue do you think I am?' The earl glowered at him before striding rapidly towards the door. 'The countess might be lying dead on the beach. Do you really expect me to stop for breakfast?'

Gazing after him, Rodgers chuckled. 'No, My Lord. I'd bet my very life on the fact that you would not.'

Jeffrey was about to ride out when his brother hurried into the stable. Politely, he nodded his head, preferring to ride alone since their blazing row. He didn't wish to be around when the coach arrived to take Willow away from Lytton.

'Ride with me,' Gerard said gruffly, his conscience jabbing at him painfully. It had just dawned on him he must have treated Willow extremely badly if she was prepared to go to such drastic lengths. 'Willow has left me a note threatening to throw herself into the sea. I may need your assistance.'

As if to emphasize the deed, Circe high-stepped into the stableyard and tossed her silky mane. Stretching her head towards him the mare gave a loud whinny, then shook her head from side to side.

Jeffrey's face drained of colour when he saw the riderless horse. 'If you've driven Willow to sow the seeds of her own destruction, I'll make you suffer,' he snarled.

The words were spoken out of fear, but Gerard knew he deserved them, as he sought to allay his brother's disquiet. 'Willow's inclined to melodramatic gestures when she cannot get her own way,' he mused. 'Her vanity will not make her risk damaging her body upon the rocks.'

'How can you be so unfeeling?' Jeffrey's voice was incensed beyond reason now. 'If you cared even a little, you'd know she's in deep despair.'

Gerard slid his brother a sharp glance. 'Allow me to know my wife better than you, Jeffrey.' Mounting his gelding, he tightened his hands on the reins. 'She does not give in to despair, rather she fights tooth and nail for what she wants. Believe me, she'll not intentionally kill herself. If she's thrown herself into the sea you can be damned sure she'll have done it to attract my attention, and jolt me out of my miseries.'

'For your own sake, I hope you're proved right.' Jeffrey didn't wait for a reaction to his threat, just spurred his mount forward towards the cliff path.

Gerard didn't bother engaging in conversation.

The least said the less damage there would be to repair, but when he heard the sound of hoofbeats behind him and saw Circe following at a safe distance, he discovered his emotions were too choked up to even try.

It occurred to him then, that he might just have fallen in love with his errant wife.

Willow struggled furiously against the bonds that held her, and stared balefully at her father.

Her head ached after he'd dragged her through a maze of tunnels by her hair, and her knees were bruised when he'd sent her sprawling through a secret panel into the ballroom of Sheronwood.

Not only that, her face stung where he'd slapped her, and her cheekbone was swelling. She'd look a complete fright when Gerard set eyes on her again, and he'd gaze upon her with distaste.

Her fingers stretched towards her wrists. If she could reach the knife concealed in the cuff of her coat and cut through her wrist binding, she intended to spring upon her father when his back was turned, and cut his villainous throat!

Never in her wildest nightmare had she expected to wade from the water and find her father waiting upon the sand. He'd spoiled her moment of reconciliation forever, and for that alone she'd never forgive him.

It had taken her days to plot the moment when Gerard would discover her lying like a beached mermaid upon the shore, her hair spread artfully about her like dark, glistening seaweed. She'd imagined him cradling her gently in his arms, telling her he loved her, then stripping away her

361

sodden clothes and making love to her whilst the sun rose in golden glory all about them.

She'd quickly discovered that making love in the sand would not be practicable. Sand, she'd discovered, had a habit of finding its way into every crevice of the body. When combined with the itch of drying seawater it was exceedingly uncomfortable.

'What sort of man does this to his own daughter?' she cried, her voice echoing to the cherub-embellished ceiling.

'You're Satan's spawn,' the marquess spat out.

'You admit to being the Devil?' A prudent tongue was not one of her virtues, sarcasm being a much more satisfying and pertinent alternative in her present situation.

The cruel eyes of the marquess slid to her face. 'You have a sharp tongue, child. Be careful you do not cut your own throat with it.'

His voice was so devoid of emotion, she shivered. It was time to change tactics if she was to get anywhere with this man. Holding out her bound wrists she invested in a moment of pathos. 'Will you not release me, Papa? The thong about my wrists is painful.'

He did not bother to respond. Taking a brace of pistols from the bag he carried, he stripped them down, cleaned them, then proceeded to load them.

She tried again. 'Why do you hate me so?'

'You remind me of your mother.' He stopped what he was doing to flick an unfriendly glance her way. 'She was an evil woman who practised the black arts.'

Pain came into her eyes at hearing her mother so maligned. 'She didn't appear evil to me; she was a most loving woman.'

'What are you saying?' Grasping her by the wrists he jerked her to her feet. 'Do not try to bedevil me, girl. You didn't know your mother; she died just after you were born.' Throwing her to the floor he turned back to his task.

She bit back a sob of pain and grief. 'My mother died by your hand, and was thrown into a shallow grave deep in the woods.'

'*Liar!*' he yelled, his boot thudding into her thigh. His eyes narrowed as they gazed at her doubled-up body. Fear flickered in his eyes. 'There's no way you could know that.'

'Unless she told me.' Despite her pain, she smiled at him maliciously. 'She belonged to the Devil, remember? And the Devil is reputed to look after his own. Marietta Givanchy rose from the grave.'

Her father's eyes now held a gratifying fear. 'Recently she returned, and revealed herself to me at Lytton House. She called herself Sapphire.' Lowering her voice, she delivered her next line with relish. 'Mama told me your soul was past redemption. Before she returned to the afterlife, she prophesied you'd join her in Hell and experience the agony of everlasting fire until the end of time.'

'Lies,' the marquess said, his voice shaking. 'You're trying to trick me.'

'Am I, Papa?' She held out her bound hands. 'Do you recognize this ring? It was on her body when you buried her alive.'

Giving a start of fear, he backed away from her.

363

She watched him pick up his top coat, then was smothered as its heavy folds enveloped her. Her immediate reaction was panic. The coat stank of rotten fish and body odour, and she thought she might suffocate.

About to kick it from her body, a sharp object pressed against her arm. A metal button, she guessed. Her mood became more optimistic: God was on her side after all. Easing herself on to her side, she carefully placed her bound wrists against its serrated edge.

Willow's cloak and boots were found where the spring tide had left a build-up of sand. Gerard grinned to himself. She'd made sure they were in plain view. For one who was supposed to be in an irrational state of mind, the cloak was neatly folded.

They found her small footprints further along the cove, coming up out of the water. They headed straight towards a larger set of footprints curving from the water's edge a little way off. 'The marquess,' Gerard muttered, his earlier relief giving way to fear. There was no mistaking the peculiar indentation of the man's twisted leg in the sand. He stared at the drag marks leading to the cave opening, then at the damp, scuffed sand scattered upon the dry. She'd not gone easily.

'She put up a fight,' Jeffrey observed, with more than a little pride.

'Much good it will do her.' Cautiously, Gerard approached the cave entrance. 'Her temper would serve her much better if she curbed it. The marquess is infamous for his treatment of women.'

'If he lays one finger on her I'll kill him,' Jeffrey growled.

'You'll not concern yourself with what is my business.' Gerard laid a hand on his brother's rigid arm. 'The marquess has challenged me, and honour dictates I meet him in a duel. He may kill me. If he does, Willow will be in the gravest peril.'

Jeffrey's eyes filled with apprehension.

'I know our relationship has not been as cordial of late as it should be,' Gerard continued, seeing his father's face mirrored in Jeffrey's. 'The fault is mine. I kept my grief close inside me, and gave scant thought that those I love most must also be grieving. I ask for your forgiveness, Jeffrey, and would know I can count on your support.'

'I'd die for her,' Jeffrey said simply.

'Do not think I'm ignorant of your regard.' He raised his hand in a comforting gesture to Jeffrey's shoulder as the youth dropped his eyes. 'It does not give me offence. Loving a woman is nothing to be ashamed of.'

'But she's your wife.'

'And as such must be treated with respect. Your honour will allow you to do no less.' The smile he slipped his brother was sympathetic. 'Willow will bear my children and provide heirs for Lytton should we survive this day. If we do not, the continuance of the tide and estates will rest upon your shoulders. Until that happens, you owe your allegiance to me. You will not challenge the marquess under any circumstances. Is that clear?'

'I understand, Gerard.'

'If it's any consolation to you, Jeffrey, I've also grown to love Willow. I would offer my life in exchange for hers.'

Their glance joined in mutual appreciation, then Jeffrey gave a rueful smile. 'She needs to be loved.'

'Then you'll understand when I ask you to go with all haste to seek out James Langland. Tell him what has happened, then alert Anthony Dowling. Go now,' he ordered when Jeffrey hesitated. 'There's not a moment to lose. I dressed in such haste, I omitted to arm myself.'

A quick, brotherly hug healed the breach between them. When Jeffrey hurried to do his bidding, Gerard turned his attention to the entrance to the tunnels. He doubted if the marquess was lurking inside. The man had come to kill him and wouldn't risk being forced to fight in a confined space.

He kept in mind that the marquess would have had him murdered whilst he slept. The man's sense of honour was dubious, and he could not now count on a fair fight. Knowing he'd be playing into his enemy's hands if he gained entrance to Sheronwood via the tunnels, he turned his eyes towards the cliff top.

Willow tried not to sob when the metal button grazed against the blood-smeared skin on her wrists. Her wrists were chafed almost beyond endurance, the lace cuffs of her shirt soaked through with blood. Yet the leather thong binding her still held.

Her father's footsteps were clearly heard. She stilled her movements when he approached her, bracing herself for any cruelty he intended to

inflict on her. She closed her eyes when he un-
covered her head, pretending to sleep.

How sweet the air was after being confined in
the coat, she thought. And how thankfully brief
the encounter when her father grunted and
threw the coat back over her again.

He was going! The footfalls moved out of her
hearing and she waited with strained breath. She
had to risk it. Throwing the coat from her body
she sprang to her feet and headed for the secret
panel.

Then she saw a pistol lying on the table. For a
moment she hesitated, then fumbled with the
catch on the panel, sliding it aside when she
heard him return.

An obscene oath echoed in her ears. The marquess grabbed and cocked the pistol in one
smooth motion. Any illusions she may have harboured about him were well and truly shattered
when she saw the loathing in his eyes.

'Dear God, save me!' she prayed, and threw
herself through the panel. The shot nearly parted
her hair as she tumbled down a flight of stairs
into darkness. Winded, she turned and gazed up
at the square of light.

Her father's outline blotted out the light. 'You'll
not escape from there. The door to the tunnel is
locked.' His laugh sent shivers creeping up her
spine. 'Eventually you'll grow too weak from
hunger to fight off the rats.'

'My husband will tear this place down stone by
stone to find me,' she shrieked, her defiant tone
banishing the conviction growing in her that
Gerard would do no such thing. He hated her.

Why else would he banish her to a lonely life in Ireland?

Tears of self-pity trickled down her face as the panel slammed shut. She'd never see Gerard again, never experience his kisses or bear his children, never look upon his beloved face.

The last thought made her scowl and her self-pity fled. She was not going to give up everything without a fight, and die in a rat-infested hole.

She gazed around at the pitch darkness, listening to the sound of her own laboured breathing. When her eyes cleared of tears, she saw it wasn't entirely dark; there was light coming through a crack in the panel.

Then she heard a scratching sound. Imagination heightened by her father's words and the darkness pressing in on her, she muffled a whimper against her hands. She tasted blood. It had saturated the leather thong binding her and caused it to stretch. The smell of blood would attract the rats with their needle-sharp teeth. Fear throbbed hot and strong through her body. When Gerard found her she'd be featureless and ugly. He'd look upon her corpse and feel only revulsion and pity. She did not want his pity, she wanted his love and admiration, even in death.

Her eyes narrowed and her fear abated when a notion occurred to her. 'Rats are not the only creatures who can bite,' she muttered, bringing her bound wrists against her mouth. Her spirits rose. 'I'm not finished yet, Papa,' she whispered. 'We shall see who dies like a rat in a trap.'

Gerard tasted real fear when he heard the shot.

Entrance to the house had been gained courtesy of the upstairs window. The shot had come from the vicinity of the ballroom.

'*Sweet Jesus!*' His heart came alive and seemed trapped in the confines of his chest. 'The marquess has killed her!' Dropping any pretence at caution he bounded downstairs and burst into the ballroom.

Expecting to see his Willow's lifeless body, he encountered only the figure of the marquess sprawled on a gilded sofa. The hand holding the pistol was relaxed, but Gerard knew it would take only seconds for the marquess to lift it and kill him.

'What have you done with her?' he demanded harshly. 'She has no part in the quarrel between you and I.'

'The troublesome brat is safe for the moment.' The pistol lifted slightly when he moved. 'Stay where you are, my friend.'

'The whole of England will know what a coward you are if you kill me out of hand.' Gerard's nostrils flared with the effort of keeping his temper under control. 'Have you no sense of honour, sir?'

The marquess shrugged. 'I find it easier to stay alive without it.'

'Then you intend to murder me?'

Willow held her breath and strained to hear the answer. Freed from her bonds, she'd climbed up the flight of stairs and had her ear pressed against the crack in the panel.

'Oh, you shall have your moment.' Carelessly, the marquess rose to his feet and crossed to the table. 'I've not forgotten the public humiliation I suffered at your hands. After I've disposed of you, I intend to murder your father and brother. Edward de Vere and your wife will be taken to France.'

'My father is already dead,' Gerard said steadily.

'So, you are the earl now. But not for long. I intend to slash you into little pieces before you die.'

'*No!*' Willow screamed, pounding her fists against the unforgiving panel. 'Release me, you rabid cur. I'll tear your heart from your chest with my bare hands and feed it to the pigs in the forest if you harm him.'

'A tedious child,' the marquess remarked, then, with as much feeling as someone squashing a bug, lifted the pistol and sent a shot through the panel.

She cried out as splinters of wood pierced her hand. Light streamed through a neat hole an inch from her fingers. She applied her eye to the hole.

'The shot was wide,' she taunted. 'And you've not had time to reload the other pistol.'

Gerard experienced admiration for her pluck in drawing the shot. At the same time, he experienced a strong urge to shake her until her teeth rattled for the risk she'd taken.

'No matter.'

Through her spy-hole, she saw her father draw the duelling swords from a case. He threw one to Gerard.

'When I've dealt with this proud Lytton turkey cock, I shall take you to France for my friends to

370

sport with. That will cure you of your bounce.'

Though her stomach churned, she managed to spit out, 'Gerard will split you to the gizzard, and I shall dance on your grave.'

'Hold your tongue, woman. You've nothing sensible to say.'

The scathing quality in Gerard's voice brought scalding tears to her eyes. Her mouth opened, then slowly closed again. He was right: shouting threats would achieve nothing except prove a distraction to him. If he was to win this duel – and he *had* to – he'd need all his wits about him.

Already, the men were circling each other. Her confidence fled. If Gerard died she'd kill herself before the marquess got to her. She had her knife. But what of Edward? She couldn't desert him.

Sobbing with the frustration of having to stand by helplessly and do nothing, she took the dagger from her pocket, inserted it in the crack in the panel and applied pressure.

Gerard put Willow to the back of his mind. She'd not come to any harm for the time being.

The marquess was in the classic *en guard* pose. He took a similar stance, but the man lunged so suddenly he only just had time to parry it. When wariness came into his eyes, the marquess grinned.

'You do not seem so confident now, my friend.'

'We're not friends.' Without taking his eyes off the marquess, he circled his foe. 'You made an enemy of me when I was but a youth.' He parried a jarring thrust to the body. 'On the day you

371

visited Lytton House in my father's absence, I recognized you were immoral. I learned to despise you, even then.'

'Your mother made herself my whore on that day,' the marquess taunted, then chuckled when Gerard swore. 'All women are whores. Daphne de Vere was one, but you found that out for yourself, didn't you?'

'Daphne became what you made her,' Gerard said hotly. 'Surely, you did not have to try and kill her child?'

'She tried to foist on me as heir, the bastard you planted in her womb.' The marquess looked incensed. 'I'd have honoured her by making her my wife, but she refused me because of Edward.'

His sword cut a swathe through the air. Gerard parried it easily.

Edward was Gerard's child? Willow's eyes flew open in shocked surprise. She flinched when the swords clashed in a furious exchange. No wonder Edward bore such a strong resemblance to the Lytton family.

She found she did not mind too much. She'd grown to love Edward, and could not find it in her to dislike the child for what was not his fault.

Gerard's mind became icy clear. The marquess had been trying to find his weakness by making him lose his temper. Instead, he'd given him an edge by revealing his own. He gave a derisive chuckle whilst they circled each other.

'Edward is not *my* son. You'd have known that should you have thought to calculate his natal day.'

Relief washed through Willow. It was stupid to

be jealous of a dead woman, and she'd known instinctively Edward wasn't Gerard's.

'Then he's truly my heir?' The marquess seemed to hesitate.

'You're pathetic.' Gerard's voice became scathing. 'Did you really think you could escape the curse of Marietta Givanchy? Of course he's not your heir. There are not enough manly virtues left in your family to produce a male.'

Do not say such things, Willow implored silently, her fingers temporarily stilled from their work. He will surely make you suffer for it.

His eyes were beginning to lose their reason, Gerard noted, going for a head thrust. His adversary's parry slid along his sword blade to the guard and the marquess staggered.

'Marietta was in league with the Devil,' he whispered, his panting breath alerting Gerard to the fact he was tiring.

The marquess was reaching the same conclusion. Damn those fawning creatures at the Academy, he was thinking, tiring himself even further by taking a wild swing at his young opponent. They'd fed his vanity with lies. He was getting too old for sword-play, and he hadn't expected the son of Ambrose Lytton to be so skilled. He *had* to goad the man into losing his temper.

'Willow is a dark-souled harlot, like her mother and grandmother before her. The French duke paid me well to rid himself of them.'

The marquess hissed as Gerard's blade drew blood from his cheek, and twisted away on his deformed leg. 'Marietta was the Devil's own. Did she not come back from the grave and talk to the

373

daughter she spawned?'

'*Your* daughter!' An unforgiving, hardness lit Gerard's eyes as he gritted out, 'You'll answer to me for your treatment of her.' His weapon found an opening and slashed a groove along his adversary's arm. A grunt of satisfaction left his lips. 'First blood to me.'

The lock clicked suddenly. Willow gave a smile of triumph as the door slid open. She was just in time to see Gerard's sword draw blood and her father stagger backwards. Then his hand slid behind his back and came out with a pistol.

Her heart plummeted with fear. 'He has a pistol!' Her cry came too late. The ball hit Gerard in the shoulder and his sword arm became useless. His knees buckled beneath him.

She was across the room almost before he hit the floor. Cradling his head in her lap, she gazed up at the swaying figure of the marquess and said scornfully, 'You're a craven coward. God rot your soul.'

'Daughter of Darkness,' he screamed. Both hands gripped the sword and brought it up over his head. 'You're about to join your husband in Hell.'

Something about the girl reminded the marquess of himself at that moment. A certain look to the eyes, a tilt of her head? There was no fear in her. Had she been a boy instead of a female...

'I am carrying your grandson in my womb,' she lied. 'Would you kill your unborn heir, too?'

He hesitated. Willow was the last of his bloodline. She would pass his title on to her sons.

Gerard Lytton still breathed. They'd be Lytton

374

sons! He shuddered, lapsing into unaccustomed indecisiveness.

He'd borne the Lyttons a grudge since his mother had taken one as a lover, and his father had been slain defending his right to her. He'd idolized his father, and when he'd taken revenge on the Lytton whoremonger by murdering him in his bed, he'd sworn to wipe out the whole family. He'd never known peace since.

What if he allowed his daughter and her husband to live, and made atonement for his sins? Perhaps Marietta's curse would be lifted from him? He could trade Willow's first-born son for Gerard's life.

Take advantage of your opponent's weakness, Willow thought, and remembered a fatal cut James had once demonstrated. She grabbed the sword from her husband's relaxed hand and went up on one knee.

For a second, she and her father gazed into each other's eyes. She was defending the man she loved, and now her back was against the wall she discovered a core of her father's ruthlessness lived in her. Her eyes were the more lethal of the two.

'Wait!' the marquess shouted in alarm.

The weapon sliced upwards, grazed under his rib cage and split his heart asunder. He was dead before he toppled backwards to the floor, leaving her staring aghast at the bloody sword in her hand.

'Willow?' Gerard groaned. Shock had rendered her husband unconscious. Now the pain of the bullet lodged in his shoulder brought him round.

'The marquess ... is he dead?'

'He is dead.' She swiftly placed the sword in reach of his seeking fingers. They curled around the hilt.

'I'll never let him take you from me.'

'La, Gerard,' she said shakily. 'You've defeated him, and are the bravest man alive.' Tremors of shock racked her body.

'Why didn't you obey me?' he said huskily. 'Had you gone to Coringal your life would not have been placed in jeopardy.'

'Did you not get my letter?' She gave him a scathing glance. 'If you send me away again you'll have to bind me hand and foot. Then I'll crawl back on my hands and knees and beg you to let me stay.'

She pressed her lips against his dark hairline, his eyelids, then his mouth. 'Have I not demonstrated I'd choose to throw myself into the sea and drown rather than leave you?'

He managed a grin. 'You have, indeed.'

'I love you.' Her mouth covered his face with feverish little kisses. 'I refuse to live without you. You must reconcile yourself to that.'

'And I adore you,' he groaned, bringing his good arm around her and burying his face in the fragrant curtain of her hair. 'Only God knows how much I love you!'

'You cannot know how I've longed for you to say that, Gerard, but somehow I knew it.' She took a sideways glance at the bloodied form of her father and said dispassionately, 'He does not look so terrifying now he is dead. His grandsons will be all the better for not knowing him.'

'You are with child?'

'Not yet. It shouldn't take long once you come to my bed and apply yourself to the task. Of course, we must allow time for your wound to heal.'

She didn't notice his grin. Her attention was caught by the sound of horses.

Rising to her feet, she staggered to a French door that led to the neglected terraced garden, and threw it open.

Clinging weakly to the door frame, she said in a voice loud enough for all to hear, before sliding to the floor, 'The marquess is dead. Gerard has defeated him.'

EPILOGUE

Summer 1757

It was her fourth summer at Lytton House. Willow gazed upon the garden and smiled with joy. It was alive with colour, scents, and the sound of insects. Such a short time had passed, but much had happened.

What remained of her father's vast estate after his creditors had been settled had become her inheritance. She'd sold the infamous French château which had caused such misery to the children who'd been taken there.

The remainder, including the Lynchcross title, was held in abeyance for her children. With

Gerard's blessing, the money from the sale of the château had funded the home for orphans she'd always wanted.

Brian and Kitty O'Shea had taken their baby son, and returned to Ireland to manage Coringal. With them had gone Circe and the Sheronwood stallion, to become breeding stock for a horse stud.

The idea had been hers, but Gerard had leapt at the suggestion once he'd seen the filly the pair had produced.

Jeffrey, John Grey and his daughter, had left for Virginia six months before. Gerard had gifted Jeffrey the deeds to the tobacco plantation. Although she missed Jeffrey's presence, she was too busy to grieve for long.

In a week's time there was to be a wedding: James Langland's proposal had been accepted by Annie Tupworthy.

'It's a love match,' she'd declared to Gerard, her romantic heart convincing her it was the truth.

James had recently inherited a large sum of money on the death of his father, and could have made a more suitable match. He'd chosen the widow, and vowed her son would become his heir should there be no issue from the marriage, which, considering the lady's age, seemed likely.

His elder brother was not of robust health and had no issue, so James was in the enviable position of now being the heir to an earldom.

'Caroline's eyes are the very image of Gerard's.' Edwina cuddled her great-granddaughter fondly against her bosom. 'Except for that, she resembles you. She's such a good little soul, never a whimper out of her.'

'She's nothing like Radford,' Willow admitted. 'I thought twins would be alike in nature.'

Her son was forever creating mischief. His eyes were violet: his hair darkly abundant: his chin firm. He'd kicked himself free from the restraints of the blanket and was lurching vigorously across the lawn on his newly discovered legs, the ginger cat in hot pursuit.

At the moment Radford was happy, but when he was displeased he roared like a bull until he was pacified. 'He's such a handsome boy, Grandmother. I'm so lucky.'

'Of course he's handsome. How could he be otherwise with Gerard for a father?' Edwina smiled. 'Radford is very strong-minded. I'm undecided from whom that trait is inherited.'

'You perhaps?' Willow suggested, her voice coated with honey.

She did not hear Edwina's indignant reply, she was watching her husband come across the lawn.

Gerard had been watching the groom give Edward a riding lesson on the gelding he'd given him for his seventh birthday.

Much to Edward's disgust, he'd been sent back to his tutor afterwards. Having recently been breeched, Edward had a tendency to lord it over the nursery at present. He was an intelligent child and was doing well with his studies.

Gerard was strong now, but the poison that had entered the bullet wound two summers previously had nearly claimed his life. The shock had painted a streak of silver through his hair at the temple. Willow thought it gave him a distinguished look.

Radford stopped when he saw his father, and let out a yell of delight. Gerard scooped him up to his shoulders and gazed towards the woman he loved.

He tossed her a grin and saw the responding spark in her violet eyes.

Willow was a constant source of pleasure to him. She was still vain, contrary at times, and stubborn. She was also as soft as a kitten, sensual, and capricious enough to turn into a spitting fury when he rubbed her fur the wrong way.

Gerard had never cared much for docile women, so they were a good match.

He stooped, picked a red rose and presented it to her with a flourish.

Her eyes fused to his. Although no words were spoken, she stood when he set Radford upon his feet, moved into the circle of his arms and laid her head against his shoulder.

Willow's loving glance went from her husband, to her children, then to her home before coming back to her husband. She had everything worth having.

Daughter of Darkness, her father had called her. That had been true. There had been events in her life that had scared her, things she didn't understand. But the darkness had been in the marquess himself. That darkness had been destroyed with him.

She smiled as the baby she carried quickened inside her. She would birth a second strong son for her husband. Next year there would be a daughter, whom she'd call Marietta.

The future had been revealed to her in her mother's crystal.

Also revealed had been a raven, trapped deep inside it. Bella had rowed her to the middle of the lake, where it was at its deepest. She'd dropped the glass into the water, and watched it slowly sucked beneath the mud.

The House of Lytton would survive for ever.

The publishers hope that this book has given you enjoyable reading. Large Print Books are especially designed to be as easy to see and hold as possible. If you wish a complete list of our books please ask at your local library or write directly to:

Magna Large Print Books
Magna House, Long Preston,
Skipton, North Yorkshire.
BD23 4ND

This Large Print Book for the partially sighted, who cannot read normal print, is published under the auspices of

THE ULVERSCROFT FOUNDATION